1893 to 1904

LETTERS TO LOUISE

A Love Story

Enjoy!

Carol Carruthers Lambert

By Carol Carruthers Lambert

Non-fiction, historical, regional work

Letters To Louise – A Love Story
Copyright © 2010 by Carol Carruthers Lambert.

Cover Image: Maria Louise Tallant - 1900

ISBN 978-1-4507-2396-1

Printed in the United States of America

A native Astorian, Carol Carruthers Lambert graduated from Astoria High School in 1949. She and Joe Lambert, a distinguished professor, have been married for over sixty years and have three children. In 1970, graduating with her older son Kal, Carol earned a BA *magna cum laude* in Spanish literature at the University of California, Irvine. She retired from the travel industry in 1994 when she and Joe moved to her parents' old (1948) home on the banks of the Columbia River in Hammond, Oregon.

O-Wah-Wauna House Publishing
Attn: Carol C. Lambert
480 Enterprise St
Hammond, OR 97121-9758
sisil502004@yahoo.com

To remember that which is worth remembering.

Acknowledgments

For their help - at different times and in different ways – I would like to express my grateful thanks to the following persons:

Dr. Tana M. Porter, Research Librarian, Orange County Regional History Center, Orlando, Florida; Heather Briston, Corrigan Solari University Historian and Archivist, University of Oregon, Eugene, Oregon; Barbara Minard, Collections Manager, Columbia-Pacific Heritage Museum, Ilwaco, Washington; Beverly Olson, former Museum/Society manager, Karla Webber and Penny Kramer of the Pacific County Historical Museum, South Bend, Washington; Lynette Thiel-Smith and Lisa Studts, former Curators of the Heritage Museum, Clatsop County Historical Society (CCHS), Astoria, Oregon; Curator Jeff Smith and Librarian/author Arline LaMear of the Columbia River Maritime Museum (CRMM), Astoria, Oregon; Patrick Webb, manager of *The Daily Astorian;* Dr. Joel Godbey, M.D. (Portland); Dr. Steven vanderWaal, M.D. (Gearhart); Theodore V. Hollingsworth, archivist, First Unitarian Church, Portland, Oregon; Chuck Meyer; Carole Karnofski; Michael Wentworth; E.R. "Bud" Goulter; and Oysterville's author Sydney Stevens.

My thanks also to Sam Rascoe (CCHS) for his willingness to help - and to Liisa Penner, Archivist, Editor of *Cumtux* and the "answer lady" at CCHS's Heritage Museum. To Carol Moore, a spry-of-mind ninety-seven year old indexer. Even though my neck is permanently bent backwards, thanks also must go to the micro-roll reader-machine at the Astoria Public Library, Astoria, Oregon – when it worked, it provided me with great old local newspaper items and articles that added much to my knowledge.

To Page & Book's Christi and Greg Payne, who gave me good advice and were knowledgeable shepherds for a lost lamb; to Diane Speakman, owner of Sesame and Lilies in Cannon Beach, my gratitude for your creative ideas.

Special recognition goes to my children, Karel ("Kal"), Kathryn and Christopher, who provided me with such thoughtful suggestions and bugged me to complete the manuscript - "Go for it, Mom," and to my daughters-in-law, Anne and ThanhNga. To my brother Richard Tallant "Dick" Carruthers, Jr., who fed me important family recollections and dates, clarified some relationships, made many helpful comments and so enthusiastically emailed me pertinent, as well as tangential, information from his own research – my grateful thanks. I valued the numerous comments and suggestions from my husband, Joe, known for his clear writing style, who tried to keep me vigilant about K.I.S. – "keep it simple" (he never used the second "S" = "stupid") and waited patiently to read about this part of the family into which he had married over sixty years ago.

To all those unnamed who gave me support along the way – thank you!

Most of all, my gratitude goes to my paternal grandparents, Louise and Dick, for writing - and saving, all these letters. I now wish even more that I had known my Grandfather Dick, but working with their letters has given me an appreciation of the man he was and a glimpse into a few of the years he and my dearly-loved grandmother had together.

Contents

Introduction

The cedar wood box! The "treasure" box. There it was amid the packing papers. Safe!

The exact age of The Box is not known nor is The Box itself truly impressive – it is a modest sized, rectangular box, painted long ago with a light gold wash, now darkened with age. It still has fine filigree brass corners and, of course, a key hole to securely lock the hinged lid, although the key has long since disappeared. But what it held <u>inside</u> is what excited me so much - that was a "treasure" indeed. It held part of the "lives" of my paternal grandparents.

My fascination with "The Box" and its contents began before I was even school age. It was stored on a lower shelf, behind the cabinet doors of the secretary, which stood in my paternal grandmother's living room. I would run down the hill from our house, dash in through the French doors of the living room of her house, and, on my way by the secretary, quickly peek into the lower shelf - just to check to make sure The Box was still in its proper place. It always was there. I had only lifted the lid of The Box two times in all those years. I knew it was filled with letters. Several bundled ones were tied up in faded ribbons - some by a reddish ribbon; others by a blue one. Many other letters were just loose. Even as a child, I knew they had to be "Love Letters."

Maria Louise Tallant Carruthers and Richard Ervin "Dick" Carruthers were my paternal grandparents. About 1904, they and their young son, Dickie, had moved into the gracious house at 681 Jerome Avenue, Astoria, Oregon. It was probably my grandmother who tucked all the letters into the cedar wood box for safekeeping. Obviously they both had lovingly saved some of their correspondence over the period from 1895 to 1904.

Letters. Personal letters. <u>Their</u> letters. To share or not to share my grandparents letters to a widening circle? The decision was not lightly made.

My brother, Richard Tallant "Dick" Carruthers, Jr., and I never knew our paternal grandfather, who had died suddenly in 1922, years before either of us had been born. Richard Ervin Carruthers and our grandmother had been married less than twenty-one years. She was left on her own with their two sons, Richard Tallant "Dick" (Sr.) and Eben Hunter. She never remarried. As I was growing up, I recall her speaking only rarely of our grandfather. I was remiss in not asking her "the questions," even though I was curious about what kind of person Richard Ervin Carruthers had been and what the relationship was between our two grandparents – what their lives were like. What was their "story?"

Dick had courted Louise for about eight years before they were finally married in 1901. Over those years they had corresponded sporadically and had saved many of their letters, as well as some from family members and friends. Although I had known where those letters were kept, I had never read them. It wasn't until recently that I felt "ready" to do so. I began transcribing them – slowly, because the handwriting was often difficult to decipher. As I typed, so many questions came to mind regarding the events they mentioned. For example: What was our grandmother Louise, at age seventeen, doing in

Chicago in 1893? What kind of reviews did Grandfather Dick get as an actor in those amateur theatrical productions? I vaguely recall learning about the Spanish-American War of 1898 in Miss Crouter's Astoria High School history class, but what was Grandfather Dick doing over in Hawaii as a U.S. Second Regiment Volunteer Engineer? How much had Louise's medical problem affected her relationship with Dick? What was going on in their lives? And what was going on around them? So many questions arose. Therefore, I began researching "background additions" to the letters to help understand the time during which Louise and Dick were writing to each other. I decided to term these "Illuminations" and intermingled appropriate quotes from their letters with short articles about some of the actual historical events.

Louise and Dick did save a number of letters addressed to one or the other, but there are an untold number of missing ones, missing pages and even missing parts of letters. In some cases letters that do exist have a portion torn off by the recipient or stop abruptly in the middle of a sentence at the bottom of a page, with no further pages to be found. When Louise's mother, Mary Elizabeth Easton Tallant, was nearing her death in 1926, she sent a household helper up to the attic in their Grand Avenue house to bring down all the letters she had saved, particularly those written to her by her husband, Eben Weld Tallant. At her direction, all of the letters were burned. It is very probable that letters addressed not only to her, but also to Eben, from their children - and from their friends - were included among those. It is likely Louise's letters written to her parents and siblings during her stay in Chicago in 1893-94 may well have met that fate, for none of hers from that period exist. Nor do many that Louise and her sister Harriet wrote home during their trips to Southern California. Two letters written by Louise from Turkey Hammock, Florida, to her parents fortunately have survived along with a number of letters from Grandfather Dick to Louise.

All letters in this volume are transcriptions of the originals. Every effort has been made to keep the sense and intent of these original letters intact. The letters were not necessarily in chronological order in the Cedar wood Box where Louise stored them; it often became a tricky puzzle as to where one letter or another fitted into the lives of Louise and Dick. Many letters were in envelopes that had mailing dates – a few postal imprints were undecipherable. But the question did arise: Was the letter enclosed in a particular envelope the one that truly belonged in that envelope? There were a number of empty envelopes for which no existing letters matched. Many letters had incomplete dates – or no dates at all - written in the heading; some indicated only the day, *e.g.* "Monday." (Thank goodness for the Java Perpetual Calendar web site!) Those letters gathered together into the batch tied with red ribbons were written during the time of Louise's surgery. Tied with a blue ribbon were the letters written by both Louise and Dick during the time Dick served in the Volunteer Engineers. A number of loose letters, with or without envelopes, were quite out of order, as if they had been chucked back into Louise's Box, perhaps after someone had read them. I have tried to fit these puzzle pieces of Dick's and Louise's lives together as carefully, and as sequentially, as I could.

The letters were hand written either in pencil, with a nib pen or, less commonly, an early type of fountain pen. Nib pens required frequent dipping into a bottle of ink, which often made the flow of thoughts transcribed onto the paper rather choppy. Of course, a blotter was essential. A rag had to be kept handy to clean the nib, as well as the hands.

Neither ink nor "stationery" was always readily available; they had to make do with an assortment - and even at times, scraps - of writing paper. The paper they used tended to be thin and the writing would blur through to the other side, so to make the reading of a letter easier for the recipient, they sometimes wrote crosswise on the reverse side. That actually did make it easier to read!

Within the body of the letters, the use of parentheses and underlining is always that of the letter writers. To retain the sense and meaning of the original words/sentences, it has been necessary to make some limited changes. These also allow a smoother read. In certain cases, for clarification, additions and/or corrections had to be made and are indicated by enclosed brackets [ ]. For example, the writer did not complete the full word, *e.g.* "Nan to[ok] Mr. Shields." The use of abbreviations is also common, as in "Stea." meaning steamer; "Pho" indicating photograph; "hdkcf" short for handkerchief and "W'hse" for the "Warehouse."

Apparently it was customary in this period to write as separate words, those that we now normally string together, such as: "to day", "good night" and "sea side." Perhaps this was done because of the need to dip the nib pen in the ink well so often. For most of these, it is easy to understand what was meant.

Almost all spellings are as they were written. For example, frequent use of "to" was written when "too" is meant by the writer – or *vice versa*. Also used were "finaly" instead of "finally," "suspose" instead of "suppose," and "quiet" when the word intended was actually "quite." Again, these misuses of words/spellings do not seem to be serious enough to distract a reader.

Punctuation had to be altered in many cases to make the reading flow easier. A period, especially that made by the nib pen, was more often than not a single downward stroke that at first looked like a comma. In so many instances, commas, dashes and periods were not used at all. Often the letter writer did not indicate the beginning of a sentence with a capital letter, which made it necessary to determine the writer's intent as to where a new sentence began. The letter writers generally omitted apostrophes and question marks: *e.g.* "Isnt it dreadfull," "Cant you get some pictures."

Western slang was used, tongue-in-cheek, such as "pardner." In their use of the expression "It's no Josh," the writers evidently often enjoyed using the word "josh" both as a verb and as a noun. Webster's Twentieth Century Dictionary defines the word as: "*v. t.* and *v.i.* [said to merge, *joke* and *bosh*.]; to ridicule in a good-humored way; to tease; to banter. [Slang]." A strange use of the word "nit" pops up now and then as a slang expression. In this period of time it was not exactly used to mean "insect egg!" Its use was to negate the previous sentence or comment as in "He is handsome. Nit." This is similar to contemporary language usage as in "I like school. Not."

References are made to numerous people in these letters. Only occasionally are names used in full. A common practice of the time was to refer to a person by a single capital letter, followed by a dash or a period, to indicate either the initial of a person's first name or of someone's last name – *e.g.* Mrs T- indicated Mrs. Tuttle; M- indicated Marge Halsted; Dr F- was Dr. Finch. The initial "L" was used frequently, mostly to refer to Louise, but other times it indicated Louise's friends Lila Sutherland or Lillie Kerckhoff. Unfortunately, these initials are not always easily decipherable at this point in time. Educated guesses, or just plain guesses, have been necessary in many cases as to the referred. Some defied identification. The letter writers knew the persons to whom they were writing - and those to whom their letters were addressed also knew them. To write out the full name of the referenced person not only "wasted" the letter writer's time, but also ink and paper, neither of which was readily available. When persons can be identified, appropriate notations have been added to the initials. There are one or two references made by the writers of these letters that are not, in our present time, considered "politically correct." These remain as originally written - they do indicate the usage of their time.

During the period of 1897 to 1898, Louise and several of her girl friends appear to have adopted names; some are those of their best beaus. Louise was known as "Richard" - even her mother referred to her by that name on several occasions. Her good friend Olga Heilborn was "Jack." Nan Reed referred to herself as "Maurice." Because she had been a member of Queen Sue Elmore's Astoria Regatta court in 1899, Pearl Holden became known as "Princess," as well as "Pearline." Pearl's sister Frances was nicknamed "Frank." But one girl friend they called "Bob" could not be traced.

Members of the Carruthers and Lambert families donated a number of family photographs to the Clatsop County Historical Society (CCHS) and to the Columbia River Maritime Museum (CRMM), both in Astoria, Oregon; a few of those photographs are used in this manuscript with the courtesy of those museums. A few others are cited with the permission of CCHS and CRMM from their archives. Inclusion of the photo of the Carruthers' Pacific House Hostelry, in Oysterville, Washington, is with the courtesy of the Pacific County Historical Society, South Bend, Washington. All other photographs are the property of Carol C. Lambert and Richard T. Carruthers, Jr.

To try to follow the lives of a few, now deceased, family members, even over a relatively short period of time, can also help one gain an appreciation for the historical events of their time – events that both affected the families and, perhaps in some cases, were influenced by them. It is not possible to accurately recreate all that happened. I have tried to be as careful as I could in doing the necessary research, but errors and omissions can occur. I apologize for any in this manuscript - they are entirely my fault.

The Forebears
Emigrating to America

Both Louise's and Dick's ancestors had emigrated from the British Isles. On the Tallant family's side, Louise (she preferred using her middle name) was descended from forebears who had emigrated from England and Ireland in the 1600s. An ancestral chart over 100 years old, in the form of a fan, gave Louise's bloodlines. Various family members had settled in the Northeastern part of America, particularly on Massachusetts' Cape Cod and in Pelham, New Hampshire. These included Nicholas Easton (b. 1593 in Lymington, Hertsfordshire, England) and wife Christian Beecher who left South Hampton in 1634 for Newport, Rhode Island. John Scudder (b. 1619, London; d. 1689, Barnstable) sailed on the *James* from London to Charleston, Massachusetts in 1635, moving to

Barnstable in 1640. Scudder was admitted as a freeman in 1654. Possibly along with his widowed mother Joanna, Trystram (often spelled Tristram) Coffin (b. 1605 in Brixton, Devonshire) and wife Dionis Stevens arrived on Nantucket Island in 1642 by way of Ipswich and Newbury, Massachusetts, then onward to Hampton, Rhode Island. He was one of the original signers of the compact for the settlement of Newport, Rhode Island. The Pelham, Rockingford County, New Hampshire census in 1790 lists a Hugh Tallant born about 1685 in County Carlow, Ireland; he was likely the first Tallant to arrive in North America, sometime before 1730, possibly with two brothers, who later traveled to the southern states. Hugh remained in the New England area. The name Tallant may actually be French; a tiny village bearing that name, and spelling, is still located in France along the border with Switzerland.

At an early date, many Scottish clans had begun to move south into Cumberland County, England, including some of the Carruthers and the Bell clans. By the Nineteenth Century, a flood of Carruthers clansmen, with numerous variations in the spelling of the name, emigrated from northern England to Canada, the United States and Australia.

According to research done by R.T. Carruthers, Jr., these years were during the Little Ice Age - the 1300s to the mid-nineteenth century. Cold and wet conditions prevailed, with only occasional warm periods. Between 1812 and 1817, there were three major volcanic eruptions in the world; the year 1816 became know in England as "The Year Without a Summer." Another set of eruptions occurred between 1835 and 1841. As the move towards large-scale "scientific" farming increased, the output of food dramatically increased, but it also put many agricultural workers out of jobs. Agriculture-dependant counties, such as Cumberland, were particularly hurt. Work was scarce. It was the time of "the troubles." In 1830 alone, an estimated 15,000 people sailed from Liverpool for North America. By 1842, the Liverpool number had grown to 200,000. That number accounted for nearly one-half of all emigration during this period.

The line of Dick's paternal grandfather, Richard Carruthers, is reasonably well documented. Born in 1776 in Irthington, England, Thomas Caruthers [*sic*], a common servant of Greystoke Parish, wed by Banns on December 29, 1808, to "Sarah late Bell"[1] of Ainstable, a single woman. William Smith, Vicar of Ainstable Parish, officiated. Thomas' trade was listed as "labourer." Thomas and Sarah's son Richard was born on August 21, 1811[2] in Irthington and baptized by Vicar Smith on September 4, 1814. Richard was the second living son of Thomas and Sarah. The family was then residing in Far Shields, near the Scottish border.

Because of the troubled times, it is not surprising Richard eventually decided to strike out on his own. He traveled to Liverpool to take passage on the *Caledonia* that sailed

---

[1] The line of Sarah Bell's mother, Sarah Whitwham, can be traced back to the 1586 Kirkoswald Register.

[2] There are discrepancies in the birth date of Richard, in his and Mary's wedding date, and in the birth dates of their daughters Sarah Ann and Mary Jane. This is not uncommon in old parish, and civil, records. No birth certificate has been found for Richard, although his gravestone in Oysterville Cemetery is inscribed with an 1811 birth year. This date is in question. Born August 21, possibly in 1811, he was baptized on September 4, 1814, per Ainstable Parish records. The Passenger Manifest of the *Caledonia*, dated June 20, 1838, lists him as 23 years old, indicating 1814 or 1815 as his birth year. His ages, as declared on the U.S. Censuses of 1850, 1860, 1870 and 1880, do not correspond consistently with any of the possible birth years.

May 5, 1838. That vessel arrived in New York fifty-two days later on the twentieth of June.[3]

The *Caledonia*'s Passenger Manifest, recorded in New York, listed Richard Carrothers [*sic*], as a 23-year old male, a farmer. Appearing immediately before Richard's name on the manifest are the names of five members of the Faint family: Agnes, age 56; John, 21, farmer; Ann, 23; Mary, 20; and Elizabeth, 12. No husband is listed. The Faints had come from the area of Westmorland, where Mary was born May 22, 1816, on a farm holding named "Wormpots." She was baptized November 23, 1820. It is not clear whether Richard and the Faints were acquainted in Northern England, or even prior to boarding the vessel, but in any event, soon after arrival in New York, they apparently left for Whitby, Ontario, Canada. The Second Baptist Church of Whitby archives recorded Richard and Mary Faint's marriage on October 30, 1839, by "publication of Banns." Mary's sister Elizabeth and a man named William Law served as witnesses. Richard's occupation was listed as "stone mason" – he was a left-handed one, unusual among masons – a trade learned most likely from his maternal grandfather, William Bell, while living in Ainstable.

Four children were born to Richard and Mary while in Whitby - sons John (1839-1851) and Robert (April 8, 1845 – November 8, 1896) and daughters Sarah Ann (1841 or 1843) and Mary Jane (1847). Probably about 1849, the family left Canada for Boonville, Missouri, where Elizabeth was born in 1849. It was in Missouri that Richard and Mary's son John died. By 1852, the Carruthers family of six began the trek westward on the Oregon Trail.

And so, the story of Louise and Dick begins.

_____

[3] Most ships bound for America were owned by the United States; each ship carried an average of 400 passengers, who were generally between the ages of 20 and 40. Steerage cost 3 Pounds 10 Schillings up to 5 Pounds each. The ship masters were required to pay One Pound Sterling for every 100 passengers inspected by medical officers prior to boarding, plus the State of New York poll tax of $1.50 for each individual landed.

Early in May of 1881, a special letter arrived in old Nantucket on the daily sidewheeler steamer from the Massachusetts' mainland. The letter was addressed to Maria Louise Tallant and the postman handed it to her in person on the porch of her maternal grandparents' home on the island. Louise had recently arrived there, traveling by train and boat from San Gabriel, California, with her mother, older brother Will and younger sister Harriet, to attend the 200th anniversary of the death of their family's patriarch.

Louise was so excited to receive a letter. Only five years old, she raced to find her mother, Mary Elizabeth Easton Tallant, to help her read it. The letter was from her father, Eben Weld Tallant, who was working far away on the Columbia River in the Pacific Northwest. Little did Louise then realize that within less than a year's time her whole family would be joining her Papa to live on the Columbia River in the fast developing town of Astoria, Oregon.

From his "floating house" moored at Eagle Cliff, not far from the mouth of the river, Eben Weld Tallant wrote the following letter - in pencil - to his older daughter Louise.

Apr 28 1881

From the middle of the Big Columbia river nearly in the Pacific Ocean

    your Papa writes to his

        Dear sweet little Louise

            And thanks her for being such a good girl on the cars. Papa was sorry to hear she was sick on the steamer going to Grandmas house for it made her cross and naughty when she got there. And almost the first letter Papa got from Mama it said Louise was cross and did not act cunning as she promised papa she would. And when Papa got that letter a big storm came and nearly washed Papa's floating house to pieces, and for two days he could not do any thing but think how his little children were not good, and that troubled him much worse than all the wind and waves did. Then the storm stoped and a steamer came to him with another letter from Mama and she wrote that Louise was now a good girl. Then didn't papa feel glad. And then he did not care for storms for he was so happy thinking of his good children that he forgot storms and only thinks how happy he will be when we can all be home again [in San Gabriel] and see Zam [most likely their dog]. And Billy Bronco and you can ride Dilly over to Margie's [Halsted]. Can you go out at Grandma's and find flowers? There are some pretty yellow dandelions there and sweet May flowers and by and by there will be buttercups and then, way by and by, there will be bright golden rods. And when you see them in blossom, you must say now Mama we must go home and see Papa. And if mama writes all the time you are

2

good, Papa will hurry home to meet you. But I know you will be good, for if you was not, Papa would not want to see you and would get on another big ship and sail away. I wrote Willie a letter and I said in it I would write you and give you a present - these little pictures. Mama will give you money for them and you and Hattie can go to the candy store and buy candy with it. Next, Hattie will get a letter from

your own loving Papa.

Louise's Father, Eben Weld Tallant
Nantucket Seafarer – Astoria Canneryman

Like so many young men on Nantucket Island, Eben Weld Tallant (1841-1932) went to sea immediately after his high school graduation - in 1858. He spent his early adult life onboard several clipper ships, circling the globe seven times and visiting all the major ports. His first ship was the *Dragoon* (probably one of the so-called "school ships") sailing from Boston via San Francisco to Calcutta for a load of jute to take to New Orleans. On April 8, 1861, at the beginning of the War between the States, the *Dragoon* arrived in New Orleans[1] just as Confederate forces took Fort Sumter. The rebels captured the ship. Twenty-year-old Eben was allowed to leave the ship and go home by boat and rail. Before he shipped out again, he sat for and obtained his Mate's Ticket. In April 1863, he sailed as fourth mate on the beautiful *Golden State*,[2] a three-masted American-built clipper ship, sailing round Cape Horn to Callao (for a load of guano), then on to San Francisco – a trip that took 121 days.[3] Eben later became the vessel's first officer.[4] He left the *Golden State* at a Chinese port very early in 1869 and traveled home to Nantucket to wed Mary Elizabeth Easton (1844-1926) on April third of that year. Returning to the Orient later in 1869, he shipped out as first officer on the *John Bright*, listed by Lloyd's of London as a small 126' long/541 ton British ship of trade registered in Guernsey. He was the purser of that ship when she carried the first tea from Japan. After numerous voyages in the Orient, particularly between Hong Kong and Shanghai, he signed off the *John Bright* and made his way to the Hawaiian Islands, where he managed a sugar plantation for several years. Other members of his family had already migrated from Nantucket to San Francisco; some of them had gone onward to settle in the Islands.

In 1871, Eben Weld Tallant sailed east from Hawaii to Los Angeles, California. He purchased land in nearby San Gabriel, where he planted and managed an orange grove. His wife Mary Elizabeth Easton Tallant and their young son William Easton Tallant (1870-1934) traveled by boat and train from Nantucket to San Gabriel to join him.

---

[1] The Port Listings of the *New Orleans Bee* of April 8, 1861, showed the arrival of the *Dragoon*, under Captain Upton, docking at the Hobart & Foster Dock, Berth 37, after an 85-day trip from Calcutta.

[2] According to the Maine Historical Society, the celebrated *Golden State* was later renamed the *Annie C. Maguire*. Returning to her Portland, ME harbor from Buenos Aires, she crashed upon the rocks near Portland Head Light, Cape Elizabeth, Maine on December 24, 1886.

[3] Cutter, 224.

[4] A family story told by E.W.T. was of the mate and he being swept off the fo'c'sle of one of his ships – believed to be the *Golden State* – and, in the violent gale, then being swept back on the poop deck by the same wave. He was lucky; the mate was lost.

During December 1872, Eben W. Tallant apparently returned to Hawaii to participate in the December 11 funeral of a fellow Mason, King Lot Kamehameha V,[5] and in the coronation of William C. Lunalilo. It is reported he also attended the 1874 coronation of the "Merrie Monarch," King David Kalakaua, a Mason and a graduate of Oxford.[6] Although he returned to the Hawaiian Islands on those occasions, Eben and his family settled down to life in Southern California. Two daughters were born to Eben and Mary Elizabeth while in San Gabriel - Maria Louise (June 16, 1875 - October 18, 1962) and Harriet Easton (January 12, 1878 – September 9, 1970).

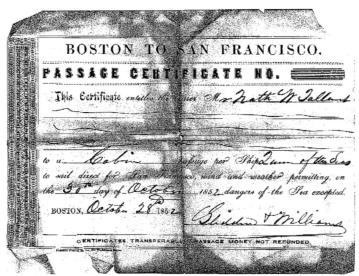

Nathaniel Weld Tallant's Passage and Cabin Certificate #64 dated October 28, 1852.

E. W. Tallant's older brother, Nathaniel Weld Tallant (1832-1899), had taken cabin passage on the *Queen of the Seas* that sailed October 30, 1852, from Boston to San Francisco. He remained in Southern California for a period of time. He then migrated north from California to the mouth of the Columbia River, where he began working in an early fish packing company on the river at Eagle Cliff, Washington Territory (W.T.). The Census of 1880 for Wahkiakum County, W.T., listed Nathaniel Weld Tallant as the manager of Frances Cutting's Salmon Cannery at Eagle Cliff. Eben and Nathaniel's mother, Lydia Scudder Tallant (1806-1890), left Barnstable not long after the death of her husband, Nathaniel (1794-1871), and traveled west. She went first to San Francisco to visit relatives, then north to Eagle Cliff. The 1880 Census also listed their widowed mother, Lydia, as residing there. She later returned to San Francisco, where she died September 9, 1890.

Early in 1881, E.W. Tallant sailed up the west coast from his San Gabriel orange grove to join his older brother and mother at the Eagle Cliff cannery.

---

[5] Lockley, ed., "E.W. Tallant," 467-9.
[6] King Lot Kamehameha V ruled the Hawaiian Islands from 1863 until his death December 11, 1872. William C. Lunalilo ruled for only thirteen months; he died February 3, 1874. King David Kalakaua was the last Hawaiian King, reigning from 1874 to 1891. He was a 32nd degree Freemason – Knights Templar. His sister, Lydia Lili'oukalani, succeeded him as Queen from 1891 to 1898, the end of the monarchy. On April 28, 1868, E.W. Tallant was vested as a Master Mason in Brooklyn, New York. He instituted the local Masonic Lodge on Maui when he was in the Islands.

View of our home, from the arroyo looking West

San Gabriel, California. "View of our house from the arroyo looking West." Louise is the child far left. Marge Halsted and her family lived across the arroyo. Marge became one of Louise's dearest friends.

Maria Louise Tallant - Six months
San Gabriel – December 1875
Photograph taken in Los Angeles.

Richard E. "Dick" Carruthers – 1Year
Oysterville - May 1875

Louise and Harriet Tallant
San Gabriel - 1880
Photo taken in Los Angeles.

Dick and Angus Russell Carruthers
Oysterville – 1879

Louise (seated) and Harriet
San Gabriel – 1881
Photo taken in Los Angeles.

William Easton Tallant with Bismark
San Gabriel – 1881
Photo taken in Los Angeles.

In 1883 the cannery burned to the ground for unknown reasons. The two brothers then moved their operation to Astoria, Oregon, where they established the Columbia River Packing Company.

In November 1887, in association with Frances Cutting, Thomas Hobson, Thomas Foster and Fred P. Kendall (Pacific Can Company), Nathaniel organized the Alaska Coast Fishing Company in San Francisco with a capital stock of $120,000 and 240 shares.[7]

Nathaniel Weld Tallant and Eben Weld Tallant became well known as leaders in the salmon packing industry, both in Astoria and in California, maintaining high standards and continually upgrading their packing processes.

In the spring of 1881, traveling by train from their San Gabriel home in the orange groves, Mary Elizabeth Easton Tallant took their three children – Will (age 11), Louise (almost 6), and Harriet (age 3) – east to Nantucket Island for the summer-long visit with their maternal grandparents, the Hon. William Redwood Easton (October 3, 1802 – May 29, 1894) and Eliza Baxter Easton (March 4, 1808 - March 9, 1889). The reason for their visit to Nantucket at that time was to participate in the 200th anniversary commemorating the death of the founder of their family tree, Tristram Coffin. Mary Elizabeth and the three children returned to San Gabriel in the fall of 1881. Soon after, the Tallant family sold their orange grove acreage and left for Astoria. Eben built an imposing home on Concomly Street, with a commanding view of the waterfront. The Tallant family lived there for over fourteen years.

Family photo donated to Clatsop County Historical Society   #26,865-960

The Tallants' Concomly Street house is in the center of this 1886 photo. Two vines grew up to the second floor windows. A close look on the west side of the cupola may show some construction scaffolding. The largest vessel - moored at the dock - is the three-masted Clipper ship, the *Tillie E. Starbuck*. The *T.F. Oakes* is also docked there. The young child on the sidewalk in the left foreground is Nat Tallant, Louise's younger brother.

---

[7] *Daily Astorian*, November 24, 1887.

Family photo donated to Clatsop County Historical Society #26,864-960.
The Tallant house on Concomly Street – 1888

The Tallants and the Eastons: l. to r.: Nat (5), Harriet (10) with their dog, Bismark; Mary Wright, domestic; Eben, Mrs. Ellen Easton Crosby, Mary Elizabeth Easton Tallant, Charles C. Crosby, Louise (13). The Tallants' older son Will (not shown), then about eighteen, was probably in school at Bishop Scott's Academy in Oswego, Oregon. Notice the plank sidewalk.

Family photo donated to Clatsop County Historical Society– #26,862-960.
Family Parlor, looking south, in the Tallant's Concomly home.

Concomly parlor. Cleveland Rockwell's
Columbia River painting was donated to
Columbia River Maritime Museum.

Nathaniel Weld Tallant and Bismark
Astoria – 1888

The three younger Tallant children: Nathaniel Weld, Maria Louise, and Harriet Easton – 1888.

Harriet, age 12; Louise, age 15 – 1890

Dick Carruthers – age 15 in 1889.
University of Oregon Freshman.

The Lost Jewel
A unique jewel of an historic house is lost to Astoria

Upon the arrival of Mary Elizabeth Easton Tallant and the three children in Astoria in late 1881 or early 1882, the family took up temporary lodgings. Eben W. Tallant, a well-traveled Nantucket seafarer, was now an up and coming cannery man. He employed Hiram B. Parker to construct a suitable house for his family at 104 Concomly Street (later Astor Street) on the northeast corner of Madison near the waterfront.[8] The two-story house was not the Cape Cod design one would have expected, but rather it was Italianate in style, with a number of tall windows allowing for lots of light into each room. Mary Elizabeth's rose bushes flanked the square front porch that extended up to the wooden plank sidewalk. The most striking feature of the house was a square cupola perched atop the two main floors. It had windows all around from which Eben could keep a weather eye over the activities at the Columbia River Packing Company cannery and on the river traffic.[9]

On May 15, 1883, the Tallants' younger son was born in the house. He was named Nathaniel Weld (usually called 'Nat') after several of his forebears, particularly Eben Weld Tallant's older brother.

The Tallants moved to their newly built Grand Avenue home sometime in 1896. The Concomly house became rooms-to-let, but stood until the 1930s, when it was torn down to allow for the expansion of the Union Oil Company. A Burger King franchise now occupies the lot at Third and Marine Drive, where the Tallants' first Astoria home had stood.

The *Daily Astorian* of October 2, 1890, ran an article dated September 23, 1890, received from the *Patriot* of Barnstable, Massachusetts:

Remains of Lydia Tallant who recently died in San Francisco arrived here Friday. Her funeral took place from the residence of Mr. Silas B. Parker Friday afternoon, Rev. Frederick Henchley officiating. Her remains during the service rested in the same room in which she was both born and married. Her son Mr Eben Tallant and his wife, from Portland, Oregon, accompanied the remains here. Funeral services were also held in San Francisco on the 11th inst. at the residence of her daughter Mrs Theodore Smith,[10] 1600 Golden State avenue.

Later, the November 2, 1890 issue of the Astoria newspaper carried a notice stating E. W. and Mary Elizabeth Tallant had just returned from the East. Following the funeral of Lydia Tallant, they had been visiting with friends and family, especially in the state of Massachusetts. The Tallants and Eastons were well-known families in the New England

---

[8] R. L. Polk & Co.'s 1890 Directory of the City of Astoria listed the home at 104 First Street. The City of Astoria's Ordinance No. 1869, adopted April 24, 1894, changed street names: Concomly Street in McClure's plating and First Street on the Adair maps changed to Astor Street; Madison became Third Street. Currently, the preferred spelling of the name of the Chinook tribe's chief is Comcomly.

[9] Goodenberger, "Cupola made Tallant house exclusive," (*Daily Astorian*, November. 26, 2004), 4A.

[10] Eben's younger sister, Sarah Frances (1844-1905), married Theodore Garland Smith (1840-1898) in Nantucket in 1865. They resided in Hawaii for a number of years, later returning to San Francisco.

area. Their forbears had emigrated from England as early as the 1600s, as had many of those families with whom they were interrelated, *e.g.,* the Baxter, Coffin, Crosby, Macy, Otis, Scudder, Smith and Weld families.

The Tallants were also related to the Starbuck family of Nantucket and New York. In 1891, Clara Starbuck, the daughter and heiress of the famous Starbuck shipbuilding family, lived with her parents in Brooklyn, NY. She visited Louise and her family in Astoria often. Both girls were about sixteen years of age in 1891.

Mailing date: Nov 7 10AM 1891 Brooklyn, N.Y.
Received: Nov 13 8AM 1891
Postage: Two Cents red George Washington Stamp
Envelope addressed to: Miss Louise Tallant
104 Concomly Street
Astoria, Oregon

Brooklyn   Nov. 7 – 1891

Dear Louise -

If you could see the great confusion I am in, you would doubly appreciate this letter, but I made up my mind that comes what might, I would write you this morning. Although I fortunately have nothing what ever to write about as it is frightfully dull just at present. The only thing that is going on that I am at all interested in is a large church wedding, the wedding of Mr. N- whose photos I showed you. Of course I shall go and you can imagine me waltzing up the aisle of the church gotten up quite regardless in my white crepe and forget-me-nots. It makes me quite tired to think of his getting married, it means a good many less theatres for me.

There is going to be a large fair in Danbury [Connecticut] for the benefit of the hospital, and I am going to help with it - expect to have lots of fun.

I am so sorry it happened so about Hattie's coat. I never was so puzzled about a thing before. I hope it will not be too late before it gets there. How is dear Dr Walker and have you seen him any more in tears and has he gone to San Francisco yet? I am dying to know if he ever married that girl. So write and tell me all the news— who are married, dead, or engaged, or anything else startling. You would laugh to see my hair. I have only done it up <u>twice</u> since I got home, and it is just as curly as can be. I know it will be hard for you to believe.

I have got to have a regular cleaning up time today, so I must stop now. I will copy the "Gobble-un will git y'o if you don't watch out" for Hattie, and will also send her the picture I promised. Write very soon and give much love to all from

Lovingly

Clara

How is Miss [Emma?] Warren? How did the dance come off? Did Ellen [Easton Crosby] stop for it? We are having the most delightful weather. If you are having it too, how I should love to be out in a boat on the Columbia river.

Early October 1892, Louise had the good fortune to travel by train to Chicago, perhaps accompanied on the journey by her father. In those years it was quite common for young women who were away from home to stay with local families, sometimes paying their board and room. Louise lived with family friends, the Adcocks, on Prairie Avenue and 29th Street. Her family felt confident she would be well chaperoned while away from home in Chicago. Accompanied by her friends, Alice W-, Sylvia Norton, Edith Adcock, and their chaperone, Mrs. Nichols, Louise was able to attend many concerts and theatrical productions while there. One of the most enjoyable and exciting would have been the piano recital given by the renowned Paderewski, who was on his Second American Tour. It was Paderewski's first recital of Chicago's 1892-1893 concert season. Louise attended the concert at the Chicago Auditorium at 2 o'clock on Wednesday afternoon, March 8, 1893. She wrote that it was "[t]he most beautiful music I ever heard."

Although no letters from her to her family survived, she did keep a very tiny, cryptic "diary" of her eight months in Chicago, noting some of the things she did there, such as the plays, concerts and lectures she attended, and the music lessons she took. She attended Plymouth Church; often made afternoon calls upon other ladies; in the evenings played card games such as Hearts and Euchre – and poker; and was frequently invited out to dinners. Louise also attended dance classes and the World's Fair - Columbian Exposition of 1893!

Bourniques' School of Dancing and Deportment   1892 - 1893
Chicago, Illinois

Fortunately, Louise did save her pamphlet of the Bourniques' School of Dancing and Deportment that she attended while in Chicago. Louise, who had turned 17 in June, was accepted into the class of "Juveniles." A three-month term cost her $20 to attend instruction on Tuesday and Saturday afternoons. In her tiny "diary," she wrote that her first dance class was on Saturday, November 5th. She wore her yellow silk dress to the Bourniques' Christmas party on Saturday, December 31, 1892. Her last class party was on the evening of April 7, 1893.

From the fall 1892 though the spring 1893, Louise attended two terms at Mr. & Mrs. A. E. Bournique's School. The Bourniques were highly regarded members of the American Society of Professors of Dancing. They had built an elegant brick building at 51 Twenty-Third Street East that was steam heated and supplied with "Edison incandescent light." The building housed separate ladies and gentlemen's Parlors, a reception room and a spacious Banquet Hall – served by well-trained caterers. It also featured a huge Dancing Hall, with "faultless waxed floors" that, as many attendees attested, provided the "most perfect dancing floor."[11]

The Bourniques' excellent reputation was known not only in Chicago, but also throughout the country. They were a "finishing school for the elite," catering to the local Prairie Avenue crowd of Chicago, offering exclusive classes for ladies and for gentlemen. Their classes emphasized "physical strength, gracefulness of motion and courtliness of deportment." Both young men and young women were taught "[H]abit is second nature." The school's strict dress code required the wearing of "thin, flexible shoes or gaiters, with moderate heels; those not worn on the street...and without nails."[12] It was mandatory to wear white gloves in all classes. Proper etiquette was also required at all times. The Grand March was always the last thing at the end of each week's classes. As the girls left, they curtsied to their teachers; the boys bowed.

The school also held "assemblies" for advanced pupils on Friday evenings. One of Louise's Assembly dance cards exists. The assemblies' programmes were simple – two small, nicely printed pieces of cardboard, tied together with orange ribbon. The dances listed were the waltz, polka, Lancers, *deux temp*,[13] and schottische. In her March 21, 1893 letter, Harriet wanted to know about an unidentified gentleman with the initials D.O.T., who had claimed a dance with Louise on her fully booked dance card - he had signed for dance number 12, the '*deux temp*'- double time, like the quick step. The young man's identity remains a mystery, because none of Louise's letters to her family were saved. Harriet, who had just turned fifteen years old, also had other concerns. She wrote her older sister wanting to know, of course, about the dances, but also if Louise had played poker (which she did), and asked her to obtain a copy of a new piece of music entitled "Daddy Won't Buy Me a Bow-wow."

---

[11]   Fox, Reminiscences: http://home.triad.rr.com/aspinks/fox/autobiog.htm
[12]   Bourniques' 1892-1893 brochure. Mr. And Mrs. A.E. Bourniques' School of Dancing and Deportment, Twenty-Sixth Annual Session.
[13]   The "*deux temp*" might use a music beat as in "Come to the Cabaret" (from the Broadway hit *Cabaret*).

A note in the Bourniques' brochure for the season of 1892-1893 mentioned that they had just "published three new dances with music, called 'The Wentworth,' 'The Manitou,' and 'The Del Monte.' . . . They are pleasing novelties." The students might also have danced to the newly composed "Crystal Palace Polka" and the "Ferris Wheel Waltz."

The Chicago World's Fair and Columbian Exposition of 1893

Louise noted in her little "diary" that the temperature of the snowy Christmas Day in 1892 was ten below zero, but she had enjoyed a sledge ride pulled by Eskimo dogs at the World's Fair - Columbian Exposition Fair grounds site. She and her friends frequently walked around the site while it was still under construction. Louise's first visit (of many during her last month in Chicago) to the Fair itself was on the ninth of May, following the official opening on May 1, 1893. Louise obtained a souvenir silver Half-Dollar Columbian coin when she visited the fair; it was the first commemorative coin of its kind to be struck from a die by the United States Mint. In a later letter written to Dick on January 29, 1896, during a trip to California, she bemoaned its loss.

Of the Fair much has been written and pictured in books and on the Internet. The major motivation for the Chicago World's Fair was the Columbian Exposition that recognized the 400th anniversary of Columbus' arrival in the New World. It was dedicated on October 9, 1892, although the fairgrounds did not officially open to visitors until seven months later. Until the late 19th century, fairs had focused mainly on agriculture, farm life and farm products. The Chicago World's Fair of 1893 changed that. It greatly broadened its social, cultural and economic appeal. Work began on the gigantic project in 1891. It was to be the "Wonder of the Ages." The total cost of the Fair/Exposition was $28,340,700 – an astounding amount for those times – but the admission price was only 50 cents for those fairgoers ages twelve and over.

The Centennial Exposition of 1876 had introduced "bread" to the populace. The Chicago World's Fair featured corn - everywhere – CORN. And much more! The Midway *Plaisance* offered amusement parks and carnivals; horse races; spectacles of all types in 65 exhibits from 46 nations; exotic pavilions; and architecturally unique buildings. John Olmsted viewed his landscaping of the fair, not as just a decorative feature, but as an integral part of the buildings. Engineer George Washington Gage Ferris, Jr. built the Ferris Wheel, the largest at that date; it carried 2,160 passengers at a time. On display were an 11-ton cheese from Canada; a 70-foot high tower of electric light bulbs; and even scandalous Egyptian "coochie-coochie" dancers who were the big money makers of the fair. The Fair's visitors wrote "post-cards" home, tasted their first hamburgers and ate "Cracker Jack" while they sipped the new carbonated soft drinks. Probably they also listened to the earliest ragtime tunes played by Scott Joplin on his coronet - <u>outside</u> the fair grounds. Buffalo Bill's Wild West Show, also located outside the fair grounds, drew millions of spectators. But what really took center stage were engineering and modern technologies. Nikola Tesla's alternating electric current drove the exhibits, ran the electric streetcars, operated the movable sidewalks and turned the Chicago night into day. And the fair's buildings glowed night and day - all were painted white, so the fair grounds became known as "The White City." There was so much to see and do. And Louise was there!

Clear images by Chuck Meyer of The Compleat Photographer, Astoria, Oregon, and K. Karel Lambert.
Authorized by the U.S. Congress, the 1893 Columbian Exposition's silver Half Dollar was the first souvenir commemorative coin to be struck from a die. On the Obverse, Charles E. Barber, Chief Engraver of the U.S. Mint, designed the bust of Columbus. The Reverse features the image of the *Santa Maria* above the two hemispheres, engraved by Morgan Silver Dollar designer, Charles T. Morgan.

Two hundred twenty four congresses were held during the Fair's run with themes ranging from Agriculture to Engineering to Women's Progress. However, only one building now remains of this fantastic Fair – The Palace of Fine Arts is now Chicago's Museum of Science and Industry.

The World's Fair/Columbian Exposition drew visitors from all over the world. Dick's father, Robert Carruthers, took advantage of this opportunity to reach a wide clientele. The *Astorian Daily Budget,* of August 8, 1893, reported he had cut and hand finished 6,000 walking canes of the Washington Territory's wild crabapple to sell at the Fair. Later, possibly Mary Elizabeth and Eben attended at some point; the Reverend and Mrs. T.L. Eliot and the Benjamin Youngs certainly did, among others from Astoria and Portland.

The Chicago fire of October 1871 had burned down a vast area of the city including the newly completed Palmer House Hotel on State Street. Although almost ruined financially, Mr. Potter Palmer and his Kentucky-born wife Bertha Honore Palmer managed to rebuild the hotel. The new Palmer House was completed in 1873. In the fall of 1874, Bertha's sister Ida married Lt. Col. Dent Grant, the son of President Ulysses S. Grant. This made Bertha Palmer the "Grande Dame of Chicago Society." On Thursday, December 8, 1892, Louise Tallant of Astoria, Oregon, attended Mrs. Potter Palmer's Columbian Bazaar. Later, she was invited to the Palmer's mansion on Chicago's Gold Coast and was "entertained in her house." In the early 1880s, the Palmers had built their massive Lake Shore Drive mansion in the turreted Norman style. The house cost $1,000,000. The Palmers' extensive collection of Impressionist paintings graced the mansions numerous rooms. Although the mansion later became a popular tourist attraction, it was demolished in 1950.

16

Mrs. Palmer was an activist. She led the fight for women's and workers' rights, organized the city's Business Women's Club and was awarded the French *Legion d' honneur* for her work on the Paris Exposition. She was elected president of the Board of Lady Managers of the 1893 World's Fair/Columbian Exposition. She not only raised impressive sums of money for the Fair, but also convinced the Fair's leaders to construct a building exclusively for women's exhibits that was designed by a twenty-one year old woman architect from Boston. When in Chicago, she gave parties for political ward workers. She presided as the ultimate hostess to royalty and international figures from all over the world at her homes in Chicago, Paris, London and Biarritz. On May 10, 1918, she died at her Sarasota Bay, Florida home.

Because the Tallants' Concomly house was located only a half block from the Astoria Wharf and Warehouse building (completed in 1892 by Richard Ervin "Dick" Carruthers' father, Robert), Dick and Louise would have been well acquainted with each other. Dick would become nineteen in May 1893. He had entered the University of Oregon in Eugene at the age of fifteen. He was a student there for one year – 1889-1890, registered in the Classical, Scientific, Literary and English Courses Department. In an 1893 letter from Oakland, he mentions he is studying and has "a row with a prof once in a while." He may have attended Stanford, the University of California at Berkeley, or even the Throop Business College at Pasadena (now California Institute of Technology, known as Cal Tech).

The following partial letter from Oakland is the first letter Louise kept from Dick. No envelope was saved, but Dick would have sent this letter to Louise in care of Mr. & Mrs. Adcock, and their daughter Edith, at 2902 Prairie Avenue, Chicago, Illinois. Louise was then seventeen years old.

Oakland   Feby 18, 1893

Dear Louise,

I received your letter Friday and was more than glad to get it. I was wondering all week what you thought of my last letter. I don't know what was the matter with me that day, but you surely knew something was wrong, but as you did not get angry but answered it I will never do anything like it again. Now you are right, never give up a sleigh ride because you have a letter to write. I can easly wait a little while. You better look out for yourself in regards to Lettie and let poor Kate [Upshur] alone, don't you think so. I received a letter from Clara the other day but Caroline [Young] where [was] out then. Now Louise you know very well I never cared anything [about] Caroline, why should I? I know I did go around with her a good deal while up home but that was all so I don't care wheather she has forgotten me or not so don't ever think C- has any strings on me, ever did have, or ever will have, although I think she is a nice girl. I know of nicer. About Jim's girl I believe he does not go with her any more. I think Jim is kind of stuck on Nan [Reed] from what he has told me but hear - this is getting to far away from our own affairs. Jim would scalp me if he [k]new I was giving things away like this. I always thought Nan a very nice girl, but I won't say she is the nicest girl of all and I am glad you know the girl who I like best for I think you ought too because it is your own dear self but Louise I think this is getting a little to severe don't you.

So you think boys are queer things do you. Well I have the same opinion of girls, but then that's all right. I am glad you are selfish about the message I sent you because that is the way I intended it to be and I send you more than twice the amount this letter. Louise, I did not mean that I did not like your letter. Now you know that I didn't mean that, don't you - you know what kind of boy I am so if I make any more breaks why just forgive me won't you? Yes, I suppose I will have to wait and see you in your new dresses to tell anything about them and I hope that will not be long. Who is Mr [Homer] Sargent, the nice looking boy at dancing school - well I don't think I will allow myself to become jealous of him shall I? Well there is not much going on now here except study and a row with a prof once in a while so I am going to close but before I do so Louise I want you not to get angry if . . .

No further pages.

Eben Weld Tallant wrote his daughter on March 21, 1893, to remind her of her promise to act as a tour guide through the Fair for Carolyn, Benjamin Young's daughter, and for other Astorian friends who would be attending the fair. But he also told her he wanted her to be home before the fishing season began to help him and her older brother Will at their Columbia River Packing Company cannery in Astoria.

Louise's father occasionally addressed his daughter by her first given name – Maria. She had been named after her father's cousin, Maria Louise Tallant Owen, a Nantucket botanist of considerable reputation, who had published two definitive books about Nantucket County's native plants.

Mailing date: Mar 21 5:30PM 1893 Astoria, Oreg.
Addressed to: Miss Maria L Tallant
                              #2902 Prairie Avenue
                              Chicago   Ill

Cutting Packing Company
San Francisco, California
Agents   OFFICE of
                              Columbia River Packing Company
                                          Packers of
                              COLUMBIA RIVER SALMON

Astoria, Oregon, March 21st 1893

My dear Maria,

I have quite neglected you in letter writing but you well know writing is a task to me and I get full enough of it in letters that must be written in way of my business. Your mother makes up for my neglect and I will also enclose material that will assist to atone for my fault. The letter from Cousin Maria you will please save as I consider her letters so valuable that I have kept nearly all she ever wrote to me. I have been greatly pleased with all your letters. Am sorry to learn from your last that Mrs Adcock is on the sick list but trust when this arrives it will trouble her to remember when she was sick.

Your mother and I have just returned from a pleasant trip to Portland where we were finely entertained by the Sutherlunds and other friends.

Ben Young often talks to me about your promising to guide his daughter through the Worlds fair. I hope you'll not make so many engagements as to delay your getting home in time for fishing season, as there will be a great amount of work for you in the office. We now have 94 boats engaged, which is far beyond any previous record and to add to this it is very probable we shall buy fish by weight instead of the old method of count; this will greatly increase the office labor of which Willie has full charge depending on you as assistant. It is expected you will earn sufficient to pay your expenses to visit Los Angeles next winter, anticipation of which is in the minds of our many friends there. You will probably see Emma & Ella[14] ere long as they plan to visit Chicago soon. They will expect you to make your headquarters with them next Winter as you have the Adcocks this.

Willie has started into business on his own account in the way of buying into the team-ing business of Prael & Co. This will put him so deep in debt that there is no chance of visiting Chicago this year. Hattie is as usual deeply in hand with Kate [Upshur] and we trust for your assistance in giving her dignity. Little Nat seems to be sincerely good and we believe he will ever be a source of comfort to us all.

With kind regards to Mr & Mrs Adcock,

I remain with love and affection

Your father

Enclosed in her father's letter was one from her fifteen-year old sister, Harriet.

My dear Louise

Received your letter this a.m. You must be having a fine time and I would not hurry home for the party for you know there will be two more and the last one will make up for the one you will miss. I first went over to Nelly with your letter to read to her but she was not at home. She is working at Mr U-. How nice of D.O.T. calling on you, no doubt but that you enjoyed yourself. _Did you play poker?_

Mama and papa are going out to tea this evening up at Mrs Flavels. I was going to ask Kate down to tea but have been out so late the last three nights that I will want to go to bed early to night. Had a fine time last night - went to the church sociable (suppose Mama told

---

[14] Louise's cousins were Ella and Emma Scudder, daughters of Daniel and Bethia Smith Scudder. Ella married E. B. Crocker; Emma Scudder wed E.C. Bichowsky, a Los Angeles-San Gabriel photographer.

you all about it as they went home early). I stayed and went home with Nettie for the night. They danced upstairs in the AAUW room. For music they had the harp and violin. I had a fine dance with Dick, two or three with Tom [Bryce] and one with Jim. Nelly [Sherman] and all the girls were there. Never saw P.H. [Pearl Holden] look so nice as she did last night – had on a brown w[ith] light blue. Mrs Tuttle went to P- [Portland] last night (maby you have seen her) and Dr T- was called away up the river some place and was away all night. We did not wake up until 8 oclock and had to cook breakfast so you have an idea how we had to cratch to get to school. It snowed last night and rained this am and made it so wet that by the time Nettie got to school she was drenched through for her bubbers [rubber boots] leake, so had to be excused from school and go home to get dry.

(Notice - excuse pencil)

O dear. Next week final examination, don't suppose I will pass but such is life in the far west. We had examination in Ivanhoe yesterday - don't know what I got but Miss B- said I passed (to my surprise).

Mama is up stairs dressing. She just called to me and said to tell you to get her a dozen hair pins - you know what kind she wants. I am going to commence music lessons next Friday from 3:30 - 4 oclock. If you have any spare chink (would send you some if I had any) will you get me "Dady wont buy me a bow wow" - not with the words but the schottice -(how do you spell it) if you can find it.

Well I must close - guess I will go up and get Kate to come down - don't feel so sleepy now as I did an hour ago. I will think of you to night as belle of the dance and having D.O.T's sweet face smiling on you.

I send . . .

Hattie

P.S. (Hope you will be back in time for the dance after this)

On June 2, 1893, Louise packed her bags, boarded the 10:30 PM train and sadly left "Chicago and all."

Although there was no envelope, Dick would have sent the following 1894 letter to Portland, care of the Reverend Thomas Lamb Eliot family[15] - the Eliots' daughters, Grace and Henrietta, were about Louise's age of nineteen, or to the J. D. Sutherland family, living at 357 W. Park in Portland, whose daughter Lila was also about nineteen years old. These young ladies often visited back and forth, as did the girls' respective parents, making the trip by steamers, such as the *Telephone* and *Telegraph*. While in Portland, she continued her interest in learning to dance after attending Bourniques' in Chicago the

---

[15] The Rev. Thomas Lamb Eliot was the pastor of Portland's First Unitarian church.

previous year. Her instructor in Portland was Madame Harriet Foreman Enrick, who was well known as the "society dancing teacher." Mme Enrick's classes were held in Foreman Hall at North 23rd and Kearny; she taught in Portland from 1882 to 1905. After moving to Mill Valley, California in 1905, Mme Enrick continued giving dancing lessons there well into her eighties.[16]

Wednesday 24 / '94   [January]

My Dear Little Girl

> *Or Big Girl which is it.*

The party being over I am going to tell you all I can about it. I missed no one who goes except your Royal Highness and I did miss you. I danced with Miss Trullinger so that made up for the high part – as for Royal, well it was a royal party and I am sorry you missed it, but perhaps you were having a better time with one of those swell fellows as you term the Portland boys, than you would have had here.

Pearl had on a new dress - a kind of a yellow. I guess the dress had been under discus-sion before you left – so you know what it was like, a kind of pale blue pink sealskin, I think. Anyhow she looked fine. Nan wore her blue and Nancy T- had a new white dress and looked the best I have seen her. Nettie had a new pair of white slippers with black heals. Miss T- was attired in dark - left the blue dress at home I guess. Tom and I danced in the same set as Miss T- and shocked her bad with our rude conduct. Nellie was there and I engaged a dance with her and she wouldn't look at me for a long time as I forgot to go around for it. Sir Thomas DeBryce was fairly in it with his new white kidds. There were about 8 boys without partners but Simon and three others of them picked up partners after they got there & it left Dick L-, your big brother [Will], Mick & myself alone so it wasn't bad for the married peoples.

Lots asked me why you weren't there, told them Portland agreed to well with you so it does too suit me.

I am going to send you my Programme & you can see what dances I saved for you. I'll be honest though and tell you that the ones that were saved were the ones I could find no pardners for, but they were saved just the same.

Coleman wasn't there so if you had been you wouldn't have to sit dying for a drink, for there was nothing but water. Mrs Sanborn wore a black dress with white satin ribbon to the extent of about 100 yards - more or less.

Well I think this about all I can remember about the dance, except that Paul was as usual ploting to get dances with the Gurls.

---

[16] Fischer, "Eighty-year-old woman still teaching dancing," clipping pasted in Louise's scrapbook, dated in pencil, September 20, 1930.

Simon and I went to the Opera [Fisher's Opera House] *the other evening and it was fine. Had a letter from W. Rikon and he asked me if we - that is I - had had a fallen out yet. I guess not, and are not likely to are we unless you stay 2 or 3 weeks more in Portland. I told Nellie I was not angry but mad at you for not being here to go to the dance. She thought I was and if you ever had a girl pleade for your cause, Nellie did.*

If you ever do, be a good girl, don't get in a row with Dunc [McTavish] *over Jenkins. Up and above all come home soon if not sooner.*

Dick

She said she was going to write to you and will probly tell you I didn't like it, but how could I do otherwise than like it after that letter you wrote and the closing part. Why, every time you write you are doing it better. Say, when am I to buy the diamond ring? Don't say this year as times are to hard. Say, the reason I rushed off so the last time I saw you was I felt like kissing you good bye, but knowing it wasn't 3 o'clock in the morning, I thought I'd better not try it, but wait till the 3 o'clock comes.

I just saw Nellie up town. She informed me that she had received a letter from you, and also told me some of the contents: ie. Glad you were going to the Skating rink with Duncan other than going to the dance with Dick. O, I knew just why you wanted to go to Portland. Well if you want to desert me that way, the whole thing is that I won't let you.

I told everything that I've known to be true and some that I won't believe so I guess I'll call my task finished. If they were all as pleasant to perform as this I wouldn't mind.

Hoping you are having a nice, nice time and that you will be home soon

I am yours

Dick

With much love etc, etc. I beg your pardon for writing with a pencil as it is all I've got to write with down here. Also for the time which I have taken in your reading this.

me.

The 25th Wedding Anniversary – 1894

Mary Elizabeth Easton and Eben Weld Tallant wed in Nantucket on April 3, 1869. Mary Elizabeth was the third of the four daughters of the Hon. William Redwood Easton (1803-1894) and Eliza Baxter Easton (1808-1889), who had married in Nantucket on September 27, 1827. Eben Weld Tallant's parents were Nathaniel (December 27, 1794, Pelham, MA – April 20, 1871, Nantucket) and Lydia Scudder Tallant (November 7, 1806, Cape Cod – September 9, 1890, San Francisco); they had married December 27, 1824, in Nantucket. Eben was one of seven children born to them.

Eben Weld Tallant

Mary Elizabeth Easton Tallant

1869   **1894**

Eben Weld Tallant, Mary E. Easton

Mr. & Mrs. Eben Weld Tallant

At Home,

Tuesday, April third,

from seven until ten o'clock,

104 Concomly Street,

Astoria, Oregon.

The printing on the invitation was done in silver. One extra envelope, with invitation, was addressed to the Misses Sophie & Eliza Boelling of Astoria.

The following letter to Louise from Dick was written on the Astoria Wharf & Warehouse company stationery.

R. CARRUTHERS   E. W. TALLANT   R. E. CARRUTHERS
President   Vice President   Secretary
ASTORIA WHARF AND WAREHOUSE CO.
Proprietors U. S. Bonded Warehouse

Astoria, OR., Jan'y 2 1895

Dear Louise:

It seems as though I'll never get a chance to have a little talk with you, so I am going to take this liberty of writing and besides I think I can explain thing a little better in writing than talking. Why it is I don't know but some how another I can't act the same with you as I can with other girls, whom I like a thousandth part as well, so here goes. Two or three weeks before Christmas morning, when I received that short little letter, I was trying to forget there was a Louise, and I guess for those three weeks I was the unhappiest mortal in Oregon, but I didn't succeed worth a cent. You'll think that was funny I suspose, but I got it in to my head that you were tired of me (and it isn't quit out of it yet) for I never could see how you cared anything for me. I am nothing to speak of, my temper, which I've an abundancy, is inclined to be of the sulky sort and it seems I am always cross. I argued with myself that it was alright for you when you were younger and didn't quite understand men, but now since you have grown to be a young lady (and I never hated to see anyone grow except you) that you would think myself rather young to be going with Etc and on that point I had to agree with you.

When all this got started I can't exactly tell but you perhaps remember the party at Van Dusens. Well I didn't intend to take you home that night, as I thought it would suit you better, but as Tom Wick went before I thought I had better ask for your company home which I was afterward very sorry for doing, because I think you didn't want it, and I never want to do anything you don't want me to. So that night might be call[ed] the starting point. I went home fully resolved that I was a big bundle of trouble to you, thinking I was done for but I fully intended to <u>like</u> you in a quiet way to myself the same time trying to help you out of what I though you had decided to do, let me slide. By keeping myself away from your company and trying to forget you were on earth, but in this later part I failed entirely and I never want to have a three weeks like that again.

Christmas eve was a deadly one, how I wanted to walk down home with you, and how I was stubborn and kept to my resolution. I went home thinking things were different a year ago Christmas eve, but on thinking I remembered that we did have a little row that night, but would have had that repeated than be as I was that night. Your note and <u>photo</u> I received Christmas morning and to me the nicest present I rec'd. I to tell you the truth could hardly believe my own eyes, but I finaly opened them and I that morning thought I was a bigger dunce, that heretofore I had been. Louise I don't know what you can think of me for all this, not much I am sure, but believe me I can't help it, it must have been born in me.

When you get this, I don't know what you will think but the only way I can do I guess is to wait till I hear from you. I suspose if it is contrary to the way I'd have it I fully deserve it, but I hope it is alright.

You said in your note that you wanted to explain two or three things if I would listen to them. I'll refuse to do this as I don't believe you done or have anything to explain that I should require an explanation, but you be judge of that. Another thing some one must of told you I made the remark that you were 'dead stuck on me.' Well I never did. If any one did say so. If I ever thought you were which I never...

No further page(s) found.

About 1887, Robert Carruthers, Dick's father, built a social hall in downtown Astoria. On November 29, 1887, the *Daily Astorian* noted that Benjamin S. Worsley (a notary public who later was involved with Robert in real estate dealings) had started a dancing school in Carruthers Hall. The fee for the ladies was $2.50 for the term of 12 lessons that met at 7:30 o'clock on Tuesday evenings. Eight years later, the newspaper printed an item that the Once-A-Week (Saturday nights) Dancing Club met at Carruthers Hall as usual on February 12, 1895. The dancing lasted "till midnight to exceptionally fine music."

In February 1895, Dick invested in homing pigeons – the purpose of which is not known. However, there is a gap in the correspondence with Louise for one entire year. Letters may have been lost or simply ceased. Or, perhaps, the homing pigeons were used as a means to contact Louise. For both Dick and Louise, life apparently continued normally. Their social life surely increased. Louise, Dick and their friends were active young people. In March of that year, Dick had been made the manager of the Astoria Wharf & Warehouse Company, the only U.S. Bonded warehouse in Astoria - behind what is presently a Burger King franchise. It is a red brick and cement, flat-roofed rectangle, two-stories high, with an interesting façade. Dick's father, Robert Carruthers, erected the building in 1892.

Astoria Wharf & Warehouse Company

Originally, both the U.S. Government (1868) and the State of Oregon (1876) held deeds to many waterfront sites on the Columbia River. By 1892, Pacific Can Company had bought some of those lots, intending to erect several buildings for stamping, soldering and storage of the tin cans used in the rapidly expanding salmon packing industry. Robert Carruthers, Dick's father, drew up plans for a very solidly built structure that fronted on the north side of what was then called Water Street. The address later became known as 114 Front Street, between Third and Fourth Streets.[17] The purpose of the building was to provide secure storage facilities for the large quantities of tin plate essential to the making of cans.

In the spring of 1892, construction began on the Astoria Wharf & Warehouse Company, a waterfront building on Tax Lot 300, Block 3, of McClure's Addition, Astoria. Robert supervised the construction; his father, Richard, still hale-and-hearty at eighty-years old, likely aided him. Richard was a left-handed stonemason, who had learned the trade in England before immigrating to America.

How did Astoria Wharf & Warehouse come by its site? Robert Carruthers might have begun construction of the brick/stone building on Tax Lot 300 while it was still wholly owned by Pacific Can Company – or possibly a gentleman's agreement by just a handshake had sufficed temporarily. It was not until the "19th day of August, A.D. 1892" that an indenture (a deed, a written agreement) was officially signed between the Pacific Can Company – a corporation existing under the laws of California, headquartered in San Francisco – and the Astoria Wharf & Warehouse Company. For the sum of "One Dollar lawful money of the United States," the A.W.&W. Co. took title to a section of Lot 300.

---

[17] Ordinance #1869 of the City of Astoria (approved April 26, 1894) changed most of the street names – Madison became 3rd Street, Jackson became 4th Street and Water became Front Street.

This deed included "[t]o wit: All the land and tide land, wharfing rights, privileges and easements to the ships channel of the Columbia River lying north of, and in front of, Lot Three (3) in Block (3) Three in the Township (now City) of Astoria as laid out and recorded by John McClure in said County of Clatsop, State of Oregon." Pacific Can's President John Lee and Secretary A.D. Cutter signed and affixed their corporate seal to the notarized document.[18]

A separate agreement, made the same day, was not recorded until October 27, 1892. It was valid for a period of ten years and set forth the obligations and restrictions for the two parties. It especially dealt with which company was liable for the construction, management and maintenance of three wharves to be built contiguously, lying north of, and in front of Lots 1, 2 and 3. (The northerly end of Lot 300 extended over the water well out to the edge of the shipping channel.) The agreement further stated that one-half of the profits derived from all wharfage business done on this large dock was to be paid to Pacific Can Company. This agreement was signed by Lee and Cutter for Pacific Can Co., as well as by Robert Carruthers, President, and W.W. Ridehalgh,[19] Secretary, of A.W.&W. Co. Witnesses were E.W. Tallant and J.Q.A. Bowlby, a Notary Public.[20]

In September 1983, the building's owners were Pat Lavis, a local attorney; Rod Grider, an Astorian architect; Captain Joe Bruneau, a retired Columbia River bar pilot; and Archie Riekkola. Lavis, Grider and Bruneau prepared a nomination/inventory form for placement of the building on the National Register of Historic Places. On February 24, 1984, the nine-member Oregon State Advisory Committee on Historic Preservation recommended that the registry include the structure. "[I]t was the consensus of committee members that this is unique not only in Astoria, but possibly in the state."[21] In a *Daily Astorian* article, dated March 6, 1984, Pat Lavis stated they were all but positive "it is the oldest remaining building on the Astoria waterfront." The paperwork was forwarded to, and accepted by, the National Registry of Historic Places in Washington, D.C.

The structure housed Astoria's only Bonded Warehouse, so-called largely because of its rock-solid masonry construction and the use of heavy-duty timbers inside, which gives a feeling of impenetrability – somewhat like a bank vault. The 50-foot wide, 105-foot long rectangle has two floors plus a basement. Total floor space is 5,250 square feet. Atop basalt stone footings, the specially constructed basement required walls thirty-six inches thick of basalt and granite (possibly ballast off early sailing ships) and a deep floor of stone. This is the only waterfront building in Astoria in which the foundation and entire basement rest below the waterline of the Columbia River.

The building's walls are constructed of brick 18-inches thick (4 courses) from the ground level to the second floor and then 12-inches thick on up to the roof. At some point

---

[18] Per the deed recorded at Clatsop County Courthouse on August 24, 1892, in Vol. 25, pp. 336-339. All documents in those days were hand written in oversized ledgers by a Recorder of Conveyance (at this time, Mr. F.I. Dunbar). Corporate seals were not actually impressed in the ledgers, only indicated by a small drawing.

[19] On April 3, 1891, Zoe Carruthers, age 19, the younger of Robert and Harriet Carruthers' two daughters, married Walter W. Ridehalgh in a ceremony held at Grace (Episcopal) Church. Early in 1891, Walter was an accountant for the Samuel Elmore cannery; later he held positions with the Union Fish Cannery.

[20] Recorded deeds: Vol. 25, pp. 667-671.

[21] "Historic nomination gets state's approval," (*Daily Astorian*. March 6, 1984), 4.

in time the brickwork on three sides of the building was lightly covered with a concrete/gunite coating to prevent deterioration and to improve water resistance. Over the years, layers of rolled asphalt have covered the flat roof, originally made of tin. Heavy steel shutters on the windows provide security. The sliding wooden doors are also made doubly secure by sheathings of heavy sheet metal. Romanesque window arches are of brick and wood with granite sills. The inset main doublewide door, facing south, has not only a granite sill, but also a special granite keystone. Reportedly quarried from the Chinook Quarry, this granite was originally used for the 1852 Customs Building that was the first U. S. Federal building erected west of the Rocky Mountains. When Astoria's original Customs House was demolished, some of the granite was incorporated into the Astoria Wharf and Warehouse Company building.

The December 14, 1892 issue of the *Daily Morning Astorian* noted that locally fired brick was used for the walls - May & Thair had produced it in their kilns on the Lewis and Clark River. Lavis, Grider & Bruneau reported that samples of several other types of brick were used in the construction to provide a comparison with the durability of the May & Thair brick. They also noted that three blue bricks from China were cemented above the main entry's granite keystone arch and some $45 dollars-per-thousand bricks from San Francisco were inset into the exterior walls.

The first floor is constructed of mainly old growth Douglas fir with heavy posts, beams and flooring. The first-floor joists of heavy timbers rest upon steel railroad rails embedded into the exterior brick walls. This added strength allows for up to "3,000 TUNS" of goods (1,200 pounds per square foot) to be stored on that level. The twelve "bays" on the main floor are still being used as storage areas.

Construction was completed by December 1892 and put into use to store the huge quantities of tin plate being brought by the shiploads to Astoria. The thriving salmon canning industry could not function without this basic material. A report in the "Clatsop County" column in the Portland *Oregonian* on January 1, 1882, estimated that each salmon cost cannery owners seventy cents - the purchase of tin plate to make the cans made up a substantial part of the cost. "In 1880, 6,188 boxes of tin plate were imported direct to Astoria. In 1881, 37,768 [boxes], while in 1882 it exceeded even that amount."[22] To pack 1,000 cases of salmon took 107 boxes. Each box of tin plate weighed an average of 109 pounds, and, in 1882, cost $6.50. Adequate and secure storage space was essential. The federal government insured the building and contents.

At age twenty-one, Dick, the company's secretary, was "placed in charge" as the company's manager according to a notice in the March 9, 1895 issue of the *Daily Morning Astorian*. A year later, in an undated letter written about March 20, 1896, Dick wrote Louise:

> *"Everyone has sold out of the A. W. W. Co now except Dr. E. C. Carter, a 1/10 owner. I am still here representing Uncle Sam[23] for a week longer. Then what I don't know."*

22 Holden, "Growth and Prosperity of Astoria," (Portland: January 1, 1882), 99. Holden, a former Associated Press agent, created a scrapbook of his articles printed in the Portland *Oregonian* and Astoria newspapers. His collection was donated to Clatsop County Historical Society.

23 The United States Government held the warehouse in bond.

On Easter Sunday, April 5, 1896, he wrote:

"I left the warehouse on the first. Since then I've been collecting for Prael Co and tomorrow I am going down to the warehouse to unload a tinship for the new company – not all by myself but just look out the same as before."

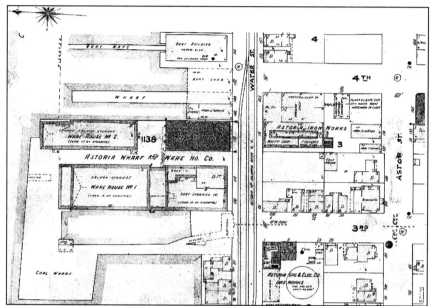

A small section of Astoria's waterfront. The Astoria Wharf & Warehouse Co. brick building with the flat roof is the dark rectangle in the center. The E. W. Tallant family dwelling - 1882-1896 - is located on the NE corner of Third Street and Astor on this 1908 Sanborn-Perris Company Insurance map.

Built over 116 years ago, the building is still standing north of the old Astoria & Columbia River Railroad track right-of-way (later called the Burlington Northern R.R.) behind what is now the Burger King fast food eatery. Over the years at least three major fires have destroyed many of the surrounding buildings, but the Astoria Wharf & Warehouse Company building was left essentially unscathed. All the original exterior and interior materials remain in good condition. Robert Carruthers, thanks to his masonry and building skills, built a building to last.

During the period 1880 to 1920, Astoria was at its zenith in the fishing and canning industry. Between 1892 and 1950, seven different companies occupied the Bonded Warehouse premises. Samuel Elmore bought the A.W. & W. Co along with all the Pacific Can Company buildings about 1909. By early 1972, Archie Riekkola and his partners obtained the title to the consolidated area. The A.W.&W. building has been leased out for a variety of purposes, including housing cars belonging to the Lovell Auto Company, storing building materials used in the construction of the nearby Columbia House condominiums and as a workshop for building outdoor log furniture. Since 1998 this historic building has been owned by Steve Fick's Fishhawk Fisheries, Inc. and used for storage.

28

Photo taken in 1894 by J.H. Bratt. On the post to the left - notice the vertical lettering "3000 TUNS" that refers to the weight the floor was built to hold.

About half of the gunite material spread over three of the walls in earlier times has fallen off – or been removed – exposing the original brickwork, which, for the most part, remains uncleaned. More recent owners spread a thick layer of material – concrete probably - over the façade of the building and painted it a pleasant rusty-red color. Disappointingly however, in doing this, some of the historic aspects of this building have been covered up. The three blue Chinese tiles and the granite keystone are no longer visible. Nor is there any definition to the bricks forming the façade wall. The front of the building has lost its original interesting historic character.

Photo taken March 2006 by J. Lambert
The façade of the Astoria Wharf and Warehouse today.

Astoria's waterfront circa 1894. The Tallant house with the cupola is in the center.
Directly behind it is the brick Astoria Wharf & Warehouse building built in 1892.
Several ships are at the dock.

The First Brick Residence in Astoria

Pasted in Louise's scrapbook is an unidentified newspaper clipping entitled "Building of Astoria has passed through several stages: new construction finest." In this article, the Astoria architect J. E. Wicks claimed: "Up to 1907 we had four brick buildings in town, a town 100 years old claiming a population of 15,000." The first commercial brick structure built in Astoria was the Odd Fellows temple, completed about 1882.[24] It is three stories high and cost close to $50,000 to build. It is still in use. The A.W. & W. building was the second commercial brick building erected.

Robert Carruthers constructed at least one other brick structure in Astoria besides the Wharf & Warehouse. Immediately following the disastrous July 2, 1883, Astoria fire, he built his own two-story brick home that faced south at 638 Cedar (now Exchange) between present day 14th and 15th Streets. The 1883 fire had started in John Farrel's sawmill, located in "downtown" Astoria; the mill was consumed, leaving only its tall brick smokestack intact. Robert bought "Old Dad" Farrel's brick stack and felled it. With those bricks, plus some left in the sawmill's burning kiln and a few bricks from Portland, he was able to complete his home before the end of 1883. Over his front door he added a special brick with the date 1883 engraved into it; it had been made at Bartoldus' farm in Young's River area – the first brick kiln enterprise in Clatsop County.[25] Uncovered during Robert's construction were a few cedar posts from the Hudson Bay Company's stockade of Fort George, erected by the British about 1813. The British had used some of the wood from the stockade and buildings of the earlier Astor group's 1811 settlement.

---

[24] Holden, *"Growth and Prosperity." 99.*
[25] "Farrel's Old Mill," (*Astoria Daily Budget,* July 27, 1907), 2.

E.C. Holden's *Oregonian* article, published on January 1, 1884, contained the following short paragraph about the Carruthers' home:

> Mr Robert Carruthers has the distinction of having erected the first brick residence in the city of Astoria. It is a handsome two story structure and cost $5000.

Harriet Hunter Carruthers, holding her cat, stands in front of their family's ivy-covered home.

The Carruthers' lot extended a full block deep, between Duane and Exchange Avenues. On the "back" (downhill, north side) of the property were a horse barn and a blacksmith's shop, which Robert used in his drayage business.

By 1884, after thirty years of residency in the Oysterville area, the Carruthers family of six moved into their new home where their third son, Robert Rex, was born in 1885. The house, later covered in Boston ivy, boasted ten rooms, two marble and slate fireplaces[26] and had beautifully carved wood double entry doors. The formal parlor of this lovely home was the setting for the wedding of Robert and Harriet's older daughter on October 31, 1894. Grace, about 25, was united in marriage to Carlton B. Allen, the son of Col. Harvey A. and Mary Julia Allen, of Ft. Canby-Ilwaco, Pacific County, Washington Territory (W.T.). William Seymour Short, Rector of Grace Episcopal Church, officiated. Mrs. Short and James Grover witnessed the issuance of the marriage certificate. Three years earlier, preferring to marry in Grace Episcopal Church rather than at home, Grace's younger sister, Zoe, age 19, had wed Walter W. Ridehalgh on the evening of April 2, 1891. Captain Al Harris gave her in marriage; Rev. Short officiated. Grace and Carleton served as their attendants, as well as their witnesses for the official marriage certificate.

As was often done in those days, the Carruthers offered rooms to let at their Exchange Avenue home. Dr. Jay Tuttle, a physician, surgeon and *Accucheure*,[27] boarded with the Carruthers for a number of years. Another roomer was Katie Wantila.

---

[26] Evans, "The Allens of Astoria," (*Cumtux*). 33.
[27] French: *Accucheure* - a physician who attends women in childbirth.

Being of brick construction, the house survived the terrible Astoria fire of 1922 relatively unscathed. Sometime after Robert and Harriet's deaths in 1917, their home became a boarding house. The Church of the Nazarene bought the building in 1936. It gradually deteriorated. In 1947, the historic brick house was torn down to create a parking lot for Lovell Auto. An overgrown rose garden now tries to beautify the site, which is next to a memorial for the 1811 Fort "Astoria" of John Jacob Astor's first settlers and fur traders.

The Carruthers women: Grace, Harriet Hunter and Zoe.
Clear image by Chuck Meyer.
Photo courtesy of Clatsop County Historical Society.
"The Allens of Astoria," *Cumtux,* Vol. 3, No. 4 - Fall 1983, 35.

A scrapbook clipping about the Carruthers' house in "The Astoria Column," printed in an Astoria newspaper on Thanksgiving Day in 1947, Harold Haynes wrote:

We have an inquiry about the background of the old brick building which has housed the Church of the Nazarene flock these last few years. Time was, we would say, when this vine covered structure was one of the show places of Astoria. Before it was a boarding house and a church building, it was the home of one of Astoria's first families – the Robert R. Carruthers clan.

Now about to be razed to the ground, the mansion was built by the senior Mr. Carruthers along in 1883, immediately after one of Astoria's big fires, the blaze that destroyed the heart of the city. The fire started in the old mill at Exchange and 14th and swept everything before it to the waterfront across a two-block front.

In the old brick house five of Astoria's better-known citizens were born, Dick, Tod, Gus, Zoe and Grace Carruthers. For many years the old house was a social center of the old town, as many an old-timer will remember.

The Church of the Nazarene, last occupant of the dwelling is holding services now at the Veteran's hall, 12th and Grand, and the old red brick building is being torn down by Lovell Auto company so the site can be used for a parking lot.

However, Mr. Haynes erred in stating the five children of Robert (he had no known middle name) and Harriet Hunter Carruthers were all born in the lovely ivy-covered brick home in Astoria. Grace, Zoe, Dick (1874–1922), and Angus Russell "Gus" (1877-1932) were born across the river in the Carruthers' home in Oysterville, W.T., where the family had finally settled after having arrived in the northwest in the early 1850s. The youngest son, Robert Rex "Tod" (aka "Babe") Carruthers (1885-1945) was the only Carruthers child born in the family's home at 638 Exchange Avenue home.

Fourth of July 1895 picnic at Lottie Bennett's family's cottage in Gearhart.
Harriet may be 4th from left; Louise is standing in front of the porch column. Both wear tams.

For Whom Louise was Named: Maria Louise Tallant Owen
A Noteworthy Botanist and Role Model of the Nineteenth Century

About 1790 Andrew Tallant (1771-1840) of Pelham (N.H.), son of Hugh and Mary Dodge Tallant, wed Amelia Weld (1771-1819). Andrew and Amelia's son, Nathaniel Tallant (1794-1871) of Barnstable married Lydia Scudder (1806-1890), also of Barnstable; Lydia was the daughter of Asa Scudder (1771-1822) and Sally Huckins (1789-1868) Scudder. Nathaniel and Lydia Tallant were Louise's paternal grandparents.

The second son born to Andrew and Amelia was Eben W. Tallant (1799-1834). This Eben married Nancy (1803-1870), daughter of William and Deborah Coffin. Eben and Nancy Tallant had four children: Maria Louise (1825-1913), William C. (1827-1861), Caroline L. (1830-1877) [28] and Henry P. (1832-1883). These four children were cousins of Eben Weld Tallant, the Astoria canneryman. Eben's daughter, Maria Louise Tallant Carruthers, was named after her second cousin, Maria Louise Tallant Owen.

Maria Louise, the daughter of Eben and Nancy Tallant, was born on Nantucket Island February 13, 1825. She preferred to spell her middle name "Louisa." She had the advantage of a private school education of exceptionally wide breadth.[29] Her parents also provided her with a well-rounded study program at home. Maria Louise had a very retentive memory and became well acquainted with scientific methods. She taught in Boston and later in her own private school. In 1853, she married Dr. Virillas L. Owen; they moved to Springfield, Massachusetts, where they remained for fifty years. "[S]he was easily the most cultivated and best-read woman of her time in Springfield."[30]

On her frequent trips back to Nantucket she was able to pursue an interest that had been established very early in her life. Her passion was the science of botany. Encouraged by other female family members, she had catalogued flora that grew on Nantucket Island, searching all the thickets, the swamps and the bogs of the island's fifty square miles. She made numerous contributions to the science of botany, as "a teacher, organizer, writer, collector, observer and record keeper. Her skill as field botanist is particularly noteworthy."[31] Maria L. T. Owen published two major volumes cataloguing Nantucket's plants. The more complete 1888 volume, *A Catalogue of Plants Growing Without Cultivation in the County of Nantucket, Mass.*, became the definitive work to which botany students and researchers still refer. "A model for all of its kind."[32]

About 1900, the Nantucket Islanders honored Mrs. Owen by forming The Maria L. Owen Society for the Protection of Nantucket Flora.

Maria Louise Tallant Owen died June 8, 1913, at the home of her daughter Amelia L. Owen Sullivan[33] in Plandome, Long Island. Mrs. Owen was eighty-eight years old.

---

[28] In the late 1850s, Caroline L. Tallant, of Boston, corresponded with John Greenleaf Whittier about her great-great-grandfather, Hugh Tallant.

[29] MLT Owen probably attended Nantucket's Coffin Lancasterian Academy on Fair Street that had been founded in 1827 by the English Baronet Admiral Sir Isaac Coffin (1759-1839), a descendant of Trystram Coffin, one of the original settlers of the Island. The academy was destroyed in the great fire of 1846. Rebuilt in 1854 at 4 Winter Street, it is now a museum. The definition of a Lancasterian school is a monitorial educational system. Introduced into some English primary schools at the end of the eighteenth century by Joseph Lancaster (of Henry IV's royal house of Lancaster), it included teaching by advanced pupils.

[30] Smith, "Maria L. Owen . . . ," *(Rhodora)*, 227.

[31] Ibid., 235.

[32] Ibid., 233.

[33] Misses S. Alice Brown and Amelia Louise Owen, graduates of Smith College, opened the Preparatory School for Girls (twelve years and over) at 78 Marlborough Street, Boston on October 3, 1887. They offered Classical and Scientific courses of study required by such colleges as Harvard, Vassar, Smith, Wellesley and MIT. Tuition for one year was $250.

34

The following is the thirty-third article of a series on fifty of the most prominent persons of Nantucket. The article appeared in the *Inquirer and Mirror* of Nantucket Island on Saturday, June 24, 1950. Louise penciled in a notation on the article: *"My father's cousin for whom I was named. L.T.C."*

Maria Louise Tallant Owen

Fifty Famous Nantucketers
By Grace Brown Gardner
33.
Maria L. Owen
1825 – 1913

Maria L. Owen was a contemporary and friend of Lucy Stone, Elizabeth Cady Stanton, Maria Mitchell and others of that brilliant circle of women prominent in the middle eighteen hundreds. Like them she was vitally interested in the welfare of women and in later years she was well known as a founder of women's clubs.

Mrs. Owen was a native of Nantucket and received educational advantages which were outstanding for her day. As Maria L. Tallant she taught for some time in the Academy on Fair Street. She removed to Springfield, Mass., with her husband, Dr. Varillas Owen, in 1850,[35] and there she made her home a center for the intellectual life of that city.

Her interest in her early home continued throughout her long life. When the Coffin School was reorganized and the scope of its work changed, Maria L. Owen gave the means to repair and beautify the old library room in memory of her grandfather, Hon. William Coffin, first President of the Board of Trustees.

Early in life she became interested in the flora of her native island, later becoming a recognized authority in her favorite subject of botany. She wrote many articles for newspapers, magazines and for scientific publications. Her great contribution to Nantucket was her pamphlet entitled "A Catalog of Plants Growing Without Cultivation in the County of Nantucket, Mass." The foundation of this work, published in 1888, was a record of plants collected and identified by her in early life. Returning to the

---

[34] Photograph of MLT Owen was taken in Springfield, Mass. in 1901.
[35] Their marriage date is elsewhere recorded as 1853.

island after a long absence she published her old list, together with additions made during occasional visits. This was pioneer work, and all later botanists who have studied the unusual Nantucket flora are indebted to her efforts. Without her notes it would be impossible to trace the history of such rare local plants as the Nantucket heathers, the cactus found on Coatue, the corema, and the sabbatia, which differs from the type found on the mainland. All doubtful specimens were submitted to eminent botanists and sent to the Gray Herbarium at Harvard, where they may be seen and studied.

The interest which was aroused by Mrs. Owen has never died out. Today the Nantucket Maria Mitchell Association with its extensive herbarium of local plants and its staff of trained workers is carrying on the work so ably started by her. Many summer visitors as well as Nantucket people visit the daily wild flower exhibit at Hinchman House, and flock by hundreds to the Annual Wild Flower Show held there in August.

Chapter Two

January to Mid-May 1896
Louise and Harriet Visit Southern California
The Ebb and Flow of Romance

The Tallants' Grand Avenue House
1895

E.W. Tallant and Bismark, their dog, enjoyed the afternoon sun.

The Eben Weld Tallant house, 1574 Grand Avenue (originally 682 Arch Street), Astoria, is listed in the Oregon Inventory of Historic Properties. It was indeed a grand and gracious home on Grand Avenue that contained a number of unusual features.

On June 29, 1895, Mary Elizabeth Tallant purchased property on the downhill (north) side of Arch Street from Edward and Elizabeth O'Connor. Per the recorded deed, she paid $1,100. The lot was one lot removed from the corner of West Seventh Street in Shively's platting of the area. On April 24, 1894, the City of Astoria had approved Ordinance No. 1869 to allow certain streets to be renamed: Arch Street became Grand Avenue and West Seventh became Sixteenth Street. Dellinger's Astoria City Directory of 1896 listed the house at 682 Grand Avenue. An official renumbering of the city's buildings took place in 1955, at which time the property was listed as 1574 Grand Avenue.

James E. Ferguson, a well-known Astoria architect, placed a Notice to Contractors in the August 8, 1895 issue of the *Daily Morning Astorian* in which he requested sealed proposals for the building, completion and delivery of a frame dwelling for Mr. E.W. Tallant on Lot 11, Block 16. His design for the house again showed the influence of the priorities of Eben W. Tallant, the Nantucket-born seafarer. In John E. Goodenberger's *Daily Astorian* article of November 26, 2004, the well-known historic building consultant notes that Ferguson's design of a "shingle style house was considered cutting edge in design, keeping up with the best East Coast architecture."[36]

In the 1890s, it was possible for contractors to complete a large house in a three to four month period, working on a tight schedule. Thus, the Tallant family might have been able to move from their Concomly Street home into their new dwelling by the end of January 1896, shortly before Louise and Harriet left for Southern California – certainly by the time they returned to Astoria in May of that year.

Viewed from Grand Avenue, only a 3-story façade is presented because the land slopes sharply down to the north toward the Columbia River, but from the northerly downhill side, a partial daylight basement is also visible. The foundation was formed of rubble stone covered with beveled shiplap. The exterior of the house was done in the Richardson wood shingle style. A complex hip-roof design with many different pitches includes a wonderful south facing eyebrow window, as well as three windowed gables on the third floor.

As in the Concomly house, there was considerable light within their new home. At the northeast corner Ferguson added a striking "bullet-shaped" turret – an unusual hanging tower - with oriel windows; the cone shaped roof of the tower rises to the top of the second floor. The family dining room was located in this area of the house. Another unusual feature, at the northwest corner of the house, is the three-story tall tower with five windows on each floor. The "half"-octagonal tower allows for fine bay windows in the Family Parlor (or Library) and in the second floor bedroom above. The parlor and bedroom each have an inset balcony facing the river to the north. Prominent on the south façade are bay windows in the Formal Parlor, facing Grand Avenue, and in the Master Bedroom directly above.

The west side chimney provided for a fireplace on each of the first two floors. A second chimney in the middle of the house served the kitchen, which was centrally located on the east side of the house. The kitchen was accessed from the outdoors by the wrap-around veranda style porch.

A squared main interior staircase with carved wood railings led from the foyer to four bedrooms on the second floor. The master bedroom faced south and west; here Mary Elizabeth is said to have spent many enjoyable hours sitting in the bay window. Younger son Nat's room was located in the south east corner. Harriet's room was in the northeast corner. Louise occupied the northwest bedroom. She had not only a fireplace and the octagonal "lookout," but also one of the two inset balconies. In her letter of May 27, 1898, Mary Elizabeth wrote her older daughter in Southern California that, from Louise's balcony, she had an excellent view of the parade of soldiers, until she "almost lost her head."

---

[36] Goodenberger, "Cupola made Tallant house exclusive," (*Daily Astorian*), 4A.

Eben and Mary Elizabeth stand on Louise's balcony.

In those early years, few other houses or buildings existed to obstruct the family's broad view of the Columbia River to the north. Facing northwest, accessible from the third floor room, is the walk-on railed balcony at the top of the octagonal tower. From here, E.W. Tallant could clearly monitor the activity on the river, which had always commanded his keen interest.

A narrow staircase that led up from the second floor landing reached the third story. Because the flooring on the third level had always been fully finished, it was rumored dances were held there. In the central part of the house, off the main hall on the first floor, next to the kitchen, an uncarpeted stairway led up to both the second and third floors and down to the daylight basement. Any household help they had often used this stairway, as well as the immediate family - especially the younger members.

A large veranda style porch extended over half of the south-facing first floor façade, curving around the southeast corner as far as the door opening into the kitchen. The verandah was a fine place to sit. Joined by their dog Bismark, both Mary Elizabeth and Eben Weld Tallant often enjoyed having their rocking chairs there on sunny afternoons and warm evenings.

On the corner lot just east of the Tallant home, Philip A. Stokes (owner of a local clothing store) and his wife Emily constructed their house in 1897 (now 1588 Grand Avenue). It was designed in the Colonial Revival/Craftsman style; the name of the architect is not recorded. On December 17, 1897, Mary Elizabeth wrote Louise:

"Stokes house is almost all boarded in. And as I said before does not interfere with any of the windows except Nat's. It will look much better than the open lot."

Eben and Mary Elizabeth lived in the home until she died on March 10, 1926, at age 81. Eben then moved into the home of his older daughter, Louise Tallant Carruthers (widowed in 1922), at 681 Jerome Avenue. Residing further up on Astoria's hill, he continued to enjoy a fine view of the river activities.

The lovely, strikingly different Grand Avenue house did not remain in the Tallants' possession. In February 1930, it was leased to A.N. Prouty for $600 per annum. Because Mary Elizabeth died intestate, it took many years to process her estate. Louise was named "administratrix" in a document dated October 18, 1935, drawn up and notarized by attorney John A. Buchanan.[37] On November 9, 1935, Harriet Tallant and her husband Frank Greenough, Nat and Florence Ross Tallant, and their niece Laura Elizabeth Tallant, "sold" the property to Louise to dispose of it as she saw fit. Later the house was divided into eight apartments until about 1986, when Charleen Maxwell purchased the property. It is now known as the Grandview Bed and Breakfast.

The letters begin again in late January 1896. Louise, then age twenty, and her sister Harriet, just eighteen, sailed from Astoria to San Francisco to spend the winter months in Southern California. The Tallant family had a number of relatives and friends who had traveled from the Northeast to make their homes in San Francisco and Los Angeles areas. Louise and Harriet had both been born in Alhambra and lived in nearby San Gabriel until the family moved to Astoria. From 1871 to almost 1882, their parents had managed an orange grove in nearby San Gabriel, so the two girls had many childhood friends in the area, as well as relatives of both the Easton and Tallant families.

Louise wrote Dick in pencil from Oakland, California. She and Harriet were probably staying with their relatives, Theodore Garland Smith and Sarah Frances (Fannie) Tallant Smith. Fannie was Eben's younger sister. The date appears to be Wednesday, January 29, 1896.

Wednesday 11:30 PM

Dear Dick -

How I wish I could be dancing with you right now. We are having a perfect time but this evening I would like to be home. You know we had a stormy trip down and did not get here until Monday but were not sea sick - that is, we were both sick for about half an hour when the storm first began - that was the first day about 4 o'clock. Mrs Robson, Will and Guss came out to see us this evening. Friday night we are going over to the "Tivoli" (guess that is spelt right) with them. It seems quite like home here with Fran Osborne and Lila [Sutherland]. Yesterday we had a gay time out at Berkley. We are going to leave Monday for Los Angeles and I want to find a letter from you there so I am writing at this late hour when I should be having my beauty sleep. Now I must say good night and you will have to say that I have begun well, only here three days and you are getting a letter already. I must go and dream now of the time you are all having. I wonder who the wall flowers are. Well good night once more

Louise

---

[37] On March 20, 1926, Judge J.A. and Madge B. Buchanan's older daughter, Mary Maurine, married Louise and Dick's older son, Richard Tallant "Dick" Carruthers, Jr., in Astoria. The Buchanans lived directly across from the Carruthers' home on Jerome Avenue.

Write to 614 South Main Street Los Angeles.[38]

Oh Dick listen to my tale of woe. What do you think I have lost – not my needle[39] *thank goodness for I hung on to that as if it were a million but my Columbian half dollar. Where, when or how I lost it I do not know and am still in hopes of finding it among my "goods and chattles." Haven't you a few thousands you would like to* put in my care, *then you would always know they were safe (don't you know). Yes I never was known to loose any thing - well… t.m.d.*[40]

Louise

Louise and Harriet sailed from San Francisco to Los Angeles. The ship stopped at Santa Barbara long enough for them to have a tour of the area. When they reached Los Angeles, they stayed with their dear friend, Lillie Kerckhoff, her brother Herman and their parents. Dick kept Louise informed about the activities at home.

Mailing date: FEB 2 5:30 PM 1896 Astoria, Oregon
Received: FEB 6 8AM Los Angeles, California
Stationery: Astoria Wharf and Warehouse Company.
Envelope addressed to: Miss Louise Tallant
       614 South Main Street
       Los Angeles, Cal

Regards to Hattie and Miss K- [Lillie Kerckhoff]

          Astoria, Or. Sunday Feb 2, 1896

Dear Louise:

I was going down to the W'hse this morning to do a little work but as I passed the Post Office I got just what I wanted so I'll answer it before I can do anything else. I was worried to death all day Friday & Sat because it was storming so hard and am awfully glad to hear you were not sea sick but it almost made me sick to think of it. I asked Small (who by the way is a weather prophet) about the weather so often that he finaly caught on and every time he sees me he remarks it must be purty rough out side, but that don't worry me any more because I know you are safe and well now. Talk about boys being wall flowers there wasn't one, but I might say there were a dozen more girls than boys so we didn't get to see who really did like to dance with us. I hardly expected to have the pleasure of a waltz with Miss [Zetta] Smith but got one just the same. She was one of the first to see my programme and when I did dance with her she in some manner triped and fell down and I in trying to save her got a fall which I'll have cause to remember for some time. Of course everyone laughed, your Mother included. I took an oath to

---

[38] Louise and Harriet stayed at the Kerckhoff's family home in Los Angeles. Louise had taken the course in the German language when a student at the Astoria Select School; she graduated in 1892. The school's principal was Miss Emma C. Warren.
[39] The "needle" is a specially shaped wooden "needle" used to make or mend fishnets.
[40] A possible translation of "t.m.d." might be "to my dear."

myself that night that I would never laugh at any one when they fell even if it was Mr Maddock. Zetta [Smith] wore her black dress and _My Pardner_ Miss Unice C- [Eunice Copeland] who was of course the bell of the ball wore a light green, ordinary sized sleeves. Mrs Tuttle wore a black dress low neck and short sleeves and looked like the dickens. Pearl [Holden] & Nan [Reed] both looked, of course; you know who Pearl took, and Nan to[ok] Mr Shields. Kate was going to _take_ Tom but _took_ the Mumps, no insult to Tom. Miss [Maud] Stockton finaly took Mr [Thomas] Bryce, Zetta took Lem [Howes], Jim didn't go but was asked by Miss Stockton and Edith C- [Copeland]. It is to bad to give him two chances to refuse. Miss C- then took Paul. Mr Kinzie went with Mrs Tuttle along with the Dr. T-, Alice W- [Wood] seen Mr J Gimer there. Olga [Heilborn] was going to take Chas Callender but he was under the weather. I wish myself you had been there. Genie [Lewis] took Cha Stone. She asked Mac but he refused. Well I don't know if I can tell you much more except the music was bum and I nearly died dancing all the dances.

So you have lost that half dollar. Are you quite sure you did not spend it for car fare. Of course if you did it is alright but mind don't loose the needle, not for the value because you can always have another but you would be some time with out one.

I haven't very many Thousands just at present but if I did I would consider them perfectly safe with you, and it is my most desired wish that I may have some day another not more than a hundred years a few Ms to let you take care of or both of us to take care of. Eaisly said isn't it.

Well I guess this is getting tiresome for you, but there is a couple of things I must tell you of. One is that when you come home you are to give Miss [Genie] Lewis a sort of shake. I've heard some things the past week - they are more than enough that you shall have nothing to do with her when you come home unless I hear differently, do you understand.

Well I must close or you will think this is a Sunday Edition of the Chronicle with 96 pages. So good bye for the present.

Yours as ever with lots of love - Dick

P.S. I send you a new cigar check. They are much nicer than the others you have in your collection I think.

No envelope. No date - probably early February 1896.

614 South Main St.

Dear Dick

I am afraid it has been more than ten days since I last wrote and I am sorry to break my promise so soon but realy the time has flown bye with out my knowing it. We had a splendid trip down from Frisco. There were several young men on board who were very nice to Hat and

I and took us for a drive at Santa Barbara. We were not a bit sea sick which suppensed us both for after our week in Oakland we were half dead. I was awfully glad to get your letter but Dick what has Genie done or said, do tell me. I can't imagine (this pen is bum, excuse lead pencil). No I am sure I did not spend the half dollar for car fare but don't know where it could have gone. Never mind about the millions Dick – there are lots of things that money can not buy. So your pardner *was the bell of the ball. I don't doubt it. What do you think - I got on a wheel the other day and rode right off - didn't have a bit of trouble (smart girl). Lillie and Herman [Kerkhoff] thought they would have lots of fun teaching us to ride but we fooled them sadly. Lillie is going to have a swell party Saturday and we are dreadfully busy getting ready. This afternoon we go to a reception, tonight to a party and tomorrow to another. Hat went to the Shilling Minstrels with Shillings brother and sister - they are friends of Lillies and wanted me to go but I knew what they were like so I got excused. I have got so much to do that I can't write any more this time. Guess you will have trouble enough reading this much and will send a good long answer soon to yours.   With much love*

Louise

Don't forget to tell me what Genie said and every thing else that has happened lately. How is "The Little Tycoon" and also how are the ballet dancers. Forgive me for not writing sooner won't you.

Mailing date: FEB 18 6:30PM '96 Astoria, Oregon
Received: FEB 22   8AM (18)96 Los Angeles, Cal
Postage: Two Cents red George Washington
Stationery: Astoria Wharf and Warehouse Company
Envelope addressed to: Miss Louise Tallant
                          614 South Main St.
                              Los Angeles, Cal

Astoria, Or. Feby 18 1896   [Tuesday]

My Dear Girl:

I received your very welcome letter yesterday morning and was very very glad you had not entirely forgotten me. Of course I'll excuse you as I know you must be having a perfectly lovely time and am quiet pleased to even hear from you as often *as I do, but that is not saying I would like to hear oftener. So you were not sea sick on the trip down - am awfully glad to hear that. You say that the time has just flown bye, not so here - it has rather dragged along. If you see the young men that were so nice to you just give them my best and tell them they are boys of good judgment. I don't think I'll ever have occasion about many millions, unless something out of the general run of things happen. Well of course my pardner was the. . .*
Page(s) missing…
But there is one thing I must caution you against - that is please don't be in such a hurry to finish a letter you are writing and forget to gum it. The one I got the other day was not sealed and of course I thought you were in such a hurry to get through that you forgot to stick it.

I don't expect to have very long letters from you but I think you might write a line once in a while, and when are you going to start home? I am getting awfully tired of dancing and going around with other girls, that is what little I do go and I still have the opinion that there is no other girl quiet like Louise. Well I must stop and write another letter to a <u>man</u> in Ilwaco, and you bet I'll cut it short to.

Well good bye for the Present

With Love

Dick

I'll send you an extra letter of love in a day or two if the postage is not raised

Astoria, Or. Feb'y 25 1896   [Tuesday]

My Dear Girl:

I received your letter this morning and of course can't do a thing till I've answered it although I've very little to do so you see it is not because I have to but simply because I want to. I often wonder if you take half as much pleasure in reading my letters (that is of course barring bad writing) as I do in writing them. If you do then it is alright. I am [glad] nothing happened to you on your ride. I was thinking when I read the first part of your letter that I'd have to wait a week to find out if any sad fate had befell you, but I see at the last of the letter you got home alright for which information I am truly thankful as I remembered my first ride, but I see you came out a little better than myself. But you don't wear bloomers yet do you? This must be answered! No or yes.

There is very little going on here now. Little Connie played here last week. The Bacon Stock Company[41] *commence to night. I would like to take you this evening but hardly think you would care to go after seeing Louis James*[42] *who is coming here the last of the week. I understand but I'd do almost anything to make up for not asking you to go to the last dance, but I'll take you to next <u>sure</u>. The A.F.C.*[43] *give an entertainment Wed Eve. Of course I am going to be in it and probly be sick the day after as usual. I wouldn't mind a bit – well I guess I'd rather like it, that is, to have you here to ask "why I didn't run a little faster". I wouldn't mind you saying that if you were only here to say it. <u>1F</u>. I hardly suspose you'll ever get use to*

---

[41] Dick probably meant the popular Baker Stock Company of Portland, Oregon. According to McArthur's *Dictionary of Oregon History,* George L Baker, a former roustabout and stagehand, formed the company in1896. He and his company traveled mainly in the northwest; he stressed family theater performances. Mr. Baker was later elected mayor of Portland, serving from 1917 to 1933.

[42] Louis James was a well-known actor of the period. One of his signature roles was that of "Othello" in Shakespeare's play of the same name.

[43] A.F.C. stands for the Astoria Football Club (also known as A.C. and A.F.B.C.). It was established in 1889. The club's initiation fee was five dollars. Dick, Will Tallant and his younger brother Nat Tallant were very active members of the club. In 1896, the AFC met in the Armory Hall located on the Flavel Wharf at the foot of Eleventh Street and Bond. They had a bowling alley and a swimming pool.

Astoria and our ways again, and for riding in a one- seated rig is entirely out of the question after having that nice evening ride with Mr Deering[44] *- say what kind of a fellow is he - tall or short, Etc. Of course I don't care but I'd like to know, does he make the 15th or 16th I've kind of lost track of things. I hope it is no more though. I am glad you are doing so nicely at whist so as you get that down as good as* <u>old maid</u> *you need not worry. Well I don't know of any thing that is really startling so will close. Of course I don't expect to hear from you every day or get very long letters because you must be very busy, but I do expect a note now and again to let me know that you are well and happy for that will help me to be, as I've never quiet missed you so much. Don't forget to tell me of Mr D-.*

With Love

Dick

Dick drew a full sized outline in pencil of a net needle on the final page of this letter. This scan of the needle is slightly smaller than Louise's original 8" long one.

Tuesday the 3rd   [March 1896]

Dear Dick

 I am not in the mood for writing so excuse a dull letter - it rained all day yesterday. Guess it gave me the blues. Every one here is rejoicing for they have been praying for rain so long. I have just received a nice long letter from Nan so felt better. Last week we went out in the country to Covina and had a fine time - drove all over the country and just rested and enjoyed life. It was a treat to be where it was quiet.

 Was glad to find a letter from you when I got home. You want to know about Mr <u>Deering</u> *- well he is real nice for he has gotten up a Tally-Ho party for us this week. We are going to start in the a.m., take our lunch and drive way out beyond Pasadena some thirty miles from here and back in the evening (seven girls and seven boys). Won't we have a fine time? He is medium hight, sandy complexion and about thirty years old. He isn't on the list at all Dick so don't*

---

[44] Charles Deering accompanied Louise and the group on the May 1896 Mt. Wilson trip; he also shows up again in her life in the 1930s.

worry. *But what do you think I got in a letter from Portland the other day – why my silver needle that I lost last summer. Where it has been all this time I do not know. Now I am blessed with two.*

A week from today we go to "Sunny Slope" San Gabriel, Cal. and stay there about three weeks so if you write in that time as of course you will, direct letters as above. How mean of you Dick to say you don't suppose I will want to ride in a one seated buggy any more, you ought to know me better than that I should go away from home if I thought I was going to be dissatisfied with it when I got back. I am having to good a time to want to be home now. Every one here is so good to us – they can't seem to do enough.

Saturday we went to see "Trilby" and it was about the prettiest play I ever saw. So you really miss me. If I should be gone a long time don't you think you would forget me?

Well good bye   write soon to

Louise

Sunny Slope   San Gabriel

Trilby

Louise noted in her March 3, 1896 letter from Los Angeles to Dick that she had been to see the current hit play, *Trilby,* (probably the production by William Brady) and thought it the prettiest play she had ever seen.

In 1894, a French-born Englishman, George du Maurier, wrote the novel *Trilby* that was partly a romance and partly a gothic horror story. The book caused a sensation. It became an immediate bestseller on both sides of the Atlantic. Du Maurier, an illustrator as well, published it in installments in *Harper's Monthly* in 1894, so it was widely read. The novel was quickly made into a long running play. The starring roles were sought by all the great actors of the day, especially the role of Svengali, a clever Jewish rogue, an evil hypnotist and a conniving singing master. The character became so well known that the name 'Svengali' was used to denote any evildoer. The great John Barrymore played the role in the 1931 film. In 1910, the French author Gaston Leroux wrote the popular novel *The Phantom of the Opera* - based, in part, on *Trilby.*

Briefly, the plot centers upon three young English and Scottish artists in Bohemian Paris, who all fall in love with a tone-deaf Irish girl named Trilby O'Ferrall, an artists' model. One of the artists, Little Billee, is completely and utterly smitten by Trilby. The evil Svengali abducts Trilby on whom he experiments, using Mesmer-style hypnosis, in order to create a split personality in her. She becomes totally dependent upon Svengali, but also, always when in the hypnotic trance, she becomes an acclaimed diva. When she is about to give a performance in London, Svengali is stricken by a heart attack. He cannot place her in the trance, so Trilby cannot sing a note and is unmercifully heckled by the audience. She cannot recall anything about the hypnosis. She becomes completely overwrought. Unable to understand how her mind could have been enslaved, Trilby falls into deep despair and dies the following day. The artist Little Billee - his true love gone - follows her into death.

George du Maurier died in London October 8, 1896, a few months after Louise had attended his play in Los Angeles. His son, Sir Gerald du Maurier, was a well-know actor in London productions, including playing the dual roles of George Darling and Captain Hook in "Peter Pan." Sir George's granddaughter, Dame Daphne du Maurier, wrote numerous novels - perhaps her most well known is "Rebecca." One of her short stories was the inspiration for Alfred Hitchcock's film "The Birds."

In one of her 1896 letters, Louise enclosed a small blue cyanotype print of six "Alhambra girls and yours truly in the middle. MLT," posing on a porch. Louise had developed this one from a regular photographic negative using a special process she was learning.

Lillie Kerckhoff and Louise.

Harriet, Lillie and Louise in Los Angeles.

Friday   [March 6, 1896]

Dear Dick

I am so glad that you won those races that I must write and congratulate you right away (good boy). I can't say this time why didn't you run faster for you ran fast enough. I am going out for a bike ride so only have **one** spare minute. Yesterday we had such a pleasant drive – went out to Sunny Slope; took dinner there and drove back in afternoon. It was just after the rain so every thing was fresh and lovely and all the mountains were covered with snow. Well good bye. Let me know what you are doing and all that is going on. Be good and think often of your –

Louise

Mailing date: MAR 15 5:30PM 1896 Astoria, Oregon
Received: MAR 19 9AM 1896 San Gabriel, Cal
Envelope addressed to: Miss Louise Tallant
Sunny Slope
San Gabriel, Cal

Sunday 15th

My Dear Girl –

It is almost a week since I wrote last but you won't mind when I tell you I've been <u>busy</u>. This change of paper is due to the fact that I am writing at home. The last letter I wrote was rather short and surly I guess but I was nearly dead with a cold, but don't worry as I am too tough to die with anything less than some thing you don't get over. Well I am about alive is all. There is nothing going on that you might wish to be home for. The Club met at Copelands Thursday last. Of course I went. Friday eve there were a few at Pearls [Holden] to spend the evening. She left for Frisco yesterday morning. Last night the two Copelands, Nan & myself took a street car ride to Uppertown. The C- went to short hand school and I had the pleasure of sitting on [Nan] Reed's steps for half an hour or so – you know where they are don't you. Two months are nearly gone since you left. You are surely coming home in time for the Fourth of July ain't you?

You congratulated me on those races. Well they were I must admit rather tame - not more than a thousand Wreaths crowned me. You ought to be here to enjoy the fine weather – out-o-sight. I've had several pressing invitations to go out in the Pilot Schooner [the *Jessie*] for a month. I am thinking of doing so as soon as I get through at the warehouse which will be in a week or ten days. It would be a good place to pass a way time till your other month is over. Lem & Jim are down in Alameda. Jim is looking up Miss Mastic I suspose. Where in the dickens is Sunny Slope – can't find it on the map. So you will ride in a one seated rig. Well I am going to have the horse up sooner this year and will you kindly pray to save him against sore legs, Etc.

Nearly every one seems to be out of town to day on bicycle rides, and that puts me in mind to thank you for not dawning bloomers, but I never had the least idea you would. Lots of new boys in town, 2 anyway and I'm almost afraid to have you come home although I want you to so bad – that's no Josh ---

Well I hope you are having a fine time and I guess there is no need of my hopeing as you certainly are. And now I must go and take you for a walk for the weather is too nice for any use except that. You said be a good boy. Ain't I always except some times. Excuse <u>bad grammar</u>, writing, Etc and remember

Yours with lots of Love

Between 1 and 16   One I hope

Dick

A partial letter from Louise to Dick begins on "page 2." No date is indicated on the scrap of her letter, but the letter is enclosed in a dated envelope.

Mailing date: MAR 20 2PM 1896 Los Angeles   [Friday]
Received: MAR 24 7AM 1896 Astoria, Oreg.
Envelope addressed to: Mr Richard Carruthers
                                   Astoria
          Bonded Ware House   Oregon

2/ "gentle men friends" who come way out from Los Angeles on their wheels to see us. Of course I enjoyed the walk with you most, however the drive we all took in the course of the afternoon was very fine.

We are going in to Los Angeles tomorrow to go to a couple of parties. I never lent my netting needle to any boy. Grace Eliot found it and sent it to me. One of the fellows here took my A.F.C. pin and kept it about a week. I nearly had a fit I was so afraid he would loose it.

Well I must stop now. It is getting so warm I can't sit here any longer. I will pick you an orange blossom for a button hole boquet – do write soon again to your

Louise

Robert Carruthers and The Mystery of the *Jessie*

The mouth of the Columbia River is referred to as "The Graveyard of the Pacific." Ever since ship traffic in and out of this river began in the 1800s, there have been over 2,000 wrecks of ships that failed to navigate the treacherous breakers, the clash of tidal currents and the shifting sandbars that guard the river's entrance. Sudden weather changes and thick fogs added to the perils of the river. Safer passages began thanks to men and women trained to guide vessels across the river's bar. The famous Columbia River Bar Pilots, familiar with the entrance to the river, are able to "read" the ever-changing conditions that threaten the safe passage of shipping.[45] Although bar pilots of today board the big moving vessels by means of helicopters and/or fast, highly maneuverable pilot boats that pull along side, it is still a dangerous profession.

In early Astoria, bar pilots boarded small pilot boats – tugs or schooners usually, and crossed the Columbia River bar – whatever the conditions - to wait out in the shipping lanes of the Pacific Ocean – in all kinds of weather - for a ship to come along that requested the services of a pilot. The wait was often long. It was always hazardous for both the bar pilots as well as for the captains and crews of their pilot boats. According to one old timer, in the earliest days, the pilots would bring a ship in or out of the river by tossing a line to her and literally "towing" her over the bar.

During the 1890s into the 1900s, bar piloting was a very competitive business. All pilots, and pilot boats, on the Columbia had to be licensed by either the Oregon or Washington State Commissioners. In 1895, the State of Oregon's pilot boat, a schooner named the *San Jose*, was operating on the river with the Union Pacific Railroad's two tugs, the *Escort* and the *Wallowa*, and the tug *C. J. Brenham* owned by lumberman Asa Simpson. Washington state pilots operated the 30-ton pilot schooner *Loyal* until the beginning of 1896, when she was transferred to Seattle for the halibut trade.

In January 1896, a feared competitor arrived on the river to replace the old *Loyal*. She was the *Jessie*. Launched at the same Benecia, California shipyard as the *San Jose*, the seventy-six-foot, two-masted *Jessie* (vessel #77266) was very fast and sleek. The 75.84-ton schooner had been built in 1890 as a private yacht for Commodore James McDonough at the cost of $35,000. In January, Dick's father Robert Carruthers traveled to San Francisco with a small crew to complete her purchase. She was a true bargain! Carruthers and his associates had only been able to gather together a deposit of $2000 of the total agreed upon price of $6000, but it was enough to seal the deal. Evidently, they expected to be able to pay off the balance from business profits. Robert Carruthers was a bar pilot licensed by the State of Washington, and as the master of the *Jessie*, he took less than forty-eight hours to sail her from San Francisco to Astoria "with enough provisions aboard to enable the vessel to stay at sea for three months."[46]

Upon arrival in Astoria, Robert placed a native of Maine, Captain James Tatton, in command of the *Jessie*. Tatton had been employed by Samuel Elmore on the *H.P. Elmore*, running their cannery vessel to and from Alaskan waters. Robert hired two bar pilots, Alexander Malcolm and George Wood, a cook and a couple of deckhands to sail the *Jessie* north to South Bend in Washington Territory. On February 4, 1896, the Washington State Pilot Commissioners issued the license for the *Jessie* to work as a Columbia River bar pilot boat.[47] Robert declared: "We're going to pilot on the bar and we're here to stay…The *Jessie* is the fastest pilot boat on the coast."[48] Her speed caused other pilots to fear they might be run out of business – and, indeed, that was Robert Carruthers' stated purpose. At that time, the pilots on the Columbia were charging a fee of $5 per draft foot – three dollars less than the fee charged on Puget Sound. The shippers

[45] The Columbia River water flows into the ocean at the rate of one million cubic feet per second and extends twenty miles into the Pacific, reported Tom Bennett in his article, "Bar Pilot Describes the Frenzy at the Mouth of the Columbia." (*Daily Astorian*, October 15, 2006), 14.

[46] Dark, *Graveyard Passage,* 74.

[47] Ibid., 75.

[48] Ibid., 74.

feared their fees would be increased, but Carruthers stated: "Our fees will be equal to the Oregon pilots and our service will be much faster."[49] She was in business – such as there was.

Even before the *Jessie* arrived on the river, Union Pacific officials had been worried that the *Escort* and the *Wallowa* were not bringing in the revenues they had expected. The *San Jose* probably broke even because she was subsidized by the State of Oregon. The competition between the Washington and the Oregon bar pilots was fierce. There was simply not enough business to go around. No holds were barred later when the Union Pacific lowered the fees for their two pilot boats to "93-cents per registered ton."[50]

For the next four years the *Jessie* managed to stay in business on the Columbia. On March 15, 1896, Dick mentioned his father's *Jessie* in his letter to Louise, who was still visiting in Southern California. He wrote:

> *"I've had several pressing invitations to go out in the Pilot Schooner for a month. I am thinking of doing so as soon as I get through at the warehouse* [Astoria Wharf & Warehouse] *which will be in a week or so. It would be a good place to pass a way time till your other month is over."*

Dick wrote, on January 4, 1898 (misdated as 1897), that he had temporarily filled in as the night watchman on the *Jessie* while she was in port. He was, in effect, the "Captain," with William Young as his lieutenant and Tom Crosby as the steward. He commented that the crewmembers of the government revenue cutter, the *Commodore Perry*, were *"not the only pebbles on the beach, when it comes to H'officers."* The young men may well have held several stag parties on board the schooner.

The following year, on September 17, 1898, when Louise wrote Dick, he was in Honolulu with the Volunteer Engineers:

> *Your father misses you. Dick, he even talkes of taking a trip down there* [to Hawaii] *on the Jessie. Do you think I could persuade him to take me along. I would like nothing better than a trip down there.*

On November 28, 1898, while still stationed in Honolulu, Dick wrote his brother Gus [Angus Russell Carruthers]: *"I hope something has been done about the schooner – is there any hope of selling her?"* Evidently business was becoming scarcer and, therefore, it was harder to make the venture profitable.

Louise wrote Dick on October 14, 1899, hoping that the *Jessie* would get off all right on the next day and wished her good luck. Then on the seventeenth, she wondered if all had gone well for the *Jessie*. Louise does not indicate whether the schooner is still patrolling the sea-lanes for business or headed for Alaska at that time. Nor do Dick's letters indicate what is happening to the pilot boat.

---

[49]   Dark, 74.
[50]   Ibid., 76.

About six weeks later, the *Astoria Daily Budget* carried the following notice in the November 24 column "About the City:"

Robert Carruthers has found that he cannot find sufficient number of people with capital to engage in the deepsea fishing business so he has found another venture for his schooner Jessie. A company is being formed to take the schooner to Cape Nome early next spring. In addition to taking a number of prospectors she will have her hold filled with the kind of merchandise that should be profitable there if it is delivered in the spring.

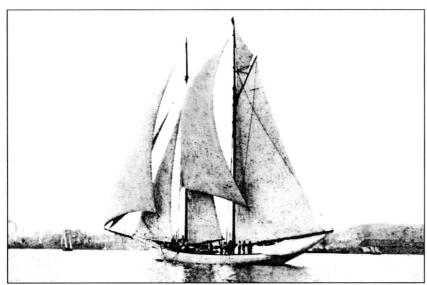

The *Jessie*   Photo #69-288 courtesy of Columbia River Maritime Museum.
Vessel No. #77266 - 75.84 gross tons; 76' length; 24.5' breadth; 8.7' depth.[51]

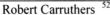

Robert Carruthers [52]

Dick - 1896

[51] *Merchant Vessels of the United States,* 103.
[52] Robert Carruthers' photo courtesy of Clatsop County Historical Society It appeared in a *Cumtux* article by Zoe Allen Evans, the daughter of Carleton and Grace Carruthers Allen, "The Allens of Astoria," 32.

According to the *Astoria Daily Budget* of January 13, 1900, the *Jessie* had been sold to a business called Astoria Deep Sea Fishing Company. She may have already sailed away to fish for halibut in northern waters. H.W. McCurdy states the *Jessie* did not survive the year in the northern fishery trade and lists her as lost near Nome, Alaska, in January 1900.[53] Had Robert sent her up to Alaskan waters earlier than the "next spring" (of 1900), as he had planned back in November 1899, per the newspaper's article? Had she no sooner gotten to the northern waters, than she was "lost?" The time line is not clear.

Angus "Gus" Carruthers

The *Jessie* at the O.R.& N. Dock.
Photo # 70-120C courtesy of CRMM.

McCurdy's account also indicates the *Jessie*'s pilot license was revoked in January 1900. He cites a collusion that was said to exist between the state pilot boards of Washington and Oregon. At some point, Washington's Governor Rogers had appointed three commissioners to his state's pilot board – "a lawyer and a saloon keeper from Ilwaco, and strangely enough, a resident of Astoria, Oregon."[54] The *Astoria Daily Budget*'s article on January 13, 1900, titled "Pilot Commission," gives a report of an apparently completed investigation involving, in part, an unsubstantiated allegation regarding the *Jessie*. Charles T. Smith, a maritime engineer residing in Astoria, made the complaint against his fellow commissioners, J.J. Brumbach, a lawyer, and Nicholas C. Kofoed, a saloonkeeper, both of Ilwaco.

Relative to the recent investigation against two members of the Washington board of pilot commissioners a dispatch from South Bend says:

Hon. Fred T. Rice sent his report to Governor Rogers yesterday, covering the result of his investigation of the charge against N. C. Kofoed and J. J. Brumbach of Ilwaco as Washington pilot commissioners for the Columbia river by the third member of the pilot board, Charles T. Smith. The charges were that the majority of the board had discriminated against Washington boats and pilots; that the two first named had received money unlawfully from the Oregon pilot board and had licensed

---

[53] McCurdy, *Marine History*, "Maritime Events of 1900," 63.
[54] Ibid., 57.

Oregon boats and pilots. The especial grievances were the refusal of the board to license the schooner Jessie, owned by Robert Carruthers, of Astoria. This boat had been under commission by the pilots holding Washington branches, and had been licensed by the Washington board, but the owner substituted scrap iron in ballast for the pig lead, which had been in her and sold the latter. The pilots then declined to go out in the boat, claiming that the scrap iron ballast would shift in a storm, and the board refused to renew her license, and licensed, instead, the Joseph Pulitzer, which is owned principally by the Oregon pilots.

The only evidence of any money having been used illegally was in the statement of Mr. Brumbachs that he had found $200 in his overcoat pocket after a meeting with the Oregon pilot board, and he had turned it over to the secretary of said board.

The report coincides with the statement that but one thing stands out clearly as the result of the investigation, and that is the lack of harmony in the Washington board; furthermore, that there are, in reality, no Washington pilots and no Washington pilot-boat, and that one of the Washington board, the complainant, Mr. Smith, is himself a resident of Astoria, Or.

Russell Dark relates a somewhat different account.[55] He states that in April 1900, a new group of three commissioners was appointed to the Washington Bar Pilot Board. Dark gives the men's names as George Hibbert, associate editor of the *Astorian Budget* and part owner of the *Chinook Observer*; Jack E. Wilson (probably John Wilson, listed as an Ilwaco saloonkeeper in 1901);[56] and Charles A. Payne, editor and part owner of the *Chinook Observer*. Hibbert wanted to license twenty-two more Washington bar pilots in order to run off the Oregon ones. Wilson and Payne objected, although no reasons were given. Referring to Hibbert's proposal, C.J. Curtis, attorney and editor of the weekly *Astoria Herald,* wrote: "None of these three commissioners can tell a full rigger from a fish trap and the only bars with which they are familiar are the ones in Astoria and Ilwaco."[57] Dark wrote that two months after these three men took office (that would have then been in June 1900!), they revoked the *Jessie's* bar pilot license. Dark does not report what happened to the *Jessie* other than that she was sent to Alaska – nor does he indicate when that occurred. Evidently, she was still considered seaworthy at that time. Could it have been a trumped up charge just to remove the competitive *Jessie* from the Columbia bar? Had she sailed north under the newly formed Astoria Deepsea Fishing Company? Might Robert have been the actual owner of that company – or had someone else formed and financed it? Might the *Jessie* have sailed northward under a completely different owner/company that we do not know about? No matter what, the main questions remain: When did she sail north? And what really did happen to her?

McCurdy also relates the mysterious disappearance of "a *Jessie*" (no vessel number given) that he says occurred in June 1898. It is known that the Klondike steamer *Lakme* had been in Alaskan waters prior to being ordered to San Francisco to serve as a troop transport vessel during the Spanish-American War. (The *Lakme* sailed from San Francisco to Honolulu the first week in August 1898, carrying 360 men, including Dick's Volunteer Engineers Company M.) McCurdy states that the *Lakme* left Seattle in May to take an expedition of some eighteen passengers as far as Kuskokwim Bay (about 300 miles south of Nome), where it met "the" *Jessie* on the 27th of June. This vessel, reportedly owned by a Columbia Navigation Company, had been hired to take the

[55] Dark, *Graveyard Passage*, 75.
[56] R.L. Polk & Co. Astoria City Directory 1901-2.
[57] Dark, 75.

passengers up the Kuskokwim River to look for gold and to trade. The *Jessie* started up river. Then she mysteriously disappeared.

The crew of the *Thomas Corwin,* a former revenue cutter, conducted a formal investigation into the matter and made an unsuccessful search for her at some point in the following year 1899. It is possible she may have been caught in the severe turbulence of a southeast gale that hit the area and could have been swamped. No wreckage was found. The fate of the eighteen missing persons and crew was never fully determined. Officials conjectured that either all persons were lost at sea, or they reached shore only to die at the hand of local Indians, or perhaps, a combination of both.[58] Could this have been Robert's *Jessie*? Or was it some other *Jessie*? If McCurdy reported the date of June 1898 correctly, this *Jessie* could not have been Robert's *Jessie*. But, McCurdy might have gotten the year wrong. Could this episode actually have happened in 1900?

Every ship built is given a unique, registered number. That number stays with the vessel forever, even if she is rebuilt or renamed. Unfortunately, the number of a vessel, even in authoritative sources such as McCurdy, Lewis and Dryden or Russell Dark, is seldom, if ever, given. Therefore, it is difficult to track a particular vessel. Conflicting reports can result. Robert's *Jessie* was number #77266. None of the recorded accounts of a *Jessie* list any number, so an error free account often is not possible.

In any event, the beautiful, sleek *Jessie* did not end her days gracefully on the Columbia River. Dick wrote the following to Louise from the Lightsey, Lewis & Carruthers cattle ranch at Turkey Hammock, Florida on March 1, 1902:

> *"Will send love on some other sheet. Sorry I can not send it on the main sheet*
> *of the Jessie you have in your drawing room. It would barely hold it, but will*
> *do the best I can."*

Unexplained is how the Carruthers family managed to obtain the "lost" *Jessie*'s main sheet.

Danger has always filled the lives of pilots, their boats and their crews, whether waiting for a vessel out in a rough ocean, crossing the bar or anchored in port. The *Daily Astorian* ran the following article on February 16, 1897, about a river mishap involving the *Jessie* during stormy weather:[59]

A lone boat drifting down stream yesterday afternoon with a strong ebb tide, without an occupant, suggested to those on the O. R. and N. dock that perhaps some one was in distress or had been foully dealt with. Investigation proved that in all probability Captain "Charlie" Swanson, of the schooner Jessie, had been drowned while attempting to go aboard from his small boat yesterday afternoon.

Sunday afternoon the pilot schooner *Jessie*, in charge of Pilot Malcolm, with Captain Swanson and crew, came into the harbor and anchored just above the O. R. and N. dock in the main channel; it being the schooner San Jose's turn to go outside. Yesterday morning at 11 o'clock, the crew were paid off in full, and the captain, according to custom, drew his wages and prepared to return on board as he is

---

[58] McCurdy, 42, 57.
[59] See also: Liisa Penner, *Salmon Fever: River's End. Tragedies,* 87.

the watchman of the vessel while she is in port. At 1 o'clock, he went down to the dock, and started in one of the small boats of the *Jessie* for his vessel. As he passed the *San Jose*, he hailed the captain and asked him to go out with him and look at his trim little ship. The *San Jose*'s skipper replied that he could not just then, to which Swanson answered that he would return in half an hour. That was the last heard of Capt. Swanson, as he was soon to go on towards the *Jessie*.

Only a few minutes after this, the small white boat of the *Jessie* was seen floating down the main channel in a direct line with the *Jessie*, but no one in it. O. R. and N. Watchman Erickson at once lowered his boat and went to capture the runaway. By hard work he succeeded in getting around the dock into the channel and despite the swift ebb tide caught the painter of the *Jessie*'s boat and rowed her to the end of the dock. There it was discovered that the runaway boat had no water in her, and that the rowlocks had been taken down and the oars placed on the seats – all ship-shape. An investigating force was at once organized and towed the small boat back to the *Jessie*, where it was soon found that no captain, or watchman was aboard.

When seen last night, Captain Carruthers, owner of the *Jessie*, said he only knew his skipper and watchman by the name of "Charlie" [Swanson] and could only account for his disappearance upon the theory that after leaving the *San Jose*, he proceeded to the *Jessie*, got alongside, took down the rowlocks, placed his oars inside; took the painter in his hand and, in attempting to climb over the rail onto the deck of the *Jessie*, lost his hold by the rolling of the boat in the gale and slipped into the swift current of the river.

The following undated letter from Dick to Louise is on Astoria Wharf and Warehouse Co. stationery. No salutation.

At a meeting of the A.C. [Athletic Club] at Olga's, Nancy & Nettie, Mr Shields and Mr Burnett, Dr Logan's new man, were elected. You are well aware who the first three are and look like; as for Mr Burnett I suspose the girls told you all about him so I'll not go into details. They intend to commence to play tennis soon.[60] *I guess they mean as soon as the weather permits. I don't know if you know Freddie Andrews or not of Portland, but on this morning's out going steamer there was a woman who received a telegram that he had committed sideways [?], all on account of her, and she staid over and is going up this eve. I saw her on the street & I think he must have been a little off to have done it. But you want to look out, for I think I'd have lots better reasons than Mr Andrews if any thing should go wrong. Mr Kendall was elected president of the A.F.C. last meeting. You see I have to dig up some purty hard news when I commence to tell you who was elected president of an Athletic Club. U&I were here and our next is John L- I believe. Of course I wouldn't miss seeing him for the world.*[61] *Prof Beggs [the dancing master] class is about busted up. The committee has been appointed for the regatta.*

---

[60] The tennis courts were located on the north side of what is now Duane, between Sixth and Seventh. The Astoria Police Department currently covers the whole south half of the block.

[61] The reference appears to be about John L. Sullivan, the first heavyweight-boxing champion of the world. He was an Irish American born in Roxbury, MA in 1858. Fans called him the "Boston Strongboy." He fought a few bare-knuckles fights early in his career, but changed to the Marquess of Queensberry rules that required him to fight with boxing gloves. One fight was in Astoria in August 1888 against a local man, "Brother" Sylvester. He lost his title in the twenty-first round of a fight against "Gentleman Jim" Corbett in New Orleans on September 6, 1892. He quit boxing after that, except for some exhibition matches. John L. Sullivan, a noted celebrity, turned to film acting roles and toured the country giving temperance lectures. It

Hope you are home in time. Everyone has sold out of the Ast W W Co now except Dr E. C. Carter a 1/10 owner. I am still here representing Uncle Sam for a week longer. Then what I don't know. Lem & Jim are home from California. I don't see any change in Jim. Lem seems the same.

I attended Herman Wise's ball, the one some while back, and ran into Caroline Young, about the only person I knew. Shields and I were coming from a call at the Copelands and just droped in to see the snackers. Caroline informed me that I used to be quite smitten on her. I told her it was her fault and not mine that I wasn't yet and whistled "There is Only One Girl in the World for Me." I didn't tell her the only reason I ever went with her was to see <u>you</u> though. She asked about you and I told her that I knew very little and didn't want to know much. This seemed to please her. What have you done anyway. It couldn't be me because she said she hated me. I haven't lost much sleep over it so far. Shields thought her a very funny girl and I don't know if I blame him. Will seems to be training again I believe to run the latter part of May. Well I can't think of another blessed thing except Gussie Gray had a spat with Chas Higgins at the last Encore Club but that's no news. Well good bye for the present. Hoping to hear from you soon

> *I am as ever*
>> *Dick*

O say is the starting of this letter o.k. this time Louise. I looked letter headings up in some bodys ready letter writer and that is the form given when writing to a friend and that is all you would ever allow me to claim of you. So I suppose I'll have to do as the book says.

>>> *Dick*

> *Sunny Slope   Sunday 29   [March 1896]*

I won't be as mean as you and will begin with Dear Dick but if you are satisfied with the way you began all right. I don't care only next time you don't get an answer. We drove down to the P.O. right after breakfast this a.m. and I was so glad when I found there a letter for me. I think I am most to good to answer it right away but we are going to be so busy the next few days that I won't get another chance. Yesterday Hat and I went into Los Angeles to do some shopping and it rained "cats and dogs" quite like home – almost made me home sick. In the evening I made candy for the children and we had a circus. There are three small boys in the family and they can make life miserable for a fellow if they want too. It is a wonder they are not all three trying to sit on my lap now – they generaly want to as soon as I begin to write.

---

is possible, although not confirmed, that he appeared in Astoria at Fisher's Opera House in March or April 1896 to give a lecture on the evils of drink, with which he had been well acquainted. He later formed a touring company that did put on a show at Fisher's on Sunday, April 16, 1899; it turned into a hilarious Keystone Cops kind of romp.

We have just had some friends in to call on us (poor people – only worth about ten million). They want us to come over and spend the afternoon with them. They live in a rather small house - <u>only</u> <u>twenty</u> <u>six</u> <u>rooms</u> in it and three people in the family. We were over there the other day and if I had been alone I am afraid I should have gotten lost going from the house to the street - the grounds are like a park.

So you told Caroline it wasn't your fault that you were not smitten on her and that you knew quite enough about me (<u>and you are the boy that doesn't josh</u>, at least so you tell me) and to tell the truth I some times wonder if you realy care for me at all. You will say I ought too but I guess I had for we have been good friends for a long time now haven't we. So glad for Mrs Tuttles sake the girls belong to our club. She will come up to the court once in a while now to see how <u>we</u> <u>are</u> getting along – we musn't dissapoint her.

Fred Andrews must have it pretty bad; hope his lady love returned and made him happy. I had a nice letter from Miss Copeland the other day. I must answer that now and write to my friend in N.Y. if I can find time before dinner.[62] I can't realize that Wednesday is the first of April (don't get fooled). We are having such a splendid time that much as I want to see all my dear friends at home I shall hate to leave all my old friends here. You know Hat and I were both born down here in San Gabriel and all the people round here knew us when we <u>were</u> <u>children</u> and we are invited to lunches and parties to meet our old play mates and mighty few of them I remember. Next week I am going to spend with an old chum in Alhambra. I sent home a picture taken out here on the lawn that has about thirty girls in it – yours truly among the rest. Lillie and I are standing together and as usural were trying not to laugh. If you should happen to be passing our house and stop in you may look at it and take your choice. I <u>must</u> stop now or my N.Y. friend whose nice long letter I received fully a week ago will "get left." Believe me to be as ever ("your friend").

Miss M. Louise Tallant

P.S. do you know the Shilling Baking "Powder" man – he is I hear a good tennis player. Why not ask him to join our club.   M.L.T.

Sunday   [Easter – April 5, 1896]

Dear Louise:

Your very nice and long letter received yesterday so I'll be as good as you were and answer it now. I suppose you are going to church now as everybody around here are starting.

I left the warehouse on the first. Since then I've been collecting for Prael Co. and tomorrow I am going to go down to the warehouse and unload a tinship for the new company, not all by myself but just look out the same as before. There is hardly any news to speak of but I'll try

---

[62]   Louise was probably writing to Clara Starbuck in Brooklyn or Clara's brother, George, in New York City.

and think some up. Nellie S- [Sherman] is home but I suppose you knew that – I've not seen her yet, but those who have say she is improved wonderfully. The Depot site has at last been agreed upon[63] and we will surely be able to take a trip to the seaside this summer without even seeing a boat. I know it will seem strange, but we'll become use to it I guess. Chas Heilborn goes to San Francisco on the 8th for a month or more. The A.F.C. are preparing for more shows, this time a drama and you must not cry because some parts do look sad. I am cast for the "villian", not a very bad one though, but I manage to get two or three people killed at the rate of $1000 per head. Mrs Patterson & Miss Jessie Jewett are the only ladies and we are trying to develop A'Dalgety into a feamale impersonator with little success so far.

We are having all kinds of weather today: sunshine, hail & rain, little more sunshine. Kate U- [Upshur] is just going by to church. Mr Gilson also.

Gussie Gray is a saleslady at McAllen & McDonalds and seems tickled to death. Tom Bryce is also a sales lady at Coopers – he's changed sides. There is going to be a strike between fishermen and the canners this year over the price of fish.

Nellie Taylor & Mr Wenig, one of Mrs Parkers star boarders, were married last week. Nellie is a lovely girl I don't think, and Mr Wenig walks as though his shoes hurt him. I guess you know him don't you – has a sort of Nate Bergman walk. They make a lovely couple. Nit!

So you don't care how I start a letter to you. Say Louise, do you really care if you get a letter or not from me. I know you never Josh. Did you get good and wet on that shopping trip to Los Angeles? If you didn't it wasn't like "Astoria". I'd like to be down in sunny south for about a week to get good and warm for once this year, and I suppose you would like to be here get a little fresh air. Tell those poor people with the 26 room house I am awfully sorry for them but don't see as I could help them out this year any, but if it is a nice place we might buy it later on but I think it a little small. I don't see why I was Joshing when I said I knew enough about you. Well I do. I know enough that there is not another girl just like you, that is to me, and as for caring for you, well I am a little bit in love with you and am quite willing to become more so if such a thing were possible and If such a thing would be permited I might sat. I know I've treated you mean lots of times but I think a girl would have to be a little bit blinder than you are to see for yourself. I some times think I've made a chump of myself over you, and think you think the same but I don't care if I have. I like you and am not one to deny it, so you see this is a little more than school boy love. I am in all probility geting sily but you will have to excuse me if I am because you wrote the words that you "sometimes thought I didn't care for you" & I was compelled to answer that I did and you know it too and I've not given up all hopes of claiming you yet, but not for a while. If anyone was to be the lucky one except me I don't know what I would do, I would surly do, I'd try and seek a more secluded spot than where

---

[63]   Scow Bay area, at the foot of 21st Street, was chosen as the train depot site.

you were and this is no <u>*Josh*</u> *nor none of it for that matter. To change the subject, although it is a dear one to me, it is raining at present.*

Miss C- seems rather smitten on the "Schilling" man. I presume she is the one who wrote of him. I know him and that is about all, but they say he is a very good tennis player. Mrs Tuttle should be happy that she can come within the portals of the A.C. and it will probly give us something to talk about as well as Mrs T-. I don't know who gets it worse – the Boy, Girls or Mrs T-.

So you are going to Alhambra. Well I guess that is a nice place, and hope you have a lovely time. Ever so much obliged for the chase of those photos and I will call and get it one of these days. You shouldn't put <u>*that*</u> *N.Y. Friend off so long. I know how I would feel and probly the friend is the same in regards to such matter. Well I must close and get dressed. I've only been down town for about five minutes this a.m. and that was to get a cigar and here it is after 12. so I'll say good bye for the present.*

From

Dick

The "Schilling" man has been asked to join the club, but he runs with Bennett a good deal so I guess the Elmores, known as the Ten for Tennis, will grab him. Was there lots of new bonnets in church this morning. And I'll bet you were the best looking girl there, never smiled a smile or whispered but was just to devout for anything.

Across an arroyo from the Tallants' orange grove lived Samuel M. and Ida Halsted, who became dear friends of the Tallants. The Halsteds arrived in Southern California from New York State in the fall of 1877, three years after Pasadena was founded. They were one of the pioneer families to settle in San Gabriel on the boundary line with Alhambra. They chose to situate their ranch house on seventeen acres at the intersection of five roads, including *El Camino Real*, because they got superior mail service there. The Halsteds' daughter Marge (Ida Marguerite, 1875-1960) was the same age as Louise and the girls were life-long friends. After the Tallant family moved to Astoria in 1881, Marge was a frequent and welcome visitor to their home. Louise and Harriet visited the Halsteds every time they went back to Southern California. Marge, a fine horsewoman, rode in the Tournament of Roses parade several times. She was very active in women's groups, such as the Girl Scouts, and drove a Red Cross ambulance during WWII.[64]

---

[64] Shoop, "Death Recalls Pioneer Days," *Auld Lang Syne* column, about Marge Halsted, dated in pencil as May 1960. The article was pasted in Louise's scrapbook from an unidentified source – most likely a Pasadena or Alhambra newspaper. Marge did not go overseas; she worked locally for the Red Cross as a driver.

Seven Alhambra "roses" at the Halsteds' house.
Louise is lower right – dark skirt.

California's Sunny Slope Ranch transportation in 1896.
Louise is in the second row from back, outside seat, in a dark dress.

Photo is of almost thirty persons dated March 1896, at Sunny Slope Ranch near San Gabriel.
Harriet, Lillie Kerckhoff and Louise are the third, fourth and fifth women from the left.

Harriet, Marge and Louise in San Gabriel - 1896.
Only the chimney remains (on the left) of the Tallants' burned home.
An old out building remains standing behind them.

Harriet, Marge and Louise in the Tallants' old orange grove in 1896.

The Great Fishermen's Strike of 1896 - Astoria, Oregon

"Time was when you could cross the Columbia river
near the mouth by stepping on the backs of salmon or
on the decks of gillnet boats."[65]

Some of the old fishermen have estimated upwards of 4,000 small boats fished in the Columbia River in the late 1880s. In 1866, on the Washington shore, William and G.W. Hume had set up the first salmon cannery on the Lower Columbia. They spent the winter of 1866 at their Eagle Cliff cannery making tin cans, "knitting" fishnets and putting together the necessary machinery. During the spring salmon run of 1867, the Hume group packed 4,000 cases, each containing forty-eight cans, each can weighing one pound. By 1883 along the Columbia there were fifty-five canneries, which produced 630,000 cases of 48 cans each (estimated value in that time was $3 million), filled with forty-three million pounds of the prized Royal Chinook. Each Royal Chinook salmon weighed a minimum of thirty pounds, so they were referred to as "June hogs." The "Kings of the Columbia" were without equal.[66]

In those days everyone thought - if they thought about it at all - that the massive salmon runs would never cease. But they did decline dramatically – in less than one hundred years. Over-fishing of the river, too many dams along the Columbia and its tributaries, logging and pollution of the waters are some of the reasons given for the decline.

---

[65] Dark, "Gillnetters: A Vanishing Fleet," unpublished monograph, n.d., 1.
[66] Terry, "Oregon Trails," (*Sunday Oregonian*, May 19, 2002).

Fishing and lumbering were the primary industries in the Astoria area. The Norwegians, the Swedes and the Hindus formed the timber industry. They settled mainly in the eastern part of Astoria, known as Uppertown. A large Finnish community settled in the western "third" of Astoria, known as Uniontown. The fishermen there, mostly Finns, had formed various unions dating from the 1870s.

The Sanborn-Perris Insurance's Astoria waterfront map of 1892 showed seventeen canneries, packing companies and offices, as well as a number of warehouses and wharfs, including the long Oregon Railway & Navigation Dock, which extended from 15th to 18th Street. J.S. Dellinger's 1896 Astoria City Directory listed only six canneries on the waterfront between Smith Point and 50th Street. There were a few other canneries further up and down the river, including the Scandinavian Packing Co. and the Eureka and Epicure Packing Co., but by this time, even more of the old canneries had been turned into warehouses.

Many of the canneries, wharfs and offices were located in the middle section of town. Here also lived a community of Chinese, who were vital to the canning industry and provided most of the hand labor, which was required then. The Chinese were the ones who made the tin cans, packed and processed them. They were the backbone of the early industry, so much so that a machine later engineered to process fish was named the "Iron Chink" – not a complimentary name, but it did indicate the importance of the Chinese workers. It also displaced most of the Chinese workers. Unfortunately, in those days, no Chinese were allowed a voice, or a vote, in the business of the fishing industry, nor were they even permitted to fish commercially.

The fishing industry, begun in the mid 1800s, was often plagued with problems - especially by strikes over the amount the fishermen were willing to receive from the canneries. The 1888 price set for fish was $1.25 per fish, but by 1893, it was changed to a more equitable per pound payment. On March 21, 1893, Eben Weld Tallant, manager of the Columbia River Packing Company (Cutting Packing Co. was their agent in San Francisco), wrote his daughter Louise the following:

"I hope you'll not make so many engagements [in Chicago] *so as to delay your getting home in time for fishing season, as there will be a great amount of work for you in the office. We now have 94 boats engaged, which is far beyond any previous record and to add to this it is very probable we shall buy fish by weight instead of the old method of count. This will greatly increase the office labor of which Willie has full charge depending on you as assistant."*

Both groups, cannery owners and fishermen, wanted to make as much profit as possible, even though neither group could exist without the other.

Dick wrote Louise on Easter Sunday, April 5, 1896, that there was *"going to be a strike between fishermen and canners this year over the price of fish."* And, indeed, there was. It was neither the first strike to take place nor the last, but, according to some, it was perhaps one of the most bitter ever in this industry. It was to last for almost three months.

In the Sunday *Daily Morning Astorian* of March 22, 1896, a report was printed regarding a meeting at Fisher's Hall of 1,000 fishermen. They voted to demand five cents a pound or they would strike the canneries and packing companies. Two thousand fishermen attended another meeting in Fisher's Hall on April 8, at which they agreed by a unanimous vote to hold out for five cents a pound for raw fish until August tenth. Further, they agreed that fishing for their own food was acceptable, but they were not permitted to sell any. Also they demanded that cannery owners were not to be allowed to hire non-union men, or any fishermen, even at five cents, unless all canneries agreed to pay the five cents to all fishermen. The commercial fishing season opened April 10, 1896. Everyone on the river feared the effects of a strike.

"A rainy day costume is a necessity for April weather in Astoria."[67]

On April 23, the newspaper noted that militiamen, called out earlier by the State of Washington to keep order, had been withdrawn from Chinook (a town across the river in Washington State), but that they were still in Ilwaco and on Sand Island in the middle of the river. During this early time of year there was usually a light run of fish, so no one was losing "very much" up till then. The newspaper reported Captain O'Connor of the steamer *Volga* said it was the most peaceful strike he'd ever seen. Dick seemed to agree in a letter dated April twenty-sixth when he wrote that the strike was still on and that things are awfully dull.

Louise received Dick's letter written on May 16, the day after the presentation of the well-received play *At The Picket Line:*

[It] *came off last night ... To say it was a success I will tell you that there was only three empty seats in the building ... But, The Fish question has not been settled yet so you won't be able to wrap cans and I won't be able to help. Everyone in town seems well and happy as the times allow."*

That was not to last.

The general feeling among union members seemed to be that there was too much competition – especially from non-union and/or non-local men - that the river could not provide a decent living for so many fishermen. A delegation of three hundred union members marched on the Cutting, Elmore and Kinney canneries, among others, to demand a twenty-five percent reduction of the fishing force (possibly as many as 500 men). They urged the owners to pay off those fishermen fairly - those who were not local and non-union men. In exchange, the union was willing to allow work for four cents a pound, if necessary. The packers/canners claimed they could not pay five cents for raw fish, but neither could fishermen survive on as little as four cents a pound. Forming a unified front, the Astoria cannery owners offered the fishermen a compromise of four and one-half cents a pound.

The June ninth newspaper stated that the Scandinavian Packing Co., up river, had offered its fishermen the price of five cents a pound for fish. Their fishermen said all demands had been met, so it was assumed the Scandinavian Packing Company's men would quickly return to fishing, but "with the understanding that no fish were to be delivered to that cannery except by men owning gear received from that cannery, and further, that fishermen should pay twenty per cent of their earnings toward the

---

[67] "Around Town," *(Daily Morning Astorian*, April 9, 1896).

maintenance of the Union."[68] The Fishermen's Union in Astoria stood firm on <u>its</u> demand for five cents a pound. The local cannery owners also stood firm and did not raise their offer of four and one-half cents.

By this time, the city's businesses, as well as the fishermen themselves, were feeling the effects of the strike. In a Letter to the Public published June 13, members of the Astoria Chamber of Commerce urged the Union to accept the proposal by the cannery owners of four and one-half cents straight. One gentleman was overheard to remark: "Now is the time for the business men to show their interest and take some steps towards bringing about an understanding in this matter. I believe it can be done and that all will be satisfied."[69] But did the public as a whole agree that all would be satisfied?

Not all fishermen were members of the official Fishermen's Union; furthermore, it was generally assumed non-union members were the ones who took a more confrontational attitude in trying to get more "by hook or by crook." In this group, violence was not uncommon. According to the *Daily Morning Astorian* of June 9, several bruised and beaten bodies already had been found floating in mid-channel. The general public became more concerned that the violence might escalate.

On Wednesday, June 17, the *Daily Morning Astorian* reported that Oregon National Guard troops had been requested. Ninety percent of the enrollment had responded to the call-up to serve as soldiers without prejudice to either side of the dispute and to maintain law and order. Under the command of Colonel O. Summers and Lt. Col. E. Evarts, seven companies of the First Regiment arrived by the steamer *Harvest Queen*. Docking at the large Oregon Railroad & Navigation Dock, the men of Battery A unloaded two 12-pound guns and two Gatling guns. The troops set up camp on the grounds of both the Court House and the Customs House squares in downtown Astoria. The establishment of the encampment (the original name Camp Page was later changed to Camp Lord) proceeded in an orderly manner and picket lines were placed. With a feeling of some relief, most Astorians seemed to take the "occupation" in stride. They welcomed the militia and enjoyed watching the military activity. However, not all citizens were in favor of the ONG taking charge because they saw no reason for their presence – no armed rioting had actually occurred. A petition was circulated requesting Governor Lord to remove the troops. That idea did not go very far because too many others feared that without the presence of the militia further lawlessness <u>would</u> occur. The Fishermen's Union had to control its members, as well as to urge non-union men to avoid engaging in any violent actions. At least one boat manned by a company of militiamen and a Gatling gun began patrolling the river, especially at night. Regimental marching and counter-marching filled the streets downtown. Artillery drills were held several times a day.

A relatively congenial meeting was held on the afternoon of June 18, attended by the ONG commanders, including General Beebe, who had arrived in Astoria on the *T.J. Potter* the day prior; the mayor and city officials; and the executive board members of the Fishermen's Union. Later that day, following their mass meeting, the union again unanimously voted to hold out for "Five cents or no fish." The nineteenth of June newspaper reports advised that military guards had been posted at several canneries by order of General Beebe.

---

[68] "Scandinavian Men to Go Out," (*Daily Morning Astorian*, June 19, 1896).

[69] "The Situation as to Fishing," *(Daily Morning Astorian*, June 13, 1896).

June 1896. The Oregon National Guard was posted at the Columbia River Packing Company.

Newspaper "comments" on June eighteenth noted the following items:
"The sunset gun jars sensitive nerves. Take Fulton's Nervine."
"Columbia River salmon was on the menu for supper" (for the troops).
"Hon. John Kopp and a member of the militia had a lively discussion over the definition of the word 'taps'."

Despite all the turmoil, some fishermen had already brought in enough to fill the first car with cases of packed salmon. On June 18, the shipment left Astoria for the east coast. Other carloads were expected to follow in short order. "Had not ample protection been furnished, it is more than probable that the fish would not have been landed at the canneries in the city."[70]

On June nineteenth, the newspaper also printed a Letter to the Public from Mr. Marshall J. Kinney denying the rumor his cannery had offered five cents a pound. His brother and partner, Mr. William S. Kinney, further stated that no cannery owner could or would pay five cents straight. He believed the majority of the fishermen understood the situation and would go out fishing at the price of four and one-half cents.

A consensus was building that the question of price per pound was almost settled. Many people were optimistic that enough fish would be packed during the season to "put enough money in circulation to meet the requirements of trade."[71] To the great relief of all the city's merchants, sales began to increase dramatically. "Foard & Stokes store was besieged with orders for fish boat outfits."[72] In Washington State, the strike was called off at Chinook Beach and men there went out for the evening drift fishing; some from Astoria went out as well. Those who did go out salmon fishing brought in heavy loads,

[70] "All is Quiet at Camp Lord," (*Daily Morning Astorian*, June 19, 1896).
[71] Ibid.
[72] "Around Town," (*Daily Morning Astorian*, June 21, 1896).

which the canneries were hard pressed to process in a timely manner. Hanthorn's Cannery hired additional crew to make tin cans, process and pack the fish. Astoria Packing Company and Elmore's Cannery tried hard to keep up with the raw materials delivered to them. The steamer *Telegraph* brought the Astoria canneries twelve and one-half tons from the up-river fishing grounds during one twenty-four hour period. One fisherman received $68 dollars in gold for his first day's work.

> "Take your wife and children in one of the new and elegant open cars of the Astoria Street Railway and go to the Scandinavian Cannery to see what 100 tons of salmon looks like; you may never see such a sight again."[73]

Weather in Astoria for June 20, 1896: Temperature: high of 70 degrees; low of 48 degrees.

At Fisher's Hall at 8 o'clock on the evening of June 20, yet another mass meeting of the union members was held. It was a long meeting with many presenting arguments, pro and con, on whether to accept the compromise of four and one-half cents straight. The "five-cents" supporters argued vigorously to uphold the original position of the union. A vote was finally called for. By a majority of fifty-eight out of four hundred thirty votes cast (244 for – 186 opposed), the members accepted the compromise. The next morning, a Sunday, Astorians were greeted by their newspaper's headline: "Great Strike Declared Off." Relief was felt even by most of those opposed to settlement.

At 12 o'clock midnight, Sunday June 21, 1896, "there will be a complete resumption of the great salmon packing industry of the Columbia river…the longest one ever known in the history of business on the river."[74] Good sense had prevailed.

Some of the militia returned to their home base that Sunday evening. A few were ordered to remain in Astoria to protect the non-union and union men opposed to the settlement. General Beebe expressed pride in the conduct of the ONG men under his command and their generally cordial relations with the fishermen. Astorians expressed their thanks all around – for the time being.

On Tuesday, July 7, 1896, an article appeared in the *Daily Morning Astorian* titled "Message of Judge Gray." It contained the text of Judge J. H. D. Gray's July sixth fiscal year report to the County Court. Most importantly, in the report he reviewed some of the events leading up to the strike and to his request for intervention by the Oregon militia. Not only had several murders taken place, but also a group of "disreputable" fishermen (believed to be non-union members) threatened "certain individuals," presumably the cannery owners. They demanded their fishing nets. The men had borrowed monies from some of the cannery owners to purchase twine to make fishnets so they could fish. According to the fishermen, those cannery owners were holding their completed nets as security against the twine-monies loaned to the fishermen. If not given back to them freely, the fishermen vowed to take the nets by force. Further, if the price they demanded for fish was not met, the fishermen threatened to retaliate by setting fire to the properties of the cannery owners. The latter – who were all taxpayers - promptly demanded that County Court Judge Gray protect their properties. Judge Gray passed the responsibility over to Astoria City Mayor Frank J. Taylor. In turn, Mayor Taylor urged Judge Gray to

---

[73] "Around Town." (June 21, 1896).
[74] "Great Strike Declared Off," (*Daily Morning Astorian*, June 21, 1896).

telegraph Oregon's Governor Lord to request that 200 troops of the Oregon National Guard be sent to prevent the fishermen from carrying out their threats. City officials believed the presence of militia would avert serious trouble, prevent destruction of property, protect the rights of those who wanted to fish in the Columbia River and allow the fishermen to land their fish at the city's cannery docks without interference.

The salmon pack of 1896 was expected to reach 350,000 cases. The cost to the county for the ONG militiamen was estimated to be $500 for Astoria alone. Many considered that a fine bargain.

Who profited most in this fish strike of 1896? Obviously the cannery owners and packers did because they presented a united front in the negotiations. The city's businessmen were reasonably satisfied. The citizens were relieved that life went back to "normal." But, what of the fishermen, the providers of the raw materials? They did return to their livelihood of fishing in the Columbia – for a while at least. More importantly, however, they had learned the lesson of power - uniting as a single voice, standing together as a single body. They would later implement that lesson to make changes in the fishing industry.

While Astoria fishermen struck against the canneries from March to nearly the end of June 1896, what else was going on in the city, the area and in the country?

J.S. Dellinger's 1896 Astoria City Directory listed 15 churches and 41 saloons. A very successful grand opening of the *Louvre* was held on June 20th (it was actually completed and opened on the 24th of April). Crowds of people attended. "Cords of bread, great platters of roasted turkeys, baked hams and roast beef were served to the visitors. The lunches, of course, were not all taken dry. An augmented orchestra performed many pieces of well-known music during the evening."[75]

A Spanish Gypsy Opera was presented on April 10 and 11 (Friday and Saturday) at Fisher's Opera House. Admission was fifty cents. On May 15 and 22, two performances of *At the Picket Line* were given at Fisher's.

People were taking an interest in moving to Warrenton and Flavel - costs were lower there - as soon as the train trestle was completed from Astoria across Youngs Bay. Workmen were busy constructing the impressive Flavel Hotel and the ship/train terminal at Tansy Point, Flavel.

"Cascara sagrada" – the sacred bark, commonly known as chittem bark – was selling for $30 a ton in Portland.

It was generally conceded Governor William McKinley of Ohio would take the presidential nomination of the Republican Party at the GOP convention being held in St. Louis. Garret A. Hobart of New Jersey would be his running mate. They would win in the election against Democrat William Jennings Bryan. Later, President McKinley would direct the U.S. involvement in the 1898 Spanish-American War.

Across the country suffragettes were marching for women's right to vote.[76]

The above article, in an earlier form, was printed with the author's permission in the CCHS *Cumtux,* Vol. 26, No. 3 - Summer 2006.

---

[75] "Around Town," (*Daily Morning Astorian*, June 21, 1896).
[76] The Nineteenth Amendment to the U.S. Constitution gave women the right to vote. It was ratified in August 1920. In 1895, Louise and her friends had marched down Astoria's streets in support of women's right to vote.

No envelope, no date.

Sunny Slope

Dear Dick

I am awfully tired and sleepy to night so excuse a dull letter but I know tomorrow and the next and next day and in fact all next week I will be to busy to write even one line. I can't begin to tell you what a gay time we are having. Tuesday we go back to Los Angeles and as Herman said he had fourty nine tickets for thing coming off during Fiesta[77] *you can imagine how much flying around we are going to do, We are going to the Queens ball Friday night. My new ball dress is "up to the limit" and Saturday night – All Fools Night they call it – we are going to mask and go in for a good time. How I wish you could be with us. Went in town to a party yesterday and didn't do a thing but get first prize and Hat got second – how is that for Astoria. I was awfully glad to get your last letter for I had made a bet that a.m. with my friend that I would find a letter for me at the P.O. and that was the only one that came. We were visiting in Alhambra and she didn't want me to drive way over to San Gabriel but I was so glad I went not because she payed the bet but because I got such a nice letter. Don't be too serious though Dick for there seems to be a* <u>long</u> <u>wait</u> *ahead of us and there is no telling what may happen – you may meet some one just ever so much nicer than Louise. I hope not though for she isn't such a bad sort of a girl after all and if you can make her love you it will be more than any one else has been able to do. Have you seen Nell and does she seem much changed. Aren't you getting tired of being in theatricals? And what are you doing now. Send your next letter to 614 South Main, Los Angeles and send it soon.*

I must say good night for it is dreadfull late. My pardner and I won the rubber at whist tonight. Yours with love - Louise

Sunday 26th   [April 26, 1896]

Dear Louise,

I have just got home from a trip to Ilwaco, and Schoalwater Bay and I had a lovely time I don't think. <u>It</u> <u>rained</u>. *I got your letter the morning I left so that explains why I've not written before. We were going to do some work on the [tennis] court this morning but the rain saved us. We've had a man working on it for a couple of days and it is going to be better this year than last. The new fence adds considerable to it. Tomorrow night there is a meeting for the election [of] officers. Nancy is to be elected President, Nettie - Treas and Sadie C- [Crang] Secy I believe. Mrs Tuttle is sure to get elected as a member and she will be given the position as hostess so I think we will have a real nice club this year. Are you going to bring Lily home with you to get*

---

[77]   La Fiesta was a popular annual event in Los Angeles.

some salt sea breeze? I think she would enjoy another regatta and this years is going to be out of sight. Genie has gone to Texas and Mr Schilling has left sorrow amongst the Copelands and we all miss Genie. The strike is still on and things are awfully dull. Prof Beggs had another show and didn't make expenses. I [will] send you a programme. I guess you must be having a nice time. How many of the tickets left? I suspose you'll start home when they are gone and I hope the show is about over. Nellie looks fine – don't seem to be mush taller but looks straight and walks better. Well there is little more to tell and I don't suspose it will be long till you are home and hear all the news for yourself. And I shall not have the pleasure of writing again so I'll close hoping you will answer this before you start back to the city by the sea.

Yours as ever

Dick

I might add that I think trips some times change people, but I can't see if there is any help for it, and I suspose the injured party must get over it the best way <u>he</u> can.

Alhambra   May the 9th 96   [Saturday]

Dear Dick

I am afraid you will have to write to me once more. The fourty nine tickets are all used up but we keep planning trips all the time or at least for two weeks a head and in that time you could write several letters to me (if you wanted to).

We start today on our mountain trip, the one planned for last week but at the very last moment the chaperone got sick and some of the party could not go so we had to give it up. Now it is dreadfully dark and stormy looking towards the mts. And we fancy it is either snowing or raining up there but we are going – our saddle bag is packed and we have sworn to go rain or shine. Wish you were here to go along with us – don't know how I will stand riding one of those Burrows twelve miles. Steve says we will have an "arnica tournament"[78] when we get up there. We are going to stay all night at a camp up there and if we can, come back tomorrow afternoon.

I started a letter to you quite a while ago but could not get a chance to finish it so as I am ready and we have some spare time before starting on our trip I thought I would begin over again. Harriet and I called on the Copeland girls aunt last week and it seems as if I had seen one of them – the girls look so ...

No further page(s).

---

[78] "Arnica, n. *Arnica montana*. The yellow flowered plants were numerous in the mountains of the West. The rhizomes and roots were used for the stimulant and local irritants effects, esp. in the tincture, as embrocations for bruises, sprails, swellings, etc.; hence, popularly, a preparation of these." (Webster's New International Dictionary - 1918). The tincture of arnica was applied externally as a homeopathic ointment for pain – in this instance, to ease the soreness caused by riding burros up Mt. Wilson.

The twelve-mile trip was to the top of Mt. Wilson. A large group of young people and a few "Burrows" appear in the photographs from Louise's album. Louise and Marge rode one burro.

On the trail up Mt. Wilson, north of Alhambra, in the San Gabriel range.

Atop Mt. Wilson. From right to left: Louise (second burro), Charlie Deering, Harriet and Lilly.

Louise is seated atop Mt. Wilson. Charlie Deering is directly
behind Herman Kerckhoff, who holds his box camera.

Mailed: May 16 - PM 1896 Astoria, Oregon
Post Office stamped "Missent Alameda, Cal," MAY 19 -11AM- 1896. Forwarded care of the Halsteds.

Astoria May 16th 96

Dear Louise:

I received your very nice letter a day or two ago and would have answered it sooner, but have been so busy getting ready for our great show - At The Picket Line - which came off last night. I['ll] send you a programme, and would send some news paper comment if I had any here but I will later. To say it was a success I will tell you that there was only three empty seats in the building, goes well I think. I hope your trip to the mountains was a pleasant one and would have been more than pleased to have been there. Thanks for the picture and Louise with out any Josh you & Hat are the swellest looking in the group.[79] Of course I would like one of the new photos. But that should go with out the asking I think. So you are going to be published are you. Hurrah for our side. Give Miss Margie my love and tell her to be sure and arrive at Astoria as I would like to see any one with whom Dick is a favorite name. Oh I guess the new officers will do, we haven't got such a nice Lease - but will have to put up with I guess.

At present I am Manager of Fishers Opera House, Astoria, Oregon. The town is at present too small to hold me. The bondsmen took it away from Beggs - and Kendall, Smith, Trullinger, Sherman and myself are running it to try and get some rent Beggs never paid. I am Manager and you will always be entitled to a box seat - this will include my friend Miss M-. This should be some encouragement for her to come to Astoria. But you must hurry home as we are going to give it up after three months. Well I don't know any news to speak of. Last night all the young people were out, but didn't see who was with who. The Fish question has not been settles yet so you won't be able to wrap cans this year and I won't be able to help.
Everyone on town seems well and happy as the times will allow. No tennis as yet.

Well I must close as I am as busy as can be. nit, but for the want of news.

Dick

Upon the back of the envelope of Dick's last letter, Louise penciled a reminder list to herself for going home:
Ribbon linen heavy linen roses laundry lace hdkf footing pictures room

Louise and Harriet arrived back home in Astoria by the end of May, before the Fishing Strike of 1896 had been settled. They, Dick and their friends would continue on their merry ways, perhaps at a different pace, with comings and goings, parties and gatherings for all, including their parents. In June, Mrs. J.D. Sutherland traveled down from Portland to visit Eben and Mary Elizabeth. It is likely that Lila came with her mother for the summer fun on the coast.

---

[79] Dick refers to Louise's photograph, from Sunny Slope Ranch, of some 30 persons, mainly women.

Louise in Los Angeles – 1896

Astoria 1898-1890. Notice The Casino Theater (white building upper left) and The Louvre Saloon and Concert Hall, just behind it. The tennis court is in the mid foreground. The Ross Opera House that burned down in October 1892 had stood on the dark area, lower left foreground.

Dick's Amateur Theatrical Career in the Late 1890s
Break a Leg!

By the 1880s, Astoria had become a theatrical "Hot Spot," along with San Francisco and Butte, Montana. A large number of touring companies, presenting a wide variety of entertainment, traveled about the west. Arriving in Astoria were such touring troupes as the Bernard Grand English Opera Company; Billy Emerson's Famous Minstrels; the Wilton Troupe, who played not only Astoria, but also Oysterville and Knappton; the

Marshfield Swedish Singing Society; and the unique Deakins Lilliputian Opera Company of Dwarfs and Giants who put on a production of *Jack the Giant Killer*.[80]

Fisher's Opera House, one of a number of buildings owned by the Fisher brothers, Augustus and Ferdinand, was a prominent theatrical house in the 1890s period. It was located at the northeast corner of what are now Exchange and Twelfth Street, across the street from the old YMCA. Their motto was "The diversion of the eye and ear is the only true medicine, after all." Fisher's Opera House had a number of directors and managers over the years, including Professor J.N. Beggs, and even Richard Ervin Carruthers in 1896. Fisher's Opera House was listed in Dellinger's Directory of 1901-1902 as then being under the direction of Mr. Lemon E. Selig, who operated it as an active theater until at least 1907. By 1917, Fisher's became known as The Astoria Theatre under the direction of F.M. Hanlin. It was at this theatre that Clark Gable, a logger working in the local woods, made his acting debut during the summer of 1922. The theatre burned down in December of that same year.

Of course Fisher's was neither the first nor the only Opera House in early Astoria. Spiritual Hall was Astoria's first one, built in 1873 on the waterfront at the corner of Lafayette and Chenamus (now Seventh and Bond). As the name "spiritual" indicates, there was considerable local interest in the occult – séances and lectures on psychic phenomena were reportedly held in the hall. During May 1873, the renowned divas, Agnes Stevenson and Anna Bishop, gave concerts of operatic arias in the Hall. On May 12, 1877, the name was changed to Liberty Hall, thanks to a long lease signed by the popular John Jack Dramatic Company. "Captain" Jack built a larger stage and added a gallery – but left the hard benches. On July 11, 1894, Liberty Hall became known as Stuttz' Parlor Theatre, under the new management of John Revelstoke Rathom.[81] Stuttz's boasted an even wider stage, the third largest in the state at that time. A well-known scene artist, Earnest Miller, painted the new backdrop and other scenery. From about 1896 to 1899, the aging Liberty Hall was used as the venue for a Chinese theatre by adding across the front of the theatre an Oriental-looking balcony decorated with Chinese characters in gold paint.[82]

August Erickson was the proprietor of the well-known Louvre at Seventh and Astor; the four story building featured a concert hall, as well as an elegant long-bar. The Casino Theatre at Seventh and Bond was listed in Dellinger's 1896 City Directory under the proprietorship of D.E. Johnson; it was gone by 1901. However, Dellinger's city directory of 1901 lists a Star Theatre-Saloon Club Rooms nearby at 507 Bond.

At the beginning of the 1880s, John Ross, a city clerk, built the Ross Opera House, a very popular theater, located on the corner of present-day Sixth and Commercial. It boasted a larger, deeper stage with movable platforms, so the theater was quite versatile for not only dramas, but also greased pig contests and boxing matches. Several accounts place sporting events being held at the Ross, in particular the exhibition match in August 1888 between John L. Sullivan and a local Greek fisherman, "Brother" Sylvester, thought tough enough by the many who bet on him to give the great Sullivan a good match. It

---

[80] Ernst, pp. 45-49. The Deakins' Company chartered the steamer *Kalama* for their water transportation. In 1884, the *Kalama* had been delivered to Astoria aboard the clipper ship *Tillie E. Starbuck*.

[81] John Rathom, an actor and a newspaper correspondent in 1896, was later a foreign correspondent for the *San Francisco Chronicle*.

[82] Ernst, 101. Ernst quotes Astorian Polly Bell McKean.

ended in three rounds – with Sullivan still standing. Unfortunately, the Ross burned down to the ground in October 1892.

It is reported the Ross Opera House could hold more than 2,000 people and had fine acoustics. One of the very few interior photographs available of any early Astoria theater is one purportedly of the Ross.[83] The seats appear to be similar to the old-fashioned "ice cream" chairs of the 1930s, with hard wooden seats and upright cane backrests – surely not comfortable for long periods of sitting. The wooden floors apparently were laid flat; there was no "stadium seating" as in modern theaters. Although there was a balcony – a U-shaped gallery, it still would not have been easy to see the "action" on the raised stage. In the photograph of the Ross, the stage does not appear to be canted, which would cause the major action to take place on the apron of the stage, close to the footlights. The Ross had gas-fired footlights, but in other theaters, some had electrified footlights, some merely candles in metal holders. The usual heavy velvet curtains of a rich color and pleasing design gave a sense of elegant beauty to the theater prior to the start of the performance. Potted palms apparently were the favored greenery. Admission prices ranged from 25 to 75 cents. For some early theatrical performances - in lieu of cash money - a large sized fish was thrown into a wooden box at the entry to the theater.

The amateur productions apparently were about the same as ones nowadays. An orchestra played musical medleys as the patrons filed in, as well as *entr'acte* selections. It is likely the actors often supplied their own costumes and did their own make-up. While professional troupes moved on to another town after only one or two performances, most of the amateur performances seemed to have been "one night stands." It is sad that the amateur crews and actors did all the preparation work for the "glory and thrill" of just a one night's appearance! After a performance, the cast and audience might well have retired to the Oriental Café at Tenth and Bond for chop suey and noodles,[84] to the Winship Chowder Club in the cosmopolitan Occident Hotel or to Daniel Crank's New England Chop House located at the rear of the Globe Saloon at Main and Concomly (later Ninth and Astor).

During these years there were a confusing number of newspapers printed in Astoria and each always displayed a number of headings and sub-headings - in various type styles and sizes - to all articles and reviews. Newspaper clippings, that often did not identify which newspaper or the full date, were pasted into Dick's scrapbook-photograph album. These clippings provide considerable information about the performances, particularly those in which he had a role. Astoria's amateur theater was thriving during the 1890s and Dick Carruthers was one of the enthusiastic actors. He studied with Professor Beggs, who at the time was the manager of Fisher's Opera House. Prof. Beggs was also listed in the Astoria directory of 1896 as a dancing master.

---

[83] See Clatsop County Historical Society photograph # 155-171.
[84] From hand-written notes by Polly McKean Bell, a lifelong friend of Louise and Dick. She was a published author and writer of numerous local newspaper articles, as well as a member of the group of actors. Her notes recalled the after-performance gatherings. She also noted Eben, Lizzie and Will Tallant - and a Jack Carruthers, "one of the so-called Englishmen"- attended numerous performances in Astoria. Polly's grandson, Thomas McKean Bell, briefly loaned her notes and several scrapbooks of theatrical materials and photos saved by Polly's brother and fellow actor, Samuel Terry McKean, to the Clatsop County Historical Society, Astoria, Oregon.

A Gathering of Amateur Performers

Back row: Sue Elmore, Nora Nickerson, William C. Laws, Floretta Elmore, Tom Bryce, Nelly Nickerson.
Mid row: Lulu Rice, Lemuel Howes, (Harriet Tallant?), Jim Bennett.
Seated: Dick Carruthers, Lottie Bennett with "a baby," Charlie Higgins, Nancy (Tuttle?) and her bird,
Kate Grant, Jim (Taylor?) and a little dog.

From 1894 to 1901, Dick, Louise, Harriet and members of their group of friends played in a number of amateur productions put on by various organizations, particularly the Astoria Football Club and the Elks. Many of these programs were benefit performances for such as the Astoria Library, and for the Grace Episcopal Church when, on May 20, 1901, a Character Concert was performed in which Louise Tallant played a role. Earlier, on October 14, 1893, the Rescue Club had sponsored entertainment; it consisted of music, songs, recitations and comedy. Harriet Hunter Carruthers, Dick's mother, arranged fifteen young women in a breath-taking Living Tableau entitled *The Vestal Virgins* for the Rescue Club production. The Firemen's Benefit Concert, sponsored by the Apollo Club, was held at the Methodist Church on July 1, 1895. On Friday, June 19, 1896, Miss Eugenia Kelly gave another Fireman's Concert; her concert offered orchestral music, guitar and mandolin selections, dances, and recitations - one by Terry McKean - and a solo by Pearl Holden.

Minstrel shows were very popular and came to town often. The Society for the Prevention of Cruelty to Children sanctioned the presentation of the "Grand Negro Minstrel Entertainment" given by the members of the Astoria Football Club at Stuttz' Parlor Theatre on Friday, December 14, 1894. The Soloists were: Messers. E. Matthews, F. Spittle, H.T. Findlay, R.E. Carruthers, D. Stuart, T.S. Bryce, J.R.A. Bennett, W.H.

Bain and J.C. Swope. Dick's part in this performance was as "R. Elephant Carruthers" in a "Daredevil Bicycle Act." At the bottom of the playbill was the notice: "No Babies in Arms Admitted Without Parent or Guardian. Curtain Rises at 8 o'clock sharp. Carriages or Dump Wagons can be ordered for 10:45 p.m." In March 1896, a quarter page newspaper ad heralded the following minstrel show that "had everything."

"Monday and Tuesday, Mar. 30-31.
Elk's Minstrels. Biggest and Best Minstrel Show Ever Seen Here.
Grand Parade Monday at Noon. Under the direction of Miller & Draper"

"Dick" Carruthers was listed as one of the "End Men"[85] in this production along with "Bill" Scholfeld; "Ed" Judd; Chester Fox; Harry Hoefler; Nello Johnson; Carl Franseen; Fred Johnson; Clint Draper; and Harry Miller. Soloists were: "Bill" Scimpff, Jas. J. Johnson, John C. McCue, Chas. H. Abercrombie, Gus Ziegler, and Miss Kathryn Shiveley.

The amateur minstrel shows were based on the popular professional minstrel troupes that came to Astoria, such as the William Laws' Minstrels who offered a show on August 18, 1896. Another professional minstrel troupe performed on January 8, 1897, under the direction of Nixon & Zimmerman.

Benefit concerts and plays were also very popular forms of entertainment. From the *Astoria Evening Budget*, November 2, 1895, [86] is the following excerpt of the review of the previous evening's play - *The Private Secretary* - presented at Fisher's Opera House. The orchestra was under the direction of Prof. Emil Thielhorn; Jesse Hansen was the stage manager; and J. C. Swope designed the stage settings.

"It is only just to Mr. T. McKean to say that to him belongs the palm of the evening for he steps far beyond amateurism, and displays remarkable talent. Miss Polly McKean is perfectly at home on the stage and was a charming Miss Edith; Mrs. W. Warren was very sweet as "Eva" and Mrs. Patterson was excellent as "Miss Ashford;" Mr. Carruthers made a very nice looking "Douglas Cattermole;" Tom Bryce took the role of "Harry Marshland."

In 1896, Fisher's presented a Spanish Gypsy Opera on two consecutive nights, the 10th and 11th of April – during the fishermen's strike. Later in that year, a November 2, 1896, clipping (probably from the *Daily Morning Astorian*) reviewed a "Karacter Concert" performed the previous night:

SWEET SINGERS MAKE A BIG HIT.
Society Turned Out Last Night at Character Concert.
Every Number was Splendid.
The Best Amateur Performance Ever Given in this City
Stage Profusely Decorated.

"It is very seldom that such an audience as that which crowded Fisher's last night is seen in this city; and rarely has there been such a display of fashion. The neat little theatre was comfortably filled, about five hundred people were present. All were anxious to see the "character" concert, as a treat was anticipated. In brief, local amateurs never did so well.

---

[85] A name always given to one of the so-called End Men was "Mr. Tambo."
[86] This review was reprinted in the *Evening Astorian's* November 2, 1930, column, "Astoria 35 Years Ago."

The stage was beautifully decorated with chryanthemums [sic], presenting a very pretty appearance.

The first number was the anvil chorus in which twenty voices took part. Following was a vocal duet, "I Don't Want to Play in Your Yard," by Messrs Richard Carruthers and James Taylor. The singers were attired in feminine costumes and made a decided hit. Responding to an encore they gave a burlesque of the Maginel-Mullin Concert Company, apologizing for the absence of their mother and Count Kosminsky..."

A small undated clipping, seemingly about the same production, reported:

In the skit "Barbara and Hannah," Messers. R. E. Carruthers and James Taylor simply brought down the house. Their sketch was replete with droll incidents and the apology of Mr. Carruthers displayed a natural talent that is likely to lead him to the professional stage some day if it is not suppressed."

In 1931, a newspaper column, titled "Astoria 35 Years Ago," reprinted another review of the above Character Concert that had first appeared in the *Astoria Evening Budget*, on November 2, 1896:

"It was quite a relief to the music lovers of the city to have something new in the concert line offered them in the Character Concert last evening. . . . A surprise greeted the audience in the second number, for instead of two little girls to sing "I Don't Want to Play in Your Yard," out came Messers. Richard Carruthers and James Taylor dressed as girls were supposed to be. Terry McKean is always worth hearing and he was particularly amusing last night His recitation was followed by a duet between Mrs. B. Van Dusen, who was never heard to such advantage, and Rev. W. B. Short. It was the artistic gem of the evening. . . . The duet on two pianos, "The Dance of the Dead," by Miss Edith Conn and Mrs. Olsen was very effective.

When the curtain rose on part two, Mrs. F. J. Taylor was discovered seated by a cradle, and very sweet was the lullaby she sang. The "Country Fair" was a delightful little scene by Misses [Alice] Wood and [Pearl] Holden and Messrs. Burnett and Griffin. Perhaps the most humorous number of the evening...The concert closed with a very pretty character scene, 'Maid in the Moon.' On the rim of a silver crescent sat a beautiful maid with streaming hair, her graceful form in flowing drapery reaching the ground. This was Miss Edith Conn. F. Barker sang a serenade to her."

A playbill announced "A Grand Entertainment – for the Benefit of the Astoria Public Library." Held at Fisher's Opera House (Lemon E. Selig, Lessee and Manager) on Tuesday evening, January 14, 1897, the actors presented "The Rattling Farce - *Box and Cox*" with Henry Weeks as "Box," Terry McKean as "Cox" and Mrs. H. J. Weeks as "Mrs. Bouncer." Also on the program was a "Charming Operetta – *A Trip To Europe*" in which Dick played the "1st Male Tourist." Terry McKean and his sister Polly had leading roles. Mrs. H. T. Crosby directed the Schubert Club choruses. Admission was 50 cents. Reserved seats were available without (additional) charge at Strauss' New York Novelty Store on Monday or Tuesday.

On Friday evening, April 23, 1897, Fisher's playbill announced yet another benefit for the Astoria Public Library Association of a farce titled *A Perplexing Situation*. Dick played the lead as "Mr. Middleton – inclined to be miserly," and Miss Tallant (probably Harriet) played "Lucy Fair – adopted niece." Nan Reed, Pearl Holden, Polly McKean, Dr. Burnett and Dr. Finch took other parts. On the same playbill, Dick was listed as "Chas. Livingston – poor but ambitious" for the second farce, *That Rascal Pat*, along with Terry

McKean, Polly McKean and Nan Reed. Both Dick and Hattie Tallant appeared later on that same evening in what were called "Living Pictures" - Harriet was in "Vision of Joan of Arc" and Dick in "Two Strings to Her Bow" with Charles Burnett and Miss Jessie Jewett.

Next to the April 23 announcement in the *Astoria Evening Budget* was one for Monday and Tuesday, April 26 and 27, featuring a "Special Engagement of the Famous Laugh Makers: Lottie Williams, Ed J. Heron and Dailey's Comedians." The evening performance also included two "brilliant" new plays: *A Nutmeg Match* and Hoyt's *A Bunch of Keys*, topped off with songs and specialties. Reserved seats cost 75 cents, gallery 25 cents. One could purchase tickets in advance at Griffen and Reed's bookstore.

In his Easter Sunday letter of April 5, 1896, Dick wrote the following to Louise: about a major theatrical production in which he had landed a good part.

> *The A.F.C. are preparing for more shows, this time a drama and you must not cry because some parts do look sad. I am cast as the "villain," not a very bad one though, but I manage to get two or three people killed at the rate of $100 per head. Mrs. Patterson & Miss Jessie Jewett are the only ladies and we are trying to develop A'Dalgity into a feamale impersonator with little success so far.*

Louise responded in an undated letter:

> *Aren't you getting tired of being in theatricals? And what are you doing now.*

How could Dick possibly be tiring of acting when the *Daily Morning Astorian* of May 5, 1896, gave such a rousing front-page preview of his next play, *At the Picket Line*!

A Grand Play   To Be Given by the Astoria Football Club Next Week

The grand military melodrama "At the Picket Line" which has been under preparation by the members of the Astoria Football Club, will be played at Fisher's Opera House on Friday, the 15th inst. The performance will be worth going a long way to see and will surpass anything in the amateur dramatic line ever witnessed in this city. The play has not a dull line in it, and every act is full of stirring situations and beautiful scenic pictures. A well-known local electrician is in charge of the lime light effects, and every detail of the performance is being carefully studied. Everything, down to the most minute matters of uniform and camp connection with the latter is being rendered the club by the officers and men of Fort Canby. Most of the scenes are laid in the vicinity of some of the most stirring combats of the civil war, and the whole performance bristles with patriotism and military ardor. It is bound to draw a crowded house. Tickets are now on sale and can be obtained from Secretary Gunn, or any member of the club. The box plan will be opened at the New York Novelty Store next Monday morning.

The Astoria Football Club players presented *At the Picket Line* on Friday, May 15, 1896, at Fisher's Opera House, during the time the city was struggling to reach a satisfactory settlement to the "Great Fish Strike." A second night's performance was given on Friday, May 22 with the same cast. The A.F.C. donated some of the box office receipts from this play to defray expenses on a project sponsored by the Grand Army of the Republic (G.A.R.) to cheer Civil War veterans on Decoration Day.

An unidentified newspaper clipping pasted in Dick's scrapbook-photo album gave a review of the play. The unnamed reviewer wrote:

THE PICKET LINE IS ESTABLISHED
Brilliant Presentation of the Popular War Drama by the Astoria Football Club.
Theater Literally Packed.
The Affair was the Most Successful Amateur Production Ever Witnessed in This City,
and Brought Out Society in Full Force.

To say that last night's production of "At the Picket Line" by the members of the Astoria Football Club was an unqualified success is but to give the proper credit to those persons who took part. Never before in the history of the city were so many people gathered together at an entertainment of this kind and never before was a play so faultlessly produced by amateurs. In brief, the entertainment was characteristic of the Football Club, inasmuch as it gave unbounded satisfaction.

Shortly after 7 crowds began flocking to Fisher's, and by 8:15, at which hour the curtain rose, the theatre was crowded. The newly organized orchestra, under the leadership of Prof. Busey, furnished the music for the occasion, which was one of the most pleasing features of the evening. The cast of characters and the fact that the play was to be given under the auspices of the Astoria Football Club, brought out an immense throng, and society was there in force. The only unpleasant feature of the whole performance was the disposition of a portion of the audience to laugh at pathetic scenes. Local talent has never appeared but what this insulting action has been indulged in, much to the disgrace – although they probably do not know it – of those who carry on so. A visitor in the city, after the performance last night, said "they acted like cattle.' The gentleman was right.

There were but two ladies in the cast, Mrs. J. H. Patterson and Miss Jessie Jewett. Both won the hearts of the audience when they appeared upon the stage. Their costumes were elegant and their acting was absolutely faultless. Mrs. Patterson has had considerable experience on the stage, having taken part in several amateur performances, and the lady played her part to perfection last evening. Her artistic ability is not without other support. For with it are beautiful features and perfect form. Mrs. Patterson took the part of "Leonora," a Union spy, who, at the risk of her own noble life, enters the rebel ranks in defense of – Her Country. The lady was an ideal heroine, and her acting elicited the warmest applause from the audience.

Miss Jewett played a very pretty part - "Silvy Holmes" - daughter, sister, sweet-heart. No more affectionate daughter, more loving sister, or truest sweetheart ever lived. Miss Jessie first appeared in the modest attire of a poor farmer's daughter, a becoming sun bonnet making her very cute. In the last act the young lady appeared in her wedding dress, and then, instead of the bewitching little farmer's girl, she was the ideal of a beautiful woman. Miss Jessie carried out her part with a natural grace which completely captivated the audience. A vocal solo rendered by her in the third act brought down the house, and the young lady was compelled to respond to the hearty encore. Both ladies were recipients of beautiful bouquets.

As for the gentlemen, they covered themselves with glory. Mr. Terry McKean, who has appeared in public several times, and who is a warm favorite with the theatre-goers of Astoria, played "Squire Holmes," rheumatic in soul, but Roman in body. His efforts were deserving of the applause he received. Mr. Duncan Stuart, owing to his humorous part, was the pet of the audience. He was slated on the program as "Hiram Lufkin," a raw recruit in love and war; and such indeed was he. His voice was pitched to High C, and as squeaky as a rusty hinge. Such an awkward, unsophisticated, but withal comical gawk was never seen, and he kept the audience in a continual state of laughter. Mr. Stuart's performance was the best, with exception of two comedians in "A Railroad Ticket," that was never [sic] seen at Fisher's.

Mr. Harry B Vidalin, a professional actor, carried out his difficult part as only a professional can. He was "Caleb Holmes," the wayward son; a man of the world, yet a loving brother; a deserter, and almost a thief, but honest at heart. Cast from his home, hunted by the soldiery, enlisted in both Northern and Confederate armies, narrowly escaping death by poisoning, he finally returned to gladden the last years of his old father and see his sister wedded to the man she loves. Throughout the play Mr. Vadalin exhibited his ability, of which the audience showed its appreciation. His makeup as a soldier was perfect.

Astoria Football Club

Presenting a Grand Military Drama of the Civil War, in Five Acts, Entitled:

"AT THE PICKET LINE."

-- CASTE OF CHARACTERS --

LEONORA, a Union Spy.................................MRS. J. H. PATTERSON.
SILVY HOLMES, Daughter, Sister and Sweetheart......MISS JESSIE JEWETT.
Squire Holmes, Rheumatic in Body, but Roman in Soul............Mr. Terry McKean.
Harvey Crosscomb, a man of Schemes...........................Mr. R. E. Carruthers.
Caleb Holmes, the Wayward Son.................................Mr. H. B. Vidalin.
Hiram Lufkin, a Raw Recruit In Love and War ....Mr. Duncan Stuart.
Albert Cherrington, a Hero of the Rebellion ....Mr. J. R. Rathom.
Sergeant O'Stout, U. S. A....................................Mr. H. J. Weeks.
Sal a Robber of the Dead.....................................Mr. C. R. Higgins.
Jerry, Her Partner in Crime..................................Mr. A. B. Dalgity.
Captain (afterwards Colonel) Harford, U. S. A................Mr. R. T. Burnett.
Corporal Dumpsy, U. S. A.....................................Mr. Jas. Meachan.

SOLDIERS OF THE AWKWARD SQUAD:

Messrs. F. Clinow, George Cherry, Chas. Ring, D. Campbell, W. Aigner, Charles Stone, Victor Giardini, A. McLean, Chester Rose, D. McCroskey.

SYNOPSIS:

ACT I. The Northern home. "The best darter that ever lived." Hiram and Silvy. A Wayward Son. Albert Cherrington. More than a brother. The mortgage. The hawk and the dove. "Too late! He has given his word." Silvy speaks. "But I haven't."

ACT II. SCENE 1. Dissembling. The wedding ring. A deserter. The awkward squad. "The gal I left behind me." French leave. The wrong man. An easy promotion. UNDER ARREST. SCENE 2. At headquarters. "A wise recruit that knows his own name." The missing witness. Crosscomb again. "I never saw that man before in all my life." DOOMED.

ACT III. At the picket line. Camp followers. The fringe of a plot. In rebel uniform. Leonora and Caleb. Outwitted. "Remember that one live woman is more dangerous than a hundred dead men." Surrendered to a girl. SCENE 2. The battle. A skulker. Playing possum A bold charge. "Another victory for the North." SCENE 3. After the battle. Robbing the dead. The vision of Silvy. THE RECOGNITION. "No! He is a Union spy."

ACT IV. The Union camp. Humors of camp life. "A drop o' the crater." A vile plot. The warning. "Here's a small bottle for yourself alone." The tables turned. "My God, the liquor was poisoned!" The traitor's death. "It means that I, who have almost starved for a crust of bread, am now a millionaire."

ACT V. The North again. A ruined home. The returned soldier. Crosscomb once more. Silvy's wedding day. Cherrington back from the dead Dark before the dawn. "Ah, it is HIS ring." Hiram lifts the veil. "Yes, Silvy, he is a-living." Crosscomb crossed. "Then her father's son will pay it." The altar and the halter. UNITED.

The A. F. C. has been established for seven years. It is the Club's boast that during that time it has given more entertainments and social gatherings than any athletic organization in Oregon, Washington or British Columbia, and has contributed nine-tenths of its earnings to worthy charities.

For the next sixty days the initiation fee will be cut in two. Take advantage of this $2.50 rate, and join the Club now.

Mr. John R. Rathom impersonated "Albert Cherrington," a hero of the rebellion. His also was a pretty part. To save the life of his friend, Caleb Holmes (Mr. Vidalin), he enlists in the Union army, leaving the object of his affections at the mercy of the man who would wed her against her will. Mr. Rathom did very well and was one of the strongest characters.

To say that Mr. Richard Carruthers incurred the enmity of every person in the house is but telling the truth, for such animosity was the only consequence of his part. He was "Harry Crosscomb," a man of schemes, and he was indeed a villain. His only object was to alienate the affections of Silvy from her lover and then marry her, thus getting control of a large inheritance. After much scheming, his plans were frustrated and on the very day when all seemed favorable to him, he was exposed.

Mr. Henry J. Weeks, an actor of no mean ability, played the part of "Sergeant O'Stout," the houghty [sic] commander of the awkward squad. As his name would imply, the sergeant was Irish, and caused no end of amusement. His rendition of 'Mush, Mush, Mush' was warmly applauded.

Mr. R. T. Burnett made an excellent "Captain Harford," and displayed marked ability. His acting was that of a hard-headed commander, always calm, but quick. Messers. Charles Higgins and Andrew Dalgity had two gruesome parts. The former impersonated "Sal", a robber of the dead, and the latter "Jerry," his partner in crime. Mr. Higgins made a perfect hag, while Mr. Dalgity, with his blackened features and attire of a desperado, sent a shudder through everyone. Mr. James Meacham played "Corporal Dumpsy," Sergeant O'Stout's right bower, in a most satisfactory manner. The members of the awkward squad, Messers Clinow, Cherry, Ring, Eigner, Stone, Giardina, and Fox, were all very good, and the camp life scenes in which they appeared were some of the best of the evening.

Altogether the production was one of which all who participated may well feel proud. Not a hitch occurred to mar the proceedings, and those who attended will speak only the highest words of praise for the enterprising ladies and gentlemen.

Captain Day, of Fort Canby, assisted in staging the war scenes, and it was due to him that those scenes were so perfectly put on. It is to be hoped the A. F. C. will see fit to again present "At the Picket Line."

The Leading Players in *At the Picket Line*

Left to right:
Terry McKean as "Squire Holmes;" R. E. Carruthers as "Harvey Crosscomb;" J. R. Rathom as "Albert Cherrington;"
Mrs. J. H. Patterson as "Leonora;" Miss Jessie Jewett as "Silvy Holmes;" R. T. Burnett as "Captain Harford;"
H. B. Vidalin as "Caleb Holmes."
Foreground: C. R. Higgins as "Sal;" H. J. Weeks as "Sgt. O'Stout."

84

Dick as "Harvey Crosscomb, a man of schemes."

"Harvey" and "Silvy" (Miss Jessie Jewett)

Possibly Act V. Dick Carruthers is on the right. John R. Rathom may be the second from the left.

The day after the play was presented, Dick wrote Louise:

[I] *have been so busy getting ready for our great show – At The Picket Line – which came off last night. I['ll] send you a programme, and would send some news paper comment if I had any here but I will later. To say it was a success I will tell you that there was only three empty seats in the building, goes well I think.*

Later in the letter, he added:

At present I am Manager of Fishers Opera House, Astoria, Oregon. The town is at present too small to hold me. The bondsmen took it from Beggs, - and Kendall,

Smith, Trullinger, Sherman and myself are running it to try and get some rent Beggs never paid. I am <u>Manager</u> and you will always be entitled to a box seat - this will include my friend Miss M. [Margie Halsted]. This should be some encouragement for her to come to Astoria. But you must hurry home as we are going to give it up after three months.

Entertainment in Astoria took on a new dimension February 12, 1897. The first moving picture ever shown in Clatsop County was presented at Fisher's Opera House. The dawn of the flickering images had arrived in Astoria. Angus Russell Carruthers, one of Dick's younger brothers, was a leading figure in the introduction of an amazing new invention – Thomas Edison's Vitascope. The life-like scenes of romance and action - all in living color - awed the small opening night audience of only two hundred persons. The entry fee was fifty cents for reserved seating, twenty-five cents for the gallery. Progress was moving forward at a fast clip indeed, but moving pictures could never completely replace "live" theatre, such as that on Broadway and in professional productions around the globe. Amateur players would continue to have their place in providing "live" theatre experiences – as in Astoria's Astor Street Opry Company's musical melodrama, *Shanghaied in Astoria*, which completed its Twenty-fifth season in 2009.

Chapter Three   **June 1896 to September 1897**
                                                                    At Home in Astoria
                                                                The Best of "Friends"

The Astoria Giant: William Easton Tallant

It wasn't until 1896 that the first modern Olympiad was held in Athens, Greece. But long before that, organized amateur athletic competitions were regularly held across the United States and in more than a dozen countries around the world.

Louise's older brother William Easton "Will" Tallant (1870-1934) was one of "Astoria's all-time athletic heroes."[87] Entering numerous west coast outdoor track meets in the 1890s, his specialties were the mile and the 880-yard dash.[88] In 1896, twenty-six year old Will became known as *"The Astoria Giant."*

Both Will and Dick were members of the Astoria Foot Ball Club (A.F.B.C., also known as the AFC and the A.C.) The group was also active in the community and put on many benefit sports events and theatrical performances. Will and Dick often ran under the club's logo, occasionally entering the same meets. Although Dick did not have Will's speed, their friendly competition probably helped each of them. Both men entered the Championship Athletic Games sponsored by the Pacific Northwest Association/A.A.U. on Saturday, September 22, 1894. It was held at Multnomah Field in Portland. The track was one-fifth of a mile less 100 feet (956 feet). Nine clubs were registered representing Portland (one bore the team name of Turn Verein), Astoria, Tacoma, LaGrande, the Willamette and Portland Rowing Clubs and the First Regiment Athletic Association. Meet rules were strictly enforced. Competitors were required to wear regulation uniforms and had to be clad from head to knee. Will (No. 6) entered the One Mile Run for the AFC. E. Coke Hill had set the previous PNW record of 4 min., 51.4 seconds. That same afternoon, Will entered the 880-yard dash that had a previous record by John Latta of 2 minutes, 8 seconds. Dick (wearing No. 8 for the AFC) ran in the Second Heat of the 100-yard dash. E. L. Bennett and A. L. Fuller set the previous PNW records of 10.8 seconds. Dick also entered the 220-yard dash (today's 200 metres) trying to beat the PNW previous record of 24 min., 2 seconds, also set by Fuller.[89] Unfortunately the record of Will and Dick's times in this meet has not been found in the available newspaper files.

The Multnomah AAC Fifth Annual Spring Handicap Games were held on June 5, 1895, at the Multnomah Field. Six clubs entered, including Bishop Scott Academy's Athletic Association.[90] Again for the AFBC, Will ran the One Mile at scratch, with no

---

[87] Tetlow, *Cumtux*, 19.

[88] Astoria's athletic field was located at the top of Sixth Street.

[89] Dick and Louise's 21-year old son, Richard Tallant Carruthers, Sr., ran the 120-Yard High Hurdles for the University of Oregon in the Pacific Coast Intercollegiate Athletic Conference and Olympic Tryouts held May 30 to 31, 1924.

[90] Will had attended the Bishop Scott Academy and Grammar School for Boys in Oswego, Oregon, just south of Portland. It was an Episcopalian school established in September 1870 by the Rt. Rev. Thomas Fielding Scott. Will Tallant may have enrolled in the military program that was introduced into the curriculum in 1887.

handicap - Will held the previous meet record of 4 minutes, 44.8 sec.; the 880 at scratch - (Will held the previous record at 2 minutes, 5.8 s.); and the 440 with a 4-yard handicap (PNA previous record was set by W.B. Laswell at 54.6 s.). Dick (AFBC) ran the 100-yard dash at scratch in the Third Heat (PNA record was the same as in 1894) and the 220-yard dash with a 3.5-yard handicap (previous record to beat was 24 sec. flat set by Fuller).

According to Dick's letter to Louise on March 3, 1896, Will apparently had begun training for a meet to be held the latter part of May. Less than four weeks after the May meet, he entered the big Pacific Coast Championship meet in Portland. On the evening of Friday, June 26, 1896, a crowd of enthusiasts sailed up river to Portland on the steamer *Telephone* to attend the track meet between the Multnomah AAC of Portland and the Olympic AAC of San Francisco. Among those on the steamer were Dick Carruthers, Charlie Callender, George Smith, Harry Hamblet, Tom Bryce, Peter Grant, C.C. McDonald, W.T. Beveridge and Cornelius T. Crosby. They were all strong supporters of Will Tallant, who was running for the Multnomahs as their strongest man. He was the Northwest record holder in both the mile and the half-mile events. Will was reported to be "in the pink," although a friend who had seen him train stated such was not the case. However, according to the June 27 *Daily Morning Astorian*, "Will has never suffered defeat from scratch men and evidently does not intend to."

Will and his coach, Peter Grant, a winning combination.

"On June 28, 1896, Astorians gathered for hours outside the *Daily Astorian* newspaper office to get the results of the Pacific Coast Athletic Championships, then being held in Portland. Will Tallent (*sic*) was running on that day for the Multnomah Athletic Club, and when the word came down that he had won the mile race, the town went wild. His time? On that day Will Tallent (*sic*) broke the Pacific Coast record, running in the then-startling time of 4 minutes, 31 1/2 seconds."[91]

---

[91] Tetlow, *Ibid.,* 19.

His official recorded time in the mile run was actually 4 minutes, 31.4 s. He competed against D.E. Brown of the Olympic AAC. "Tallant's performance was splendid. In fact it was wonderful," according to the *Daily Astorian*'s reporter. Within hours of this record mile run, Will ran the 880-yard dash. Pitted again against the Olympic's Brown, Will won that in 2:04.4 s. – not his best ever time, but enough to win. When the news of "Billy's" half-mile victory reached Astorians, they were ecstatic. The newspaper reporter went on to say: "(T)here is considerable satisfaction in the thought that the great city of Portland had to send to Astoria for a man to win two races. There is still more satisfaction in the fact that Tallant broke the Pacific coast record in the mile, . . [and that] the great Californian's scalp is dangling at Will's belt, and the city of Astoria is truly proud of her speedy son." He was indeed Astoria's Giant!

Will, who had both speed and strength, was also a regular member of Astoria's local Rescue Hose Team volunteer firemen. Rescue Hose Teams were yesterday's fire fighters. The firemen had to run from the firehouse to the fire sites pulling behind them the awkwardly heavy and cumbersome wheeled equipment upon which the fire hoses were reeled. Most of the streets then were merely hard-packed material. The surface of streets along the waterfront was planking atop pilings. Here, it was relatively easy to pump any amount of water necessary right out of the Columbia River. But with the many steep hillsides of Astoria, getting the hose reels up to those parts of the town was a daunting task. The firemen's speed and ability saved many a business and home in a town where wood was the major building material. Daily practice was required. Will's Astoria team often practiced by having organized meets against other hose teams from various cities. More often than not, Astoria's team won those competitions.

The outfits worn by both the runners and the firemen were quite similar: each wore sleeveless or short-sleeved cotton tops. "Trousers" (which in photographs looked like the material used to make long-john underwear) usually extended to the knee or just below – similar to the style of today's basketball players; the firemen wore a padded athletic supporter over the pants. Neither runners nor firemen wore socks. Their footwear was a soft soled, flat, little tie-up shoe. The shoes of the runners had spiked soles and it is likely the shoes of the firemen had spikes as well to give them better traction in pulling. Pomaded hair might have cut down some of the wind drag, but the big moustaches many young athletes wore in those days probably negated that edge.

Louise's older brother was a dedicated sports fan. He played cricket, English football (soccer), and baseball. He attended every boxing match he could. When asked to be best man at his good friend Charles Callender's wedding to Pearl Holden on October 12, 1898, he was hard pressed to choose between that and seeing "Gentleman Jim" Corbett fight, but he attended his friend's nuptials.

Not a fellow who hesitated to try new things or to put new ideas to the test, Will was apparently quick to see the advantages and the profits to be made as a businessman. In April 1898, his mother commented that *"Will ought to succeed if work tells for as Papa says he is a worker and nothing discourages him."* The Klondike Gold Rush that began on the West coast in July of 1897 gave him a great business opportunity. Alaska gold miners arrived in San Francisco heralding the huge Dawson City Bonanza strike at Rabbit Creek. Alaskan miners named "Skookum Jim" and George and Kate Carmack had discovered the gold. Word spread like wildfire. Almost immediately two hundred thousand men

89

stampeded northward. So many of Astoria's fishermen left for Alaska's gold fields, it badly hurt the local fishing-cannery industry. Everyone was wild to pan for gold and become rich. All of their families who were left at home also hoped they would become wealthy.

Will - a student at Bishop Scott's Academy.

Will - Astoria's 1896 champion miler.

Dick and Will with their coaches, Tom Spencer (left) and Peter Grant.

AFC team (1894)   Family photo donated to CCHS - #565-584
Back (left to right): Walter Ridehalgh, George Smith, Frank Gunn, John Rathom, Harry Bell, Will Tallant.
Front: C. Addin, J. Ashbury, Frank Spittle, B. Gibson, A. Bartholemew, Charlie Higgins.
Spectators directly above Will and Harry Bell are Carleton and Grace Carruthers Allen.
Peeking around the right post, on upper right, is Will's mother, Mary Elizabeth Tallant.

Will had apparently been ahead of the main movement north. The 1897 strike was not the first gold strike in the Alaska/Yukon area. Gold was found in 1886 on big strikes at Circle City, Forty-Mile and also on Cook Inlet. Off and on, Will Tallant spent about seven years up north; he knew Skagway, Dyea, St. Michael and Nome in Alaska, as well as Dawson City and Lake Bennett in Canada's Yukon Territory. He had gone up and down the Yukon River as he tried his hand at gold mining and panning for gold. While there, he had learned some of the native languages and dialects. He also had learned to herd the reindeer pack animals. As early as 1891, the Sammis of Lapland had been transporting reindeer to Alaska and the Yukon Territory. The reindeer were well suited to the climate and to the hardships as pack animals. They also were a source of food for the miners.

Many who went prospecting were unprepared for the climate and conditions they encountered. During December 1897, one thousand men, women and children were caught poorly prepared for the bad weather, with heavy snows and icy winds, on the infamous Chilkoot and White Passes. Most had insufficient supplies to last through the severe Alaskan winter. So many humans and pack animals perished that the U.S. Government formed a mercy expedition to Dawson City. Will volunteered as a guide for the "reindeer drivers" in the rescue attempt. Possibly it was on this occasion that Will, along with Grant Trullinger, sailed to St. Michael, south of Nome, on the *Eliza Anderson* and then pressed onward to Dawson up the Yukon River.[92]

---

[92] Penner, *Cumtux,* 26.

By the end of 1897, Will caught a different kind of Alaska fever: he found a partner, George Johnson, and the two men started a team and drayage business in Skagway and nearby Dyea. According to Mary Elizabeth's letter to Louise January 18, 1898, they had bought two horses and a truck, but could not get them on board the over-crowded steamer *Elder*. Making reservations on the steamer *Oregon*, George, and a fellow identified only as Jake, took the horses up to Dyea. The port of Dyea was mainly a tent city in 1898, populated by 10,000 men and 5,000 mules.[93] It became a ghost town by 1900 as the gold fields lost some of their lure. Several aerial tramways had been built to haul men and goods up the Chilkoot Pass and the White Pass from Skagway and Dyea in 1896. The one from Dyea was operated by gravity and weights; Skagway's horse-powered tram became a steam operated one. However, when the number of customers dwindled to "no riders," the trams were closed. Gold seekers were taking the train! By July 1900, the new White Pass and Yukon Railroad was making two trips daily from Skagway to Caribou Crossing and Lake Bennett. The railroad made connections with all of the steamers docking at Skagway and Dyea.

With his Alaska business settled in March 1898, Will used $3,000 of his Klondike money to begin a new venture – seining on the Columbia River. He had six boats and nets, seven men, eight horses, and a floating "mess house." His seining grounds were up river. The 1901 Dellinger City Directory listed his occupation as "seiner." In 1902, he took over his father's management of the Columbia River Packing Company in Uniontown (the western one-third area of Astoria). Will later formed a partnership with Peter Grant, his friend and former track coach, and established the Tallant-Grant Packing Company built out on pilings at the foot of Columbia Avenue. A news clipping saved by the family reported Tallant won a state land board judgment in 1904 against the Sanborn-Cutting Packing Company and gained the rights to seining grounds between the Spencer and Barrel Beacon grounds near Altoona; Tallant paid $10 per acre for those rights. In the 1930s he still retained some of the seining rights – at least one in Young's Bay was in his name and another in his wife Clara's name. For many years his company remained as one of the major salmon packing companies of the area.

During WW II, the facility was run by Paragon Packing Company; in 1966, the Oregon Fur Producers (clients of Bioproducts, Inc.,[94] then owned by Richard Carruthers, Jr.) used the buildings for a few years to make mink feed out of fish offall. The abandoned buildings were included in the Uniontown Historic District formed in 1990; within a year, some of the pilings and buildings, then known as Overbay's Landing for kayaks, collapsed. Early in the morning of Wednesday, April 24, 1997, a fire of undetermined origin destroyed the remaining structures and most of the wharves, leaving only the pilings.[95]

Apparently Will liked cars. For a few years, he chauffeured some of the Regatta queens, including his sister Harriet when she was elected Queen of the Astoria Regatta in 1907. Harriet rode in his auto in great style, with the top down, of course. Will's automobile was as gaily decorated as were the parade floats. He owned one of the first

---

[93] McCurdy, 146.

[94] Richard Ervin Carruthers founded By-Products, Inc. in 1911. His son, Richard Tallant "Dick" Carruthers, Sr. (1902-1965), later formed Bioproducts, Inc.

[95] As part of the present day surge of restoration and construction in Astoria, investors purchased the site, perhaps with the possibility that the remaining pilings might form the foundation of a waterfront project.

"Moon" cars and on April 12, 1911, the *Astoria Daily Budget* reported that Will had purchased the highest powered car ever delivered to Astoria to that date. It was a sleek Pope Hartford Torpedo with four cylinders and fifty-two horsepower, capable of great speed.

Clara Wiederholdt Starbuck

William Easton Tallant

Clara Wiederholdt Starbuck (1873-1948), the daughter of Sydney Starbuck, had visited the Tallant family in Astoria a number of times over the years. Clara, descended from a brother of Benjamin Franklin's mother, was an heiress to the famous Starbuck ship building family of New York. Both Clara and Will had been born in Nantucket and shared a common ancestor – Trystram Coffin, who had founded the well-known Cape Cod family in 1642 and established a highly regarded school in Nantucket. In mid October 1903, Will left the west coast for New York City. On December 12, 1903, Clara W. Starbuck and William Easton Tallant were wed in a ceremony held in Brooklyn. Louise and her mother, Mary Elizabeth, gave a reception for Clara on January 5, 1904, when the newlyweds arrived in Astoria.

Will and Clara's daughter, Laura Elizabeth, was born in 1909.[96] In 1911, the family bought the stately Astoria home of Senator Charles W. Fulton. The Colonial Revival style house still stands at the southeast corner of Irving and Seventeenth. After one fire in the house in 1931, another in 1932, the large house was converted into the Tallant Apartments. Will's younger brother Nathaniel (1883-1968) and his wife Florence Ross Tallant occupied an apartment in the W. E. Tallant house until Florence's death in 1955. The spacious house has had several owners since then and was restored to a single-family dwelling.

Will retired in 1922. Twelve years later, on Friday, September 28, 1934, William Easton Tallant was found dead at his home on Irving Avenue. No cause of death was listed. Clara soon moved to nearby Gearhart, Oregon. She died December 10, 1948, leaving no will. Two of her pallbearers were Richard Tallant Carruthers, Sr. and Eben Hunter Carruthers, the two sons of Louise and Dick.

---

[96] Laura Elizabeth Tallant married Richard Schroeder in 1941.

The only photograph found positively identifying the *Tillie E. Starbuck*
is from a long ago newspaper article.

The Starbuck Connection

The family name of 'Starbuck' is a familiar one not only in coffee, but also in early shipbuilding and in literature. In his book *Moby Dick,* Herman Melville named Captain Ahab's first mate "Starbuck." The leading character in Bernard Cornwell's Civil War series, *The Starbuck Chronicles*, is Nathaniel "Nate" Starbuck, a Boston-born swash-buckling Confederate action hero fighting in Virginia.

W. H. Starbuck was known for his sleek and beautiful clipper ships. He built the first iron clad sailing ship, originally named the *Oliveto*. She was renamed the *Tillie E. Starbuck* - (#116057; 2,157.46 gross tons; 266.5' length; 36.5' breadth; 20.4' depth; 200 hp.).[97] She was a fast, three-masted screw steamer constructed by John Roach. Launched in Sunderland, England in 1881, her homeport was New York. She sailed to Japan and India, specifically designed for the North Pacific trade as an American merchant vessel. She was purchased by the Lewis and Edward Luckenbach Line Steamship Company of Long Island, NY and became a part of their fleet of 42 British ships, 14 American ships and 9 others. In 1883, the Luckenbachs selected the *Tillie E. Starbuck* to inaugurate their new service from New York around Cape Horn to Astoria and Portland. She made the trip at least once each year. On one of the trips, she set a record for the fewest days at sea – 106. The Luckenbach brothers claimed that record was never beaten during the era of the Clipper ships.[98]

On her first trip to Astoria, the *Tillie E. Starbuck* arrived on January 10, 1884, carrying a 3,000 ton, million-dollar cargo, consisting of twenty-two locomotives and rails for the Northern Pacific Railroad - and the huge Oregon Railroad & Navigation

---

[97] Merchant Vessels of the United States, 1896, 297.
[98] Barber, "Reduced Rail Freight Rates," a clipping from the *Oregon Journal Sunday*, December 20 (no year), 36.

Company's ferry that ran between Kalama, Washington and Goble, Oregon.[99] Later, she sailed as the largest of the Columbia River grain fleet. Another W.H. Starbuck vessel, the *T .F. Oakes,*[100] later renamed the *New York,* also frequented the port of Astoria. The *William H. Starbuck* took the first load of northwestern lumber from the Columbia to New York.[101]

1896 Fourth of July. Everyone got together for a picnic on Scarborough Head.

Scarborough Head

Well known in the 1890s as an historical Indian site, Scarborough[102] Head (or Hill) was also a popular picnic area for Astoria's young people. They would have had to either rowed/sailed themselves across the Columbia or taken one of the scheduled steamers over to Chinook, Washington, and then trekked or ridden horses up the hill. It was located on the north bank of the Columbia between what is now known as McGowan's Church and Chinook. Dominated by a mammoth boulder in earlier times, the hill had been used as a landmark. Of course the land originally belonged to the Indians, but, at a later date, the land somehow became the property of the Scarborough family. In the late 19th century, Fort Columbia, a U.S. Army installation, was built around and on Scarborough Hill. In May 2007, the U.S. House of Representatives passed the Columbia-Pacific National Heritage Study Act; its purpose was to officially combine Fort Columbia, Station Camp, Cape Disappointment-Ft Canby area, Dismal Nitch, Knappton, Knappton Cove and Fort Clatsop into one multi-site honoring the Lewis and Clark expedition. The Senate postponed discussion of the bill in June 2008.

---

[99] Lewis & Dryden, 224.
[100] Barber, "Reduced Rail Freight," 36.
[101] *Ibid.*
[102] Sometimes written "Scarboro" (or "Scarboo," as Louise wrote it on the photograph.)

The Chinook Indians inhabited the north side of the Columbia. The tribe was led by the powerful one-eyed Chief Comcomly, who became a fast friend to the Lewis and Clark Expedition members and to later settlers of Ft. Astoria (later known as Fort George during the occupation of the British). Chief Comcomly dominated the Clatsop and Tillamook tribes on the south banks of the river by using fear and intimidation. He convinced the other tribes of his invincibility, declaring that as long as the huge boulder remained in place atop the particular hill later know as Scarborough, his sacred power – and that of his people – could not be challenged. Comcomly died in 1830. Sometime later, some of the young warriors of the Clatsop and Tillamook tribes rowed across the river, climbed to the top of the hill and toppled the great sacred rock off its perch. It tumbled down, as did the Indians' belief in Comcomly and the Chinook tribe's power over all others.

Part of the culture of the Chinooks included a "rite of passage" that required each young person – male and female – to find his/her own "guardian spirit" to give them special powers. The spirit manifested itself to each person in a vision, as each kept a lone vigil of long days and nights on the then thickly wooded "Scarborough" hill. The Clatsop Indians, led by Chief Cobaway, also believed in this traditional ritual – their young people spent their days and nights alone in the woods on Saddle Mountain.[103]

Louise probably wrote the following letter in the late summer or early fall of 1896. The dance she planned would have been held on the third floor of the Grand Avenue home.

No date. Envelope addressed to Mr Richard Carruthers, City

Thursday evening

My dear boy

I don't know how many square miles I have walked the last few days in hopes of seeing you. Where do you keep yourself? I am glad you do not stand around on street corners and cigar stands and still some times I wish you were there. I could see you oftener and would know where to find you. Nothing special has happened but I wanted to see you the day I asked Gus to tell you to phone me. I thought I was going on that trip to the Dalles. Hat was anxious to go because Laura [Knowles] & the Sommervilles are there and we had tickets given us. I thought it would be lovely if you could go too, but other wise I didn't care much. I should have gone tho. on account of Hat only my cold got so bad Papa wouldn't let me. That night I felt pretty sick – don't know when I ever had such a cold. I only stayed a little while at the cannery and when I met Hat she said you had just gone into Charlie's. I rushed up there thinking I would be in time to say Hello, but you had gone – at least I didn't see you around. Charlie was busy so I went back down town and shopped for about an hour. That night I saw by the paper you had gone to Flavel so the next morning I was supprised when you phoned and I guess you thought it funny that I had so little to say.   - excuse pencil – it goes faster - I went down town

---

[103] Miller, *Clatsop County, Oregon*, 11, 13, 62.

yesterday and surely thought I would see you and tell all I didn't say over the telephone and again today I didn't see you, so that is why I am writing. Expect my luck will still be with me tomorrow and our rooms won't be papered on time to have the crowd up to dance until Friday night (be sure and come – it is all in your honor) fare well a la Will Sherman. We can easily find 25 girls to dance with about 10 boys (how nice). Well I expect when you are up at Rooster Rock I will be sitting up nights like this writing to you. But now I must stop and get to bed before my cold gets another cold added to it. So will say good night and I love you in the same old way and hope to see you as I pass by tomorrow.

Yours for always

Louise

Thursday P.S. Be sure and come up tonight. The men are through with the paper. The party is <u>very</u> <u>informal</u> but you can come in your dress suit if it isn't pressed. I wish it was a party for just <u>two</u> – don't you. . . L

Hello! Hello! Are you there?

Two tin cans connected by a taut string can still provide limited communication. In 1876, when Alexander Graham Bell unveiled his invention – the telephone - a wonderful new world opened up.

On March 26, 1926, the *Astoria Evening Budget* ran a front-page article commemorating the fiftieth anniversary of the invention of the telephone. The article featured a photograph of Eben W. Tallant, who was one of the very first subscribers, possibly from the late 1870s. According to his daughter Louise, he was the first private subscriber in Astoria with continuous telephone service. The 1926 photo also shows Miss Esther Lokan, a veteran operator employed by the Pacific Telephone and Telegraph

Company, explaining to Mr. Tallant how she places and connects calls on her switchboard.[104]

Astoria's telephone service was not officially put into general use until April 1, 1884. By then, there were forty-eight customers, including E.W. Tallant. However, at least two business telephones had already been placed in service six years prior to that according to the *Daily Astorian* of June 22, 1878: a business on Main Street (evidently the newspaper office) with a connection by a cord line, and the other was the telegraph office that connected its line to the wires of the Western Union company. On June 23, unidentified reporter(s) wrote they had tried "telephoning for the first time at Brookfield where Mr. J.G. Megler had an excellent good pair." They had "a conversation with Col. John Adair in upper Astoria," on June 26. They further noted that "[p]ractice is necessary to perfectly talk and understand this wonderful means…This instrument is in use at various points along the river, and a conversation can be carried on between the points quite understandingly by those who have experience."

Although city directories giving name, address and occupation were in print, telephone directories were not published in the 1880s. By 1900 subscribers numbered more than 500. Accurate information is not readily available because the Astoria fire of 1922 destroyed so much of downtown Astoria, including the *Daily Astorian* office and its stored newspaper files.

Few letters were saved during this time period. Possibly few were even written. Both Louise and Dick were in Astoria so there was really less reason to be writing to each other. An undated note from Louise accompanied an unidentified Christmas present for Dick, along with a letter.

Merry Xmas

*This thing isn't as good as it looks Dick but you must not put it
in your top drawer and let it stay there. I send my love with it and
best wishes for a Merry Christmas and a prosperous New Year
Yours as before Louise*

Mailing date: 26 DEC 5PM 1896

Saturday

Dear Dick

Please come and see me again. You said you would not but I know you will and don't you think we ought to understand each other better. Don't you see how different it is if I had let you do as you wanted to, it would [have] ment so much to you, more than I would want it to for although I like you very much and you know it, I can not promise for the future and although you care so very much for me now (I never knew before how much) some day it may be

---

[104] The switchboard is similar to one owned by the Clatsop County Historical Society; it is not currently on display.

different. However we can't look into the future so let's be good friends for a while longer any way.

I am so sorry Dick if you feel badly. Here is my kiss. You may take yours some other time – no one has more right than you.

as before   don't be too serious

Louise

"Hotel de Chafe" Party menu - dated February 8, 1897

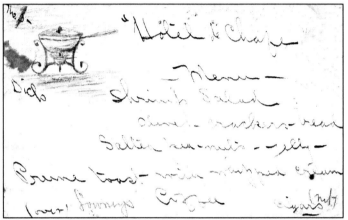

The chafing dish is hand drawn in brown ink by Louise. The menu included Shrimp Salad; olives; crackers; bread; Salted peanuts; jelly; Prune toast with whipped cream; Lowneys; coffee and cigars. Note the word "(nit)" after "Cigars" on the menu! Lowneys chocolates were very popular. On the reverse side of the card are listed the Chefs: Nan (Reed), Olga (Heilborn), Harriet, Pearl (Holden), Clara (Lionberger) and Louise. They were assisted by: Tom Bryce, R. T. Burnett, Charles Heilborn, D. Prael and E. J. Smith.

"Hotel de Chafe" Party Menu **March 22, 1897** Louise's hand drawn figure of a Wading Girl in red and green inks decorated the menu.	**Yacht Club Dance** **March 26, 1897** *"A Farewell to Mr. John Grover"* Committee: W.A. Sherman - G.J. Smith - R.E. Carruthers

Oysters fried in batter; Crackers; Bread; Pickles;
Quince with whipped cream; Cake and Coffee.

Dances. Dances. Dances. These were given by various organizations such as the University Association of Women, The Chrysanthemums and The Assembly. They were well attended by young and old, singles and couples. Will Sherman, George Smith and Dick Carruthers were the organizers of the above one that was held at the Yacht Club on March 26, 1897. A few colorful signal flags decorated their program to carry out the nautical theme. The initials "LMT" on Dick's card should have been "MLT" for Louise.

On June 16, 1897, Louise celebrated her twenty-second birthday.

June 20th

Dear Dick

I didn't thank you very kindly last night did I but I do now thank you very <u>very</u> much. You could not have given any thing I would have liked better realy – didn't I tell you I always liked every thing you gave me, that is right too and you have given me far more than Xmas and birthday remembrances and I appreciate it. Dick never doubt that I am so unfortunate about saying the right thing at the right time that you think I don't care at all about how much you like me but I do and I would be so glad if we could always be good friends, as we have been so long, and never think of any thing else – don't you think that is a good plan to <u>try</u>. I am sure Miss Askmore would. Well Dick this is the first note from me in a long time isn't it and I don't suppose I have said the right thing now but don't <u>josh</u> me. And I must stop short for Hat is anxious for this pen and ink and I have realy nothing more to say except Thanks again.

> *As before*
> > *and always.*
> > > *Louise*

Mailing date: SEP 19 6:30 PM 97   Astoria, Oreg.

Sunday   Sept the 19th

Dear Dick

I can't tell you how sorry it made me feel to get such a letter from you but proberly you are right and I deserve to feel badly, but Dick I didn't realize that I acted <u>so dreadfully</u> last night. I was some what supprised that you walked up with us and was a little angry at first (I may as well admit it) for it didn't seem necessary for you to leave [the Commodore] Perry to come with us, but you know best about that. I know I should have acted differently to you (and I am sorry). I can't ask you to forgive me because I know you can't do it. But I hope some time you will when you are not so angry with me as you are now.

I can't expect you to take me to Lottie's so I will <u>not</u> <u>accept</u> <u>my</u> invitation as I shouldn't enjoy going at all now and if I don't feel better than I have the past few days, I couldn't go any way, So <u>please</u> <u>don't</u> decline your invitation on my account. You have given up enough for me Dick. You think I don't care <u>but I do</u> and I only hope to some time prove it.

As ever

Louise

P.S. please don't call me Miss Tallant again unless you want me to feel that you are not even my friend and we have been good friends to long to think of that I hope. L

The photographs above show the interior of the Tallants' living room and parlor. The left photograph is looking south toward the bay windows overlooking Grand Avenue and the right photo looks north toward the river. Both Louise and Harriet played musical instruments. Louise was especially proficient on the guitar and was often asked to play for guests, her friends and family.

Mailing Date: SEP 20 4:30PM '97 Astoria, Oreg.

Monday

Dear Dick

I felt that you would be sorry and I didn't blame you for being angry and I will be only to glad to have you take me to Lotties if it is possible for me to go, but I am quite lame today and Mama says I <u>musn't</u> <u>think</u> of going unless my foot is <u>much</u> better for it is quite a long walk home and you know how tired I get lately when I go to parties. But I am going down now to have the massage treatment and I hope it will take the soreness all out so I can go for I <u>honestly</u> <u>want</u> <u>to</u> now. I don't know how I can let you know for sure. So come up for me and if <u>possiable</u> I will go, if not Dick you <u>must</u> <u>know</u> that is the only reason why I do not. I must go so must stop now

as ever

Louise

A Probable Case of M. *bovis*

In Louise's letter to Dick, written from Sunny Slope, California in April 1896, she cautioned:

" *Don't be too serious though Dick for there seems to be a long wait ahead of us and there is no telling what may happen.*"

Louise had been bothered for over a year and a half by increasing lameness and pain in her left ankle. Dancing, which she loved to do, had become too difficult. Walking caused her considerable pain. Her physicians in Astoria, probably Dr. M.M. Walker and Dr. Fulton, had diagnosed the problem as a type of tuberculosis that infected the bones and joints – at least, so she and her family were told. Surgery was advised as necessary to correct the deformity, to drain the inflamed site and to remove the infected bone. She was referred to Children's Hospital in San Francisco under the care of Dr. H.M. Sherman. The surgeons there were believed to be more experienced in performing the necessary procedure. The hospital was considered better equipped to give Louise the best possible chance to recover her health.

In the latter part of the nineteenth century, surgeries of this sort were more difficult and required skilled orthopedic specialists. The infected area(s) on the bone had to be carefully and completely carved out. Most often the complete removal of a bone (or bones) was required, as in Louise's case. Anesthetics and painkillers were nowhere near what we have today. In the 1890s, physicians and surgeons were limited in what they could provide a patient to combat infections or relieve pain. The time required in the operating room to complete this type of orthopedic procedure made it very hard on the patient, both during and following the operation. A long recuperation period was necessary with little, if any, physical therapy given the patient. A rosy outcome was not necessarily guaranteed.

Many types of mycobacterium exist - and have existed since very ancient times. TB has been prevalent for a long time. M. *tuberculosis* has caused epidemics, for example, during the Industrial Revolution, when it is estimated that more than thirty-percent of the deaths were the result of overcrowded, unsanitary conditions that allowed bacteria to be easily spread. In 1882, Robert Koch,[105] who was a physician and a scientist, identified the bacterium that causes TB. This type of bacterium affects the respiratory system and is sometimes termed "consumption" or the "white plague." It is a slow growing chronic disease. Stronger health care standards for people, for livestock and their environment - especially in cleanliness, sanitation and sterilization - helped to stem the spread of the disease both here and abroad. Discovery of the first antibiotic – streptomycin – did not occur until the 1940s. It was used during WW II, but did not gain widespread use until well into the 1950s. This, and later discovered antibiotics, microbiotics and the use of chemotherapy – particularly when used in combination(s) - helped make certain types of TB rare occurrences in the United States. Even so, well into the 1960s, numerous TB

---

[105] Dr. Koch was honored with a Nobel Laureate medal in 1905 for his discovery and research. He is called "The Father of Bacteriology."

hospitals existed in the United States to care for TB patients. The disease has still not been eradicated.

Web sites and medical books, including the Merck Manuals, describe extra-pulmonary mycobacterium TB-like inflammations that infect parts of the body other than the lungs. One type infects the bones and joints. Airborne transmission from infected cattle or contaminated cows' milk was determined to be the probable cause. Thus the organism is named *M. bovis.* This particular bacterium is communicable cow to cow, cow to human, or human-to-human. It produces arthritis-like symptoms, especially in the weight-bearing joints such as the hips, knees and ankles. Although it is not life threatening, it is a degenerative disease and usually quite painful. In the 1860s, Louis Pasteur and Claude Bernard discovered the method of "pasteurization" that destroyed, or at least reduced, most disease-producing bacteria in liquids, such as milk. In 1904, Denmark passed Europe's first pasteurization act. But it was not until after WW I that the amount of available pasteurized milk increased in the major cities of developed countries.[106] This greatly reduced the transmission of bovine TB, but even today, *M. bovis* can be passed to humans in air droplets, by ingesting milk from contaminated cows or from being in contact with infected cattle - especially in under-developed/Third World countries, particularly to children.

Bovine tuberculosis was relatively common in the United States (and globally) during this period. A number of Astorians kept cows and regularly herded them through the "built-up" areas of Astoria. Raw milk and raw milk products were all that anyone commonly had available.

On Thanksgiving Day, November 25, 1897, Louise, accompanied by Harriet, left Astoria by steamer for San Francisco to prepare for the surgery on her ankle. They stayed with their father's sister, Fannie (Sarah Frances Tallant Smith) and her husband, Theo Smith, at 912 Page Street. Louise entered the Children's Hospital early in December. Dr. H.M. Sherman performed the surgery on December third (or fourth), 1897. The surgeon(s) removed at least one infected bone in the left ankle. Louise was required to remain in the hospital for about eight weeks. After Christmas, she wrote her first letter to Dick. Her hand was so unsteady. . .

> *"that unless you know that I had not left this dear little <u>narrow</u> short white*
> *iron bed of mine for over three weeks or even turned over in it for the last two*
> *- that you might think in gay S.F. I had been having too gay a time."*

Her dear sister Harriet dutifully kept Louise company almost every day, although Hat did find time to do some sightseeing and attended various social affairs in San Francisco. Their father, who also had been with Louise at the time of the surgery, sailed back and forth between Astoria and San Francisco numerous times. He surprised the girls by

---

[106] Orland, *"Cows Milk and Human Diseases. Bovine Tuberculosis.*
http://www.zgw.ethz.ch/pdf/orlandCowsMilk.pdf

arriving back a day early in order to spend Christmas Day with them. He was able to combine his frequent visits there with his own business for the Columbia River Packing Company and the Cutting Packing Company, headquartered in San Francisco.

Finally, Louise was allowed to get up. A cast had been placed on her foot and ankle. It would remain there well into April. After being taught to use the "hated crutches," she was released from the hospital late in January 1898. On January twenty-sixth, Louise wrote:

Dick, I am afraid we have had our last dance together. I didn't know until yesterday just what they had done to my foot."

She and Hat stayed in San Francisco with the Smiths for a week or so. Louise had decided she would recuperate in the warmer climate to the south. She felt reasonably confident - even on crutches – that she could manage to travel by rail on her own to the Los Angeles area to visit her friends and relatives. The surgery had given her some hope that she might be able to walk normally, without pain, and maybe to dance again. But, by April 1898, the surgical incision still had not fully healed, causing frequent cleansing of discharging matter. Nor had the cast been removed yet either.

Harriet returned home to Astoria by a steamer leaving from San Francisco on February 8, crossing the reasonably calm Columbia River bar before daylight on the ninth. Safely back home, she wrote Louise, then in Alhambra, the following on February fourteenth:

"My eyes have looked so badly since I have been home that Mama made me go to Dr Walkers yesterday; about all he did was to talk to me about your foot. Dr S- etc showed me a picture of a foot and explained which bone it was they took out."

Early in June, Louise returned to Astoria, having regained strength in her body if not yet in her foot and ankle. Although the surgery did help her, Louise continued to use crutches for many months. She was thankful she did not have to wear a brace. Special shoes, costing $15 a pair in 1898, became a necessity. Her knowledge of this thing that she called "her defect" seems to have been the major reason for her reluctance to marry Dick earlier, despite his numerous proposals. Seemingly, she did not want to be a "burden" on anyone – especially a husband - and believed she could not be a true partner to Dick.

Later, in early September 1898, Louise was still not able to walk without crutches. She wrote Dick, who was then in Honolulu, that her foot was getting stronger all the time, although she had to sit out dances and not attempt to walk long distances. Finally, in October, her doctors told her she could try putting full weight on her left leg and that the ankle should become more flexible. Harriet and Louise left Astoria on October 15, 1898, for Louise's check-up with her doctors in San Francisco. They stayed with their cousin Sydney Smith on Castro Street. At the November 5 doctor's appointment, Louise did get good news. Although her surgeons had told her that they had never expected her to "have to try to walk," or that her foot would be as strong as it had become, she told her doctors - "I am tougher than I look."

Almost one year after her surgery, in her November 29, 1898, letter to Dick, she boasted that she had thrown away those awful crutches the day she left San Francisco and had not touched them again. However, Louise suffered from pain, lameness and numerous other problems in that foot and ankle for the rest of her life.

Family photo donated to Clatsop County Historical Society - #26864-960.
Grand Avenue house – 1897.
Mary Elizabeth and Eben are on the porch.

Chapter Four   **December 1897 through January 1898**
Children's Hospital
Rough Going

While Louise, accompanied by Harriet, was in San Francisco for her surgery, Mary Elizabeth (Lizzie) had to remain at home in the Grand Avenue house with young Nat. She worried terribly about her older daughter, who was so far away and in pain. Following Louise's surgery, she sent frequent letters to her "Puss" in care of the Children's Hospital in San Francisco. She did her best to help Louise keep up her courage and endure the pain, particularly during the Christmas-New Year's holidays. On January 6, 1896, she wrote: "*When I think of what Dr. H- [Harry Sherman] and B- [Dr. Bishop] did it makes my blood run cold.*" Later, Louise would realize how close she came to losing her foot altogether at the "house of horrors."

Sunday, a.m.   Dec 5 th   [1897]

Dear Louise.

The telegram rec'd yesterday made us all feel very happy to know that the operation had be[en] so successful. And I cannot be glad enough that we started you off, but I am not going to write any more about your troubles for we have had enough of them. And I do not want to tire you with a long letter as Mama wants you to keep quiet and not exert yourself any until you feel real well and strong again. Hattie & Papa can do the writing for you. Lila is invited out on the [U.S. Government revenue cutter Commodore] Perry to dine with Mr S-. Capt P- & wife & Miss P- [Irene Phillips] go with her. Will proposed I went up to Mrs K to dinner and let Annie have a holiday. So telephoned and asked if she wanted Nat & I to come & she said yes. So I shall go. It is near twelve and they dine at 1/30 so I shall have to get dressed as it is quite a climb up there. We have not been to the [Bowling] Alley or at least I have not, but L- [Lila Sutherland] goes with Miss P-. When I hear you are all well, as I trust I shall by my next 2 letters, I shall go out more. Dr W. [Walker] says it will not take your foot long to heal, he does not think. Keep up a good heart for now that they have removed the cause, I feel sure you will gain very fast. And be sending home for new dresses on account of getting so fat. Tell H. I will write to her soon. Nat says "tell Miss Puss I will write to her soon" – Lila is going to write too. Well Puss here is a <u>big</u> <u>hug</u> and kiss from one who loves you dearly and is anxious to give them in person.

Mama

106

Mailing date: DEC 6 5PM 97 Astoria, Oreg.
Received: DEC 9 11AM '97 San Francisco.Cal.
Postage: Imprinted green Two cent
Envelope: Columbia River Packing Company, Astoria, Oregon.
Addressed to: Miss Louise Tallant
             Childrens Hospital
               California Street
                 San Francisco, California.

Monday. 2. P.M.

My dear little Puss and Harriet.

If I don't blow over I will write you just a few lines so you can get a letter every morning from home. I shall write a note to Papa and send to Aunt Fannie's [108] so H. will see that. So I direct this to you Puss then if you are alone when the mail comes it will take up your mind until Papa & H. come. I shall send you a note every day, but don't want you to try to answer them if you are at all weak or tired for you must just give up everything and rest so you can at least get to Aunt F's for Xmas. And perhaps you may get to Margie's but you must not try to hurry too much. Dr Walker says he thinks when Dr S- [Sherman] lets you go you will be better than you have been for some time.

You would go wild if you were here feeling as you did the last week. I think it blows ever harder than it did the night of that hard storm. And Puss my chair fairly rocks. This a.m. I went down to Mrs H. while L- [Lila] went down town. She could hardly get home. I did not get a letter this a.m. as there is no morning mail but hope when Will comes up he will bring me a letter, altho it cannot tell about the operation, but the telegram made us all feel so happy. Do you know this writing desk fairly shakes - it almost frightens me. Wish Papa and you were all at home, but I will stand anything to hear that my little Puss is getting along. And I know down there in the sun shine you cannot help feeling well soon. Don't hesitate to call on your nurse to rub you. Mama wishes she could, but the nurse will do it better than I can. Yesterday Nat & I went up to Mrs K's., took dinner, tea. Came home about eight and had just gotten gas & fire lit when L- and Capt P. came in. Capt only stoped to inquire for you. And everybody Puss was so glad to hear of the success of the operation. Dr Bishop telephoned this a.m. while we were at breakfast. Will answered it.

O My - it almost makes me sea sick the house rocks so - do hope it will go down - I mean the <u>wind</u> *- before night. Will said he was going to write to day. Nat talks of it - you know how hard it is for N. [Nat] to write. Well I am going to write to Papa now. And do not want to tire my dear Louise with too long a letter but if Mama told you how much she loved you and wanted to be with you it could fill volumes. But I know you are in the best of hands. And that*

---

107 Aunt Fannie was Eben's younger sister, Sarah Francis Tallant Smith (1844-1905), wife of Theodore Garland Smith (Uncle Theo). The Smiths resided at 912 Page Street in San Francisco. Their son, Sidney, was born in Nantucket December 7, 1865.

before we know it you will be going down to L.A. where you can have sunshine & open air exercise –

   Sealed with kiss for my dear girls from Mama

                              Tuesday. Noon.   [December 7]
Dear Girls,

   Have just written a note to Papa so will write you one that it may go to hospital where you can read it together. Nat was glad to get H's letter this morning and it did us all good to hear how nicely Puss was getting along. I am glad Papa stayed - for five days more will see such an improvement in L. that she will not mind his leaving her for she will know when he goes she is on the road to recover rapidly. Louise, Dr Bishop has just called, wanted to hear all about you and wished to be remembered. Well to day is just lovely. It seem splendid to sit here and not being every moment afraid the windows would blow in. Lila went down town this a.m. with Olga and Alma who came down last night. Last eve it was a howler. Just after dinner, door bell rang – it was Mr & Mrs Chutter. They took off things. Soon after they came, Olga & Charlie; then the two Drs F. [Finch] & B. [Bishop]. All spent eve. Charlie brought L- [Lila] a nice box of Lowneys chocolates which with apples furnished treat. Yesterday P.M. in all the storm Mrs Sanborn came in with work. This a.m. Madam Van Dusen took her work and came and sat until lunch time. Am anxious to see Louise's handwriting then I shall feel she is getting along finely – Shall send the package by Stea[mer] Sat to Aunt Fannie's. Don't fret about Xmas for we shall not make anything of it this year. Nat can hang stockings. Mrs Sanborn says they are not going to do any thing - all her money she says she has had to give Lighter to go East with. All we want is for Puss to be comfortable and you and Hat can be together and it will be happiness for all. We are too big now to make much of Xmas. That is, if it is so we cannot be together, we can be happy knowing that it is all for the best. And can be with with each other in spirit if not in person. H., I am going to send you the net and floats then you can get ribbon there and send from Frisco. I think I will send the basket & hdkf case to Mrs H & Margie from here. I send a spool case to Aunt C- [Clara Foard] and hdkf case to Ella [Scudder Crocker]. That will be the extent of my presents there. When L. is at E's she can give the boys some trifle.
   Well it is time this got to box so will close hoping to continue to hear good news.
      There is the door bell—
      Sealed with kisses from your loving
                              Mama
Just rec'd Papa's telegram with good news. Now Puss. Don't do <u>anything</u> but <u>hurry up</u> <u>and get</u> <u>well.</u>
   Mama.

Grace Eliot – Portland

Lila Sutherland – Portland

Mary Crosby – Nantucket

Tuesday afternoon.

Dear Puss and Hat.

O you don't know what a comfort papa's telegram to Will yesterday gave us all. It was one of the worse storms I ever saw. Never knew the wind to blow so hard. The table in round window [in the family parlor, northeast corner] *fairly shook. We went down stairs about five, lit the lamps and sat there feeling forlorn when Will came in and threw the telegram into my lap. I knew by that it was* good *news. O Louise I am so happy to hear you are doing so well and now I know in a little while you will be feeling as you have not felt for a long time, but do not try to do too much when you first get about. Your foot will be tender and need petting for some time. Glad you like the hospital so well for it certainly is the best place to have anything like an operation attended to. It was so nice that Hat could stay with you the two first nights, but I think perhaps it is as well for her not to stay all the time as you certainly need rest. And when night comes you can go to sleep knowing Papa & she will be down in the a.m. Glad you like your nurse. Wish Mama could step in and see how cosy you look, but I try to think I did the right thing staying home. But Puss you will never know how Mama loves you and how lonely she felt when you all went out of the house that night. But it is all over now. And the dark clouds I trust have passed over leaving only the gilt linings for us now. Rec'd letters from Mrs H.* [Halsted] *and Ella. Both say they are anxious to see you down there and will receive you in their open arms.*

Last eve in all the storm Mick [Prael] *came up and spent the eve. We played Grabouche. Foard & Stokes just sent a very pretty calendar. My it makes me think Xmas is coming but all the Xmas I want is for Puss to be well then we will have a merry Xmas.*

Hattie when you are down town look and see what you can get a ring for Nat for. You know about the style he wants. Should think you could get one for $3 or 4, say not over $5.00, but think a cheaper one will do. I think what would fit Fred would fit Nat. I have asked papa what he wanted I should do about sending money or whether he had some. I do want to have something for Will & Nat Xmas. Wish you would see what you can get a dressing gown for Papa for. Has he gotten an over coat? Will & I were going to give him one, but it seems to me as tho he needs a jacket more. This weather any old coat will do and in the Spring he could get a light one. What do you think? Can you find any little things cheap that will do for the K's – or some little vases I could give to Mrs T. [Tuttle] or S [Sherman]! Anything that is pretty and cheap. See if you can find some and send up by Papa. I must have a few trifles or I should be lonely Xmas. Nat wants neck tie.

Louise I have been fixing your night dress this a.m. and want to finish it to day as Rozetta is coming up tomorrow to show me how to make those spool cases. In the package I send I shall put that Indian basket for Mrs. H. [Halsted] & you must tell her about it being made by the last one of the tribe & all. And the hdkf case is for M[arge], just a little token of love – that is all this Xmas. I am going to write Mrs Adcock [in Chicago] before Xmas. Hope by & by when you will send her a picture or piece of fancy work. Try to write her by & by when you feel strong.

Well I don't have much to write for I have not been out except to Mrs K. Sunday since you left. When the weather is better, now that I hear such good news, I shall try to go out. Was so glad to get all your letters and look every morning for one from my dear little girls –

Here is a good nights kiss for both

From Mama

Nat says he is going to write tomorrow.

Wednesday, just done lunch   [December 8, 1897]

Dear Eben, Louise, & Hat

Mama is going to address this letter to her little Puss. And she can have the pleasure of opening it if Papa and Hat are not at the hospital, then when they come you must let them read it for there is nothing going on but what I can tell it all in one letter. Rozetta came this a.m. and is still here helping me make some of those spool and pin cases. So I thought I would get excused and answer my letters I got this a.m. before anyone else comes. Dear Puss, Mama's heart aches to be with you. And wishes she could take your pains herself, but the idea that the trouble is <u>all</u> removed and will not have to be <u>done</u> <u>over</u> must help you, and all of us, to bear up. And I feel that each day you are getting better and stronger and before long it will all be over and you will among your friends in Los A. and will soon forget you were ever at the hospital. Such weather as we are having would have driven you wild. Saturday after I mailed my letter the storm increased; we had thunder & lightning, wind, rain, hail, and in fact all kind of weather. In the afternoon about four o'clock, Mrs Upshur, Mrs H. Allen, Mrs. Chutter &

110

Mary Ed all happened in together. When Mary Ed went, she went down into the cellar and just as she got to bottom of stairs, such a bright flash came it lit the whole place up. We were alone in the eve. Nat, Lila & I played cards, then at nine started off to bed for we had not been able to sleep the night before. About ten, such a thunder storm, lightning so you could see all over the room. Nat had fallen asleep so I had to stand it alone. I wished Papa was here. Hattie writes that he looks like a different person.

Hattie you are a good sister & nurse. Go out when you can and don't get sick. As L. improves, you must go around and enjoy your visit all you can.

Mama

Mailing date: Astoria. Oregon DEC 19 6:30PM '97
Received: DEC 23 1:30PM '97 San Francisco, Cal.
Addressed to: Miss Tallant Children's Hospital San Francisco California
The envelope was sealed with wax and forwarded from Astoria. The letter is from her cousin, Mary Crosby, the younger daughter of Ellen M. Easton Crosby and Charles C. Crosby.

Nantucket   Dec 12th

My Dear Louise,

I only learned yesterday of the severe trial which you have undergone with your foot and I hasten to send you my sympathy for your suffering and congratulations that the operation is safely over and that your foot can be saved. The journey down to San Francisco must have been very tiresome to you as well as painful and you must have been glad to reach your journeys end. I can realize some thing of the discomforts which you have bourn for I once hurt my foot. Injured one of the muscles by falling in a roller-skating rink and I well remember the agony of mind and body which I endured when I had to stay shut up in the house and all the other girls were going about and having a good time; finally managed to hobble after them with the help of a cane but did not find that very satisfactory. However, it did not last a long time as yours has done and I hope soon to hear that you are able to walk about again and enjoy yourself without enduring pain.

Your mother wrote that you were expecting to go South and spend the cold weather where you could be out of doors. No doubt that will benefit you as I am a firm believer in fresh air as a cure for ills – mental and physical.

It is lovely and warm here nearly all Winter. I am sitting now by an open window and the wood fire in my room is rather uncomfortable. I wish you could be here as there is no purer air in the world than in Nantucket. I have a lovely little horse and open carriage and could drive you about. Also a bicycle, but I much prefer my horse, although I find my wheel very useful especially for getting out to the Golf links.[109] Has the Golf fever reached you on the Pacific Coast? We are all rank mad on the subject and have some fine new links, which are said to be the most like the old Scottish links of any in the country. Every body plays here – old and young. There are several ladies over sixty that played several times this summer. I had little Alice here and she went wild over it and played in one of the junior tournaments. But if I get to writing about Golf I should never stop and if you are not a convert you can not understand a golfers enthusiasm.

Give my love to Harriet, also to Uncle Eben, who I believe is with you. It seems a long time since you were here as little girls – and I suppose you have all most forgotten old Nantucket. Wishing you a Merry Xmas and a brighter New Year, I am

Your affectionate cousin,

Mary Crosby

Wednesday. Noon. 15th   [December 1897]

Dear Hattie & All.

I am going to address this letter to you Hat for it seems a long time since I have done so but then all are for you, but I have imagine[d] that if they came addressed to the hospital you would get them quicker than tho sent to Page St. Recd Papa's Sunday letter but am glad that I recd a telegram with later news yesterday. So hope now Puss will not have any more set back, but will gain rapidly. I am in such a hurry to see her handwriting then I shall feel she is getting better but don't want her to write until she is rested and a good deal stronger. After I closed my letter to you yesterday we had a regular run of callers. Mrs Berry, Violet Bowlby, Gemma Lewis, Mrs Gus Kinney & Fannie. So the afternoon slipped away quickly. After dinner it did not rain so they insisted we all walked down to Mrs Berry's which we did. Sat there until little after nine. Came home and went to bed. I slept better for having been out altho I think the telegram had lots to do with it. It was the first time I had been below Mrs H's since you went and seemed quite like going to a city. Stores kept open until nine now but I did not see anyone in them and very little to buy if one goes in. I do hope you will be able to find some little toys for the Kendall children. You don't say anything about getting ring and had I realized how L was should not have asked it of you, but that first telegram gave us such hope, that I almost imagined her out of the hospital by this time. As it is, don't do anything about it for I am going to see if Will will let me have the gold chain he says Suzanne has to sell for something for Nat.

---

[109] It is believed golf might have been invented many years ago in Scotland. One of the early rules apparently was "Gentlemen Only – Ladies Forbidden" and thus the word "GOLF" entered the English language.

This afternoon Lila and Miss [Irene] Philips take their work and go down and sit with Violet. Tomorrow they go to Genie's if it is pleasant. I shall go up to Annie's while Lila visits G. Our Euchre Club meets at Mrs Stokes this eve. Annie is going over this eve to help her girl. I shall not go as I do not care to go without Papa. It seems nice not to hear the old wind blow. You will see by paper that they say it has been the hardest & longest storm ever known. This a.m. I did mending and let down sleaves on Nat's over coat. Don't know what I shall do if he grows any more. Lila says give girls my love and tell them I will write soon. Tell Papa there is nothing to write - but not enough for two letters. So he will have to take this as his.

Everything goes on smoothly at home but I shall be very glad to see him I assure you. Fred [Kendall] does not know when he shall come down but I guess now not until after Xmas. I am afraid you will not get home by Xmas but it will be all right for we shall not do anything. Will says he rather wants to go to Portland to the games Xmas but does not want to be away from home, but perhaps I shall insist upon his going for there will be nothing to keep him at home.

Give Papa a good kiss for me. I am going to try to get dressed before L- goes - or any one comes for most every P.M. I get caught before getting clothes changed. Nat was pleased to get your letter Hat. Now Puss here is such a <u>*big kiss*</u> *that when H- gives it to you, you will think there is an earth quake, but if she leaves anything of you, just give her as good as she sends and tell her it is from*

Mama

The four daughters of Nantucket's William Redwood Easton (1803-1894) and Eliza Baxter Easton (1802-1889): Left to right - Ellen M.; Louise's mother, Mary Elizabeth (*aka* Lizzie); Harriet Richmond and Charlotte Ann. Charlotte wed Fred Wellington of Boston. Ellen M. Easton married Charles C. Crosby in 1860 – they visited the Tallants in Astoria and may have been related to the Crosby family on Bond Street.

Eliza Baxter Easton   - Nantucket -   William Redwood Easton

Six Easton Women. Mary Elizabeth, center.

Mary Elizabeth Easton Tallant – Astoria

Harriet Easton – Hartford (1885)   Ellen M. Easton Crosby – Nantucket
(No portrait photo is found of Charlotte Easton Wellington as an adult.)

Friday 17th 1896 [Lizzie meant 1897]

Dear girls,

When this reaches you papa will probably be on his way home, and you will miss him, but Louise you must try to <u>feel happy</u> over his <u>going</u>, knowing if you were not a great deal better and well on the road of improving, he would not have left. So that alone must give you courage and cheer you. And it will not be long now before your suffering are over and you are on your feet again. You have had a great deal to go through with, but have come out all right which had you lingered much longer at home might have been a great deal worse. So <u>cheer up</u> and when you get to L.A. and are driving around you will soon forget all your pain and trouble and the world will look bright once more to you. This noon Pearl came in and took lunch with us. She said she was going to send you a Xmas present. So is Olga & Nellie, so you will have a good many presents after all. When Aunt C's box comes I will send hers to you. Shall send my package tomorrow to the express as the Stea. leaves Sun. Shall send it to Page St. and Hattie will see that you get your things, if you are not at Aunt F's. Papa wrote Fannie is sick. I do hope she is better by this. Lila is going down to the *Perry* with Miss P-, Violet, Nellie & Olga. Says she will write tomorrow. I was down town this A.M. with L-. and Miss P- when Miss P- got your letter, H[arriet]. She was glad to get it. I have had a chapter of accidents lately. Last eve Nat ran against the umbrella holder & broke it. Just now I was dusting the hall, knocked over lamp, round shade went into a thousand pieces, then I went to move table – over went Nat's Chinese boat & that went to smash. So I called L[ila] to come & finish dusting for me. Guess now that L.[Louise] is improving so rapidly, that my nerves will get quieted down soon.

It rained hard when we were down town but it is trying to clear off now. Nat has finished your net H. And I will send it by mail today so you can use it if you like before Xmas. It would be a nice present to give Fannie. I send Aunt F. one of those spool cases in your package. Nat is going to send that bright net & another he has made to Alice & Edith. That is all I shall send them. Shall try soon to write Mrs Adcock. Shall only send a spool case to Aunt C. & hdkfs case to E. Shall not try to remember the others. Will put that basket into the package & L. can give it to Mrs Halsted when she goes down. Shall not try to remember the Ks this Xmas, only by letter. Tom is up now trying to stop the leak in bath tub. It is now most three and I have not changed my clothes so will close this. And shall write every day if only a few lines for I do not have much to write about. The Stokes house is almost all boarded in. And as I said before does not interfere with any of the windows except Nats. It will look much better than the open lot.

Now dear girls you must try to amuse each other. And don't get blue. Only think how much worse off you might be. With your good nurse, friends, Uncle Nat [Eben's older brother] and Aunt F. [Fannie] and family, you will have a <u>good</u> Xmas wherever you are. And all we want to make us happy is to know that Puss is out of pain, Hattie well, and we all will be merry if we cannot be together. It might have been much more lonely for all. So only look on the <u>bright</u> <u>side</u>. Sealed with kisses from us all to our dear <u>little</u> <u>girls</u>.

Mama.

Saturday 18th   2.30.

Dear Girls.

I rather imagine Louise setting up in her chair to let Papa see how <u>grand</u> she looks before he leaves. Well the letters today are the best yet. No more chat. which means so much, for now that the wound is healing the pain will soon be over. I do hope Puss when you get up you will not try to over do. I think when you can sit up in a chair & be wheeled out into the air you will gain your strength rapidly. As lovely as it will be if you can get to Aunt Fannie's by Xmas, I would not have you think of it unless the Drs say it is perfectly safe. Don't be over anxious for no matter where you are on Xmas you and we all have so much to be thankful for that it will be a pleasant day any way. I have just put up the Xmas package. You will think you are <u>going to get something</u> when you see the size of it, but Puss's dress, your ball dress H. make a big package. I have made a present for each. Louise, I want you to <u>examine</u> yours very carefully and see if you don't think Mama quite an artist. L. you must take your waist and sleeping gown for your Xmas - for that and the money to get to L.A. is all I can do this time.

Hattie, I hope you will enjoy your gift. I took much pleasure in making it. And you can count the stitches to find all the love it contains. Nat sends a little gift. Hope H. you attended to <u>his</u> <u>order</u>. I sent the net by mail today as you will want it to send to L.A. & I don't want you to open package until Xmas.

Papa in his letter says he "shall not leave until L. can sit up." but Will read telegram Thursday which is later than letter saying he is coming. If he does not come this Stea. he cannot get here by Xmas, but as lonely as I should be I will not complain if he stays on Louise's acct., but from todays letter I feel L. is getting along so rapidly now that she will not mind his coming for I think he feels he ought to be here. Sorry to hear they are all sick at Aunt Fannie's. If they are not better I do not think I should want L. to go there anyway – but it might be only a cold. If it is fever of any kind should not want H. at there.

Olga sent a little gift to each of you which is in the box with some others. Aunt C's [Clara Foard] or Ella's package has not come, expect it will be on the Stea. Tues. If so will open and send yours to 912 Page St. Tuesday so you can have it Xmas. Pearl asked where to send & told her at Hospital so you will have to call them if L. does leave. L[ila] will go home Wed whether Papa comes or not as she wants to get home by Xmas. Now Louise don't worry because Papa left. Eat all you can, the more you eat & the more cheerful you keep, the sooner you will gain strength and get down to L.A. where so many dear friends are anxious to have you. Don't I *wish I could see you after all this suffering and give you a mother's love & kisses, but you know you & Hattie both are always in my mind, and the best Xmas present I can ask for is that you both are well & Louise free from pain.*

All send love & kisses

Mama

Eben W. Tallant was enroute to Astoria by steamer for a very short visit with Mary Elizabeth and his younger son Nat before returning to San Francisco to spend Christmas with Louise and Harriet. He wrote his letter on the Oregon Railroad & Navigation Company's stationery.

Mailing date: DEC 21 4PM 1897 Portland Ore.
Received: DEC 23 130PM '97 San Francisco, Cal.
Addressed to: Miss M. Louise Tallant at Children's Hospital

[December 21 was a Tuesday]

4.30'

Drawing dark. Getting Rough and quite cold. Mrs Gunn has severe headache so I have had to hunt up other lady acquaintances. Just after lunch I got into conversation with a very pretty girl [next to] my room. A Portland girl, she gave me her name but it sliped my mind. She is from Mills College going home for Christmas vacation. She knew of [our] Will Tallant; also that he had two sisters, friends of the Sutherland girl and the Johnson boys. So I put in considerable part of the afternoon with her and her friends.
We shall be in Astoria very early in morning. Will close now. Give my love to Miss Philips, McKee, Murphy, Munroe and others. A week from now I will be with you if nothing happens to interfere.

Good Night, Puss & Hat

Your affectionate father

Xmas Day 4. P.M. At Freds [110]   [Saturday]

Dear Eben & Girls –

My thoughts have been with you all day wondering if you Eben were having a pleasant trip and thinking of the girls, hoping they were opening their presents which they have; whether Louise was out of pain – etc etc. We came up here last eve. Will went up to Portland. We had a very pleasant eve. The tree looked very pretty. Mr & Mrs Troyer, Mrs Cooper and her two girls, Dr W- were here. All had a number of presents. Some of Fred & Annie's were very pretty cut glass & silver. They were delighted with the bell. Fred said it was the best present he had.

---

[110] Fred P. Kendall was the superintendent of the Pacific Can Company, adjacent to the Astoria Wharf and Warehouse. He and Nathaniel Weld Tallant formed the Alaska Coast Fishing Company, headquartered in San Francisco. Fred and his wife Annie resided in Astoria at 372 Franklin during these years.

We did not get to bed until after twelve. I was very tired, never woke until I heard the church bells, then found I never had turned over for the night. The first thing when we awoke Nat & I sat up in bed and opened Louise & Hattie's packages. Olga had told me about the lace, Louise. I shall be delighted to have it and will try to have either a new black dress or waist as you propose by the time you get the other done. Accept a good kiss & thanks for it and the thimble. Harriet your hdkf is a beauty. I don't wonder your eyes are troubling you. As much as I like to have these pretty hdkfs. I should not want you to do them if your eyes trouble you. You must give them a rest now. And here is a good big kiss as thanks.

Nat was delighted with the ties. Wore one down to breakfast. He will thank you by letter. After I had gotten through with your packages, Nat gave me a little box with the cutest little silver pencil for purse. Then I gave him his ring & watch chain. He was happy over the ring. And it would amuse you to see him work his hands so as to show it. Hope Fred is as pleased with his.

Nat went to office but was just too late to get package. I had a letter from Alfred [Alfred Wellington, a cousin; son of Charlotte A. Easton and Fred Wellington, Boston] saying he had sent a big package, so Nat is going down at five and will mail this and try to get it - he brought me H's letter. I am so sorry Louise to hear that you have had another abcess which has caused you so much pain. Mama hopes & prays you may be spared anymore. I was so delighted to see your writing, but don't try to write if it tires you. While Papa and H are there let them do it for you. As much as I have enjoyed your notes I am willing to wait until you feel better. I expect you will be surprised tomorrow to see Papa as from your letter you seem to think he left here this a.m. He has a lot of pretty presents for you and the girls have sent you lots which I have not seen. So if Louise is only free from pain you will have a very happy day tomorrow with papa and all those nice Xmas gifts.

Annie & the children have gone over to Mrs Cooper's tree with the children. Fred & Nat are down stairs. And as Nat has to go up to house and then to office I shall close this as it does not rain now (although it has been a dismal day - rain & wind) - so he can go & get back before it gets late, as they insist upon our staying here tonight, for which I am very glad for it would be dismal at home.

I have made a list of presents as well as I can remember and will add others when I get them as I know of one or two more coming. Will send any that come to you and enclose yours to Papa's. Eben, as I cannot give you a Xmas kiss in person, the girls will have to give it to you. And if you give them all I sent they will be pretty well kissed. Will said he ment to have written yesterday but would when he got home. Fred goes to Portland tomorrow night, returns Tues. Annie & children go to beach. Will address this letter to the hospital as I expect you all will be there. Am anxious to hear how L. is, so do write every day with out fail to you loving wife &

Mama.

118

Mailing date: DEC 26 6:30 PM 97 Astoria, Oreg.
Received: DEC 30 11 AM 97 San Francisco, Cal.
Addressed to: Miss Louise Tallant at Childrens Hospital

Sunday. At Freds.   [December 26, 1897]

Dear Eben & Girls.

Well Mama felt happier this a.m. than she has for a long time. Nat went down to office and came home with Harriet's letter. It did me good to hear that Louise even felt well enough to <u>try to</u> play cards. I know this a.m. you must have been very much surprised when Papa walked in as your letter says "can't wait until Monday to see him." It will be all the pleasanter and such a lot of nice presents as you will have to look at to day. Louise it will repay you for having to stay alone part of Xmas.

Louise that colar [collar] came this a.m. It is a beauty and I don't know of any thing that would have pleased me more for I admired it so when you were working on it. I surely should have to have a new dress to wear them on. Many thanks. That & H's hdkfs. show what industrious girls I have. I sent a letter off by Nat yesterday P.M. and when he came home Mr K & I were keeping house while A- & children were at the C's [Cooper] tree. When Nat came in it looked like Santa Clause coming - he had so many packages. Mrs Starbuck sent Papa a picture in water col[or]. - Nantucket snow scene – and the funny part is in one corner of picture is 'L.T.' – letters look just like the ones L. makes. I almost thought L did it. If it is admired we shall have to say now see who did it. When H. gets home will let her fix a glass over it. Mrs S. sent me a very nice linen center piece or rather <u>platter</u> piece hem stitched and very fine nice linen. Clara – a very pretty cut glass olive dish. Mrs Adcock's present pleased me as much as any I recd as it seems so nice to think they still remember us. It is a very handsome pair of ivory glove stretchers with very heavy silver handles. Louise she sent you a book which I shall send. Lila sent me a very pretty piece of Battenberg. And Sadie sent Nat a little perl letter opener with silver handle. This a.m. in mail was L['s] lace & a Pho[tograph] for L. from Seattle. I looked at it. It is very good, shall mail it tomorrow.

Nat brought up notice for reg[istered] package which we shall get tomorrow, then I shall send all the things as I think the bags will have something in it for you. Should like to have been with you when you open the boxes. Don't you think your belts fine? Eben, I shall send L. & H.'s gift to you as it will be very useful & just what you wanted. H's letter makes me feel as tho now L. would go ahead & get well quickly and I do hope nothing more will come. There is Fred so I will go down as it is dinner time & finish for him to take to P[ortland] tonight – he goes on the *Lurline* at 6 P.M. Annie just came into room – said Fred wanted her to go to P. with him & wanted us to stay to night with Miss M. & baby, so we shall stay. – After dinner it has come on such a storm – blows a gale. They have decided to give up going to P. until *tomorrow. We shall stay as Will is in Portland, though he should come home on day boat. Dr Walker is here so I am going to give this to him as it is too stormy for Nat to go out to mail it. This must ans[wer] for all. Nat is going to write during the week. We both send love & kiss and hope to hear a great improvement in L.-*

> *Good night kiss from*
> *Yours only,*
> *Lizzie*

How are H's eyes – she did not speak of them in letter?

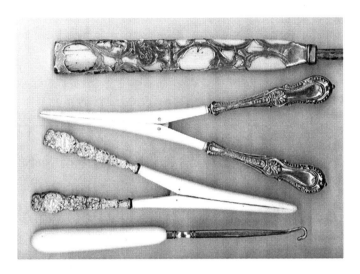

Mary Elizabeth received the gifts pictured for Christmas 1897. Her son Will gave her the ivory handled silk umbrella. The handle is wrapped with a fillagreed sterling silver design on which her name is etched. The date "25 Dec '97" is etched on the end of the handle. Mrs. Adcock (Chicago) presented Lizzie with the ivory glove stretchers with sterling silver handles and the ivory handled buttonhook. Buttonhooks were necessary to help do up the tiny buttons on both gloves and high-topped shoes.

The letter written by Louise's mother on the 26 December included the following list of Christmas gifts received by her and young Nat:

List of Presents   Christmas 1897

To Mary Elizabeth	From
Handsome patterned rocker	Papa
Fine silk umbrella. Ivory handle with lace work of silver all over it	Will
Bedstead. hair mattress & springs	Brother Nat
Nice silver pencil for purse & umbrella stand	Little Nat
Lace collars & thimble	Louise
Hem stitched hdkf.	Harriet
Table cover Delft	Little James
Handsome night dress	Clara [Foard in San Gabriel]
Very pretty work bag	Cousin S. [Sarah] Parker
Lovely hdkf.	Mrs Stokes

Pretty center piece wild roses	Fannie
" " " Battenberg	Mrs Sanborn
Picture in silver frame "Two Farewells"	Fred [Kendall]
Pretty box lined in yellow silk	Annie [Kendall]
Bag made of hdkfs, blue ribbon sewn in corners	Ada
Four little mats	B & L Scudder
Xmas card	Miss Mason
Handsome white silk pin cushion	Mrs Ellis
----yellow silk & lace----	Ella
Burnt leather Pho[tograph] Case	Mrs Berry
Calendar, Nantucket Historical scenes, Island Home	Aunt Ellen
& view of Nantucket	
One of those calendars that are tied with ribbons & close	Aunt Harriet [Easton]
up to drop down long with pretty little	
pictures & verses	
Center piece spanish work	Mrs Kerckhoff

Nat's Presents   Christmas 1897

Ring – stone something the style of Will's only smaller	Papa & Mama
Silver watch chain	Will
1/2 doz hdkfs with "T"	Aunt Clara [Foard]
Two neck ties	Foard, F. & James
" "	Louise & Harriet
Drinking cup	Mrs. Kendall
Puzzle	Neal
box cartridges	Fred
Pretty calendar	Aunt Hattie Easton
Lovely pair light blue silk suspenders -	Dr Walker
hand-painted blue violets	
White chair for room	Papa & Mama
Whisk broom & case	Louise & Harriet
Vaseline jar - silver top	Nat [his uncle]
Neck tie	Aunt Clara

With considerable difficulty, Louise wrote the following letter to Dick - in pencil.

Mailing date: DEC 29 6 AM '97 San Francisco. Cala.
Received: Jan 1 7 AM 1898 Astoria. Oreg.
Addressed to: Mr. Richard E. Carruthers
               Astoria
                 Oregon.

Dec. the 27th 1897

Dear Dick

   It was so nice of you to send me just what I wanted that I am going to write and thank you right away even if my hand is so unsteady that unless you knew I had not left this dear little <u>narrow</u> short white iron bed of mine for over three weeks or even turned over in it for the last two - you might think that in gay S.F. I had been having too gay a time. I wanted to write Xmas letters to the girls and you but could not. Just the last few days I have [been] much better. This writting and the rate at which I go remind me of when I first went to school.

Dr Sherman tortures me ever[y] other day – how I dread to see him come. He says tomorrow I must get up in a wheeling chair. My bones seem to be coming through – I only weighed 108 when I got here and I must be a shadow now. It is a good thing I did not know what sufferring was before me or I wouldn't have enjoyed last summer much.

We must all have of troubles and our pains in this world, Dick, and I tell you some of them are mighty hard to bear as you know. I can't realize that it is about two months since I have walked and goodness only knows when I will walk again.

Harriet is a perfect treasure; she stays with me all day long. Papa come[s] out to breakfast with me at seven and stays with me in eve until they give me my sleeping dose. I haven't had a minutes natural sleep since I have been here. But dear me seems to me I am writing lots about my troubles and now that the worst is over I ought not to think of them. My address will be Childrens Hospital for some time yet –

We had lots of Xmas presents and I do realy thank you so much – you are extravagant to send so much. Did you and Sadie enjoy the dance. I hope you can read this – I have been a long time trying to write it and "clean tuckered out" now so good bye from

Louise

I address this to L. as I sent last to Page St. L.

Sunday Jan 2, 1898.

Dear Eben & Girls.

Recd your letter finished by Harriet this a.m. Don't understand why you have not heard as there never has been a day since you first left that I have not sent a letter. I believe there <u>was</u> one night that Will forgot to mail it and I put it into express package so it got there just as soon. What good news from Louise - how she must have enjoyed being out of doors. Now I feel she will pick up quickly. Hope next thing to hear she is getting around on her crutches. Was disappointed not hearing how the girls liked their Xmas package but suppose the exertion of getting Louise out, etc was too much for them to think of anything else. It is rainy again & looks dismal enough out. Nellie went home this a.m. I have invited Mrs Heilborn up to dinner for five o'clock dinnr makes a long evening although I guess we shall be glad to get to bed early for every night we have been up or kept awake until late.

Last eve after I finished your letter Nell & I walked down to mail it & went into Mrs Berry's. It was a perfect moon light night. Came home about ten o'clock. Will got home this a.m.. I have hardly seen him for he ate his breakfast before we were up. He asked me to ask you to bring up some more Quail. I don't know anything about the boats, but Will was over there Thursday. I will tell him what you said when he comes to dinner. We are going to have our New Year's dinner. Roast beef & plum pudding. Hope to hear Louise still continues to improve.

Will she have to have the Dr come to Aunt Fannie's and check her foot? Won't it be nice when she can get around her self even if she does have to use her crutches for a while. Recd a letter from Aunt Ellen. She sends much love to all, particularly to Louise. You must have enjoyed the concert. How glad I am L. could get out there. I should think it would give one the horrors to see so much suffering. Very kind of the W's [Worths] to call.

Hope to hear Miss Philips [Louise's roommate in the hospital] is better. Please remember me to her and tell her I hope to hear fond reports from her. By the way girls – Miss Philips [Irene Phillips, Astoria] has entirely forgotten me – never telephones nor comes to see me. They say she has quite fallen in love with Nelly. Can't let her move with out her. Dr. T [Tuttle] telephoned to see how Puss [was doing]; said "he & Nettie were coming up but every eve Nettie was taken up with Miss P-." Jay has left school and gone to be with his mother & I hear Nettie is going to stay here all winter. She has moved into Mrs Green's. I met her Xmas eve as Nat & I were going up to Annie's. She said she & her father were up one eve while Papa was here the eve we went to the Sanborn's. I invited her to come see me & she said she would.

It is most time for postman to be around so I will close as I like to be sure and get them mailed & it is three o'clock. Shall be glad when I hear you say when you are coming but hardly dare look for you next Stea. Can't get letters tomorrow but hope to in the P.M. Kisses all around & lots of love & sympathy to Fannie & family. Love to Bro[ther] Nat.

Your own

Lizzie. T.

Dick wrote a New Year's letter to Louise.

Astoria, Or   Jan 4 '97   [meant 1898]

Dear Louise:

Your very nice letter received and was glad to hear that you were improving and hope by this time your foot is stoped giving you any trouble whatever. Of course we all keep posted in regards to your health, Etc. and are pleased or dissatisfied according to the news received.

It was real good in you to write me, and under the difficulty which you had to do so. I am glad that you liked what I sent although I was not any too sure about what to send, and am only sorry that it was not nicer.

I received my cigar ribbon tobacco pouch and it was a dandy, also a few other smokers articles from Marg – it was kindness on her part, I am sure.

Grace [Dick's older sister] gave me a very pretty water color of Hug Point and I bought a little oil of Hay Stack so you see my room is a gentle hint of a good old ten days gone bye never to be forgotten. Your mother was look[ing] well when I last saw her "We use her as a sort of storm signal in regards to your self." I don't know if she would like that comparison or not but must be taken the right way. I am getting along finely and at present am night watchman of the *Jessie* ranking as Capt while *Wm Young* as Lt., and T. Crosby as steward - we've had some very good times on the old ship and several stag parties. So you see the *Perry* crew are not the only pebbles on the beach, when it comes to 'Hofficers. The next dance will be Friday. The last was very nice and I had a very good time indeed. Of course it could have been added to by the presence of your self and good nurse Harriet. Harriet will have to be hard up for all her work when she arrives home. When she does which I hope will be soon as that will be another good sign.

Well there is very little news, and as I am not around much I am probably not on to what little there is. But the girls I guess keep you posted on every thing. I might add that Flavel's gave an afternoon to us, we boys, New Years day, and it is the only place I've been here lately. I've not been up to Heilborn's for so long I am to tell the truth ashamed to go, but will have to make a start in that direction soon for aperance sake at least. I think 1898 or at best the fore part of it will be a dull one for me, but now I am getting to troubles so I'll quit.

The next dance comes off Friday and as yet I have no pardner, so I will have to content myself with the latest song "Everybody has a Lady but me."

Well I presume you are good and tired of this so will close hoping that you are about recovered and will soon be on your way to Los Angeles. Hoping to hear from you

I am your Etc

Dick

The *Commodore Perry* was a U.S. Government Revenue Cutter, stationed in Astoria and Seattle. It was primarily used to interdict opium smugglers on the high seas along the West Coast.

Angus "Gus" Carruthers

Charles Berkeley and Dick Carruthers

Thursday 6. P.M.   [January 6, 1898]

Dear Girls.

Have just now come in from Mrs Sanborn. Sewed until five then went in there, found Mrs Megler there and we have just come home together. Recd Papa's letter this a.m.

So sorry to hear of Louise having more pain & Dr S- having to attend her again, but she seems to bear up under it so much better. It shows how much stronger she is getting. Papa wrote about your brief trip to Park and the fun you girls had. And Louise's boquet the gardner gave her. I sent you quite a long letter yesterday but have not been anywhere to get much news. Mrs C- [Harriet Carruthers] and Mrs [Grace] Allen called this afternoon to hear about you girls and sent lots of love. Said Margie sent Dick such a nice Xmas present.

Last night or rather this morning at three o'clock the fire bell rang. Nat looked out, saw a lot of smoke. We telephoned Control and they said it was the "Astor House" but today found out it was that blacksmith's shop opposite Fisher's hall and next to the Prael's barn. Mrs C- [Carruthers] said Mr C- got up and went down [so] that they got the horses all out but the building did not catch as the wind blew the fire down Street. I hope Papa is having such a nice day on the ocean as we have had. If so he will have a nice trip up. Last trip of the State she got here at 9.30 in the a.m. Hope she does now. Here comes Will so I shall have to hurry up and get him to mail this. You will miss Papa very much but I hope before long Louise will be getting around on her crutches. Can you wheel the chair for her? I have so many things I want to ask Papa about seems as tho I can't wait for him to come. Has L. done anything about getting a jacket? I should think you could order some out for her to look at, as I should think she would want to take advantage of sales. Papa did not say anything about Flora [Kimball-Parkhurst] so I guess she must be getting better. Let me know what they hear from Frank [Smith]. I do hope he will not have to give up and come home sick. Give them all lots of love and sympathy from me.

Nat wants to go down to Pasey this eve and play a while. The eve's are long when we sit here alone after dinner. Louise, do you think you could get my fountain pen fixed – it needs a new pen! And they are so nice to write with & just what you need as you can write in bed or in lap and not have to have ink around. If H. thinks she can have it fixed I will send it.

Nat says if Papa does not come and fly around a little he will not get the pilot com[mission] as there are so many after it. I do hope he will for we shall need all we can get this year. When I think of what Drs H- & B- did it makes my blood run cold. Well this not much of a letter but it will be something to get when the postman comes. When L. gets out of hospital I shall not write every day for realy there is nothing to write. Nat will run down and mail this. So will close with love & kisses

From Mama

Friday   11 0 a.m. at sea

Dear Children

Here I am on my lonely trip the pleasure before me of getting home, the pain in my mind of leaving you girls. Here's my journal to date. I have Room X a newly built room on upper deck. I had hoped to have a room all to my self. For first half hour after leaving Wharf was confident I had for there was no baggage but my own in room and no one else had entered. I then pressed the button, called the room boy, gave him a half dollar, told him to put my three dozen quail into ice house then lower middle bunk down to give me good breathing room. He came back, reported I was to have a room mate but the man had no baggage. Soon he showed up. The only baggage he had was a bottle of linement (that smelt to heaven) and a spare collar button. His only additional incumberance was a sprained ankle. Goodness! Will I ever get rid of hospital work, was my thought.

At 11. 0 30 I went to purser's room for meal tickets. Got seat #96 --- on Columbia I had table 1, seat 2, at Capt's right. This seat however proved to be the best in the State. Pursers right. - two ladies between me & him. Captain's table not set, nor has it been yet. Meals were good and I enjoyed them. Took a siesta after lunch   Did not see much of room mate but at 4'0 invited him to try some of Joe Marshal's whiskey. It struck him happly - he took about three fingers - swallowed it straight. This steamer is not as comfortable as the Columbia. [111] Officers and boys less attentive. rooms cold. no electric lights. Meals however about as good. I ate hearty dinner. had a smoke. went to bed at eight. soon fell asleep. partner came in later. closed door and windows. pulled his curtains. I woke up at 9 o 30 [9:30 p.m.] smothered. Seems they have a steam pipe under the lower bunk which thus give full force at night. I got out. opened window wide. went back to bed and slept fairly well balance of night. got up at 7. boy had not cleaned my shoes and did not bring coffee & toast.

Harriet - time your return on *Columbia*.

4 o P.M.   Had a long afternoon nap. woke up to find we are in Oregon weather. a driving rain S W wind with Rain. nothing interesting to report.

Saturday 3 .30 a.m.

Inside Astoria harbour.   will be home by four o'clock.

Fine smooth trip and I am about clear of my cold

Give my love to Miss Phillips, Dr. Murphy, Miss Hancock and others.

hastily closed by

your loving father

Saturday   2. P.M.

Dear Girls.

Well Papa came walking in upon us this morning at four o'clock. I heard the Stea. when she whistled. Had not been asleep since three - heard the cuckoo strike three and soon after the whistle sounded. He had a lovely trip smooth all the way - everyone at table. I was glad to see him I assure you. We lay and talked until light when the gong sounded. Wasn't I glad to hear such good news from Louise; Papa says she will be able to go to L.A. by the last of next week. I know L. you feel badly to think you will have to use your crutches while there, but don't let it take away any of your pleasure. It is a small thing when you realize how near you came to loosing your foot - and perhaps life.

Now that you are stronger you will realize now what you and the rest of us all have been through. And coming out as well as you have should make us all happy. The Drs here say you can have your shoe made so that you will not limp and think how much better you will be in health, probably better than you have been for years. Dr W- says it will not be long before you are dancing and getting around the same as ever, Anyway Louise we all can't be happy enough that you are well & soon will be stronger than ever. So don't worry about anything. And we will come out on top yet. Will will get rich at Klondike & all will be happy. So let's try to forget

---

[111] The steamer *Columbia* was the first passenger vessel to install electric lights on board.

the past three months or more and thank God for his kindness in restoring our dear Louise's health.

What a lot of nice presents Puss sent. Isn't the vase lovely? The table cover is beautiful. Such work. Did you see the four tassels in box to be sewed on? They are small. Shall use it on state occasions this winter & save it for summer wear & company. The night dress I think lovely, but I know it is too small. Guess I shall have to give it to the <u>first</u> <u>one</u> of you that gets married. Will was wild over it. Said he was going to see if Puss could get him one. The hdkfs are fine. Nat claimed one right off. Olga came up to see them this a.m. – was delighted. Says Puss is all right. That picture L. did it. I hope you will be able to do some work while in L.A. – you may be able to find someone to take a few lesson of. I want you sometime to make some little sketch for Dr Fulton for I feel L. we owe him everything. Dare not think what might have happened had he not spoken to Will when he did. Will sent him some of the Quail Papa brought up. Papa says the men all think he will get the office. Johnnie Fox is working for him. You will see by the paper there are several after it. I hope he gets it. I think Will is in a fair way to make money. He has now gone to bank to see if he can get $300. Not many young men that can wire money as Will can. You will be amused at the piece in paper about the <u>brick</u>.

Hattie, Papa says when you sign this check, sign it "H.T." not "H.E.T." as they did not put the "E" in. I wish if you see anything cheap that will make me a pretty waist you would get it. I think a black silk (India) for summer would be pretty, but you might see one something the style of my new one. Anything cheap & pretty. If you have money enough. Mr Kendall expects to leave the last of next week and will only be a few days in Frisco. I hope you will be ready to come home with him as he will be nice company. We will let you know just when he leaves & he will see or send word to you when he gets there. I think the jacket a beauty – just what I wanted him to get. And how cheap. Well if I write anymore I shan't have any thing to put into tomorrows letter. Dr Tuttle and Nellie called last eve - very pleasant call. Must mail this for the postman as the letters don't go tomorrow a.m. so must be sure and have it go to nights boat. Don't get lonesome without Papa. I don't believe there ever was a papa that did more for a child or children than he has. Now L. you must show your affection by not worrying over what has happened. Only think of what <u>might</u> <u>have</u> <u>happened</u> and I know you will be happy. And here is a good kiss for both my dear girls from their

Loving

Mama

Regards to Miss P. [Phillips – Louise's roommate]
Papa says he didn't know what you should have done without her – he thinks she is a <u>brick</u>.

Olga Heilborn - Astoria

Harriet Tallant – San Francisco

Lillie Kerckhoff – Los Angeles

Cutting Packing Co.
San Francisco,
Agents

Columbia River Packing Co.
PACKERS OF
COLUMBIA RIVER SALMON

Astoria, Oregon   January 18th 1898

My Dear Girls -

Presume you think it's a long time between letters but the fact is your mother and myself are each too busy to write much; besides there does not seem to be much to write about. Your girls probably give you all the doings in your circle of friends and my mind is entirely on business. I can report for Will as he is not likely to write. He has got a new Alaska fever - this time it is to be teaming business at Skagway. Geo Johnson and Will are in equal partnership in it. They start with two pairs of horses and one truck. Tried to get them up on the last trip of Str. Elder but she was so crowded they could not get them on. Have now secured passage on Str. Oregon which is to sail about first of February. George and Jake go up with the teams. They have secured the drayage of Ross, Higgins, Foard & Stokes, Fisher Bros and others who have stores there. If they meet with profitable employment will send up more teams as fast as Will can raise the money to buy them with which he hopes to do by earnings and sales of his nets, boats and Seines. I hope it will prove profitable that he may get out of this uncertain cannery business as it looks now as the bottom had droped out of it. If it does I don't know what I shall do as I am rather old to try new ventures. I got disappointed in Pilot Commission business – personal friendship of Gov Lord and Chas Wright gave the job to him.

All business in Astoria is exceedingly dull as the active workers are giving their entire attention to Alaska, fishermen in particular – all leaving and it looks doubtful about getting anything like a full crew. Received letter yesterday from Bro Nat written 13th reporting arrival of Frank [cousin Frank Smith] and Wife and that they were going to housekeeping by themselves; that Uncle Theo remained in the Islands. I can imagine there was a lively time at Aunt Fannie's that Thursday I left. I am anxious to learn when Louise can start for Los Angeles and whether it will be necessary for you to go with her. I hope Louise will able to go alone. Alice Wood goes to S F on this Steamer to be there a week and return by Rail. She hopes to have Harriet's company back. We told her we thought it would be about right time for Harriet's return.

We received your postal card Sunday and were pleased to learn that Miss Philips had nothing worse than a bad cold. Yet that is bad enough – hope to learn she is better as Louise needs her encouraging voice to cheer her up. I hope Frank can spare time some afternoon to take her to the Park.

It's well Louise is not up here for there would be small chance for an outing as it Rains almost continually - today being particularly severe. S E gale - 50 miles an hour with steady downpour of Rain –

Mary Elizabeth continues the letter. Her writing in light pencil on thin paper is very difficult to read.

Papa just brought up this letter – was glad he had written as I have left my sewing and started on slippers then [too] if H. and Miss P- come up I should not have time to write.

It is an awful storm. Don't know as they will come. I was going down to get Mrs H. to show me how to crochet a slipper so I could do it quicker, but was afraid they would be too thick to wear all the time. The knit ones are light. Such good news from L. makes us all feel fine. When you get to L.A. you will soon get so you can walk. And as soon as you get strong you can have your shoe made and you will never know anything ailed your foot in a little while. I am glad Hat you had a good time at dance. Papa says, if he was L. he would be careful how she let Fan[nie] wear her things for he says she is one that takes no care of anything and you will have to look out L. for no knowing when you can have another satin. Not until we get returns from Klondike.

I wish you would measure your ankle L. and give me some idea how big to make slipper at top. Will try to finish it this week, but I am a slow knitter. If the girls were not coming I think I should go down to Mrs H. and crotchet one. Keep on Louise trying to walk and you will soon get about. What is the cause of not letting people in to hospital? Is there some contagious *sickness there? If so do hurry and get away from there. Hat, look out – don't come down sick again. Lunch bell so seal this with kisses from*

Mama

Evidently the following is a draft of a tongue-in-cheek letter to the hospital nurse, Miss McKee, who cared for Louise and her roommate, Miss Phillips, at the Children's Hospital. Louise, Miss Phillips and Harriet had gotten to know Miss McKee very well during those many weeks. Miss McKee was likely the nurse for Louise and Miss Phillips.

Dear Miss McKee.

Deeply appreciating the fact that we are on the rapid rd. to recov. & we will soon be able to dispense with your services, & being deep ext. grateful for the latter fact, as you have a very depressing effect on our nervous system, we present you this token of our gratitude for your unturning efforts in making our stay here as miserable as possible.

Hoping that every time you have oc. to look at this calendar you will think of the unfor. who presented it to you and will endeavor to mend your ways and try to render the lives of your future victims a little more endurable. We are

Your[s] Sincerely

L. Tallant

H. Tallant

M. Phillips

Mailing date: JAN 20 6.30 PM 98 Astoria, OREG.
Received: JAN 24 4.30 PM San Francisco, CAL.
           Second receipt date: JAN 25 6.30 PM
Addressed to: Miss Maria L Tallant
           Childrens Hospital, California St. is crossed out. Written below is:
           912 Page St.
           San Francisco Cal.

Astoria, Oregon, January 20th 1898

My Dear Children

We were greatly disappointed today at not receiving even a postal card as we received nothing from you yesterday.

Received letter from Uncle Nat this morning under date of 17th in which he reports Louise progressing finely. Otherwise we should have worried. If you cannot find time to write letters you must certainly send postals for we are all extremely anxious to hear from you and your mother gets quite nervous if she does not.

Will is exceedingly busy getting off George and Jake with their horses for Dyea. Will goes to Portland tonight – he speaks of his errand as business connected with Alaska outfit but I surmise the greater call is to be present at the prize fight – Billy Elmer[112] (Willie E. Tohiss?). Nat is busy studying for his Examination which comes off tomorrow. If he passes I have promised to take him to Skipanon Saturday on a gunning trip. He is working hard to go.

We have enjoyed a bit of pleasant weather today. Very little wind - cloudy but only occasionally Rain. Saw Kate this morning, she was looking better than when I saw her Saturday. Your mother was down to Bowling Alley yesterday – played three games – lowest score 21 points. Don't know as you are interested in my work but it seems good now to have something to do. I have six men repairing our roadway and Oscar repairing boats. Tomorrow I have seven hundred cases of Salmon to ship. If I get that all done and have a successful hunt Saturday shall be able to enjoy Sunday rest.

Has your mother ever written about the dogs? Well they are fat and happy. Weighed Harry yesterday – 71 pounds. Harry slept with Annie last night and Trilby with Nat. Your mother heard a noise early this morning which proved to be Trilby barking in his dreams. Investigation found her top of Nat's bed. Of course she was put out in a hurry.

Give my love to Aunt Fanny and all the cousins. Hope to hear good news from Miss Philips.

Affectionately

Papa

Mailing date: San Francisco, Cala   JAN 26 – 6 AM '98
Received: JAN 29 7AM 1898 Astoria, Oreg.

Jan the 24th 1898

Dear Dick

So you had a "sweet little letter from Louise" did you? Well here is another – perhaps it won't be very sweet though for I don't feel very gay but I am glad and thankful to be out of the Hospital. That is a thing of the past even if the future doesn't seem very bright. I suppose I ought only to think of what _might_ _have_ _been_ and how near I came to losing my foot altogether and from – well I am after it all for I do feel well. Every one that saw me a few weeks ago say they never saw such a change and when I get to Los Angeles -- and I plan to leave here next Monday [31st Jan] on the Sunset Limited which leaves here at 5.50 PM and arrives there at 10. AM. Not a long trip is it. I think I can go alone with out any trouble, but I was going to say I think I will soon get my strength back down there driving about with Marge.

Dick I am afraid we have had our last dance together. I didn't know until yesterday just what they had done to my foot.

---

[112]   Billy Elmer fought Dick Case on January 21, 1898, in Portland, but police intervened for an unknown reason. Elmer later played a major role in George Bernard Shaw's play, "Cashel Byron," that opened on Broadway on December 28, 1900.

Hat is anxious to get home for the next assembly dance. Have they desided when it is to be. She has been to several dances down here and had a fine time. I hear Miss Phillips and Nettie are as thick as "Oregon Mist." How do the boys like Miss U. - as much as when she first came? It is so lovely and warm out that I am going to try and get out on the sidewalk and walk on my crutches - don't know whether I can go more than three steps but I am going to try.

Write to me when you can and direct to Alhambra. Give me all the news. If it was only sunnier and warm at home I don't believe I would go to Los A. - it seems as if I had been away ages.   *With love as before*

Louise

Jan. 30, '98   *Portland, Oregon*

Dear Maria -

I just put up all my things to go to bed, and then I hauled them out again, because I felt I didn't want to let another day go by without writing to you. I want to tell you how awfully sorry I am for all you have had to go through, and how glad I am that you are on the road to recovery at last. I was going to tell you about the Marie Antoinette Fete that I am going to take part in - but I don't know but what it would be kind of mean to when you can't dance yourself. I won't tell you about the dance, but about the dress rehearsal. You see this affair is a great big thing for sweet charities sake and half the people in town are involved in it - it is to represent a great fete that was given in honor of Marie Antoinette at some court - and where there were a great many fancy dances given in her honor. There are about a hundred and twenty dancers and dancesses. So you can imagine what a brilliant effect the dress rehearsal was - with all the bright costumes. I am in the shepherdess dance and have a regular "pinky, curly" Bo-Peep costume. Ellen is in the Spanish dance - with yellow petticoat - black bespangled bole-role [?] & black lace mantilla. I have a week's holidays next week between the two terms so the fete won't kill me.

I haven't seen Lila for the longest time. I guess because I am in school at the time that I used to see her so often going down town. Or perhaps she has been keeping your dear mother company again.

Now I must to bed for the Fete cometh when no man can sleep. Think of me cavorting around on the Marquam Grand Stage in short petticoats. Oh, what would my Hood River Methodist land-lady think of me - paint & powder and wig too!!

Your own

Grace.[113]

---

[113] Grace Cranch Eliot is the older daughter of Dr. Thomas Lamb Eliot, who was the first pastor of the First Unitarian Church of Portland. Grace and Louise were the same age.

Dick sent the following greetings to Louise, who had just arrived at Lillie's in Los Angeles to begin her recovery:

Jan 31, 1898

Dear Louise:

Your letter Saturday and I am going to write you this morning. Well Louise I hardly know what to say – that poor foot – and no more dances. Well I know it is awful hard but then there is lots of other things besides dances you know and if it will be of any use to you I'll offer my services to try and make you have a good time. Now I suspose I've made matters worse by writing as I've done but when you arrive home, why I'll receive you with open arms and perhaps if I've made you feel badly upon your receiving this letter I may be able to atone for it. – for really I am going to try and be the same as I use to be. If things do not go against me while you are down in Los Angeles, for really I am a little bit sore at that place and some, say one of its citizens. I know I have no right to be and you need not tell me so either but neverless this thing of getting over certain things is not quite so easy as it might appear to some people, and as long as some lucky fellow has not made his appearance, I am going to try and hang on and when he does, well I want to kill him for your sake, but Jim Corbett and his lonely life by the sea will be my lot. But for goodness sake give me next summer anyway when I'll try.

The next dance is on the 10 th or 11 th. I am going to see that Miss McBride gets there OK. I rather like this little girl although she is not so very handsome she's got good sense and it is the only chance I had for a pardner for this dance. I've only been up to Olga's once since you left – it seems so funny as I use to be there so much before, but I guess I've fallen from grace.

The Library show was a success, it was good there was about 50 people in it and the marching was fine.

Well there is little more I guess so I will close hoping to hear from you soon if it is not asking to much. Regards to Mrs H- [Halsted] *and love to Marge. Keep a little or as much as you think you could stand for yourself. And don't worry but what you are alright.*

Dick

P.S. Well in reading this over I see I said I would receive you with open arms and fearing you might think I was getting quite free, I must explain of course I didn't mean as some might think I did but when you come home I'll try and explain myself. But if you will just kindly consider yourself kissed about 20 or more times, hugged good and hard and let me know the result, it will help me out, i.e. I'll know how to treat the dearest girl a going when you arrive. This is no Josh.

Chapter Five   **February to June 1898**
                                                Recovering in Southern California
                                                          Among Old Friends

An Invitation to Louise:

> You are cordially invited to attend the first Social Gathering
> of the Alhambra Tennis Club,
> February eighth, eighteen hundred and ninety eight, at eight P.M.
> Residence of Mr. J. A. Green
> First Street and Commercial Ave.

The Alhambra Tennis Club issued an invitation to Louise to join their group when Louise was just beginning to recover from her ordeal. She was struggling to get around on crutches and to keep up with her own group of old friends. However, to attend the social gathering of the tennis club would likely have allowed Louise to meet many new people and, thus, kept her busy going places, with less time to dwell on her misfortunes – or on her lingering pain.

An Astoria friend, Nan Reed, *aka* "Maurice," writes Louise, who is now visiting Marge in Alhambra.

Saturday Feb 5 - 1898

My dear Louise:

Guess you are wondering what is the trouble with "Maurice" - nothing only she has not been feeling well all week - been real near the hot water bottle most of the week "so good as new now."

Last night we had our party at Knappton but it wasn't much of a "chafing dish party." Pearl did the inviting and you know how she is, starts out and is only going to invite two or three but ends up with two or three doz. She was only supposed to invite fifteen for last night but twenty-five went and that wasn't all she invited. It rained cat's and dog's but it did not stop the fun. We had a splendid time - danced and played cards. I went with Brother Tom. I think it so much nice[r] for a girl to go with her brother, don't you

So glad you and Marge are enjoying beautiful sun shine. Well the rain is staying with us for the last few days. Getting to be to much of a good thing.

Kate tells me Hat will be with us in a few days. Wasn't she a [dunce?] not to want to go to Los Angeles with you. I wish I could get half a chance like that. I would come a running.

I do wish you and Marge could have been with us during the snow. I just had a circus with dear little Rev. Marcotte.[114] He was out in all his "Glory" and took me down about a doz.[dozen] times. I went down with Chas Higgins and we had a "up tip"- it was funny. Oh, no they didn't josh us. It seems like year's ago when we were all out coasting on the old <u>box</u> we had to pull down the hill. That was in the days of Lem and Dick. <u>Ha</u>. <u>Ha</u>.

I was going to have a party on the fourteenth of this mo. – wish I knew something real new to have for my friends. Can give them all a Valentine and send them home happy may be.

Assembly next Friday – I wish it would get a move on. I am wild to go. I am going with Paul and may be Lewis Peeples is coming down from Portland to go with us. He was lovely to me while I was in Portland and I think him fine. He is a splendid dancer.

Now Louise I am a little sleepy so guess I will stop for to night – didn't get home last night until almost 2.00 a.m.

Love to all and you

I am as ever

Nan

Louise's father wrote this letter to "MLT" on his Columbia River Packing Co. stationery.

Astoria, Oregon, February 8th   1898

My Dear Louise

We were just delighted this morning at receiving your first letter from Alhambra and learning of your rapid gain. We hope you will continue the good work and soon be using both feet to sustain your accumulating growth. We appreciate the kindness of your many friends and hope we can have the opportunity of returning some of their many favors. I presume your young Englishman was fully rewarded by your thanks and smiles. Regret to learn of annoyance of Frost and Drouth in Los Angeles Co – wish we could send them a portion of our downpour of rain for we see little else but rain. Sat & Sunday was a soaker – steady rain with violent gale. We all worried over it on two accounts. Will's outfit leaving for Alaska with fear the horses might die in the rough weather. And Harriet to start for Astoria by steamer. Much to our satisfaction the wind changed from South to North and then East which made a smooth sea. Bar today is reported to be smooth, so we feel easy about Harriet. We expect her arrival before daylight tomorrow. Nat and Gus Wood plan to be down to receive them. Your mother thinks there is no need of my going but I hardly think it possible for me to remain in bed after telephone informs me Str. is near dock, much as I may need the rest to prepare me for tomorrow

---

[114] The Reverend Henry Marcotte was the pastor of Astoria's First Presbyterian Church from 1896 to 1901. He may have married Nora Nickerson in 1901, but verification has not been found.

night's dissipation for you must know the Euchre Club meets at Meglers' Brookfield tomorrow night that means we will get home daylight next morning.

Now about that box. I marked it Emma Bichowsky, Santa Monica. That being his house, intending to write him to distribute it between the Kerckhoffs, Halsteds and self. I have neglected to write as yet. But to make everything safe will now send another invoice with better assortment direct to you at San Gabriel. Plan to put in some Smoked Salmon. That should atone for my neglect.

You would be surprised to see Nat; he is getting to be quite a beau; we no longer have to tell him to keep his hands clean. Since he got that ring, he aims to keep his fingers to compare well with it. I feel ashamed not having written an answer to Miss Philips jolly note to me. Do apologize to her for me – tell her I shall never forget her and hope some day to have her under our roof and supply her active brain with an abundance of fish diet.

Recd. letter from Mr Eliot with promise of visit. Glad as I always am to see him, hope he doesn't come this week as we are to have some important cannery meetings and they always unnerve me. Love to all with lots of kisses for you from

Your Affectionate Papa

P.S.

Curley inquired for you yesterday. I told him how you had improved and were now in L.A. He asked is she at Margie's? I said yes. Oh! Margie is a nice girl - was his answer.

Dissipations At The Euchre Club
And Other Pastimes

In her December 15, 1897, letter to her daughter Harriet, Mary Elizabeth mentions she will be attending the Euchre Club meeting at Mrs. Stokes that evening. This popular club in Astoria was made up of persons who regularly enjoyed a 'trick-taking' card game known as Euchre. It was a fast-paced game that requires rapid, decisive decisions by the players. To win the game, a team of two players has to score a total of ten points as quickly as possible by taking 'tricks,' either in trump suits or non-trump suits.

The card game is believed to have originated in Pennsylvania in the nineteenth century with ties to the Pennsylvania Dutch and to German settlers in the Midwest, especially Iowa, but it was known throughout the United States. It quickly spread to Canada, England and Continental Europe, Australia, and New Zealand. Even now it can be played on-line for team play or competitive league matches. This game has been especially popular in the pubs of Great Britain, so much so that each pub often has its own team to enter in matches against other pub teams.

Each table usually has four-handed play comprised of two teams, although Olga Heilborn and her friends played a six-handed Euchre at her Chafing Dish party on February 9, 1898. Originally 33-34 cards were used – only the higher cards of Aces through sevens, leaving out all the lower cards of a deck. Today's Euchre game usually has only 24-25 cards – Aces through nines. The rules of the game are many and varied depending upon where one plays and who is playing – and thus quite confusing to a beginner. The rules may include such terms as "farmer hand," "blind doubles loner," and "No Ace-No Face-No-Trump." Many references are made to the game's rural origins, *e.g.* "barn door opened" and "in the barn," with players sounding "moos" at the appropriate points. German players may call the Jack the "bauer," meaning farmer, while the British use terms such as "Right Bower" and "Left Bower," and play with twenty-five cards, plus an extra card called the "Benny.*"*

Various letters to and from members of the Tallant family and their friends mention that they played Euchre on many evenings. Apparently Eben Weld Tallant and his wife Mary Elizabeth were regular players with others in the Astoria Euchre Club. The game requires mental dexterity and certainly provided entertainment, good food and social contact, especially during stormy winter evenings. These evenings were not just playing cards! They were not for the faint of heart, mind - or stomach. E.W. Tallant's letter dated February 8, 1898, noted:

> *"I may need the rest to prepare me for tomorrow night's dissapation...The*
> *Euchre Club meets at Meglers' Brookfield[115] tomorrow night - that means*
> *we will get home daylight next morning."*

On February 17, he wrote:

> *"Perhaps your Mother did not give away the giddy times she had last week - all*
> *night out at Meglers; afternoon and evening bowling Friday winding up in a*
> *ballroom. There was more bowling Saturday; tramp to Fred Kendalls; card play-*
> *ing in evening and winding up with severe cramps and sickness lasting over*
> *Sunday, I tell her she is as indiscrete as Frances and wonder at what age when*
> *girls get to age of discression."*

Despite another very full week of evenings out for both of them, Lizzie:

> *"...was able to attend the usual card party last eve and get home this 2.am stuffed*
> *with coffee, sandwiches, oysters, cake, Ice cream, etc, etc. She stood it better than I -*
> *my poor stomach was completely disgusted with the abuse. I am alright on exercise,*
> *but coffee, cake, ice cream and midnight smoking kill me quick."*

Louise's note to Dick at the Presidio, San Francisco, written from Astoria on Thursday, September 29, 1898, added the following:

> *"Well nothing startling has happened only Dr Finch called last night. Mrs White*

---

[115] Meglers' Brookfield place was only a boat ride north across the Columbia from Astoria.

& Virginia were here to dinner. Mrs Halsted & Marge came up in the evening and we all played cards. I nearly hurt myself laughing over that scientific game called "Pig." We made Dr Finch a hog – you remember that game don't you? It is lots of fun."

Other popular card games of the period were "Old Maid" and "Whist." In an early April 1896 letter from Sunnyside, California, Louise remarked on how well she was doing in playing Whist. Whist, or *Whiste,* was so named because of the way "tricks" were rapidly whisked or scooped up off the card table. It began in the 18th or 19th century and was derived from the English card games known as "Ruff," "Triumph" and "Honours." There were numerous variations of using a fifty-two-card deck; some kind of bidding was added later. During the twentieth century, Whist evolved into the game of Bridge. People at this time also enjoyed bowling. There were several ten-pin bowling alleys in Astoria, usually located in the social clubs. Lizzie enjoyed going bowling often at the Club.[116] Occasionally Eben accompanied her.

Crokinole or *Croque'nole*

Louise played this game while she was visiting in Southern California in 1898 and enjoyed it very much. In many ways, crokinole is a cross between shuffleboard and pool. The antique boards were octagonal in shape; the modern ones are likely to be round. Both are card table size. The game is for 2, 3 or 4 players (or two teams of two players). The smooth playing surface itself is a round shape with a "gutter" or ditch around the edge of the board. Concentric rings denoting ascending values are marked as lines on the surface and division lines quarter the circular board into four 90-degree sections. In the center of the playing surface is a small sunken "nole," a depression the size of one of the playing discs. Eight rubber-coated pegs, termed "Dodmen," surround the "nole." These pegs form obstacles to reaching the center "nole" with one's crokinole discs. The discs are like mini wooden pucks with a small hole drilled in the center of each disc. Some nowadays are just thin, lightweight rings.

Each player is given six discs. The object of the game is to score the highest number of points by "shooting" your "man" between the pegs/Dodmen into the center hole and by "*croque*-ing" or flicking your opponent's men <u>off</u> the board into the gutter while you remain <u>on</u> the board in scoring position. Easy? Not exactly! Ricochets off the Dodmen pegs and off of other discs add to the fun.

In a February 21, 1899 letter to Dick over in Hawaii, Louise wrote that she and Harriet had gone down to Charlie's house to enjoy a "rare bit" he and Dr. Finch had cooked up. While at Charlie's that Tuesday evening, she wrote:

[They] *"had a fine time playing croconole (don't know how it is spelt, but any way that is how it sounds). You remember we played one night at Nans and laughed so much – you, Charlie, Dr. Burnett, Olga, Nan and I. It makes my fingers hurt."*

---

[116] Astoria's Irving Club had ten-pin bowling lanes, as did the Public Bowling Alley.

A player may shoot either right or left handed, provided that the buttocks of the player do not leave the chair seat and that a player does not begin "the shoot" outside of one's own quarter arc of the board. The shot is made by placing your disc on the outer most ring and "flicking" your index finger so it propels the disc forward (hopefully). However one must hold the tip of the finger firmly against the disc – otherwise, by the end of a game, the fingernail will be black and blue, as well as very sore. Snap <u>with</u> it, not into it! Players with arthritic hands have successfully "swooshed" the discs and won games.

There are numerous crokinole clubs. In 1932, Canadian businessmen, who played in coats and ties, founded the oldest continuously operating club. They have a statistician who has kept a record of every game they ever played. However, crokinole is really a family game, a rural game played in the kitchen or parlor. It is never associated with gambling or with drinking. It <u>is</u> associated with lots of laughs; (bad?) jokes; genial joshing and jibbing; "suggestions" on how to play the next shot; and, of course, urging your opponent to try for a totally impossible shot.

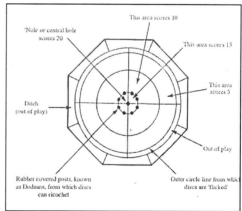

Photographs are reprinted from Michael Webster's article in *Harrowsmith* Magazine, December 1994.

Strangely, its history has not really been documented, although it appears to be a combination of other board games. In India, in their game of "carums," the pieces were flicked with a finger, but the game board had snooker table netted pockets. In England, the game "squails" was derived from one called "shove ha'penny" in which a coin placed on the edge of a board is struck with the palm of the hand toward a target.

Research indicates that the game probably originated around 1867 in a Canadian Mennonite community near Ontario. The oldest known board in existence is a Canadian one dating from 1875, made near Stratford, Ontario. The game's name derives from the French "croque'nole – meaning "a flick" or a "small, hard biscuit." In Canada the discs are often called "cookies." No one can figure out "how it came about that German immigrants crossed a British pub game with an Indian board game, gave it a French name, and then thought the story too uninteresting or too unimportant to record."[117]

A personal note: Families who own Crokinole boards treasure them and hand them down in the family. Our maternal Grandmother Madge B. Buchanan brought her family's board across the plains from Missouri. Another member of the family inherited it. So, both my brother's and my families each purchased modern Canadian ones in 1997. Our younger son and his wife later found a 19th century antique one in England and presented it to us.

Nell Sherman   Lottie Bennett   Nan Reed

Mailing date: FEB 10 630AM '98 Astoria. Oreg.
Received: FEB 13 1898 9AM   Alhambra. Cala.
Addressed to: Miss M. Louise Tallant
                Alhambra
                    Los Angeles Co,
                        Cal

Feb-9-1898

My dearest Louise –

By the time this reaches you – you will be thinking all kinds of things about me. It was impossible for me to write last Sunday – we had company from early morning till late at night, couldn't even go to church. The son of an old friend of papa's and mama's was in town and spent most of his time at the house. He was quite a nice looking chap – over 6 ft tall, blonde, wavy hair and blue eyes. Well I must tell you about our chafing dish party to Knappton. Of course we expected it to be a nice moonlight night and of course it just poured so it came through the umbrella. You never saw such a downpour. It was quite rough going over but no one was sick; we struck the sands and talk about screeching – you never heard such a noise. I was somewhat frightened myself. But at last we arrived all safe and sound. Mrs C- [Callender] had almost given up hope - she thought we wouldn't come. First part of the evening we played

[117] Webster, "They Shoot. They Score. . .," (Harrowsmith Magazine, December, 1994), 86-100, 103.

six hand euchre then had music. I was called to the kitchen to help make the rarebit and set the table - the rarebit turned out just delicious. We had rarebit, coffee, olives, lovely bread & butter, 2nd coffee, cake and Lowneys and then just before we went home all those that wanted them had raw oysters - I didn't. Then we danced and had more singing until 12:30, then got ready for home. My but it was rough coming home - may be I didn't feel sick. We got home at just 1:30. Haven't done anything since -

Friday night is the last Assembly party. I'm going to wear my new white organdy - just about finished it today. I hope it will look nice. Saturday night am going to a party at Higgins and Monday night Nan has a Valentine party and then the Chrysanthemums are going to have another party next week so we will be quite gay. Well, How is Los Angeles and how's Louise & how's Marge & how is _that_ foot. Is it nice and warm? I can just imagine smelling lovely orange blossoms and other flowers. Now you will have a fine chance to sketch and make pretty little water colors.

Hat and Alice got home this a.m. but I haven't seen them yet. Nettie Tuttle is still here; I don't know how long she is going to stay. The cutter [the _Commodore Perry, a_ U.S. Government revenue vessel] will leave very soon now for the Sound. I think Miss Phillips will be glad to get away from here.

Mr Sturderant goes off on his vacation next Saturday.

Mr Ross is quite attentive to Genie Lewis. And Mr Turner is quite attentive to Nettie Tuttle.

Did sweet Alice Benbolt tell you any of her tales of woe? _Brother Tom_ asked me the other day to be sure and send his best when I wrote.

Well dear girl I must light the lamps - this is German night. "Bob" hasn't arrived yet - she generally arrives early - perhaps it's a little too juicy for her.

Give lots of love to Marge & share the letter with her like a good boy & tell her its her turn next. Love to Mrs Halsted and a whole lot for yourself.

From your loving

"Jack" Olga

Louise's friend Olga Heilborn signed herself as "Jack." A few of the girls referred to themselves using male names – apparently those of their "beaus." For example, Louise was "Richard" and Nan Reed was "Maurice." Pearl Holden called herself "Pearline," although her friends often referred to her as "Princess." Apparently Pearl's sister, Frances Holden, called herself "Frank." Unidentified is a girl friend who called herself "Bob."

There is no date on the following partial letter from Harriet. She included a small "blue print" of an interior room in the Grand Avenue house. The Cyanotype photograph was not properly processed, so is of too poor a quality to reproduce. Harriet did not sign her second letter to Louise in Alhambra. It was dated the fourteenth of February 1898.

Forgot to tell you Nan called up yesterday to get a picture of me taken when I was au infant - said she had one of every one she had invited to the party - & gave her that tin type – no one would guess who it was. Every one is dead struck with my fur, strange to say. Olga's cape is very pretty, dandy high collar. She hasn't been up to see me yet - thought maby she would come up this afternoon but guess its too stormy. Mr P A Stokes house is getting along slow but sure it isnt in it with our's.

Nat wants me to write out some invitations for him - his PDQ Club is going to meet here Friday night - don't you feel for us? And its almost four o'clock and I haven't changed my dress yet so good bye. Hope you won't get tired reading this letter – better take a day off. Will send this seal for Marg's fan - give it to her with my love.

Dick was telling me about some thing he sent you girls but couldn't quite make out what it was - expect it was some thing funny.

Good bye again. Give my love to Mrs Halsted. Write soon to

Harriet

My dear Louise

I suppose half of the girls in town are writing to you to day and telling you about the dance so I'll make my description short. Can't say that I had such an awfully good time - there were only 20 more girls than boys in the first place - put that down – and Tom and I didn't get there till the second dance - but think – did well too only sit out three dances. I wasn't alone either – always had 20 or 30 to keep me company. There were about a dozen girls from Portland came down to bowl with the A.F.C. ladies in the afternoon and were all invited to the dance. The Chewing Gum girl was there with Sadie Crang and another Portland girl with Maggie Higgins and not one new boy and lots [of] the Astoria boys were not there (Mr Sturdent or Mick or Charlie Chewder & Burt Fergerson of Ft Stevens). Mr Turner came in late with Miss Phillips - she had on her shirt dress & hat; they danced two or three dances together and that was all – she makes me <u>sick</u>; do you know she hasn't as much as spoken to me since I got home – passed her on the street once or twice but she didn't stop - she is engaged to Mr S-. has a lovely diamond ring so I hear - he went last night. The Perry leaves some time this week. Every one is down on Miss P- for some reason she had the nerve to tell Mrs Upshurr she thought the Portland girls put the A-girls in the shade at the dance. Well no one else thought so and I noticed most of the Portland girls had a dance with Mr Hitchur Thomson. Etc. Both of the Barker girls were there - the youngest one spent most of her time flirting with Will - it was too funny to watch her. Will took Frank again - Olga had an awfully pretty new white dress but Kate looked the prettiest of any of the girls & though don't know who came with who for it was so late when we got there - had to wait for the carriage. Wasn't going to write much about the party but after I got started couldn't stop - Oh yes Mrs H. Allen looked dead swell in black. I had a fine dance with Mr A-. Tomorrow night is Nan's party - wish I had a new waist to wear with my silk skirt - think I'll send you a sample and see if you can get some cheap stuff to make a waist to wair [sic] under my white swiss with the silk skirt - but don't suppose there will be any more parties now for a while except the Chrysan—s, they give a dance next Monday night. Don't care much about going.

I am sick of Astoria already - for goodness sakes don't come home till you have to - its hasn't stoped raining and blowing since I got here and there isn't a d—thing to do. Mama was awfully sick last night - she & papa were up to K-s to dinner in the evening - she had such cramps she thought she would have to stay there all night but she didn't. She came home about 10:30, went to bed and about 12:30 she was taken with them again and papa & I were up a long time with her. She didn't get up till 12 this noon and is feeling much better now. She was going to write to you to day but will wait now until tomorrow; thinks she will feel more like writing then.

We will send your guitar down on the next steamer - as freight it costs $3 as express will, and the music with it.

Hope you went to Steves and had a lovely time and wore your silk dress. Marggie H- had a party last night - everyone in town was invited but Frank, Pearl & I. Pearl first returned from Knappton yesterday - haven't seen her yet - will tomorrow night at Nans. I am going with Dick - expect I'll have to talk a left arm off and tell him all about you but I am used to that now. Dr Finch took two dances with me Fri evening so as to hear all about you but Dr B- didn't even ask for one much to my sorrow. My eyes have looked so badly since I have been home that Mama made me go to Dr Walkers yesterday; about all he did was to talk to me about your foot. Dr S- etc showed me a picture of a foot and explained which bone it was they took out - he gave me an eye wash - hope it will do some good for my eyes look bum.

Have been cleaning out my desk so thought I would use up all the old paper on you.

Gosh Louise I would like to be driving around with you and Marg. I never was so discusted with Astoria before in my life. This rain is some thing awful. Don't know how mama stood it all winter.

Mrs Knowles was down Friday & stayed till Sat night with us. Ma & pa & she went to the club Friday evening. Then came up to the hall for a few minutes. After wards she said Laura is as happy as a lark. She is to be married this fall and will live in Haycreek. Frank says Pearl will be married this fall she thinks and she & you will be bridesmaids - Frank was up to dinner yesterday and stayed all night with me.

[Harriet]

Irene Phillips

Dick, Mick Prael, Bob Bennett and George Smith

Dick and Charlie McClarity

Dick and Tommy Bryce

Feby, 17, 1898

My Dear Louise

We have been greatly pleased to learn by your recent letters of steady improvement and are now most anxious for you to be able to report that you are free from pain and able to enjoy unbroken sleep. How extremely fortunate it is your having such good friends as Mrs Halsted and Margie. It's hardly possible to conceive of a more favorable spot for you to rest and recover in.

Your letter received yesterday instructing us not to send your guitar came too late to stop it. I am rather glad it went any way as I would suggest your trying to make some trade with it for a better one. Say you could get a more perfect one for Twenty dollars, the[y] might allow six or eight for this one and you pay the balance in cash. Will was speaking about your old one when you wrote for it and said it was too bad you did not have a better one. I think if he were not so hard up by investments in Alaska he would furnish you the means, but later on either he or I will try and do it. It would be very pleasant next summer to show Papa your new guitar and tell him you got it with his Twenty. So I will aim to replace what you spent of his present and let it go for a guitar.

Mama mailed you yesterday Bfst [breakfast] for 2 Boxes – Salmon, 1 Guitar. The large Salmon box contains an assortment of Salmon which you can share with the Kerckhoffs and Halsteads; the smaller box contains a variety of stuff, even a few pots of preserves – the latter sent under protest of your Mother and Harriet as they said Mrs. H. had loads of such stuff and wouldn't want it; however I thought it would do to take on picnics and we have a greater quantity here than we have use for. I was disappointed in getting good Smoked Salmon, so sent but a very small quantity and Puget Sound Salmon at that. I am now trying to get some new fresh fish which I plan to salt and have smoked here. When I get it done will send you some. You will note the Box containing Guitar is of excellent material and workmanship. Oscar made it from Spruce boat lumber. Open the box carefully and keep it to ship new Guitar home in.

Mama, Hat and girls probably write you all that's going on. Perhaps your Mother did not give away the giddy times she had last week – all night out at Meglers; afternoon and evening bowling Friday winding up in a ball room. There was more bowling Saturday; tramp to Fred Kendalls; card playing in evening and winding up with severe cramps and sickness lasting over Sunday. I tell her she is as indiscrete as Frances and wonder at what age when girls get to age of discression. However she was able to attend the usual card party [of the Euchre Club] last eve and get home this 2.am stuffed with coffee, sandwiches, oysters, cake, Ice cream, etc-etc. She stood it better than I – my poor stomach was completely disgusted with the abuse. I am alright on exercise, but coffee, cake, ice cream and midnight smoking kill me quick. Getting late. Will close this scrawl. Love to all

From your affectionate father　　Papa

Mailing date: FEB 28 1898 4PM   Alhambra, Cala

Feb the 27th 1898

Dear Dick -

Your last letter was rather a hard one to answer so I put it off – the fact is I am just to that stage of my illness where I am very lazy – the pain is so much less now that I can get some rest and forget all about the foot & etc and sleep. Oh what a blessed thing sleep is, and just think of it, I gained five Lbs this week – pretty good gain for one week isn't it. I am beginning to feel and look like myself again – that is when the crutches are out of sight – horrid things – I hate them but I ought not to say that for I would be helpless with out them. Marge I believe wrote you all the news only a few days ago. She is a dear girl I tell you – takes the best kind of care of me, cooks breakfast for me when ever I feel like getting up and waits on me so that I am afraid I will be spoiled for ever – nothing could be better for me than this place. Think I have gained over twenty pounds since I left the hospital or the "house of torture" as my room mate used to call it. Every day we take long drives and the country is simply lovely now. I enjoy driving more than any thing and it is warm enough to sit on the porch so we are out of doors most all day and my appetite is some thing to wonder at. This is surely the place for me but I would like to be in Astoria just a little while to see you all and let the folks at home see how much I had gained. I don't know about being received with open arms though, it wouldn't look – well you know and then you would have to embrace crutch and all. But to be serious Dick you must not think of such things and please try not to think of me – it is easier to forget now that I am far away. And when I come back it will not be so hard to be good friends as we used to be and I am so sorry - I can't tell you how sorry I am Dick if I make you unhappy but it is too late now, we can't go back and do differently. I wish we could though for I feel how much I am to blame. We have been foolish and must make the best of it now however. You know I sealed that contract, do you regret how you begged to do it – you did you know that it would be easier for you and I hoped it would (don't do any thing rash that you will be sorry for some day). It must be very dull at home now Lent has begun and I often wonder what you boys find to do. I suppose the Club is your refuge. I must stop now and write to Nan & Olga – they are so good about writing to me and I haven't written them for so long. "Be good and you will be happy" so they say.

Always your loving friend

Louise

Mar 8   '98

My dear Lou

Have just written to Mama. Papa came home this morning; he says mama is having a fine time and the weather is simply lovely – it is clear and cold here to day and we haven't had any rain for four days – put it down – expect the oranges came on to days steamer. Papa has gone down to see. Every time a wagon goes by I jump up to see if its there. Just feel like eating a dozen. Received a letter from Miss P- to day - guess she wrote you she had left the hospital – expect she is happy now although she has to go back again soon. Havent a bit of news to write to day – it is more than quiet here now. Heard the other day they were going to have another

Assembly dance right after Lent and the Chrysanthemums are going to give one also. What shall I wear? Will wear my white with pink ribbons at one of them.

Why don't you get a bicycle pillow and have the people you meet in Cal put there names on it and then finish it up when you come home. Think I had rather have one with a pattern but for my self but get some thing easy. Every time I see Dr Finch he stops and asks for you. Papa said to tell you Paul B- asked to be remembered to you. Last Thursday was Kates birthday – Frank, Grace and I were up to dinner. Nan came up in the evening, brought her a basket of home made candy which was (soon) out-of-sight.

Received a long letter from Fran S- [Smith] a day or two ago. I about split my sides over it. Has she written to you yet? She said she was going to as soon as she finished music, but you know Fran. Uncle Nat has an awful cold – got it the second day he was here – that speaks well for Astoria doesn't it?

Ana Westdahl came up on the last steamer five days ago. She is going in the millinery store with Mrs McK- to learn the trade. She said to send her love to you. W-a-l-l, I must close or this wont go to day. Write often to

Harriet

The following letter is from Louise's friend Pearl Holden, *aka* "Pearline," *aka* "Princess."

Mailing date: MAR 18 1 PM 98 Astoria, Oreg.

Give my love to Marge & her mother & also to Miss K-
My dearest Louise -

No doubt you think me very naughty for not writing to you more often, dear, but when I tell you how very busy I have been & how a great deal of my time is taken up with Charlie [Callender] you will forgive me wont you? Being the last of the year I have had a long statement to make up & letters to file but if God is willing I guess it is the last time I will ever have to do those things again as I intend to stop working about June or thereabout. Don't tell anyone as I told Mr Lownsberry I would keep it quiet. He has had a number of applicants for the job & they are all perfectly welcome to it as far as I am concerned – you have no idea dear how happy I am. Charlie is just "goodness" itself & can not do enough for me. I never thought it possible that anyone in this world would love me as he does. I cant hardly realize it yet & I only hope that someday you will be just as happy, as you must not forget that you will always be my twin sister whether I am married or single & must come over to Knappton to see me just as often as you can wont you? Charlie has given me the Winona for tonight & I have invited twenty four of the boys and girls to go over & have a great time & have a Chafing dish party. I only wish you were here to go with me but never mind we will just have lots of parties after

148

you come home & I will see that you have a better time than any one else as you will be a pampered person I can assure you. I will write and tell you all about the party some time next week. Well dear I must go to work if I want to get off early tonight so will close. Hoping you are better & will write soon, I am lovingly your friend

"Pearline"

Astoria, Oregon, March 19th 1898

My Dear Maria

Yours enclosing one to Hat. rec'd on time and now at home so refer only to memory. Note your going in to Kerckhoffs where of course you will have a good time tho you may miss the good air of San Gabriel. I notice in newspaper reports that you have had a severe frost there. Hope it did not occasion loss to our friends. Glad to learn of your continuous improvement in health. When people inquire about you here I tell them you are the most healthy member of the Tallant family. At present we have quite a hospital – Uncle Nat is very sick – in fact I fear he never will fully recover from his present attack [refers to his older brother Nathaniel Weld Tallant]. Our [son] Nat has been on sick list and out of school two days – felt better yesterday and was on street in afternoon and again last eve but today is laid up again. Harriet keeps well and for the most of her time sticks close to the house but she, Kate and Frank did turn themselves loose Sat. night, March 12th, Did not get home untill 2' AM Sunday, thereby creating great gossip downtown and nearly causing Kate the loss of her job at Booth & Co.

Will is exceedingly busy. Geo. Johnson returned and Alaska business about settled. He – Will – now turns his attention to new ventures – has half a dozen boats and nets in preparation for fishing on his own account and going into seining deeper than ever.

Mama of course keeps you posted of her doings. Last we were at Club, she bowled three games. I bowled two – 19 & 34. NO! I have not been to Dr Logans for store teeth – my old stumps are too good to loose. I am inclined to think that if I had false teeth they would be more often in my vest pocket than in my mouth. We have greatly enjoyed the oranges – have about enough left to last us over tomorrow – did not notice any just bitter ones – all were excellent.

Have you got your new guitar. How are you off for funds – let me know when its ebbing. I send by this mail Astoria papers that give all items that occur.

Let me know all about the Kerckhoffs – do call on Will. Remember me to them all. Tell Will he must hunt me up a job for I expect the bottom to drop out of the Columbia River and I must return to Los Angeles

Affectionately
Your father

Miss M. McKee, one of Louise's nurses at Children's Hospital, kept in touch with her.

Monday, Mar. 27, 8 p.m.

My dear Miss Tallant: -

I wrote to you so long ago but I am ashamed to say, have not posted it yet. I will add this, as an appendix. I have just read the letter through that I wrote you on the 7th and find that there is no mention of the operation - well, Dr. Sherman decided to operate and so she was duly prepared. I gave the anesthetic and do you know, that as soon as she was fully unconscious, her leg came down perfectly straight - you know, there is really nothing the matter with that leg - it is imagination! Dr. Sherman knew this beforehand, but he thought of the mental affect of an operation. He however, decided it would be better not, so put the patient's leg again in P.P. [plaster of Paris] and there it is now, perfectly straight. She has not been told she has not had an operation, so don't you mention it to her. The greater part of her trouble is hysteria. I begin to doubt now that she took as much morphine as she said. Anyway, her leg is alright - she could walk if she only thought she could. She seems in about the same condition to me as when she entered the Hospital, except that she has had no morphine for weeks. This is a hard case because everything depends on herself and she can't or won't help herself. Enough of this - how different this note from the previous one, but this is the result of observation. I told Dr. S. how well you are doing and he was delighted.

To come from the ridiculous to the sublime - I went to hear [Madame Nellie] Melba last week and she is grand - mamma says she does not equal [Madam Adelina] Patti, but, she is superb. The toilets worn at the opera were beautiful, and the jewels magnificent. Everybody endeavored to look her best. The Bostonians are here now;[118] I am going to see Rob Roy this week. Did you ever go to The Chutes, when you were here? They are very near us, and the other night, a party of us went - we had more fun. It was amateur night - any one who thinks he has any histrionic ability can appear that night, and such costumes & such acting - it is fun.

Are you as enthusiastic over Kipling as we are in S.F. - he is quoted continually - the 'Vampire' particularly -

". . .A rag and a bone & a hank of hair. . . "

Write very soon & believe me

Lovingly

M.M.

I have been talking about Miss P- without ever mentioning her name.

---

[118] *The Bostonians*, a novel by Henry James, had been adapted for the stage some years earlier. Louise attended a performance of the play in Chicago on February 15, 1893.

Sunday April 3 rd /98

My dear little Puss.

Twenty nine years ago to day I left home to make a new home for myself with your dear papa. Could we then have looked a head all these years and seen ourselves pleasantly settled in our pretty home, four fine children. No family ties broken by death and all in as good health as we now are – we should have thought there was nothing more for which to wish but I am afraid we don't half appreciate all our blessings. This is such a world of rush, everyone trying to out do the other, Money the chief aim in life, no one contented with what they have so that our blessing which we do have are over shadowed with the desire to get more. For my own part I think I could be perfectly happy if we could only feel settled and sure of having the same we now do but every year it is the same old chestnut "Close the Cannery' – it don't pay". Uncle Nat said this a.m. that he could not see why Mr Cutting did keep running unless they could show <u>some profit</u>, which they had not done for several years, but we will hope on. Still it makes me nervous and unhappy.

We recd your nice letter yesterday; it seemed as tho it had been a long time on the way, but it was just as acceptable. And this a.m. had a note from Hat with yours to her. So we had a double pleasure. Glad you are feeling so well. You didn't speak of your foot at all. Has it done paining you? And has it entirely healed so you don't have to dress it? How much longer will you have to keep the cast on? Does the lame leg get fat? You say the other is getting as big as mine! Remember I always told you you had a better start at your age than I had at the same age to get <u>fat</u> so look out. Mrs Ferguson at the [bowling] alley said the other night, "she went to school with you and that I reminded her so much of you, that I moved and looked like you". Think what a compliment that was for me.

Papa wants I should come down and help get lunch. So you will have to wait a while.

When I sent the box I looked around to see if I could see anything I thought you wanted. Remember[ed] about the China bracelet - could not see the Alaska one any where. I can send it in the mail for a few cents if you want it and know where it is. Isnt it too bad Papa's diary Nat gave him Xmas got lost – he paid a $1.00 for it. I told him at the time a cheaper one would do as well.

Wonder if your <u>minister</u> is the one Mr Marcotte is trying to get to take his place while he takes a vacation. He said he was trying to get a friend from Southern Cal to take his place for him to get a months vacation. You are lucky to have that silk dress, it is just what you need. I will send H's note and you can see what she says about shirt waist.

Will is head over heals at work getting out a seine; he has two or three men working for him- one at $100. per month. Will gets up & goes off early and some times does not come home to dinner. He has put all his Skagway money into this venture. I do hope he will be successful for he has $3,000. in it. It is make or break with him.

Papa was saying this a.m. he should be so glad when you had gotten through with your foot and had that old cast off. Won't it seem funny to get up and dress it with a shoe the same as the other? Do you think it will be long now before you can come have shoe fitted? I expect you will have to learn to walk but if you get along as quickly as you have done, it will not be long before "Richard is himself again." [she refers to Louise]

Tell Lillie I think you and she are very complimentary about my letter writing, Am afraid you will not be able to say as much about this!

After I finish this Papa and I are going to walk down to the new depot. I expect next week will be quite a lively one here with all the republican delegates. And the R.R. finished. It ought to help Astoria. Perhaps I can get a chance to sell out. How would you like to move down to L.A.? Am afraid we would be like the O's, have to be content with a smaller house.

I hear F- is coming to visit the Elmores this summer. Glad Will and Louise [Kerckhoff] called. Do return it at the first opportunity and give them our love. Guess we shall not be able to invite any of our friends here this summer. We shall have all we can do to make both ends meet. Perhaps by another summer we will have fond news from Klondike, then can entertain friends. Uncle Nat is so blue & sick that it is enough to drive me crazy.

Recd papers and notice of Mrs H's death. Shall write Aunt Clara [Foard] soon. When you see her give her lots of love; if you are over at P[asadena], call and see her. When do you think you shall go to visit Ella [Scudder Crocker]? Are they going to have a Fiesta this summer?

Guess we shan't tint walls at present. All the kitchen is very satisfactory, but I can't get hold of men long enough to get carpets up. Perhaps when you are up home. Next fall we can have the men and then it will lost but little.

When do you think you shall be able to come home? Do you think you could stay over with Mrs Westdahl when you were having your shoe fitted?

Mr W- is ordered to Alaska & Flora will be all alone and I think I could get her to let you board there and it would be so much cheaper than to go to a regular boarding house. Can't know whether you could stay at Aunt Fannie's or not.

Will send Hat's note in this so that will make up for the stupidity of this. Nat down to Jamie's. Now we are having good weather it is harder than ever to get Nat down to writing but will try. What do you think of the war out look? Give my love to Mrs. H. and Marj, and Stevie & wife – and all inquiring friends.

Write soon to your loving

Mama

152

Envelope addressed to: Mr. R. E. Carruthers
Astoria, Oregon

April the 7th

Dear Dick

I guess I wont try to answer your last letter to me because I don't understand it very well and might only make matters worse so I will try and tell you what I have been doing since I wrote last. I spent two weeks in town and had a fine time considering that I don't find it interesting to be an invalid but every one is so nice to me I cant help but have a good time. Marge came for me last Friday and we drove out together – we are getting to know the road between here and town pretty well. Saturday we spent the day down at Redondo – it is an awfully pretty place but the wind blew a gale and the ocean was grand – it was so very rough, it made me home sick for the beach at Elk Creek. Oh I wonder if we will ever have another trip like that. Driving out from town last night Marge talked all the way about her trip down there with you and what fun you had. We are all going on a moon light picnic tomorrow – a drive out, "not a walk out." Moon light nights down here are some thing grand – the sky is always so clear. Marge shakes the bottle of Oregon Mist all the time but the charm must be off for she cant make it rain. Some one told me Geo. McBride was going to be married – is that so, and who is he going to marry. I hear that Mrs Page & Clara leave soon for the east and other startling news such as the R.R. being finished. Just think I can come home all the way on the train – wont that be fine. Marge is practicing her singing lesson and it is rather distracting. She is getting along fine though; her voice is much improved. We practice once in a while on our guitars. I have a new one – it is a daisy and I enjoy playing so much more. I still gain in weight and strength and feel pretty well.

Well I have got to close now to get this in todays mail. Marge sends her love and I send mine – that is, if you want the love of your friend

Louise

Harriet, Lillie and Louise at Redondo Beach, California – 1898.

Elk Creek, Clatsop County, Oregon

Under the listing for Elk Creek in the State of Oregon Immigration Commission's 1915 Oregon Almanac, an official pamphlet, is the following information:

> **Elk Creek.** Altitude is 10 feet. Population 50. Nearest railroad point Seaside, 9 miles north. ... Near Cannon Beach, summer resort on Pacific Ocean. Good fishing. Splendid scenery.[119]

Elk Creek cabin. Olga and Louise are standing 3rd and 4th from left. Dick may be second from right – with a cigarette.

Courtesy of CCHS archives.

In the early pioneer days of the 1800s in the Pacific Northwest, whenever an explorer or trapper saw elk near a streambed, they promptly named the waterway Elk Creek. Hence, numerous Elk Creeks existed in Oregon then, and still do. The Elk Creek that is the site at which Louise, Dick and a group of their friends camped is in Clatsop County. It empties into the Pacific Ocean, just north of Cannon Beach, Oregon, forming a fine "singing sands" beach over eight miles in length between Tillamook Head and Hug Point/Arch Cape. Haystack Rock, a 300-foot high volcanic monolith, dominates the beach.

Lewis A. McArthur, in his book *Oregon Geographic Names,* notes "Captain William Clark was the first white man of record to visit the vicinity of this stream, which he did

---

[119] *1915 Oregon Almanac*, 108.

on Wednesday, January 8, 1806. He called the stream *Ecola* or Whale Creek."[120] (The Chinook Indian word for "whale" is variously written as *ehkoli/ekoli/ekkoli).* For many years it was commonly referred to as Elk Creek and was listed as such on the maps of the area. However, in 1974, the Official Commission for the Oregon Lewis and Clark Trail replaced the Elk Creek name with Captain Clark's *Ecola* name.

Early settlers also named the village Elk Creek, but, in 1910, their first post office was designated as Ecola for surer delivery of the mail. However, again to avoid confusion, in 1922 the post office underwent a name change - this time, to Cannon Beach.[121] This name was to memorialize the discovery of an iron cannon that had washed ashore near Arch Cape. The cannon was determined to be from the schooner *U.S.S. Shark.* Under the command of Navy Lieutenant Neil M. Hawison, the vessel was headed out to sea from Astoria. She had to cross the treacherous sand bars at the mouth of the Columbia River, which came to be known as "The Graveyard of the Pacific." In the rough seas, the *Shark* lost her steering rudder. Despite numerous attempts to build a new rudder, the *Shark* ran aground and broke up on Clatsop Spit near the mouth of the Columbia River on September 10, 1846.[122] Debris from the wreck drifted down the coast.

Although no letters have been found to determine the exact dates Louise, Dick and friends camped at Elk Creek, one might assume they had been to that beach more than one time. Louise specifically refers to this beach in her April 7, 1898, letter to Dick written when she was visiting Redondo Beach, California. She wrote:

> *"...[T]he wind blew a gale and the ocean grand – it was so very rough it made me home sick for the beach at Elk Creek. Oh I wonder if we will ever have another trip like that."*

This reference is probably to a trip taken in the late summer or the fall of 1897. It is not known how many of their friends went on this camping expedition or exactly how they got from Astoria to Elk Creek. The Astoria Depot site had been agreed upon by April 1896, although the first passenger train between Portland and Astoria did not officially began service until May 22, 1898. Meanwhile however, on August 3, 1896, the entrepreneur A.B. Hammond had completed the Astoria & South Coast RR to Seaside. Trestles with drawbridge sections had been constructed over two bodies of water – all the way over Skipanon Creek, but only half way over Youngs Bay. The Astoria and Columbia River Railroad did not complete the other half of that trestle until 1898.

Dick wrote Louise on Easter, 1896:

> *"The Depot site has at last been agreed upon and we will surely be able to take a trip to the seaside this summer with out even seeing a boat. I know it will seem strange, but we'll become use to it I guess."*

---

[120] McArthur, 245.
[121] The Tillamook Indians' name for Cannon Beach was shown as "Ne-cost" on Capt. Clark's 1806 map.
[122] Miller, 23. Note: see also a fictionalized article titled "The True Story of the Wreck of the Shark," by Norman Howerton of Ilwaco, WA., that appeared in the *Evening Daily Budget,* Tuesday, March 1, 1938.

On their trip to Elk Creek in 1897, it is probable that the campers had to take a boat from Astoria west across Youngs Bay to Warrenton. There they boarded Mr. Hammond's railroad south to Seaside. In Seaside, they probably hired horses with carriages - or drays - to complete the journey in a southwesterly direction to the Pacific Ocean. Roads of a sort did exist a good part of the way into the camping site. The Elk Creek Toll Road had opened across the coast range of hills in 1890. The camping party would have had to take most everything they needed with them, although the village south of Elk Creek was not far away. The young people may have had the use of a roughly constructed cabin. Dick and Louise refer to the camp site in several of their letters written during the latter half of 1898, always remembering it with pleasure and referring to the good fun they had there, even with Dick taking his turn as the cook. Louise wrote on July 27:

"Oh, those good old Elk Creek days, I love to think of them,"

In Dick's August 8, 1898, letter – written while at sea on the *Lakme* headed for Hawaii – he told Louise:

"I can't help but think of Elk Creek...and when I get back, there is the first place we will have to go to – just see if we don't."

Louise and Dick's Elk Creek group certainly included the following persons: Olga Heilborn, Pearl Holden, Zetta Smith, Edith Copeland, Clara Lionberger, probably Harriet, Mick Prael, Dr. Burnett, George Smith and Charlie Higgins - and the Reverend Henry Marcotte of the First Presbyterian Church. Unfortunately, as happens, the group all too soon began to break apart as each person later set out to make their own lives.

Rev. Henry Marcotte and some of the campers.

Will – home from Alaska.

Easter Sunday   [April 10, 1898]
At home

Dear Puss.

I thought of you this morning opening your box and being reminded of those who love you. And send lots of love and kisses to you. Hope you are having as pleasant an Easter as we.

This morning was bright and pleasant. Papa and I went to hear Mr Marcotte who gave us a fine sermon and fine music. Reba [Hobson] sang beautifully. So did Mrs Ross. Each song a solo - and the choir sang very nicely. This eve we are going again. Mrs Taylor is to sing and she is always fine.

Well Louise yesterday when I was out in the kitchen trying my hand at nut candy, an express package came. I did not have to wonder long who sent it. And will return many many thanks from us all. They were in good order fresh and very fragrant, but the carnations were not as large as those Marge sent last year. So many buds. I guess I cut off a hundred <u>little</u> ones as Papa said the others might mature if the little ones were taken off. It seemed strange they would let so many buds grow - particularly send them on cut flowers as of course they take the life from the flowers. We are enjoying them very much. I shall have them on dinner table to night - also had them on for breakfast. Dr Walker is to dine with us. Here is a kiss for the pinks & one for Easter.

This is the opening day of the canneries. Will held his Easter service at the Cannery although I think it a poor excuse. He has gone into the seining with his Klondike money - has gotten grounds up river; has seven men, eight horses, mess house - our old Skipanon Sam for cook - and wants to hire more horses. Will ought to succeed if work tells for as Papa says, he is a worker and nothing discourages him. I do hope him success.

We heard from our Klondikers yesterday. G. Johnsen had letters from the Petersons, our men and the 7th from G. They were frozen in the river but in the best of spirits, well and said "they would not come home until they could make us all rich." Dick Humphreys wrote to the man who staked him that A.G. the butcher, who they said one of the Powell girls was engaged to, that he need never do another days work, that he had a claim that would give them both more money than they could spend in a life time. Hope our men will be writing us the same. They had to pay $2.50 for a letter to be brought out.

Your letter smelt so sweet. I have just written to Mrs S- and enclose the orange blossoms in it. Glad the hats arrived in good order. How does it happen your letters take so long to come - yours written Monday, got here yesterday, Sat. Don't you get discouraged Puss. You will come out all right. You have been very brave all through your troubles, so keep up a good heart and you will soon forget you ever had crutches.

Guess that Hat will be home the last of the week. Shall be glad to have some one to speak to. You ought to see Nat - he came out in his Easter hat - the shape Jamie wore when you were here, only a _light_ _one_ - very becoming. I have forgotten what the name is. Well Puss if I take this to the box now it will be in time for postman, so will close it with love to Mrs H- & M. and seal it with a kiss from

Papa & Mama

Mailing date: MAY 4 6AM 1898 from Santa Monica, Cala.
Received: MAY 8 9AM 1898 Astoria, Oreg.

May the 3 rd 1898

Dear Dick

Such a good joke on you not to tell us who you were going to be the best man for I fear you have been telling Babe [Dick's youngest brother, Robert Rex] your troubles and secrets again. You know you always told me you told him _every_ _thing_. Any way the secret is out, so now write and tell us all about it - who the bride is to be and where she lives and etc. I bet she cant compare with Nan - he must have forgotten her pretty quick. I am dreadfully disappointed in him – didn't you think he cared more for her than that. Marge and I are making a visit at Santa Monica. She is going home tomorrow and I will miss her terribly. She kindly shared her box of Lowneys with me - they tasted fine.

I hope you are not called into service and now that we have destroyed so many Spanish boats I guess they cant spare any for this coast, hope not any way sure. Well I hope Mr Berkely will be happy but I don't go so much on a fellow that can forget a girl so soon - where does it come off?

As ever your friend

Louise

Mailing date: MAY 10:30PM '98 Astoria, Oreg.
Received: MAY 15 8AM 1898   Alhambra, Cal.

May 10 1898

Dear Louise: -

I am afraid you might start for home soon, not that I would not like to see you do so, but then it would spoil my chance of writing to you soon, or perhaps not again I'll - if you will pardon me - such matters a little and again we might be called out and then of course I know you would like to have a letter from me before I go to get punched through and through with cruel Spanish bullets, and I can only stand a certain amount of that kind of trouble. (Of course the assertion that you would like to have a letter from me is a conjecture on my part.)

Well I don't think we will have a call and I only wish it were otherwise, because I would really like to go. I never have had my curiosity satisfied on that part of human events and presume I can't rest well untill I do - and I always have been sore at Spain and heir [to the throne] since a little fireworks took place near Havana, and today I am more than sore at any Spaniard to think you could be so cruel as to marry one of them - this is a dream the Princess [Olga] told me of to day: You married a citizen of Spain. Well I have heard of blows almost killing another but to tell you the truth this _knock_ almost killed Richard E. Well, I only hope you have not done this cruel hard thing; don't bring him home with you, not even for your sake would he be safe from the hands of the Naval Rescue of Astoria - we have not _smelt_ _blood_ and I am afraid the sight of him would put us on the war path.

A Miss Young told me at the last dance you were engaged to ----- I will not mention the party. That was bad enough for me to hear, but this last - well say, awful, don't mention it, about the Miss [Caroline] Young engagement - I'll tell you later ---

Well I suspose if you know Buckley is going to be married, it is no use of me keeping still as everyone will know it now - you never could keep a secret - always had to tell Olga. I don't know which one of the boys told as several of them knew about it. I don't know the girl so wouldn't pass between her and Nan but I'll wager she is none better - just the same if this was none of my pie or I would have fixed things up differently - I only hope she is nice and they are as you say, will be happy forever and a day. He said they were to be married in September. Of course I don't blame him much as you do - you say men soon forget - then what are you folks to expect but I don't think he should hang on to shoe threads [laces?] forever and I don't think Nan cared for him very much anyway - and then this girl whoever she is, is an old girl of his.

And to tell you the truth, I don't know what I am a-talking about. He said he was going to be married, well let him, and further more, I can't find time to take care of any one else's trouble and my country's and then my own at the same time.

Well everything is so so in Astoria. Electric lamps are still 25 [cents] each, a 12 for $3.25. How many do you want? If I could only print as fast as I can write I'd make a good typewriter and I trust you can read what I've written as it is so interesting (the last word on the top line is 'interesting'- had hardly enough room up there so brot it down).

We are going to ride to Portland Monday on the _train_ - you ought to hear me say that - sounded fine, Well I hope you will be home soon, so soon that this will never reach you but fall in the hands of some Spaniards or _Spaniard_ who will kill himself trying to read it.

Well you know...

Dick

Friday 13 – 1898 [This Friday the 13th was in May]

Well Puss -

I think you deserve a letter on my company paper. We certainly all rejoice with you and feel we have lots for which to rejoice. This a.m. Mrs Sanborn came for me to go to ride. While I was getting ready, telephone rang. I could hear Hat say – Why, isn't it splendid, why she will come get home. I kept saying "what is it, who is talking with you", then she said it is Papa. Says he got a letter from L. etc etc. My, I was delighted. As I went out I said now Hat you must raise the flag for that. We had a nice drive – Madam Van D. [Dusen] went with us and we went and got Babsey. She soon got tired & we took her home. Mrs S. goes every a.m. & takes turns taking the neighbors. This was my second trip. When I came home Papa was here and I got your letter. I had been feeling anxious since you wrote you did not feel well & that foot was discharging so I made Papa write Dr S. [Harry M. Sherman] Sunday to see if it was all o.k. and then I wrote for you to come home. Of course if you can have your shoe fitted by staying a few weeks longer we should advise doing so, but we hope you can arrange to board with the K's. Suppose the Drs are going to the medical convention as Dr Walker is. He told Papa after he told him about your letter this a.m. that he thought Dr S. would fit the shoe right away. Of course your leg will get stronger as soon as you can use it. Guess you will soon be as good as new.

Nellie was here last week and had on a <u>regular</u> <u>shoe</u>, *just like the one on [her] well foot, and said she could walk just as well & thought better for it was lighter. She was feeling very proud. When we came by the house saw Hat had flag waving. Said Papa telephoned to put it way up – on Louise's* <u>victory</u>. *Why, it excited us more than Dewey's!*

Will got up this a.m. and went up to his seine on the stea. There does not seem to be many fish. Four men get them – they are selling them. Hat wrote yesterday about the bureau cover etc.; if Ella is with you, tell her I want to get some yellow that her Xmas pin cushion will go with. Last eve H. & I went down to see if I could get a hat as H. wants mine, but could not find any thing, so shall have to keep it. H., when in P. [Portland], got a sailor & said it was all she should want, but now she wants a nice one or one more trimmed. Don't you think you could get a hat - something like my black one - cheap - and trim it for her? and bring it for a present. I will send you some money. Would think you could buy flowers & trim so much cheaper there. The hat she wants is $4.00, but I think we could buy a hat & fix it for less. Write on a slip of paper and tell me what you think. Don't know as I can afford one but you might let me know about what you could get up one for. When you come home would be plenty of time for she has two or three new that she can wear. How I wish Mrs K. [Kerckhoff] and Lillie would come up to see us. Do tell them that I shan't like it at all if they come so near and do not come to see me. Do you think it would make any difference if I wrote to them? I have asked so many times.

[Mama]

Mailing date: MAY 27 6.30PM 98   Astoria, Oreg.
Received: MAY 30 98 San Francisco,Cal.
Addressed to: Miss Louise Tallant
          c/o - H.M. Sherman M.D.
            1303 Van Ness Avenue
           San Francisco
           California.

Friday. May 27 – 1898

Dear Louise. –

Your letter this a.m. has made us all wild with delight. I can't realize that you will really be home in a week. Was so glad to hear the K's were coming as far as Frisco with you and have written a note which you will find in this to them asking them to come up and make us a visit, I do hope you can persuade them for I do long to see Mrs K. and have a visit from her as well as Lillie. I shall rather expect from your letter to hear Marg is with you and we will be glad if she can come as we shall feel easier about you on the trip, but all you will have to do on the stea. is to wait until some of us meet you. We will have them ring us up and we will ring up H.S. [Henry Sherman's livery service] so you will not have to walk up. I can't believe this is my last letter – or I may write one more if I hear where you are in time to send one.

Today has been one of excitement – first your letters. Then Mr & Mrs Strong came down [from Portland] on cars at noon & we decided to treat them to broiled salmon this eve. Then Nat has just been in & packed up to go to Gearhart with Ross, Paul Park, G. Ward & that Ohler boy to stay until Monday night. This noon Will sent up for his hat, coat etc as he was going up for his seine & was going to take the new minister who is taking Marcotte's place & they will not be home until late to night. The family all seems to be stuck on P. [Presbyterian] ministers – might be worse. The high school presented the boys with a silk flag this P.M. I watched them from your balcony until I almost lost my head. Last eve they gave a concert for them. I sent you a paper with act.[account] of fire but it went to H.[Harriet]. The Clatsop Box factory got a fire & took everything from it until it came to brewery where, being brick, they stopped it but it jumped from there to the old Lienenwebber [sic] cannery. Caught Booths [Cannery]. Telephone & Relief [the steamers] went to Booths & put it out – quite exciting. Then yesterday, Dick Merrion's horses ran – he was drunk, fell off and was killed – only lived long enough to be taken to hospital but was conscious. Well another call. Nat off, so now I will try to finish then go down to fix table. Never mind Puss if you can't use your foot quite as soon as you thought. The boys & girls would be disappointed to see you come home all o.k. – they want to pet you they say. You will have lots of chances to ride, although they will not be any such rides as you have been having. I know Hat will be delighted with her present – she always has wanted one so much. I do wish she would practice but she does not touch the piano from one day to another – it seems too bad after all the money we have spent.

I have not been feeling well so have not ans. Aunt C's or Mrs H's letters. Have taken 10 grains quinine three nights running. Guess the good news to day will make me feel so well that I shan't have to take any more. You won't know your neighborhood. Stokes new house, & J. Welch is putting a new front onto his house – has a <u>stone</u> foundation. Swell front, large windows, liese eru [leisure?] parlor and looks as tho it was going to be <u>quite a house.</u>

If you are at Aunt F's give them all my love. I hope to hear that Sid & L. [Smith] met you & that you are there. Remember me to Miss P. I hope some time when she is better and we are not so crowded to invite her to visit us. Hat is going down town now as I will have her mail it. Remember me to Dr S. & tell him I hope to meet him in Astoria.

Callers...so seal with a kiss.

Mama

The following article about the fire is from the morning issue of *The Daily Astorian* on Thursday, May 26, 1898.

FIRE FIEND'S WORK IN ASTORIA
Clatsop Mill Box Factory and Other Property Destroyed
ENTIRE SECTION THREATENED
Flames Started in Engine Room   Heroic Work of Fire Department
and Many Volunteers   Some Accidents

The most disastrous fire in years occurred in Astoria at 3:30 o'clock yesterday afternoon destroying completely the box factory of the Clatsop Mill Co., the Columbia cannery, the Pacific Union cannery, the old Lienenweber [*sic*] cannery and damaging the roadway of Exchange street, the Booth cannery and the railroad trestle.

The fire started in the engine room of the box factory and in a moment the entire building was a mass of flames. The fire department was soon on the ground with all the available apparatus in the city. The firemen were quickly joined by hundreds of volunteers and despite the heroic efforts of all it was soon evident that the box factory was doomed. A high wind from the west prevailed at the time which saved the sawmill from destruction. The attention of all was now bent to protect the spread of flames to adjoining property, but notwithstanding hard and brave efforts the flames caught the Columbia and Pacific Union canneries, which were burned to the water's edge. Then came the tug of war. John Kopp's new brewery was next in the line of march of the fire monster and for a time seemed certain of destruction. Additional men, under the leadership of Albert Seafeldt, took off their coats and worked as never before. Here there was some system observed and with satisfaction the boys saw that their hard work was not in vain. The brewery was saved.

In the meantime the wind carried sparks half a mile away to the Booth cannery, which caught fire, but the flames were quickly extinguished and no damage was done. Not so with the old Lienenweber [*sic*] cannery near by. Sparks set the roof afire, which burned 40 minutes before the department could get to it. By that time the whole building was burning and little of it was saved. The railroad trestle was scorched but General Manager Curtis had a gang of men stationed there with buckets and no damage was done. The steamer *Telephone* steamed down about that time and passed a line of hose ashore and helped keep the flames in check at this point. The damage to Exchange street was not great, but the planking had to be ripped up in places to get at the fire which was below.

The tug Relief, Captain Randall, steamed down to Hanthorn cannery and protected that from flying sparks.

As near as could be estimated last night the losses were about as follows: Clatsop Mill $16,000, insurance $10,000; Columbia cannery $20,000, insurance $11,000; Pacific Union cannery $2,500; Lienenweber [sic] cannery $2,500; net and boats belonging to fishermen stored in the canneries $10,600. The estimate as to nets could not be made accurately, but fishermen stated a large number were lost and damaged.

Police Officer Settem lost 145 fathoms of small mesh net, which was stored in the burned cannery. During the fire a number of accidents occurred, but accurate reports have not yet been received.

A man named Charles Johnson, who was on a boat near the box factory, was hit on the head by a timber, knocked overboard and would have drowned had not R. Adams jumped in and pulled him out.

One of the employees of the factory, young Connor, had to jump overboard to escape the fire, and Ernest Oberg was badly burned.

Mayor Bergman and others who watched the fire asserted that not one-half the damage would have been done under the old volunteer system and with experienced men under systematic methods. The paid fire department is too small to handle such a blaze as that of yesterday, and had it not been for the good work of volunteers that whole end of town would have gone up in smoke. The fire department companies did splendid work, and were promptly on the scene, but alone would have been unable to cope with the emergency.

Louise did not leave the Los Angeles area until June 5, 1898. She stopped in San Francisco for a short visit with her relatives and to see her physician, Dr. Sherman, for a final checkup. With her splint removed at last, she boarded the steamer for home with great anticipation and happiness.

Chapter Six   **July to early August 1898**
                                              Dick Volunteers

A mustached Dick
The Presidio, California

Portland, Oregon
July 2d 1898

Report in person at the Armory at Tenth & Couch Sts Portland
at 10 o'clock A.M. July 5th Tuesday prepared for mustering.

Kenneth Morton
2 Bt. 3 Arty. Mustering Officer

Unbeknownst to family and friends, Dick had signed up on April 19, 1898, for three years in the State of Oregon's National Guard, 2nd Division, Naval Battalion, as a Boatswain's Mate, 2nd Class. He was listed as "an electrician; born in Oysterville; age 24; 5'11 1/2" tall; with dark hair, blue eyes and a dark complexion." He remained in Oregon's National Guard officially until March 20, 1900, when Lieut. Commander Wm. A. Sherman of the ONG signed his honorable discharge from service to the State of Oregon and Dick was "removed from station."

The Spanish-American War 1898 to 1902

In 1885, Cuba began seeking autonomy from Spain – *"Independencia o muerte"* (Independence or death). Cuba's desire for freedom from Spanish rule spread to other areas, especially in the Spanish dominated Philippine Islands.

The year 1898 was an eventful and important one, which had a large impact on American lives. By February, while Maria Louise Tallant was recovering from her surgery in the Children's Hospital in San Francisco, some of the Spanish fleet remained in Cuban waters, still trying to quell the rebels. Although the U.S. Government did not officially recognize the insurgents, it was open to U.S. intervention and ordered a United States battleship to Cuba. On February 15, 1898, the Spanish attacked the American battleship, the USS *Maine*. She was destroyed, and sank in the harbor of Havana, Cuba, taking some two hundred sixty-six American lives. At home, Americans began to take notice and the rallying cry: "REMEMBER THE *MAINE!*" echoed across the nation. President William McKinley sent the battleship USS *Oregon* to Cuba from San Francisco on March nineteenth. Louise's mother worried about the onset of war in her April third letter, but most Americans probably did not feel truly involved quite yet.

President McKinley's demand that the Spanish immediately withdraw from Cuba was ignored. The President then ordered a blockade of Havana harbor by the United States fleet out of Key West, Florida. On April 20, 1898, an official State of War was declared against Spain. The U.S. Army and Marine Corps ground troops were deployed to help stop the Spanish and, to bolster the Army troops, President McKinley issued an authorization for the formation of a volunteer force.

From Santa Monica, California, on May 3, 1898, Louise wrote Dick of her concern that he would be called into service, but hoped the destruction of so many Spanish "boats" would keep the war away from the West Coast. Dick referred to events in a joshing way in his letter to Louise dated May 10, 1898, implying he intended to join the Volunteer army forces.

Meanwhile, in the Pacific, some of the Spanish fleet was still gathered there to defend their holdings in the Philippine archipelago. Ferdinand Magellan had claimed the islands in 1521. Spanish settlers had formally established the city of Manila by 1574. It was an uneasy history for the region with complex relations, open hostilities and wars which occurred with so many nations - Portugal, Holland, China, England, to name but a few. Almost everyone was vying for possession of at least a piece of the Islands. Generally, the Philippines were considered under the rule of the Spanish. But the Insurrection of 1896 had pitted the Filipinos' demand for change – for control to create their own national identity - against the domination of the Spanish. The Filipinos fought hard for their independence from Spain and finally were able to declare a provisional government on June 12, 1898. Later that year their national assembly ratified it.

In April, U.S. Naval operations to aid the Filipinos had been put into effect under Commodore George Dewey, who was ordered to maneuver his flagship, the USS *Olympia*, and his squadron of fighting ships into the area near Manila Bay. Their mission was to capture and/or destroy the Spanish ships. In Boca Grande Bay near Luzon, Dewey's group – with the famous quote "You may fire when ready, Gridley" - opened fire early on the morning of May first. By midday, Dewey had destroyed all the Spanish ships. By the seventh of May 1898, Dewey's squadron controlled Manila Bay.

Louise's mother, Mary Elizabeth (Lizzie) Tallant wrote Louise on Friday the thirteenth that, as exciting as Dewey's victory was in the Philippines, she felt more excited by Louise's "victory" over a difficult recovery from her surgery and the news of her impending return home after so many months away. *"Hat, you must raise the flag for that!"* And later, in her May 27 letter, she noted, from her daughter's balcony at their Grand Avenue home in Astoria, she could watch the parade of the young boys who had joined the army, as more men marched away to war. They carried a silk American flag, a gift from the high school, and the night before, they had enjoyed a concert given in their honor.

But the fighting in the Pacific was not over. Dewey realized he needed more troops – infantry troops – if he was to hold the area around Manila. He requested immediate aid. On May 25, one detachment left San Francisco bound for Manila via the Hawaiian Islands. A second group arrived in Manila on July 17 under Brig. Gen. F.V. Greene. The U.S. government ordered a third contingent of five transports under General Marrett, which reached Manila on July thirty-first. The U.S. Third Battalion, Second Regiment of the Volunteer Engineers, which included Dick in Company "M," boarded the wooden steam schooner *Lakme* in San Francisco on August 5. The ocean voyage to Honolulu took thirteen long days on that slow vessel. Dick arrived in Honolulu harbor early on the eighteenth of August 1898.

However on August 13, realizing he faced a formidable combined force of the U.S. Army, U.S. Marine Corp and the U.S. Navy, the Spanish commander in the Philippines surrendered. Thus the loss of lives on both sides was greatly limited.

Relations between the Filipinos and the Americans were not much better than with the Spaniards. During the night of February 4, 1899, armed combat broke out between the American and the Filipino troops around Manila. It ended in short order with the defeat of the Filipino forces, whose government promptly declared war against the United States. The U.S. then signed a treaty with their ex-enemy, Spain, and more soldiers were sent to the Philippines. Pres. McKinley appointed William Howard Taft as Governor of the Philippines in 1900.

The Spanish-American War did not officially end until April of 1902, when Cuba's first assembly took control of their government.

On the Fourth of July 1898, sent off by Louise and Marge with hugs and kisses, Dick, age twenty-four, left Astoria by train for Portland on the first leg of his journey as a member of the Third Battalion, Second Regiment Volunteer Engineers. This battalion was attached to the expeditionary forces, a part of the Eighth Army Corps. The Regiment was made up of four companies: I, K, L and M. Dick belonged to Company M. Their commander was Maj. W.C. Langfitt (Capt., Corps of Engineers of the U.S. Army.) Assigned to the Presidio in San Francisco, Dick waited for orders, hoping to cross the Pacific to join the battle. His battalion would remain at the Presidio until August 5, 1898.

SPANISH-AMERICAN WAR
Period July 1898 to May 1899

Envelope addressed to: R. E. Carruthers
    Not to be opened until the second day out on the ocean.
Envelope shows a color photograph of the USS *Maine* in front of the American flag.
Louise wrote in ink beneath the photo: "**Remember the *Maine*.**"

July 4th

Dear Dick -

I am a little excited over this sudden news of your going so my hand is not very steady but I know I wont get a minute to talk to you and when you are out on the deep blue sea and perhaps are a little blue yourself and maby sea sick too it might cheer you up to know that I am thinking of you – yes, I am sure I will be thinking of you no matter where you are or where you read this. This is so sudden Dick I haven't even had a chance yet to thank you for my birthday present which is a bute and I like it so much. I wish I had, or could do something for you but I don't know of any thing but what would be in your way. You will have so little room for your things although you said you would take a trunk & box. Please Dick forgive me for what I said about that box – it worries me so ever[y] time I think of it. We intended giving you a send off and asking all the old crowd up to have one of the good old times again and give you our blessing. You have mine any way and will pray for your safe return and we will celebrate your coming back instead of your going, for we haven't the time now to do that. Be good and brave and take care of yourself as much as you can. I will be one of the many who will be glad to see you back. I hope they put you off at the Hawaiian Islands. I hope you don't have to go to Cuba. Write to me when you can and when I know where to send a letter, [I] will write you all the Astoria news.

We will all miss you this summer. I am fraid there wont be many picnics & etc but I shant care much. I will go to S.F. in Oct. and then spend the winter trying to walk. I am having hard luck trying to celebrate the holidays this year. It began with my getting ready to go to S.F. on Thanksgiving day, then Xmas & New Years in the hospital. I said then I wondered what would happen on the 4 of July and now you are going to leave us and go so far away but we will have a celebration that will make up for them all when you get back and you will have lots of wonderful things to tell us about.

Well I guess Harriet & Marge are wondering why I am spending all the morning writing letters when there is so much excitement down town and if they knew it was all to you, would send so many messages and love that I wouldn't be able to close the envelope and I want all the spare room myself so am not going to let them know. I shant like it a bit if you open this before the time mentioned on the envelope although it may be a long time before that day for no doubt you will spend some time in S.F. I hate to have you go and still I know it is the best. Perhaps I can find time to write more later but must stop now. With best love to Dick and Remember the Maine and remember

Louise

P.S. As I cant be with you myself I send this small photo along to let it share your troubles and dangers. I am sorry that I had my eyes down for I would like to see you now. hope there is nothing mean in this letter – if there is it is not meant to be so and I hope I am forgiven for mean things said in other letters. Here is a parting kiss in case I don't get a chance to give it to you today. And what ever happens for the sake of good old times remember Louise. I can hear you say "no need to tell me that." Well I'll not forget you no matter how long you are away.

L.

Don't you fret about Dr F. for he is not in it with R.E.C.

The following is a portion of the article that appeared in the *Daily Morning Astorian* newspaper on July 5, 1898, about the Fourth of July celebration.

THE NIGHT CELEBRATION

In the evening after the news of Sampson's victory had been made known, a grand parade was held, forming on Eleventh and Commercial streets. The Columbia Marine Band headed the procession and discoursed some particular music, then came a squad of police under Chief Hallock, the Second division, Oregon naval battalion, followed by a large number of citizens, many people falling in line as the procession moved up Commercial street. Returning the procession halted in front of the Occident Hotel where speeches were made and rousing cheers given for Sampson, Shafter, Dewey and the boys in blue. The Columbia Marine band played some patriotic music and the crowd dispersed.

A large gathering was in attendance at the dance at Foard & Stokes hall last night, over two hundred couple [*sic*] being present. The hall was appropriately decorated with flags, the work of Miss Tallie Levy, of San Francisco, assisted by Alfred Cleveland. Crispin's orchestra furnished the music, which as usual was excellent.

The naval reserve yesterday evening assembled at the gymnasium to escort one of their departing comrades, Richard Carruthers, to the train, who successfully passed the examination for the engineer corps at Portland. Mr. Cyrus, son of A.R. Cyrus, has also joined the engineer corps. From Portland it is expected they will be ordered to San Francisco. Both young men have a host of friends in this city who wish them success in the United States army.

168

Mailing date: JUL 5 6-30P 1898 Portland Ore.
Received: JUL 6 7AM 1898 Astoria, Oreg.

July 5 [Tuesday]

Dear Louise:

Rather soon, but a line to tell you how it all happened. We will leave tomorrow night or Thursday night sure. I have got nothing to say but that all you girls are too good and I felt purty near breaking down last night, and I love you all, of course some more than others – mainly, well you know – two guesses. The "Ditty" bag is a daisy. I have looked it through and will try and take care of it as well as the money bag. Thank your Mother for the roses, and bless you all.

My address as near as I can find out:

R. E. C.

2nd Regiment Vol. Engrs.

San Francisco

I don't think you would reach me with a letter here. I should write more thanking you all for how good you were, but you know I appreciate it, and will....thanks, thanks. . .

Love to all and to you

With lots of, and lots of love for yourself.

Dick

Before Dick left Astoria, Louise gave him a lovely small soft chamois bag with a black drawstring top. The sturdy cord was long enough to be put over the head so the bag rested on the chest. Her tiny, tightly folded note inside read:

To wear round your neck to keep your money safe.

Hope it is big enough. "for richer or poorer"

yours

Louise

Mailing date: JUL 8 6.30AM 98 Astoria, Oreg.
Received: JUL 10 2AM 1898 Presidio
Addressed to: Mr R. E. Carruthers
                    2nd Regiment Engineers Corps
                    San Francisco
      Volunteers.   Cal

Thursday [July 7]

Dear Dick

I was glad to hear from you yesterday. Realy we did very little for you. We would all have been glad to have been able to do more. I think we all found it hard to swallow when the train pulled out – curious, isn't it, how that lump gets in your throat. I wonder if you left Portland last night or if you are getting ready to start now. We had our Fourth July picnic today – just eight girls and Griffen, Elmores driver. We had a splendid time – it is a perfect day.

Todays paper tells us the Hawaiian Islands belong to us – I hope you may be sent there, but then I guess Manila is a pretty nice place too. How are those cigars. Please Dick don't smoke so much, and that bottle you speak of I hope you didn't take it with you. You know I have a pretty high opinion of you and I should feel dreadfully to have to lower it even a wee bit and that is no Josh either. I always liked you best for that reason – at least that was one of the reasons, but that doesn't worry me. I would like to know though where you are going and when you are coming back – perhaps you would like to know yourself. We met your mother on the street yesterday and she said if we wanted to go camping she would lend us a tent – isn't she kind? Marge has gone to write a line to send with this. Every time we drive past the Depot now our horse wants to go in – she seems to like the place for some reason or maby she thinks we like it – just wait till we go down to meet you when you come back. I suppose people are making remarks about our kissing you good bye but we don't care and I only wish I had given you two. I will when you come back so be prepared.

I hope this reaches you in good time – let us know when you sail and just where a letter will reach you at the last minute. And if you get sick with the fever down there and need a nurse, just send for me. There isn't a [better] fever nurse than

Louise

That last is a mistake – I guess there are a few better than me.

Included with Louise's July seventh letter to Dick is one from Marge Halsted, who was visiting Louise in Astoria.

My dear Dick

We have just come home from the finist picnic and for a wonder we had the finist kind of a day for it to. If you had been here we might have asked you to go along but as we couldn't have you we concluded we would not ask any of the boys. I cannot tell you how much I miss you although we did not see much of each other this year, but the fact of knowing you were here was far better than thinking your going farther away all the time. I wish to goodness you wouldn't go to Manila. Now that's real mean isn't it? When you want to go so bad.

I have heard lots of fine trades for you the last two days and hope some day to tell you a few of them. Hope you are over the effects of the shock us girls gave you the night you left; but Dick you ought to be more used to such things than you are. I didn't suppose you would be so surprised when your sister would kiss you. Don't flirt with more than two Spanish girls at a time, for if you do there is liable to be trouble.

There has nothing happened since you left. I had a letter from home today and mama said she did hope you wouldn't leave before she got here, but alas, alarks. If you stay any time in S.F. she may see you on her way up.

There goes the six o'clock bell so I must go down to dinner. Now Dick drop me a line when you get a chance and be sure and take good care of yourself and come back soon.

With best love from

Marg.

Camp Miller encampment at the Presidio, San Francisco. Dick's tent is at the lower right corner.
(This original photograph is a cyanotype. The iron salts were not fully washed off.)

Dick stands in front of his tent at Camp Miller.

Five music makers: Harriet and Olga in front of
Louise, Lillie and Marge.
(Original image is a cyanotype)

Mailing Date: Jul 10 6PM 98 Astoria. Oreg.
Received: Jul 13 3PM 1898 Presidio. Cal.
Addressed to: Mr R. E. Carruthers
                                2nd Regiment Vol. Engineers
                                        San Francisco
          Company M.   Cal.

July the 8th 1898   [Friday]

Dear Dick

I fear you only stay in San Francisco for a few days I am going to write again (so soon) to make sure you get a letter before starting. Yesterdays Oregonian gave a list of the Company and about it, except the most important part, where and when you sailed but we will expect to hear that from you before long.

Well how do you like it as far as you have gone. Hope you got all the coffee and sugar you wanted with your twenty-one cents. Olga has invited all the boys and girls to have supper with her down in her back yard. Wish you were here to go. Last evening we had quite a musical. Olga came up with her mandolin and Mr Decum & Dr Finch called. Mr Decum plays beautifully on the mandolin & he seems very pleasant. Did you meet him? Marge & Hat have gone with Will up to his seining grounds. I have been out all morning driving Olga around to the different houses asking the people up tonight. If you are going to stay long in S.F. let me know where you are camped and I will write Lillie Kerckhoff to go out and see you. She would like to I know. I suppose lots of your Oakland chums will be down to see you off. Some of your Astoria friends would like to be there too, but we will be with you in spirit and if your right ear doesn't burn it ought to. Marge feels pretty bad because you have gone and she won't miss you as much as will

Louise

Mailing date: Jul 11 9AM 1898 Presidio. Cal.
Received: Jul 14 7AM 1898 Astoria, Oreg.
Envelope addressed to: Miss L. M. Tallant

Camp Miller   June 9 - 1898   [meant July]

Dear Louise:

I thought you might like to know how I like to be a soldier so I will write a few. Don't expect too much though as we have hardly got fixed up. Well we left Portland Thursday night after having been well cared for by the emergency corps and got here this morning having lived on ham sandwiches, cold meat and coffee but when I say we had a good trip I mean it. We had a cup of coffee and a sandwich from the Red Cross so early this morning at the ferry landing and then transferred six miles to where we are now; got our tents, blankets, straw and then started to pitch tents. Then there was searching for boxes, boards or any old thing [to] fix up with and you know I am not slow some ways myself and I hope I have my share of straw, boxes and planks. My pardner, who is pretty good himself, is Jackson of Portland[123] - a very good fellow so far. I don't know how it will last through. Say, I rather like the business so far and think I can stand it ok but then it would be nice if I could only call on a certain party once and, well say twice a week. How long we will be here I don't know but for some while I think to be drilled.

The food so far is alright and if it keeps up I shall never kick, but you know how it was at Elk Creek - so hungry you could eat any thing. We have all got a tin cup, plate and knife, fork and spoon, and when mess is called, line up single file and get coffee, no sugar or milk, bread with butter - "nit", bacon and well of course we have salt and pepper. Tonight we had fried meat and when it came time to wash my plate, etc, which everyone does his own, there is not much left to clean off. O yes, we get a spud handed out to us as we go by, and everyone goes to his tent to eat - four to the tent. - (well, wait a minute while I get my pipe lit) Say, but it seems funny, this business. O, when we left Frisco we each and every one of us got 21 cents, not dollars, and if I tell you that besides this I had the sum of 5 cents you would laugh but its so; and I've got 16 cents left and I am going to send you 11 cents for pocket pennies. I therefore have 5 cents left. Say I am getting so saving that when I get home I want [to] know how to spend money. The 11 cents is part of the first money I received from the government so I'll divide. Well I hope you are ok and happy and that Dr Finch is well "etc" and I am going to close but when I write again don't open the letter till you receive it and I'll make it a long one. I am going to write Marge in a day or two - tell her and thank her for the ditty bag etc.

Well I close on this page. If you see 'babe' give him my address and say to him I will write in a few days for a dance, etc.

With love and lots of it   Dick

                                Co. M. U.S. Vol. Engeers

                                Camp Miller

                                Presidio, Cal   Well consider it!

Mailing date: Jul 15 3PM 1898 Presidio. Cal.
Received: Jul 18 7AM 1898 Astoria. Oreg.
Envelope imprinted in red on reverse: Catholic Truth Society, S.F., Calif.

                        San Francisco June 14 - 1898   [meant July]

Dear Louise -

Just a line. I received your letter and you cant write to me too often. I have been doing my kitchen work today; tomorrow at 11 [a.m.] I go on guard and come off at 11 Saturday when I will have the afternoon to myself. THEN look out for a letter - it will be a good one. I guess

---

[123] Perry E. Jackson, a 24-year old Lineman born in Korkoma, Wisconsin, joined up in Portland, Oregon.

you received my letter since you last wrote. Don't wait for me to write as sometimes it is hard to get time although you need not think I am worked to death. I have to get back to camp in a few moments – am writing about 1/4 mile from [camp] at a very handy place indeed. Will not go before 23rd July, if then -

Love to all

Dick

Well I came near forgetting - you just consider yourself hugged good and hard and then, well – no need of telling you the rest. Cook, well – I am a dairy, coffee, bacon, soup, spuds, bread – all cooked in a washboiler and very nearly thrown at 90 hungry poor fellows who didn't have sence enough to let the Army be. Well I must sneak – just wait till Saturday and then, well say 10 cents Postage - I forgot to send you your share of 21 cents but will do it Saturday – haven't it with me now. Will answer you[r] letter then

Dick

I am out of sight in dust and never felt better in my life

Mailing date: Jul 16 4.30PM 98 Astoria. Oreg.
Received: Jul 19 3PM 1898 Presidio. Cal.

July 14th 1898   [Thursday]

Dear Dick

I was so glad to hear this morning from you. Guss told me yesterday they had heard so I was looking for a letter. Hope you got mine although they were not addressed just as you wrote to direct them. Yours is dated JUNE 9 – where were your thoughts, back in June somewhere – June 9th you were up here in the evening. Well you seem to be pretty comfortable. I do hope you had that 11 cents in your money bag and didn't loose it for I haven't gotten it yet and I want it very much. I will put it out at interest and we will spend it together having a good time when you get back. Cant you get some pictures of your camp. I wish you had our little Kodak. I would like to see how you are fixed up. Hope "Jackson of Portland" is a fine fellow and you will continue to be good friends. Give him my regards.

I am O.K. and happy as I can be under the circumstances. We are having rather a "hot time in the old town"; some of the young set of boys have gotten into trouble and Mama is broken hearted because Nat's name got mixed up in it through the kindness of Guss Woods. I guess you know what kind of a boy Guss W- is – troubles, troubles always isn't there Dick. I try not to worry because they say worry makes people thin and I don't want to get thin.

I spend a big part of my time driving around and we have a good deal of fun that way. Tonight there is a church social at your house. I hadn't intended going but I saw your mother this morning and she wanted me to come so Marge and I could play for them, so to be obliging I am going, but I wish you were going to be home. Every one had a fine time at the Knapton

174

party. I didn't go of course so I don't see why they all enjoyed it so much, but they say they did. Now Dick, please let up about Dr Finch – he was well the last time I saw him and very happy because he was talking to Sue.

Thanks for the eleven cents and <u>don't</u> forget to send them. It is kind in you to divide and I hope they will be lucky pennies "for us." I wished you'd send me one when I read in the Oregonian about your great wealth but did not expect so much as 11 cents. I am afraid you are denying yourself too much for me. Say Dick there is a friend of mine Fred Westdhall (you know Mrs Wadlieghs oldest son) in camp out there at the Presidio Camp Merritt with the Tenn. Troops – look him up. He is a fine fellow and awfully jolly. And Dr Walker stoped me this a.m. to say that he had a telegram saying to come and go off to Manilla and he said if they would give him until Sunday to get ready he would go. Hope he goes with you. I'll tell him to take good care of you.

I would like to see you washing your tin plate and etc, but realy do you get plenty to eat? And I am glad you like it all but agree with you it would be nice if you could come in once or twice a week to see

Louise

Stationery: Catholic Truth Society, Presidio.
Mailing date: Jul 17 6 AM '98 San Francisco Cala.
Received: Jul 20 7AM 1898 Astoria, Oreg.

Camp Miller, July 16/98   [Saturday]

Dear Louise

In keeping with my promise of the other night, I am going to try and write you a long letter. In the first place I'l glance over yours for the fourth or fifth time to see just how to answer it. I hardly think it will be much trouble, not near as much as one letter I had to answer and right here let me say I am not going to wait always for a letter and hope you will not wait before receiving a letter from me. If you only knew how much pleasure it is for me to receive one you would never hesitate in writing one; if it only be a few lines, it fills up the right spot. Well after one more thing I'l answer yours. Be good to me and perhaps some day I'll get even although I am perhaps far behind now.

<u>Well</u> your letter begins <u>so</u> soon. All I have to say is that makes me tired. I hope you all had a nice time at Olgas and am very sorry that I am not able to say I also had a nice time, and your wishes in regards to my being there are very gratefully received - I wish I had too. I have just met Mr Decum and my opinion which was very good of him will be somewhat lowered if he don't quit going with some people. Never mind names. I would like to see Lillie Kerckhoff but I don't know if she would consider it much of a pleasure or not – you will see the reason why later in my description of my personal appearance. I was over to Oakland Sunday and saw a few of the boys. They were all glad to see me except Chas. C. McClereity whom Stan Cullin and I met

while out driving. He was with his intended and was somewhat taken back I think at my appearance. The other boys took it, my being a soldier, as [a] good joke and came back to camp hoping to see me put in the guard house – now don't misconstrue this and think I had drunk the bottle you spoke of nor any thing else. They thought I was late for the roll call and I thought so myself. Your last letter I think as I have thought before, that is you have a pretty poor opinion of me. Well never mind girl I am not quite so bad and I think there are even worse than I. Don't let any body josh you too much about that good bye, and then be sure no one can josh you about bidding any one else good bye soon – not till you bid a welcome first. Now be true, if you don't – well, I don't know, but then something will drop.

Now I am going to try and tell you part of my experiences since arriving. First I will say there was nothing much happened in Portland or the way down to Frisco, but the Red Cross people, they used us fine and helped out a whole lot. Hardly know how we would have done with out them, nearly threw things at us. Gave us three or four dinners and when we left the Armory in Portland for the [railroad] cars, gave us a package which contained soap, towel, housewife,[124] Bible, wash rag, comb, sleeping cap (and it is alright), and a handkerchief for our necks and then came a fine bunch of flowers. The only people I met there were Lila and Miss Black who I think was a little susprised at seeing me at a Red Cross hand out. Well we had a good boys time on the train down but girl – or girls - suits me a little better. When we got started we all commenced to size each other up – I am not through with the details yet.

We arrived in S. F. Saturday morning, had fine coffee and so-so at the Red Cross and then marched six miles to the Presidio, Camp Miller. The two companies of Engineers were showed us, each four men were given a tent – and the whole bunch had them up in no time. The cooks were busy getting ready for dinner - dug a hole in the ground, place a stove over it something like Micks [Prael?] patent, got out four wash boilers, 4 or 5 pans and there is a first class company kitchen. Then came a fellow with straw - we go[t] our share, then shelter tents which we use in marching were handed out as sheets I guess. Then a blanket and dinner was ready. We all got in single file, were given a tin cup, plate, and knife, fork and spoon. Then after a dip of the dish or pan in a barrel of water to get the dust off we got one share of bacon, hardtack and coffee and all made a rush to our tents and "done the eat act," and I guess the bacon was alright and every thing else as far as that goes. Well we are going down to that kitchen three times a day; the meals are better as they have more time to prepare them. We get our stuff, go to our tents, eat and go wash the dishes, everyman his own, then a smoke. I believe I am [a] natural born soldier.

---

[124] Housewife: a little case or bag for needles, thread, scissors, pins, cloth for patching, etc. - also called: *hussy*. Sometimes spelt *huswife*. *Webster's* 1918 New *International Dictionary of the English Language.*

This place is fine except sand – I've seen sand but never before sun, wind and sand over everything, so much as here. It is no use of trying to keep clean although I do, but sand land[s] all over. Well we get up at 5.40 to the tune of an old tin horn. roll call - six. breakfast - 6.20 clean tent; roll call and drill from 8 to 11. dinner at 12. drill - 3 to 5. supper - 5.30. have to be in the lines at 9. in tents - 9.30. Taps at 10. This is your work if not otherwise appointed.

Thursday I was kitchen police - that is help the cooks; Friday at 11 [a.m.] I went on guard – have to be at the guard house for 24 hours straight - you are on duty all the time but only have 2 hours of guard work and then 4 hours off. I went on at 1 [pm] Friday afternoon, was relieved at 3, went on again at 7, was relieved at 9, went on at 1 Saturday morning and relieved at 3. Then my last trip was 7 to 9 this morning. You do not have a chance to get much sleep as there are no beds in the guard house - bring your blankets and sleep on the floor. This guard duty only strikes you twice a month and you have the afternoon off on the day you come off. I am taking mine now. Will have to report back at 6.30 for roll call, and by the way, I might say supper. O yes I must say we buy extra things such as butter, caned milk, etc and I am getting fat besides a fair starter of a mustache, of which I am very proud and our camp barber, who by the way is the cook, says it will be one of the best ever.

I wish I had a Kodak but then they wouldn't allow one in the post, but I would like to send up a picture or two. But when I get home I'll take one or perhaps several evenings off and tell you of all the good times we had. Because I realy enjoy it - enough work to make the food taste good and so you want to be lazy. I so far have not been fortunate to receive any non-commissioned office, but I am to tell you the truth glad of it as they have so much more work to do. And I have enough and Uncle [Sam] is good in giving me so much money for my work I am satisfied.

Well I think this is a very long letter although it might not be very interesting, excuse. I am purty tired from my 8 hours walking and telling gay fellows to halt and yelling like an Indian for a Corporal of the Guard Post No 4.

Well the main thing is that I am happy, not so much so as if I were only in Astoria for a day or two. Am perfectly sure I'l live on the U.S. rations and that I love a certain _little_ girl as 'bout as much as ever if not more and want to hear from her when ever she can spare the time if but a line. I am writing this you will see at The Catholic Truth Society. The Truth is I don't care much as long as I can get out of a sandy tent and in to one where people have a table and ink – where about 100 of the boys are busy as bees all day long writing letters. Well there is lots I could write, but then you know how that feeling comes and this I guess will have to do, besides I have some few lines to drop home yet to day.

Some say we go on 23 - sure I don't know. A large lot of one town went yesterday, but their places were taken by 1300 from New York. Well I hope to have a letter from you this evening and I'll soon write you another when I get a chance to run over here, for this is a snap. I don't know how you like the rubber stamp yourself but everybody takes advantage of <u>Ink</u>. I want to say of the several house wifes I have, two from home, two from Red xxx [Cross]. There is only one that I can do any thing with.

              With love and lots of it   *X*

                    Dick

    Love to all the girls and Marge, regards to every one who might have interest enough to ask. Never mind the joshing. We won't do a thing to the natives when I get home

    If you can't read this - keep it by and I' [will] translate it some time

    I am still remembering the Maine! –

    And that's about all. Is the war over. I couldn't tell for sure.

KP Duty

The Door Plate Dick and the three other engineers nailed to the their tent post.
The sign was made on a scrap of cardboard.

178

Mailing imprint and stamp torn off
Received: JUL 26 7AM 1898 Astoria. Oreg.
Addressed to: Miss L. M. Tallant
Stationery: Catholic Truth Society Presidio

I got your letter ok . Thanks   *San Francisco July 22 1898*   [Friday]
Dear Louise

Just a line to say we are now to go to. Honolulu is one port first and as we are told to be ready in from 3 to 10 day[s]. I write this so you will try and get a letter to me before we sail – address same - it will be forwarded if I have left. I am going to write you tomorrow, but this is a warning as soon as I could give you so I will surely expect a mate for the one I've already got in my inside pocket. I would write more but have not the time. Tomorrow, one day off, I will see you are not forgotten and I hope you will be glad to be remembered by ----. Well lots of the same old thing you know

           Dick

Will have several relics for you as soon as we break camp – will send them together. How is Dr Finch. He is awfully nice I think. Remember me to all, and Marge I think owes me a letter. Well - till tomorrow.

Mailing date: JUL 27 5.30PM 98 Astoria. Oreg.
Received: JUL 30 3PM 1898 Presidio. Cala.
Return address on envelope: Return to Box 54 Astoria, Oreg.

                    July the 27th 1898   [Wednesday]

Dear Dick

Your letter saying that you would leave in from 3 to 10 days came yesterday and I should have answered it right away but I was so tired from being up the night before when Mrs K- and Lillie came that I fell asleep right after lunch and did not wake until callers came and then after they had gone I drove Hat & Marge around the point to the picnic Violet Bowlby gave – a "walk out." They went over the new eights street road down on to the beach at the end of the road and the girls say they had a fine time. Lillie has been half sick with a dreadful cold so she could not go.

I do hope this gets to you before you leave. So you realy are going. I am glad for I know you will be. People have been saying all along that they wouldn't send more troops and that you would not go, so I am glad you are realy going to get the chance and hope so much that it will be of benefit to you and that you will be lucky in having good companions. I hope we will hear soon what boat you go on and the exact date. Babe[125] said he had a long letter from you the day before yesterday and you were cooking for the officers. I wonder what they have to eat but

---

[125] The Carruthers' family referred to Dick's younger brother, Robert Rex, as both "Babe" and "Tod."

I remember you are some what of a cook – at least you got breakfast while at Elk Creek for some of the boys that were going to town. Oh, those good old Elk Creek days – I love to think to them. I rather looked for another letter today but guess it will come tomorrow. I have a dreadful headache today and have got "the blues" so I am afraid this wont be much of a letter but I couldn't let another day go by. I had so many things I wanted to say and now I cant think of a thing and my head feels like a lead ball.

The Perry is here again – they say there are lots of nice young officers on her this time. Mr Ross & Mr Sturdevant are the only ones that were here before. We are having a hot time voting for a Regatta Queen – 5 cents a vote. It seems to me the craziest thing Astorians ever did and they have done some pretty funny things some times too. I wish I didn't feel so stupid but I will try and write again very soon and do better. Marge is shocked now because I have written so many letters to you already, but I tell her it is all right – I am just trying to be good and I have been haven't I.

Well Dick I simply cant hold up my head any longer. I have been about an hour writing this much and I haven't said any thing bright either so guess I must close. This is a warm day, a little too warm to suit me. Lillie didn't get my letter that had your address so she did not get out to see you as you must know with out my telling you. If this is the last letter you get before starting. - Well good bye   good luck   and God bless you and bring you safely home to your friends & family and

Louise

The August fifth edition of the *Astorian Evening Budget* printed a notice that Robert and Harriet Carruthers had received a letter that morning from their son. Dick told his parents that the command he was in had been ordered to break camp to go aboard the transports for Manila. Many rumors circulated through the camp continuously, so no one really knew what was going on or when they would actually be shipped out. This particular "rumor" turned out to be accurate – at least about being shipped out.

Mailing date: Aug 12 6.30AM 98 Astoria, Oreg.
Received via San Francisco: Aug 27 1PM 1898 Honolulu
Addressed to: Mr R. E. Carruthers
           2nd Reg. Vol. Engineers
           Honolulu, Hawaiian Ils. U.S.A.

August 8th Monday

Dear Dick

Your short note received yesterday saying you were going. Sorry we did not know in time to send a telegram with our last farewells. Hope you had time before the Str. left to write a few lines more. <u>Thanks</u> for the photo, buttons, 11 cents and etc. The picture doesn't do you justice but I am awfull glad to have it just the same. Is that your swell pipe you have in your hand?

I kept all the love you sent but divided the buttons as you must have meant me to do. We will have them made into pins I guess. I think Marge is writing so we will probably tell you about the same things. Mrs Halsted comes tonight - you can imagine Marge is happy.

Who made the door plate - it is great. Give my regards to Jackson Hendershot, Fairchild's Dr (love to the Dr). You probably read my letter today - stale wasn't it - it was written so long ago but it isn't ever[y] one who gets mail the second day out. It seems so strange to think that when this reaches you you will be way off on the Hawaiian islands or even perhaps gone on to Manila. What do you expect to do - stay there in Honolulu or go to Manila? I am glad you are well, there has been so much sickness - poor fellows. It is hard luck, think of all the fever there is in Cuba. Isnt it dreadfull. I wonder if you are sea sick. No doubt you will look up Mrs Burbach [Bierbach] while you are down there. How do you like it all. Any way, write all about it.

Friday Mrs Kerckhoff gave us a treat - she took us all to the Sea Side house to stay over night. We had a splendid time. They had a mussel bake and who do you think was there? Why Jim Corbett[126] - and he very kindly brought the mussels to me, opened them for me, told me all about where he got them down at Elk Creek, what nice salad he could make out of them. Oh I assure you he was quite attentive and we had quite a chat. How does that strike you? Poor Jim, I wonder if he realy is crazy, he <u>doesn't look as if he was.</u>

It is near dinner time now. We have been baking cookies all afternoon. How I wish I could send you a lot of them - just think we made over 70 doz. And that is the truth. Mrs K-, Hat & I. I think they will last a while don't you. We went by a receipt and had no idea it would make so many. We are dead tired now so I will finish this tomorrow. We are all well. I am feeling fine - foot is ok. Good bye for today. Oh yes I forgot to say your postal came this a.m.

Hat just tumbled down stair with a lamp in her hands - excitement is over now and no damage done except to her crazy bone and the lamp chimney.

Your postal was dated <u>Aug</u> 30th - you were rattled but no wonder. Only wish I could have said good bye again.

Marge & I made a bet this a.m. about your coming back in 6 months.

<u>Tuesday</u> ---

Mrs Halsted came this morning or rather last night but as I could not go to the depot did not see her until this a.m. She is looking quite well; said she wished she had known which boat

---

[126] This Jim Corbett was from a local Astorian family. He was not the famous boxer, "Gentleman Jim" Corbett.

you were on – and we haven't been able to find out yet. Why didn't you say? Went out for drive last night as usual; met your Mother and Zoe down town and had a long chat with them. Both are looking well; Zoe looked especially pretty. Wish she would be Regatta Queen. The voting is quite exciting. Maude Stockton is ahead now. Do you have the papers sent you? I will send them if you don't. I guess Guss is down in S.F. I got a paper "The Wave" this morning sent from the Grand Hotel and Hat says it is Guss' writing on the wrapper. It is fine. Has all the pictures of the troops, you among them and the camps of the Engineers.

<u>Wednesday</u> ---

This letter goes on the installment plan. I will finish it up this time and send a photo along Lillie took of us all on the porch. I know you will be glad to see us all (Mamma, Mrs K, Marge, Hat & I and Harry).

Yesterday we four girls spent the day at Mrs Meglers – had a good time but got up so early to catch the boat that we nearly went to sleep befor lunch time. Will has his horses down from the seining grounds and yesterday eve we hitched up Billy and had a great ride; he is a stylish looking horse, holds his head high. It was great fun. Well Dick I must close now – sure write lots of love because if I write more the envelope wont hold it. Good bye. Don't get homesick but think of us all, often. We, at least I, think of you every day and hope you keep well, happy.

As before, and write soon to

Louise.

I forgot to mention the fact that Dr Finch called Tuesday and was here this a.m. helping Lillie develop pictures. He had <u>nothing</u> to do with the one I send, however, and I cant tell you you neednt be jealous of him.

Yours!

Co. M. 2nd. Reg. U.S.V. Engineers,

Dick is just to the left of the flag – with a small "X" above him.

Roster of Company M, As Mustered in on the Seventh Day of July 1898.
All mustered in as Second-Class Privates.

Names.	Age.	Where Born.	Occupation.
Batter, Frank	43	St. George, Canada	Carpenter
Baxter, John C.	21	Orange, N. J.	Fireman
Bell, Chas. W.	38	Newburg, Ind.	Carpenter
Bishop, Asa	31	Duncans, Va.	Miner
Bittner, Austin H.	22	Marshall, Mich.	Machinist
Blackburn, Frederick R.	38	Fall River, Mass.	Steam engineer
Blevins, Thomas	27	Warrensburg, Mo.	Railroad trackman
Bodinson, Gus.	29	Soderhamn, Sweden	Railroad laborer
Butler, Ernest I.	21	Luverne, Canada	Electrician
Bynon, Benjamin J.	28	Moss River, Ohio	Miner
Carney, John J.	38	Portland, Me.	Railroad carpenter
Carroll, William	25	San Francisco, Cal.	Laborer
Carruthers, Richard E.	23	Oysterville, Wash.	Electricalworker
Clark, George	23	Lansing, Mich.	Telegrapher
Clark, John C.	33	Bridgeport, Ohio	Chemist
Coffin, Jacob E.	32	Haycock, Mich.	Wheelwright
Connertin, F. David	28	San Francisco, Cal.	Fireman
Coulter, Alva S.	38	Olympia, Wash.	Miner
Covington, Wm. H.	24	Lexington, Ky.	Railroadman
Craig, James D.	28	New Prospect, Tenn.	Railroadman
Crow, Augustus	26	London, England	Cablesplicer
Crowel, Charles	23	Burnettsville, Ind.	Miner
Currier, Frank K.	27	Locks Mills, Me.	Railroadman
Curry, Geo. G.	30	Union, Ind.	Clerk
Cyrus, Henry W.	26	Clakamas, Ore.	Electricalworker
Doolan, Peter E.	27	Palermo, Canada	Miner
Dugdale, George E.	27	Batavia, Ill.	Clerk
Dunlop, David	43	Monaghan, Ireland	Carpenter
Elwell, William F.	31	Decatur, Ill.	Civil engineer
Erickson, Charles	35	Leffele, Sweden	Butcher
Fairchild, Louis E.	31	Morrow, Ohio	Electricalworker
Fletcher, Ormand	39	Toronto, Canada	Topographer
Francis, Charles H.	24	Chicago, Ill.	Bridge carpenter
Francis, Ed. R.	21	Chicago, Ill.	Bridge carpenter
Grau, Claus C.	36	Skoten, Norway	Miner
Hall, Wendell	37	Juda, Wis.	Civil engineer
Hanna, William	21	Irvine, Scotland	Railroad trackman
Harris, James F. L.	36	Columbus, Wis.	Telegrapher
Haws, Herbert	21	Charleston, W. Va.	Machinist
Hendershot, Grant	19	Salem, Ore.	Steam engineer
Howell, George L.	21	N. Yamhill, Ore.	Bridge carpenter
Hunt, Floyd P.	37	Independence, Mo.	Steam engineer
Inglerock, Charles S.	26	Pendleton, Ind.	Railroadman

Names.	Age.	Where Born.	Occupation.
Jackson, Perry E.	24	Korkoma, Wis.	Lineman
Johnson, William	33	Dalles, Ore.	Laborer
Jorgensen, Jorgen	31	Frobjerg, Denmark	Telegrapher
Kieth, William G.	34	Iola, Kas.	Carpenter
Kellogg, Bert A.	32	Whitesville, Mo.	Steam engineer
Kissell, William F.	38	Johnstown, Pa.	Telegrapher
Kitchen, Frank P.	28	Hull, England	Concreteworker
Lanka, Robert	22	Chicago, Ill.	Draftsman
Linn, Ellsworth P.	38	Van Wert, Ohio	Steam engineer
Logsdon, Charles E.	26	Benton county, Ore.	Carpenter
Leister, Archie C.	24	Wheeling, West Va.	Railroadman
Lynn, John C.	32	Big Rapids, Mich.	Blacksmith
Mason, Charles A.	35	Cambridge, England	Laborer
Meyst, William, Jr.	25	St. Paul, Minn.	Carpenter
Miehlstein, Joseph	23	Treverton, Pa.	Plumber
Millar, William E.	24	Trenton, Canada	Metal polisher
Moriarty, James	36	Winona, Minn.	Bridge carpenter
McCarty, Walter L.	26	Fort Scott, Kas.	Railroadman
McDermott, William	21	Bridge Station, Ill.	Boatman
McFarland, Adolphus G.	24	Delaware, Ohio	Railroadman
McReynolds, Sterling	35	Santa Rosa, Cal.	Marine fireman
Nolan, John	39	Du Chien, Wis.	Teamster
O'Heary, John F.	20	Springfield, Ill.	Railroadman
Reed, George H.	27	Indiana, Pa.	Carpenter
Rodabaugh, Thomas W.	23	Coquele, Ore.	Railroadman
Seyde, George A.	35	Chemnitz, Germany	Clerk
Shea, Daniel	41	Milton, Pa.	Railroadman
Shepard, Sylvenus F.	43	Proonuba, N. Y.	Blacksmith
Simpson, Frederick A.	33	Wenham, Mass.	Carpenter
Smith, Fred W.	21	Oregon City, Ore.	Draftsman
Sproul, William W.	30	Doniphan, Kas.	Carpenter
Stephens, Clarence W.	24	Pleasant Home, Ore.	Operator
Sweetser, Edwin S.	24	Portland, Maine	Carpenter
Turner, William H.	33	Chardon, Ohio	Blacksmith
Wallace, Frank J.	28	St. Louis, Mo.	Carpenter
Waller, Sampson	18	San Francisco, Cal.	Clerk
Welsh, Maurice D.	24	Rossville, Ill.	Miner
Warness, Edward	36	Stzerton, Norway	Stonemason
Welch, Michael	44	County Curry, Ireland	Miner
Westlake, Fred W.	24	Florence, Col.	Sketch artist
Wheeler, Valentine	39	Camppelton, Canada	Carpenter
Wikander, Gustavus A.	19	Keokuk, Iowa	Blacksmith
Wilson, William P.	30	Grayson, Cal.	Steam engineer
Stratton, Orin H.	25	Elk Point, S. D.	Civil engineer
Anderson, Charles A.	27	Kyrke Falls, Sweden.	Carpenter
King, Charles R.	30	Milwaukee, Wis.	Carpenter
Wilkinson, Frank	26	Alcampa, Cal.	Surveyor
Weaver, Lawrence M.	26	Mattoon, Ill.	Railroad fireman

Note: The four last named men were mustered in at the end of July.

The list is printed from Captain William Mayo Venable's *The Second Regiment of the United States Volunteer Engineers. A History*, (Cincinnati: McDonald Co., 1899), pp. 144-145.

Chapter Seven   **August to October 1898**
                                                                   Westward Ho

The Third Battalion, under the command of Capt. F. J. H. Rickon, and the New York Volunteer Infantry marched from the Presidio to the San Francisco docks on the fifth of August 1898.[127] Cheering crowds lined their passage along the streets. Thirteen officers and three hundred sixty one men were assigned to an older Alaskan coastal steamer, the *Lakme*. In Dick's letters he misspelled the vessel's name as "*Lackme*;" another member of Company M, Michael Welch, misspelled her name as "*Lakine*."[128]

The Klondike Steamer *Lakme*

In the late summer of 1898, the U.S. Government commandeered the Klondike steamer *Lakme* to transport some of the troops from San Francisco and Honolulu. She was definitely not built for that purpose.

The *Lakme,* the first wooden screw steam schooner built in the Pacific Northwest, was vessel No. 140944 (gross tons 529; length 176.8; beam 38.8; hold 12.6; speed 8.25 knots).[129] In 1888, T.H. Peterson built and launched the steamer from Washington State's Port Madison shipyards for G.H. Hinsdale of San Francisco. On her first trip from her homeport in September 1889, she was chartered by the Oregon Railroad & Navigation Company and served that company for many years.[130] In 1898, the *Lakme* had delivered the ill fated expedition group to Kuskokwim Bay, where the group boarded a vessel named *Jessie* and mysteriously disappeared.[131]

Dick reported in a January 18, 1899 letter about a fire that almost destroyed the *Lakme* while she was docked in Astoria. She apparently returned to the northern waters later in 1899, providing service to St. Michael and Nome, Alaska under the auspices of the Seattle & Yukon Transportation Company. She was listed as wrecked later in 1899 on St. George's Island, Alaska, but apparently was repaired and returned to service. [132] The *Lakme* appears again in January 1911, when, carrying a load of lumber from Coos Bay to San Francisco, she was damaged in a violent storm and almost ran aground on the beach. She was saved by a passing steam schooner whose crew was able to get a line aboard her and towed her to a safe harbor.[133] She continued as a lumber ship until 1927 or 1928. The *Lakme* was scrapped after forty years of service - a sad end for any vessel of the seas. However, the troops who had sailed on her in August 1898 would not have mourned her passing.

---

[127] Venable, 103.
[128] Michael Welch's web site: www.spanamwar.com/2ndengineerswelch.htm).
[129] Merchant Vessels, 265.
[130] Wright, ed., *Lewis & Dryden's Marine,* 356.
[131] McCurdy, 42.
[132] Ibid., 46.
[133] Ibid., 195.

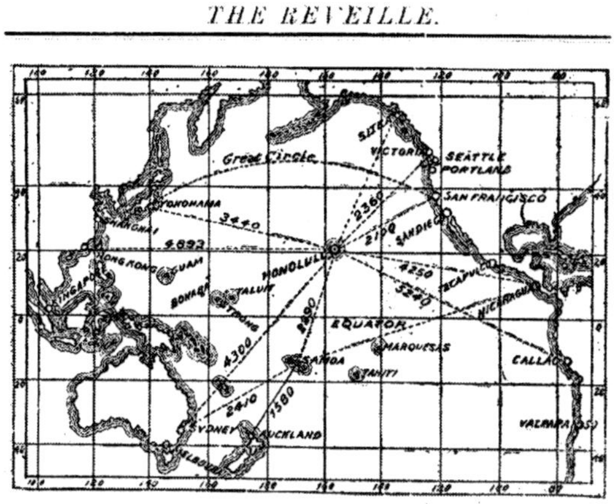

San Francisco to Honolulu – 2100 Miles.

Setting sail from San Francisco.
(original image is a cyanotype)

Dick's correspondence of August seventh and eighth, written in pencil on very thin "tissue" paper, was difficult to read. The "letter" he refers to at the start of this is the one Louise gave to him before he left Astoria on the Fourth of July. She had instructed him not to open it until his second day out on the ocean.

Spare time on the Lackme - Or What I did with part of my time -
Page 1

> On Board the *Lackme*
> Pacific Ocean Aug 7, 1898   [Sunday]
> 2nd Day out

Dear Louise.

I am going to try and amuse myself now and hope that which will help pass my twelve or fourteen days will entertain you some in the near future. If I write too much you need not read it all. Well first let me say I have opened the letter and received the photo. I had one with me already but am glad to have another. Thank you for it, as well as the letter.

One of your wishes came out alright I see, i.e. you wished I would be put off at the Hawaiian Isles. You wish you could have done something for me - well I think you have done a big lot. Well there is lots of nice things said in the letter and I am awfully glad that the x [kiss] was delivered before now. You cant tell how things are going to come out sometimes can you. I don't know if I shall always remember the Maine, but there is surely no use in you telling me to remember Louise. I think I shall. Well I guess you have forgotten half what you said in the fourth of July letter, so I will keep good care of it and show it to you when I return. The next thing is to answer the last letter I got before sailing. It was one from you and I was glad I got it for if I had a notion you were tired of writing to me, it put a stop to any such idea. I got it about a half hour before we went in to the stream Friday afternoon. I am afraid I am a little bit larger in the head since I read it. I surely ought to enjoy receiving a letter from you after the time you have writing one. Girls. Phone. Doorbells, etc. Girls were always troublesome and I have at times known doorbells to be troublesome. Well I realy appreciate a letter from you, and you know it.

The mustache is a goner and I will try and keep it in trim. Well I guess I would that you were along only I would want you a little better situated. Well I am glad I got the letter before I left as it made [me] feel a whole lot better. I have been busy sewing most of the time today so will close and tomorrow will start on the trip from the time we broke camp. Well so long for a while. Well I guess I wont [write] more [of] this today. Will add more tomorrow.

Aug 8th 1898   *Third Day Out*   [Monday]

Well here goes for some more. We broke camp on Friday morning at 7 oclock. They were roused at 4.40. I was on guard that night and was stationed at the Christian Commissioners tent which was being used as a guard house as the old one was too small. I had 16 prisioners under charge during the time and had a real nice time of it. At 8 the signal was given to break camp; at the sound of the last note every tent came down at once and what had been our camp was a small file of tied up canvases. Co 'L' won, got through in two minutes with 'M' a close second. Then in about an hour came our march to the dock - six miles with 40 pounds on your back and only two hours sleep the night before. Well I made it with my spirits well up from the cheers and attention we received on the way. Upon arriving at the dock about 12, I was much susprised to see Gus and spent most of the time talking to him. We went aboard about five after a meal from the Red Cross and lay in the bay a mile down from town that night. The next morning we started on the old *Lackme*, a steam schooner, and the room we have is more than you would think - 400 on this small ship. Well when I first came on board I thought dam several times but like every thing else I am well use to it. I have one of the best bunks on board and with the aid of a hunk of salt water soap keep purty clean. The weather has been fine and today bids fair to be warm as we are fast coming in to the tropics - tomorrow it will be hot. I have not felt the least bit sick and few are I am glad to say.

We get an early breakfast served on deck as are all other meals. One company served at a time taking turns - if we are first at one meal, we go last at the next and keep going the rounds. The food so far is better than army rations. The boat feeds us and they are doing very well so far. We still hang on to our plates and sit any old place as long as we can eat and do our own washing. We have a fair wind and with all sails set are perhaps going ten knots so you see we *are not so fast. Yesterday we passed a sailing ship and today so far nothing but a lot of flying fish. It will take us about nine days longer but we are very liable to have fine weather the rest of the way. I spent a good part of my time putting a pocket in my new white suit, which was not supplied with any and it is a daisy I tell you. The buglers are at practice; Co. 'I' at setting up exercises and it is, with the call of the tramp, hard to think of much. We bring our bedding up next and take our exercise and thank goodness go to dinner first today for I am as hungry as well you know me. I can't help but think of Elk Creek every time I look out at the water, and when I get back there is the first place we will have to go to – just see if we don't.*

Well there is not much to say but I [will] write some when anything happens to write about, and if I happen to get a chance to mail a letter on a passing steamer I will add a few lines at the last moment. Well this will I guess be all for today. Well they say we are going to meet a mail steamer today so I'l close this and have it ready to go on board. We are still on the move and have good weather. Well I say good bye for this one now and send lots of love and just wish you were here for well say a day or two.

Dick

If I do not get a chance to send this I will put a '1' on the outside of it, so read this one first and don't open it until you get it.

THE SANDWICH ISLANDS

In 1555, the Spanish navigator, Gaetano, was the first European to reach the group of islands in the mid-Pacific Ocean now known as the Hawaiian Islands.

By the early Eighteenth Century, comparatively little of the Pacific Ocean had been explored or mapped. However in 1768, the British Admiralty selected the young Lieutenant James Cook to head several voyages of discovery into this vast region. For his first voyage Captain Cook chose a flat-bottomed, shallow draft *collier* vessel, the *Endeavor*, to allow him better flexibility to investigate shallow waters and inlets. He engaged two *colliers*, the *Resolution* and the *Adventure*, for his second expedition. Cook was an expert surveyor, mapmaker and navigator, so was able to deliver volumes of scientific data and knowledge to the British Royal Society, which in turn was able to create far better charts of the Pacific Ocean – many blank areas were filled in. Cook discovered and named numerous islands, large and small - as well as the Antarctic and the Arctic Ocean. He claimed many islands in the name of Great Britain, including the North and South Islands of New Zealand.

Each of his first two voyages had taken three years. It was not until 1776 that he began his third and final one – with the *Resolution* and the *Discovery*, another *collier*. His mission on this voyage was to determine if a northwest passage did exist across the northern part of North America. Sailing east from England around Africa, south of India and then north in the Pacific Ocean, Cook found no such passage. In 1778, he did stop at a chain of islands in mid-ocean, which he named for his good friend, John Montague, the

Third Earl of Sandwich. Although Cook was at first welcomed as a representative of one of the island peoples' gods, Lono, relations with the native people deteriorated. Fighting erupted. Cook was killed – the rumor he was eaten has never been substantiated.

However, thanks to Captain Cook, this chain of islands was accurately entered on official British Admiralty charts of the Pacific as the "Sandwich Islands" and remained thus named for many years. The Islands were, and still are, a "stepping stone" of major importance in the vastness of the Pacific Ocean.

Distance to the Hawaiian Islands from San Francisco – 2,100 miles.
Latitude: 21 degrees, 18' Longitude: 157 degrees, 51'
Dick and his fellow soldiers on the *Lakme* reached Honolulu on August 18, 1898.

Honolulu Aug 18 / 98

Dear Louise

Just a line to say I am here and that the intended long letter on the boat was a failure due to the fact that there was not [a] thing to write about. Got here about 4 this morning and so far I like the place. A steamer leaves this afternoon so I send this to say I am well, completely happy, a little homesick and want to send a little love. Will write soon -

Dick

A small notice from a local newspaper (neither the name of the newspaper nor the date is known) was pasted into Dick's scrapbook. There was no heading. It would appear the military on Oahu had not been well prepared for the arrival of so many more soldiers and volunteer engineers.

The letter received from "Dick" Carruthers gives a pretty hard description of the life that he has to lead in Honolulu. When four hundred of them were herded together like swine in the *Lackme* on the trip over he took it good naturedly because he believed it was a war necessity, but on the arrival they expected better treatment but for days they were given but coffee and bread three times a day and the bread was limited. It is a little better now but not much.

Honolulu Oahu

August 21 1898   [Sunday]

Page 1

Dear Louise:

I am going to try and write you a good-sized letter. I'll start in with when we left the old Lackme as the less I say about the trip on her the better. It was a hard one; I like to rough it but that was a little too much. We are camped at the fort of Diamond head about four miles from Honolulu and if it was not for the ants, "thousands of them", bugs and dust I would consider it a very nice place. We are as usual very nicely fixed, matting on the tent floor and a dining room in the rear made of our shelter tents fitted with a table, made of what was a fence before we came. There is a tree, a small one, at the back of the tent which gives us some shade in the afternoon. I am now using the dining room as a very good writing place. The shade tree we have is one that was introduced by the missionaries, has a bean on it that is used as feed for stock. It also grows a liberal supply of thorns. The only use we put the tree to - it furnishes us with toothpicks. We are within five minutes walk of the bathing beach and we have sun in every day. It is fine. We have as good water as any one but it is always warm and nothing extra. There is enough slope for good drainage so all around I think we have a good ground. How long we will be here is a question now that we hear the war is over but I hardly think we will be here 4 or 6 months, at any rate as we will be the last to be discharged. Then if I like the place and find something to do I might stay a while longer, but that is looking ahead a long way.

We had mail yesterday and I am sorry to say I did not get a line from any one, but next steamer will surely expect a letter or two. So far I like the place and only wish I were able to write, as I think one who could would be able to write a good letter from here. We have of course sampled all kinds of fruit that we have been able to get a hold of. We have had our fill of Pineapples, bananas, Mountain apples and a half a dozen other things, to say nothing of Pineapple and banana pies which the natives sell us. The oranges are black and are nothing extra. There are about a dozen stands at our gate looked after [by] Chinamen, Japs, natives and whites, all after the soldiers' nickels, who have everything from soda water to coconuts.

Well I'l try and say what I think of the town. We landed in a very funny dock, just room for us - I guess it was saved for us. I did not see much until yesterday as we were not allowed to leave the dock until we all marched out, although I did get a small view when I was sent after a bucket of water. The line of march was out King street by what was once the Queen's palace. It was a hot old march with fifty pounds on your back and 85 [degrees] in the shade. And our ranks were well broken by the time we reached here. It will be needless to say I staid with it to the last, but when I struck the camp I was about gone. The road we came out is simply grand - talk about homes, Palms, ferns and every old thing - they are surely in it. It is the purtiest place I ever saw and a great deal different than I expected. I am somewhat disappointed with the natives - they know too much and are not half wild looking - in fact I have seen several of the girls and they are realy good looking and dress in the very latest, but I hardly think I would be likely to go any further than admire them. Although some of them are they say loaded with rocks.

I went down town yesterday - took the horse car about three quarters of a mile from here and had a fine look at the road we came over when I was to tired to look at it. We passed several banana plantations loaded down with that fruit and houses all along that were nothing less than fruit orchards - you cant see the houses. I looked up Otto Burbaugh and he was that kind that I went out with him to dinner and I had a fine feed, as we call it now, as well as a good talk. They are nicely settled in a nice little cottage and are as happy as can be. I had the pleasure to see Olga & The Princess [Pearl] hanging upon the wall and it did me good to see two such fine ladies out - well, where ever you would call this. I was also pleased to renew my acquaintance with a lot of blue prints taken around Astoria, Coxcomb ridge, three girls in an arbor, etc, as well as several other scenes.

That had a little tendency to make me feel a little homesick. The star boarder was out for a day or two so I did not meet her, but I am promised that pleasure soon. After dinner Otto went to work and I staid and gave Mrs B- all the news I could and went down to take a look at the place. Well it is a queer one – narrow streets, low houses and indeed it has a different look from the U.S. Nearly two-thirds of the stores are run by Japs & Chinamen. All the drivers for the natives are driven about by Chinamen. It looks queer to see a Chinaman driving a native in a swell carriage. The native is not dressed as well as the driver and generally seemed to have a mess of fish done up in a big green leaf. They say if they had 50 cents, 25 cents is for fish and the other 25 cents to ride home on. Then he is broke after looking around for an hour and buying a few things for camp.

I made for the drug store where I was to have Otto's wheel for a spin. In the meantime Mrs B- had come down and we walked over to the fish market. Well I saw about a hundred kinds of fish, one that I knew: a bunch of salt salmon. Well of all the funny fish they have them here – red, white and I don't remember but what there were blue. Green though in a dozen shades. Well to go to this market is worth a week of any soldier's time. We went from there to the drug store where I went for a ride. I came to camp about six. So you see I have not been around much, have not eat[en] any poi and so far I am stuck on the place and am thinking of staying here. If I do you will have an invitation to come and see me. The climate is even, the nights cool, bugs plenty, butter - $1.00 a roll, eggs - 50 cents a dozen, fruit - 5 cents worth does us for a meal.

The natives are not pleased with our coming and there was hardly one at the flag raising which took place three days before we arrived. They even hissed us as we passed them and said in an undertone that we were the ruin of their country. The Americans are all pleased though. Whisky is 25 cents a drink; beer - 15 cents, so you can see I am not drinking very hard. Well I am going to close and when I see more I'l write again and only wish I could write a more interesting letter of an interesting place.

I hope every one at home is well and that you are doing fine and having a good time. Write when you feel like it and remember me to all. How is Dr Finch. And love to yourself in a lot that would suit -

    Dick

P.S. The shooting stars are too many to mention, and ones that you can see. I only wish you were here. I would take advantage of them.

Queen Lili'uokalani and Hawaiian Sugar

Following years of bloody battles, which eventually unified the Islands, the Kingdom of Hawai'i was established under King Kamehameha in 1795 as a monarchy form of government that lasted almost until the very end of the nineteenth century when in 1891, their last monarch, Queen Lydia Lili'uokalani ascended the throne.

Born in Honolulu in 1838, Lydia was the third of the ten children of high chief Kapaakea and chieftess Keohokalole, but was adopted at an early age by Abner Paki and his wife. The Pakis saw to it that she was well educated at the Royal School, learned English and found her faith through the missionaries of the Congregational church. She attended King Kamehameha IV and his wife Queen Emma. Lydia Lili'uokalani married John Dominis, a foreigner – a *ha'ole* – in 1862. Dominis died in 1891.

Lydia was quite talented musically and wrote several songs; in 1884, she composed and published the famous "Aloha Oe" – "Farewell to You."

Following the death of her brother, King David Kalakaua early in 1891, Lydia Lili'uokalani became the Queen of the Kingdom of Hawai'i. In 1887, King Kalakaua had been forced at gunpoint to sign a new Constitution limiting the powers of not only the monarchy, but especially that of the native peoples. It placed much of the administrative powers in the hands of Americans. As Queen, Lydia Lili'uokalani's primary mission was the preservation of the islands for the Hawaiians themselves. Immediately upon assuming the throne, she tried to establish a new Constitution for Hawaii to counter the "Bayonet Constitution of 1887" and to protect her peoples' right to vote.

The United States government had taken a keen interest in the sugar and whale trade of the Islands, but the McKinley Tariff was assessed in 1890 on the U.S.-Hawaiian sugar trade. A recession ensued. In order to counter the tariff, rumors of annexation were rife, especially among the many *ha'oles.* Annexation would mean the tariffs on sugar would not apply to exports going to mainland U.S. and Americans' profits would be protected. By 1893, many annexationists were also advocating that Hawaii become a Republic. A group led by Sanford Dole began to object to the "monarchy" itself. The American Minister - then appointed to Hawaii, ordered troops to occupy the government buildings and the Iolani Palace. The Queen was dethroned. Later in 1893, because the Hawaiian people so strongly supported their monarchy and their Queen, President Grover Cleveland's new minister to Hawaii, James Blount, recommended to the President that the Queen should be restored to the throne – with conditions. Although she acquiesced to the conditions demanded of her and pardoned the annexationists, Pres. Cleveland decided Congress should debate the "Hawaiian problems" anyway. The Hawaiian Islands were officially recognized by the United States as the Republic of Hawaii on July 4, 1894, under a then established provisional government.

This was not the end to the problems of Queen Lili'uokalani. In 1895, at the age of fifty-seven, she was arrested and convicted on an apparently trumped up charge implicating her in a plot by royalists. It was said that numerous weapons had been found on the grounds of her Washington Place home. She was fined and ordered to spend five years at hard labor in a prison. The sentence was commuted to "incarceration" in her bedroom in the palace. She remained under house arrest in Iolani Palace for five months.[134]

On July 7, 1898, Hawaii was officially annexed to the United States by a joint resolution of Congress, creating the U.S. Territory of Hawaii. This took place just prior to Dick's Regiment's arrival on Oahu. He mentions in his August 21 letter that apparently at the raising of the U.S. flag a few days before he arrived, few Hawaiians, if any, attended the ceremony. Nor did the native people take kindly to the arrival of U.S. troops.

"They even hissed us as we passed and said in an undertone we were the ruin

of their country. The Americans are all pleased though."

After Lydia Lili'uokalani's release, she lived in her Washington Place home for the next twenty years. She never remarried nor had any children. In his letter of August 29, Dick notes that he passed by her home and sat on the lawn awhile, but did not see her – he commented that she might be " busy ironing."

On November 11, 1917, former Queen Lili'uokalani died of complications following a stroke.

Hawaii was officially admitted to statehood as the fiftieth state on August 21, 1959. In January 1993, on behalf of the United States, President William J. Clinton issued a long overdue official apology for these events to the native peoples of Hawaii.

Mailing date: Sep 1 4.30PM 1898 Astoria. Oreg.
Received: Sep 14 7 am 1898 Honolulu
Addressed to: Mr. Dick Carruthers
        Co M 2nd Reg. Vol. Engineers
        Honolulu
            Hawaiian Isles   U.S.A.

August 28th 1898   [Sunday]

Dear Dick

Your nice long letter came this morning. I had been looking for it for several days. Hope you get the last one I sent you but I made a mistake and only put a two cent stamp on it, but know you will think it worth paying three extra stamps for. Dear me, I don't see how you stand such days as the one must have been when you broke camp and had to march so far after being up all night.

Wednesday –   Two days have gone by without my writing more (forgive me). I have just been for a long drive and am awfully tired. Marge and I took Miss Strong and Virginia White over the new Eights St. road and around Smiths Point. The Eights St. road's a dandy, planked

---

[134] The Iolani Palace was built originally of coral blocks in the 1860s by King Alexander Liholiha Kamehameha IV. King David Kalakaua rebuilt the palace. It remains a museum.

all the way to Young river but the road around the Point, well you know what that is like and it is no wonder my back aches. Then we drove to Uppertown.

It has been rainey and cloudy for two days but has cleared off fine now. Marge wants to go on a walk out but it is to late now to get up a crowd, any way my days are over getting the crowd together. I say let some one else do it. Mick and Tom were up last night. It is all off with Mick & Marge. <u>Don't mention it though</u>. She thinks Mr Kueckler the <u>nicest</u> man in the north west. It might be different if you were here but I am not sure of that even.

I hope you don't mind red ink. The other has given out & I am tired of tipping the bottle to get the last few drops.

I sent some blue prints in my last [letter] that I hope got to you O.K. Let me see, it is such a long time ago that I wrote that letter I forget what has happened since of interest. I have been playing dress maker and have made a waist for Mama that I am proud of. Goodness, Oct. will soon be here and I will be off to San Francisco. Think of tomorrow being the first of Sept., how time does fly, but I suppose the summer has been a long one for you [with] lots of work and not much play.

Yes I hope we can go to Elk Creek but we will never have the same old crowd - you and I are the only ones to represent it. Mick to be sure is here and Clara Lionberger. Dr Burnett and this house don't jibe worth a cent. Dear George Smith is in the far north where he is welcome to stay. Zetta Smith I believe is here but I never see her (thank goodness). Havent heard from Edith Copeland this summer.

I wish I knew when the mails went to Honolulu so I could send letters regulary. I am so glad you got my letter just before you left S.F. I hoped you would. Well Dick will add more tomorrow when I am not so tired. I was glad you were not sea sick and hope you will like Honolulu and keep well there. Good bye for today. Take care of your self.

Louise

Wednesday evening

The family have all gone out with exception of Harriet but Kate is here and they are sitting up stairs not at all sociable. So thought I would write as long as I can see but it gets dark so early nights now. The first signs of winter. Last night we had to light the gass before we had finished dinner.

There is going to be an old fashioned church sociable over at C. J. Trenchards tomorrow night – "grounds lighted with electric lights and the band playing for dancing." Of course it will rain in spight of its clearing of so fine today, it always does rain where the Episcopalians have any thing. You know, guess I wont go for I cant dance with you.

Pearl and Charlie are to be married the 12th of October – at least that is the day set now. Charlie isn't well and they have put it off once. Olga and I are the only girls invited. Will is to be best man I believe.

Lillie and Mrs K- left us a week ago. We miss them very much. For a while we had twelve in family and now only six. Dark room – cant see any longer so will go down stairs and light the gass and amuse my self by looking at the new Cosmopolitan which came today. All the magazines are full of war sections.

Well war is over now so you cant distinguish your self by fighting.

> *Good night*
>
> *L.*

Thursday –

Well I will finish now and mail this today. Hope it gets on a Str. bound for Honolulu and doesnt have to stay a long time in S.F. It is a most perfect day. Last night the moon light was grand. We sat on the porch after the folks came home - it was too lovely to stay in the house. Tomorrow we have planned a trip to Olney in a fishing boat – if it is like today it will be fine sailing.

The Regatta this year was alright and the Queen Mrs Normile was very handsome in a <u>*beautiful*</u> *satin gown. We watched the fire works from our up stairs window and I thought of the year before when we all were up there and how different every thing was then; little thought then that a whole year would go by and I would not yet be able to walk - and little you thought you would be way off on the Hawaiian Ils. How little use it is to make plans when one can never tell what the next day may bring.*

Well, good bye –

Sure this time Olga's letter from Lolly said Otto[135] *had seen you – you had been in the store or some thing like that.*

Write us all about Honolulu and what you are doing. With love from

> *Louise*

On August 27, upon the receipt of Louise's letter written August 12, Dick penciled a "reminder" list to himself on the back of the envelope - things about which he wanted to write home:

> *Plants,*
>
> *Climate,*
>
> *People,*
>
> *Town*
>
> *and Curios.*

---

[135] Laura ("Lolly") Heilborn and Otto Bierbach wed March 12, 1895, in Astoria. They moved to Honolulu where Otto, a pharmacist, was employed in a downtown drugstore. In their home, the Bierbachs displayed a photo of Lolly's sister Olga and Pearl Holden, aka "Princess."

Laura and Otto Bierbach - Honolulu

Dick at the Bierbach's.

Marge Halsted

Sadie Crang

Edith Copeland

Harriet, Frank (Frances) Holden and Kate Upshur

August 29 1898   [Monday]
Honolulu Oahu

Dear Louise:

I got one letter Saturday and that was from you. I also got one from Mother and one from Marge yesterday, Sunday. This is more thick and fast for this place I can tell you. A transport, the *Arizona*, brought the two yesterday, yours came on the regular boat bound for China. There is no need of my saying they were received with a yell as are all letters we receive. When a steamer is reported we can hardly wait until our first Sergent calls mail, then there is a rush, and when the letters are delivered many a one goes away feeling sore as their names had not been called. I have missed one mail steamer so I know how it feels to get left. As I got (Page 2 - it might be a book) yours first I am starting one to you first but don't know how soon it will start, soon I hope. I hope you have received my two letters and note I wrote upon arriving. Well I will try and answer your letter the first thing I do. But wait till I ask how is Dr Finch.

I left a telegram to be sent home as soon as we started. Perhaps it was not sent. But then you know I have started by this time. Glad you liked the photos, etc. That's right - I am glad you divided the buttons. You say you kept all the love I sent - well that is what I sent it for. The 2nd day out letter was not bad at all, only things turned out a little different on the fourth than you expected. I hope though that you were not disappointed - well were you? I hardly think we go any further but the only thing you are sure of in this lay out is what you are very liable to have for dinner. I think we are good for three or four months here then will be discharged. I think I shall have had enough by that time; seeing there is peace it is liable to seem different. You will see by my last letter that I saw Mrs Bubach. I have only been to town twice and was there once the time I mentioned in my last.

I was not seasick a second, but was good and "Lackme" sick the last six days of the eleven. Mrs K- is alright and I am sorry I was not there because I know she would have taken me and then I could have kept an eye on James C-. I am a little sore at him anyway. Did he give you any shells besides the ones the mussles came in? Don't think I have been sheding tears but it is enough to make one do so. - dirty paper, from ink, a bad pen - have to keep a rubber band around the tablet to keep it from blowing away sheet by sheet - then have a next door neighbor come over and spill water over your letter. Hard ships, we'll say. Well do the best you can to read it. I think your cookies will last you a while and indeed I would like to share half and half. Thirty five times twelve, grand total of 420, say. But if you had seen us on the *Lackme*, you wouldn't think they would last long.

I was standing near one of the boats on deck and had just discovered I knew Houston, who at one time was watchman at the cannery, our cannery you know. We had been sizing each other up all the way – this was about the 9th day out. We were having a good old Astoria talk and a quite [quiet] smoke when I heard Jackson calling for 'M-23, my official number. We used numbers in finding a fellow in the crowd as the four companies crowded the deck. When I answered 'M-23 - life boat 8" he came up and said he and Foley had located three big boxes of crackers and they were about to be condemned by the committee of six, so we increased that committee to the extent of two more, us being some what hungry. It was tins. They were busted open. The boxes were only four feet from a guard so the com. met on deck and decided Foley, "the grafter of Co. K of Salt Lake" was to condemn them, i.e. bust the box. The others arranged themselves in front to form a shield as well as sing, talk and act unconcerned. We did it as you will see; it took a good hour to get at the first box, then one at a time did the grafter hand out sodas to us. They were stowed away in our blouses and then in our bunks. One at a time we made the trips to return at once to our posts to keep the not very wise guard off. The box was empty. We, and our friends, those who had at some time divided their spoils with us, filled up with soda crackers and were they good! A guard on one of the other beats saw us but he being wise and a friend helped keep the other one off for the sum of a hat full of crackers.

Then we had to have the other box and the same old thing over, only imagine our joy when they turned out to be gingersnaps. We had got about half of them when the crowd commenced to get on. Well it was off in two minutes – what was once three boxes of crackers remained three big wooden boxes. The guard was on by this time, but every body sang "On the Wabash" so he could not call the Corprl of the guard who would in turn have had the armed squad after us. Still it was bad enough as we had to eat all we had that night for fear of a searching party in the morning. The last thing I saw of Houston, he was trying to climb in his bunk full of crackers and gingersnaps – a fullness that we had not enjoyed for a long time. He could hardly walk. I was no better off, but my I felt fine. You don't know what a sence of feeling it is to be empty for 9 days, get filled up all of a sudden and so unexpectedly. I woke up Fairchilds three times in the night to eat a few more and he would wake me. In fact it was sleep for five minutes and gingersnaps, five minutes. We got away with them and it was three in the morning when I finaly went to sleep, blessing the man who made two boxes of sodas, a box of gingersnaps, the longshoreman who did not put them out of reach, and Foley who had done the most locating the boxes. I hope I have not tired you but this is just to show how long 70 doz. cookies would have lasted and to show one of the many things a soldier does. You might think it wrong, but be half hungry for a week it changes your mind.

I am glad you are well and the foot is ok. Keep the good work going. Tell Hat I would give most any thing to fall down stairs. The pictures are fine and I believe I could put up with them even though the Dr. had done the work. You all look natural to say nothing of the familiar spot. Many thanks. On the side of your letter you say in speaking of the Dr. 'He had <u>nothing</u> to do with the ones I sent however and I cant tell you you neednt be jealous of him L. Well that was what I always thought, you couldn't tell me I neednt be jealous. Well I received all the love you send ok included and will remit receipt at the last of this letter. I am going to write to Babe soon although he owes me a long letter so tell him when you see him I have not forgotten him. We are still at Diamond Head near some name or other park[136] and are a little more comfortable than at first - an application of water every night has helped the dust some what. I (and one of the boys) are getting a small camera and if we have any success I will have some camp scenes as well as some place of interest for you. I hardly see why we wont be successful as a better man never had hold of one than R. E. C. so keep low on the weather bow. Since I last wrote I have eaten Poi and I do not think it bad. When mixed with a little sugar and baked hard, I am fond of it and buy a Poi pie quite often.

Tuesday

Yesterday I went to the funeral of our first dead, Fletcher of Portland.[137] He was given a swell burial by the Masons, we assisting. If we had had full charge he would have had a mule team, a cheap coffin, an American flag, three volleys and Taps. He was alright with the Masons though. He was a quiet fellow and had made very few friends; had gotten sour on army life and took his discharge a day or two before it was given him.

I hardly know what I have written before but I'l try hard not to contradict myself. One of my tent mates wrote home after the march out here that he had passed down a long road shaded with pineapple trees; he has since seen pineapples growing and is sorry he wrote. Saturday a party of five of us went six miles up a valley. This is not considered the finest island but there are a goodly number of things growing. We first went through about two miles of rice and taro fields or marshes owned and run almost entirely by Chinese. A rice field looks as bout as nice as any thing I saw growing. We then struck higher ground and had pineapples, bananas, mountain apples, etc till we could eat no more. We had several chats with the natives at different places and they all treated us royally - nothing to good for us. Coming home wet, got leave to pick some "Tamarind" which we did, filling a flour sack of it. It is a sort of stuff, but I guess you have seen it. We have had "Tamarind ade" every [day] since and it improves our not-over-good water a good deal. Speaking of water we are allowed to drink only not fit for this place - to much meat, not enough vegetables, but we get them ourselves.

I remember of hearing your Mother and Mrs Halsted talking of Guava Jelly - I know what it is such as has been boiled so you see they take fair care of us in some ways, but U.S. rations are like now - it is fine but so sweet that a little goes a long way. We get it from the peddlers here and very cheap too. They also sell Poi pies, or full meal pies as they call them, pies that are nearly all crust and most anything you want.

---

[136] Kapiolani Park is between the city and Diamond Head.
[137] Ormond Fletcher had joined up in Portland. He was a 39-year old topographer born in Toronto, Canada.

I heard this morning that the New Yorkers would go home in six weeks but I think it will be longer before we get started. I think we will move to Pearl Harbor. I will be glad if we do – it will take us away from the New Yorkers, whose conduct keeps us locked within bonds. We will there be on our own merits as it is some twelve miles from here I am told. Longer from the city, but I care very little for Honolulu. Perhaps if I were a citizen I could have a better time, for a soldier I have found, is a soldier be he a regular or a volunteer. Well I am not looking for much as my interests are some ways from here. Honolulu – good enough for some, but she never could get my game. I guess it is a good place for people with money, but no place for a working man. And anyone would be foolish to start from U.S. to come here as he would find nothing to do .

I am so sorry Astoria has an Irish Queen; our old queen [Queen Lili'oukalani] is so much nicer. I have never seen her, but it wont be my fault if I don't. We went over to her house the other day and sat down in the lawn, but I guess she was busy ironing as she never showed up. Well we examined her carriage that a Jap was washing in the back yard anyway. I'll see her yet if she don't die and then I'll go to her funeral and take a chance. I have not met the young lady who stays at Mrs B- and am getting worried about it. I must spruce up and go around some night.

We all had Mosquito ban hats and covers issued to us the other day. The hat as I called it looks like a bird cage when you put it on. The covering I guess you know what they are like – I use mine for a pillow. Well I was going to say we had very little to do the other night so a gang got out their new stuff and after taking off most – well nearly all of their clothing – put on mosquito ban and had a dance by moonlight. One guard was scared of his post and there was a great row all over camp. So you see we have a little fun once in awhile.

I saw Mr B- down town yesterday and he said his wife was laying for me for being out walking with two Knabse [knacke] the other night. It surely is a josh as I am hardly fortunate enough to have one let alone two. He claims she saw me so I'l write next time how I come out, but let me swear here and now that it is false and I can prove my innocence as I have not up till yesterday shaved for 10 days so you see I could hardly have two girls when there are 900 good looking New Yorkers below us – and they do say "them New _Yorkers_ are fine people." I don't know I am sure but will leave that solely to your own judgement. You I guess are good and tired, so I will if I can think of anything write a little more to make you a little tireder so you will rest well after you receive this. I never did have to do much to make you tired and I would give 10 cents to have a chance to have a row [in a boat] with you tonight or perhaps pay day I would give more. Well I don't know of much more to say except I might say from pictures and etc, you are a "purty good looking girl," write fairly well, use good, very good grammer when speaking . . .

No further page(s) found.

Sept. the 17th 98   [Saturday]

Dear Dick

Your nice seventeen page letter received. It was a full long one – took me quite a while to read it but then I am not rushed for time and enjoyed it all. I was a little disappointed that you don't have more to do and don't seem to like it as much down there as I thought you would. I went to see your Mother; she was disappointed not to hear from you. I gave her all the news. She invited Marge, Mrs H- and I down to spend the evening and we had a splendid time. Babe and Will Sherman were there, also Mr & Mrs A. V. Allen. Your Mother told our fortunes with the cards and talk about having troubles, my fortune is full of them but I rather think I have had a big share of them already, don't you?

Marge is getting up a walk out for tonight and she isn't doing a thing to the telephone – she is doing the inviting over the phone. Wish you were here to go with us – walk outs are no fun with out you and Mick to play "Monkey."

We had a fine picnic out to Olney last Monday - four carriages: Marge, Mrs H- and I drove out with Mick; Hat took Olga, Nan & Posey in our carriage – big load for one horse wasn't it, but Fanny is all right. Then Mr Marcotte, Nell & Violet Bowlby in a single reg. three on one seat, and Will Sherman and Charlie had a double carriage and took Virginia White and Anna Westdhall. The boys are quite smitten on Anna. You must josh Babe about going fishing with her.

Well there is a theater co in town. Last night quite a party went – this puss were not in it. Of course I couldn't go but it makes me pretty mad that no one asked Marge and she had just given a party and invited every one to it. You know she and Charlie celebrate their birthdays together, but such are the ways of Astoria. She is going to leave us next week and go down to the boarding house with her ma. I don't like it much after she has been with us all summer to go off down there just the last week she is here. They leave on the 1st of Oct. for home, but her ma is lonesome and wants her.

The weather is simply fine - couldn't be better. Well I guess I will write more later when I think of something else.

Sunday –

Dear Dick again,

I should give you a little sermon being as how this is Sunday morning but I guess you wouldn't enjoy it so all I will say "be good and you might be happy." Be good for my sake for you know I go a heap on what you do and don't you let Mrs Burbach even think she sees you out walking with two Kanacke girls unless they are pretty nice girls, then it is all right. Excuse those blots – accidents will happen.

Well we had the walk out last night. There were nineteen to supper. Babe & Mrs Kueckler came late just as I was leaving. I came home before nine because Nat had to go way down to the barn with the horse and I didn't want to make it late for him. Then I didn't care about staying longer; I get tired of sitting around and not being able to do as the others do, but my foot gets stronger all the time. The Drs say I can use it next month. Havent decided just when I will go to San F. yet. Say Dick read my letter over again and see if I didn't say "I _can_ tell you you neednt be jealous and etc," that is what I meant to say _sure._

Do you know the difference between Uncle Sam, a rooster and an old maid? If you don't I will tell you next time – and ask some of your soldier friends if they know "why Sampsons fleet was moved from Key West - if they don't know, tell them it was because they couldn't afford to keep them in _Florida water._"[138]

Oh say I saw a picture the other night down at your house that I would give a dollar to have. What do you think? Well it was one of you taken I guess just before you went to Eugene to school. You have your hands in your pockets and a tourist cap on - it is a dandy.[139] I spent half an hour looking at it, and another of you and Gus taken together in your first long trousers and your hand on Gus's shoulder – he is standing beside you and you are sitting on an old fashioned chair.[140] Also saw one of you taken with your best girl. I guess no one would know it was you so I am not jealous. We had several selections on the organ that evening. I bet you wish you could grind out a tune or two on it and maby you think I didn't think of you a time or two that evening. Your Mother had the nicest supper for us. I wont tell you of all the good things we had for it would make your mouth water to hear of it, but she made what she called Oregon Naval Reserve Punch and we all drank to your health and safe return home. Cracker cake – my but it was good, much as I like it though I would have been glad to have sent it all to you. Your Father misses you. Dick, he even talkes of taking a trip down there on the _Jessie._ Do you think I could persuade him to take me along. I would like nothing better than a trip down there.

Last night the boys planed a hay ride for tomorrow night. They think they can get twenty people in the big dray of Henry Sherman, use four horses and go around Smith Point, back over Eight St, then up to Alderbrook and around town. Hope we live to tell about what a good time we had.

The Princess [Pearl] weds Charlie on the 12th of Oct. Charlie says Will must be best man and Will says it is pretty mean for them to set the date the same time to get married that Corbett ["Gentleman Jim"] has set to fight – and he has either got to miss the fight or the wedding. I don't know which he has decided to do. Hard luck isn't it.

---

[138] Webster's 1918 Dictionary: "Florida water - a kind of (proprietary) toilet water." It was a trademarked name. For the answer to the first joke, see Chapter Eight, page 219.
[139] This photograph may be found in Chapter One, page 9.
[140] See Chapter One, page 5, for this photograph.

I had quite a long letter from our friend Mr Teal; he is up in Dyea[141] and he said he would buy me a gold nugget. Isnt he all right. And Solis heard that Windy No 1 was making quite a fortune up there some where. Well I am getting so hungry that I must go down and see if lunch isn't ready. Can imagine how good those crackers must have tasted to you, poor fellow. I think it is a shame that you don't get more to eat. Do you feel well all the time? I have just had some lunch so I feel better myself but I do hope you keep well. Take as much care of your self as you can and write soon again and tell me all you do.

As before with love

Louise

Glad you got the pictures and liked them.

Marge, Harriet and Louise with Olga standing.

Hat, Louise, Olga and Nan in Astoria

The *Daily Morning Astorian* newspaper printed the following letter September 25, 1898:

ARMY LIFE AS SEEN
Richard Carruthers Sends a Noway Letter from Honolulu
Every Day Life in Camp.
The following interesting letter has been received by Mr. And Mrs. Robert
Carruthers from their son Richard, who joined the United States engineer
corps and is now stationed in Honolulu.

We are still at Diamond Head and are now under the command of Col. Barber, the New Yorkers and engineers having joined forces. It saves us from considerable guard duty and they are a good way from us. I have been to Honolulu twice since I last wrote you – well, three times, but once to see

---

[141] Dyea, Alaska, a port near Skagway, south of the Chilkoot Pass, was a major starting point during the Gold Rush.

where Fletcher was laid to rest. You spoke of coming to live here. Well, for my part, no; it is a poor place for me, I think, and so far I am quite disappointed in it. Nothing seems to grow to a profit unless irrigated. Fruit is high; they claim that so many soldiers passing through have more than cleaned out the crop. If any one was to say it was a tropical country I would be liable to dispute them. It is not, from my point of view, and I have gone around considerable. Three or four of us a week ago went into the country and expected to see wonders; we did not. Rice and sago seem to do well and a few bananas and pineapples were about all we saw. They say this is not the finest island – I guess not. We got a flour sack of tamarinds, though. They look like a bean, but have meat in them something like the China nut, only it is sour enough to make a good lemonade – tamarindade, I presume would be correct. We also on the trip ate prickly pears, mangos and guavas. Mangos I like, guavas are fit for jelly only, I guess, and prickly pears, excuse me. Our company was given a ride of 18 miles to a sugar plantation and mill. Again I was disappointed as the cane was not ripe and the mill was being repaired. We go on trips Saturdays and get wild tomatoes, which are a change, and at first not only a change but something to fill up on, as there was trouble over the supplies at first and a cup of coffee and a slice of bread was given us for meals for three or four days. But things are better now. I myself went into the kitchen for a week and I am famous for my boiled rice with dip. Dip is made from sugar, vinegar, water and nutmeg, but they all said it was fine and as I ate a good deal myself I guess it was. You can imagine the work of cooking for ninety men on an open fire. You get up at 4 o'clock and go to bed at 8. You, of course, are excused from everything else and have two men to help (kitchen police) detailed for the day. I was second class cook, but was the head guy while I was there, as the first cook, a second class man, was an Irishman and couldn't read – was unable to read the army cook book. A bucket and a half is enough rice, two of beans, and a boiler (wash boiler) full of spuds will do. Well, I think I did better than most of the cooks, as so many wanted me to stay.

Thursday I went to town and had dinner at Bubaugh's. Friday I was with a mule train – a regular government outfit – hauling stuff from town. Today I am supernumerary - that is I am to stay around so if any of the guards take sick I fill their places. As we only mounted three men on guard today, I guess I will not be called for, but must stay at home. Camp life is bout the same here as at the Presidio, only it is warmer and our mail is so irregular. For instance, you might write two letters and the one you wrote and mailed last would perhaps reach me first. I do hope you get all my letters, and I think you will. We are faring very, very poorly, as this is so hard a place to get stuff; but it is improving as we go along. The days are good and warm, but we are nearly used to them, and our work is light. The nights are fine – cool enough, but not cold. So far we sleep on the ground, but are going to make canvas bunks as soon as we are sure we are going to remain in this camp.

I generally am asked "What are you doing here?" Well, there are lots the same way. In the next company there is a senator's son who is so homesick that he has turned yellow, so he is now known as the "Yellow Kid." I am not quite so bad as that, although army life is very liable to make me so, but I guess will be able to stick it out. We have a good stock of books, and I am at present reading *Old Curiosity Shop* and am very much interested in it. I am still with the same crowd, and on pay-day we are thinking of buying a chafing dish that we saw down town to do a little side cooking. You might think we have all the fruit we want; but no; it is too high for us; they say so many soldiers have cleaned them out. For the last two or three days I have been feeling sick, but am all O.K. today. There are about twenty of the boys going home tomorrow, when this letter goes, on account of sickness – all old complaints, so it is not the climate. About our being mustered out, it won't be until the commissionery meet in November, as we understand, to settle peace. So I hardly think I'll be home for Christmas. If they do not show any inclination to muster us out then I will write for a discharge, but am willing as long as there is any chance of further war to stay, and then give them time to muster out. I hardly think they care to hold us after that. The officers, of course, would like to stay, as it is pie for them. Well we will wait a while before we kick, as I guess Uncle Sam will do the right thing if we give him time, for there is no telling how soon he might need us again, and we, if treated wrong, might refuse.

204

Received: San Francisco Oct 4 1898
Received: Honolulu Oct 12   9 am   1898

Oct. 27th 1898 [meant <u>September</u>]   [Tuesday]

Dear Dick

I haven't any letter to answer but am going to begin a letter to you just the same because I know you don't always wait for one from me before writing, and one may come before this is finished for I like to add a line or so each day. I got the news from Marge's letter and am anxious about you because you said you were not feeling very well. There has been so much sickness among the soldiers; I hope you would escape. Part of your letter to your mother was published in the *Astorian*. We read it Sunday morning and enjoyed it very much. I had hoped you would find there was to be a good opening for you down there but I will be awfully glad when you get home again. You say it will not be before Xmas but I hope you will have occasion to change your mind about that. <u>Realy</u> <u>we</u> do miss you a lot. Last Fourth of July seems a year ago. Mama says I must stop because she wants to sweep her room and I am in her way so will go and print a picture for you.

later –

Marge has just gone up stairs to write to you so she will no doubt give you all the news so I will wait a few days before writing more then I can tell you about the dance which comes off next Thursday night at the Fishers Hall – that is if I happen to be there which is doubtfull as no one has asked me and I don't know as I would go any way. It is just a little more than I can stand to see all the boys and girls dancing and not be able to even walk myself. If you were here I would go for I am sure you would sit out a dance or two with me, wouldn't you? And we could have a good old fashioned row – no, I believe I would be so glad to see you that I wouldn't <u>even</u> <u>think</u> of a mean thing to say.

I am getting ready to go down to San Francisco. Don't know just when I will go yet but it will be a happy day if I get there and the Dr says my foot is ready for use once more. He wrote Papa that he felt sure it would be and it gets stronger every day now and gradually the stiffness is coming out. But oh it has been such a long time and I am afraid it will be such a long time yet before it is real strong again and I wont be lame. You don't know Dick how hard it has been for me.

I am making a book of blue prints for you but I cant say when it will be done. You know the sun doesn't shine every day and we are out of paper now and there is none to be had in town.

Marge leaves us tomorrow to go down and stay with her mother – perhaps they will be here all next month. I will miss her more than I can say.

Wednesday-

Dear Dick

I am so afraid you are going to be ordered to Manila - our paper this morning says the Honolulu troops are going but I do hope it isn't so for that seems such a dreadfull long way off it will be ages before you get home. I hope another mail will come along soon and bring me a letter from you, and you will know what they are going to do with you.

Mick and Tom called last night - they are great chums. I wont be able to tell you about the party for I am not going and Hat has not been sufficiently urged either. Marge is going with Paul B. Will has gone out to the Nehalem and taken the wagon and Fanny [their horse] so there is no way for me to get out and I have been putting in my time sewing. By the way I have a new dress - that means the cloth for a dress and the dress maker is engaged to make it (when it is done I will tell you if it is becoming or not).

Those were great trades you gave me in your last letter. Thanks. Babe [Robert Rex, Dick's brother] isn't well at all, at least he doesn't look well, and last Sunday he nearly frightened the family to death by falling down in a faint - perhaps it is indigestion, but I guess not. I think he does to much work nights on his books when he is tired from running around tending store all day - don't say any thing to Mrs Burbach about Babe.

Dr Burnett leaves us next week to open an office of his own in Medford - sad news isn't it. How I will miss him. Just think, he wont be here to walk home with me from Chafing dish suppers any more and leave me down on Commercial to come alone the rest of the way. Oh there is no doubt about his being missed, but realy Olga feels badly over his going. He must have had a good side that I never saw, or she would not like him so much. He is going to take her to the party. Charlie takes Anna, I think. Dr Finch - of course you want to know about him - takes Sue Elmore. She goes to Oakland next month for the rest of the winter. Mr Stokes next door has a good looking young brother visiting with him by the name of Tom. Hat & Marge are quite struck or pretend to be. Nora is back, joy of course for us to see her again, and school has begun - that means Mr Thornton is here but I have not seen him yet. Polly came up the other day and brought me a maiden hair fern growing nicely in a jar - wasn't that nice of her?

Pearls wedding day is drawing near; she says I cant go until after she is married, so of course I will stay for that. It is the 12 th. She gets funnier every day - realy I don't know what to make of the girl but perhaps it is only because she is in love that she does such queer things. If it is, deliver me from ever getting on that bad. You know how much I care for you - that is about twice as much as I care for any one else. Do you think there is any danger of my getting to act like Pearl? Charlie has catarrh awfully bad and doesn't look well; he is so very thin and pale.

Well I must say good night for it is six oclock and company coming to dinner -

L.

Thursday –

Well nothing startling has happened only Dr Finch called last night. Mrs White & Virginia were here to dinner. Mrs Halsted & Marge came up in the evening and we all played cards. I nearly hurt my self laughing over that scientific game called "Pig". We made Dr Finch a hog – you remember the game don't you? It is lots of fun. I am glad you can get a good home cooked meal once in a while at the Bierbachs. How good it must seem to you to sit down to a nice table. I guess camp life has a demoralizing effect on table manners hasn't it. I would just like to sit down to a table <u>loaded with good things</u> and have you sit next to me and watch you eat. I guess I could keep you company for the first round but after that would just watch.

Well Dick I will say good bye for this time and go for a walk as far as the corner and mail this. Take care of your self and write me another nice <u>long</u> letter and don't go off to Manila but come home soon if not sooner.

As always with love from

Louise

Oct 1st. It has just rained all the time and I haven't been able to even get to the corner to mail this. I will let some one mail it for me now

L.

Dick wrote a reminder list on the front of this letter's envelope:

Camera

Bubach

Erickson

Dish Wash

Chapter Eight   **October 1898 to February 1899**
                                                      Life goes on at home and abroad

The United States eventually won the Spanish-American War. In the process, it learned some valuable military lessons. The U.S. Navy was much more efficient in keeping sanitary conditions onboard the ships at sea, and therefore, had less loss of life overall. The U.S. Army and Marine Corps, of course, faced depravations and hardships as a land force that caused significant losses of American lives. However, not only had the United States government not provided the regular infantry and volunteer troops with proper preparation in training and equipment, but also the men were not prepared for what they were getting into in "The Tropics." In the worst of the hot, soggy summer wet season, limited knowledge of how to deal with tropical diseases was a major cause of relatively high death rates among the land troops.

Some Tropical Problems in Hawaii

Soldiers in the warm, moist Tropical climates of Hawaii and the Philippines – as well as in Cuba - were subject to contracting some nasty diseases, especially malaria, parasitic infections/dysentery and typhoid fever. Known remedies were not the most effective in combating the parasites. Antibiotics did not exist yet for use against typhoid bacteria. Illnesses were more serious. Contraction of many diseases could be avoided, just as with tuberculosis, by taking care of oneself and keeping one's surroundings clean. However, army camps often became the source of epidemics.

All the U.S. troops in Hawaii were issued a type of mosquito ban, plus what Dick termed a Mosquito ban hat and covers that "looks like a bird cage when you put it on." Mosquitoes, in vast numbers, made life miserable for everyone. Any person in the tropics could be exposed to the bite of an infected female mosquito and, from that, contract malaria. The single-celled organism infects the body's red blood cells, creating a roller-coaster pattern of fever, sweating, chills and shakes. Quinine was probably available in the late 1800s and has been used for many years to counter the effects of malaria. More recently, derivatives of quinine have been marketed. No drug therapy, even today, can fully prevent the infection.

After nearly a month of no letters from Dick, on October 3 he wrote Louise that he had contracted the "camp sickness." He had been so sick he had lost 10 to 12 pounds of weight and felt utterly exhausted for weeks. But at the time of this letter, his health had improved.

"I am perfectly well and we are being fed real well now. It was brought about by everyone going to the doctor and we were all put down 'too hungry to drill.' Well of course they had to have time to get things down to working order."

Parasitic infections can run rampant through any group of people. A one-celled organism, a protozoan – like a worm, can enter the body and attach itself to the walls of the intestines causing infections. Infected stools, unclean food and water from poor sanitation are the culprits leading to Amebiasis (in the large intestines) and Giardiasis (in the small intestines).

Typhoid fever is caused by the bacterium *Salmonella typhi*, which finds its way into the lymphatic system and intestines and, thus, is spread through the feces and urine of infected persons, as well as in the handling of soiled bed linens in hospitals. Flies, poor sanitation and poor personal care allow the contamination of the water supply and food. Eight to fourteen days after the infection enters the gastrointestinal tract and the bloodstream, symptoms occur. Inflammation spreads and can cause extreme exhaustion and dehydration. Fevers up to 104 degrees F. might last ten to fourteen days. The bacteria are exceedingly hard on the human body. If proper treatment is not given quickly, complications can occur – possibly leading to coma and/or death. For those who recover, relapses are possible.

This disease is highly contagious – a regiment could be infected in no time. In the First New York Regiment, typhoid fever began shortly after the regiment's arrival in Hawaii and quickly became an epidemic. Apparently when they established their Diamond Head camp site, they did not take adequate care in locating the latrines away from the water supply and the food storage/preparation area; in providing constant care of the latrines; in insisting upon proper and frequent hand-washing; and in drinking only boiled (or chlorinated) water. At the end of October, Dick wrote Louise there was considerable sickness starting in camp. The situation in the New Yorkers' "filthy" camp was so bad, so contaminated with typhoid germs, that the chief surgeon (or as Dick called him – "the board of health") had condemned the camps. The New Yorkers were moved to Waialea.

Even though the Engineers had been camped alongside the New Yorkers, only a few cases appeared in their units. They had received top ratings for cleanliness and attention to prescribed sanitation regulations. To be on the safe side, a new encampment was constructed by the Engineers at the corner of Kapahuhu Road and Kanaina Avenue, near Kapiolani Park - one-half mile away from the condemned encampments.

At this time Dick was in good health, but Louise worried about him getting ill again. The newspapers back home contained many articles about the typhoid fever deaths on both fronts of the war, even though the war had wound down in the Pacific. The New Yorkers were among the first to be ordered back to San Francisco in late November and early December 1898. Unfortunately, they left behind some 250 men (out of 900) who were too ill to travel – and some thirty dead.

The United States government decided nurses were needed in Hawaii. Dubbed the "Christmas Ship" - or the "Santa Claus Ship," the *St. Paul* left San Francisco for Honolulu and Manila on November 18, 1898. The hold of the vessel was full of Christmas packages from relatives at home and California pine Christmas trees. It also carried the very first female trained nurses ever sent by the U.S. government <u>outside</u> the mainland United States. Some of the thirty-four nurses on board were associated with the

Red Cross, while others were attached to the White Cross organization that was headquartered in Portland. Half of the women nurses disembarked in Honolulu to help with the sick and injured soldiers at the Buena Vista Hospital. In early December, Dick and 25 other engineers were assigned as nurses-aides at the hospital. Most of the patients were suffering from typhoid fever, including about thirty in Dick's own regiment. Dick remained there for four weeks, working twelve-hour shifts daily - "the hardest work I have ever tackled." Some Red Cross men from San Francisco finally arrived on January 2, 1899 to relieve them, even though all the trained women nurses wanted the engineers to stay – saying the engineers were better than the Red Cross men. Dick was next assigned to "fatigue" duty and, later, to office work.

Sources:
Merck Manual of Medical Information, Whitehouse Station, N.J.: Merck Research Laboratories, 1997. 870-900.
Simeon Margolis, M.D., Ph.D., Med. ed, *Johns Hopkins Symptoms and Remedies*, Redding, CT: Medletters Association, 2003. 546, 707.
William Mayo Venable, "The Third Battalion," *The Second Regiment of United States Volunteer Engineers*, Cincinnati: Printed for the Author by McDonald & Co., n.d.

Honolulu   Oct 3 1898   [Monday]

Dear Louise –

I am ashamed that I have not written to you long ago. Well my plea is I was sick, not so sick but what I could attend to duty except the last day or two when I was confined to quarters. I am perfectly well now and although my cheek bones are quite prominent I am fast picking up the ten or twelve pounds I lost since I arrived. I had the camp sickness that nearly all have had but don't worry, you cant lose me. I have written home only once more than I have to you so I guess they are all a little worried but there is no [need to]. I felt mean ever since I got your last letter - [part of page torn away] - to think I had [just] mustered up courage enough to answer your first long ago and I am afraid this is not going to be any thing extra, but I will answer both your letters and mail this tomorrow and within the next four days I will write more complete.

Well yours of Sept 1 received 14th good time. In the first place only use a two cent stamp – it is enough for a letter. The first thing I know you will have that 11 cents all spent. A soldier's letter only needs 2 cents - in fact we seem to be favorites of Uncle Sam – well we should be. We stand trips because we have too.

So it is off with Marge & Mick and I am all but forgotten. I thought Marge thought more of me than that but I hope all will not forget me soon. Now you wont will you. Well I'l take two guesses. So you were dress making. Well I could give you a job or two if you were here. I guess there is not much telling when the boats sail from here. Indeed I often think of different days and say it will be by the 14th of October when you receive this. Well I have not answered your first letter very fully but it was so long ago that I guess you have forgotten what you wrote.

Now I'l take up your last of Sept 19 received here Oct 1, 1898. Glad you gave my mother the news in my last and wish I could have been home the eventful night but it is mean to be hunting up ones picture when he is so far away. I must write to Babe soon and I'll Josh him about Miss Westdhall – he owes me a letter or I would have written before. Don't fool yourself about me running around with any girls. I do not like their style. The only girl I know here is Miss Kelly – she is real nice but there are others. I am so glad you are doing so well but be careful please – don't go to fast, creep first. I read your letter again. I guess you made a mistake but it is alright, but I have another kick that I will register later on.

That's a good one on Florida water, but I give the other up so write the answer next time. But it is mean to hunt up those pictures and as far as you having one simply out of the question. You are not the only who does some thinking and lots of it. I know my father would take you if he started out but then I guess he wont and besides there is a chance of our going to Manilla. Well I have taken in the sideshow I might as well go to the circus and I will be alright there if we go.

Dr Walker - and I'l bet I would be glad to see him after 12 or 14 days on the sea. If we go there of course we go on a big transport and will go about twice as far in the same time as we did on the Lackme. We know nothing of all this now of course, just a rumor and surmises are common things around here.

So Pearl and Charlie are to be married and will be before you get this. When you see them give them my best and wish them all the happiness there is, but you can put it a little nicer. I am glad the Windy No 1 is making so much money – some one should.

I am perfectly well and we are being fed real well now. It was brought about by everyone going to the doctor and we were all put down "too hungry to drill." Well of course they had to have time to get things down to working order. I have just lit my pipe and am going to register the kick: The idea of you saying <u>one</u> friend in - in writing of a certain young man I wont say who, but he lives in Alaska and deals in gold – I think I want you to understand that he is not my friend, in fact he nearly drove me away from Elk Creek once I remember. Should I consider him my friend? If it is not a Dr in one letter, it is a James Corbett or a gold seeker. Well I guess I ought to be satisfied with a letter once and a while but don't mind me – keep up the good work but I can't say who I wish the luck too. I dislike them all so much I think I will pray for Jim and if I get home soon I may be able to "maroon" him on some dark and dreary ile [isle] where he will pass the remainder of his days. This will cause you pain I know but woman I must, I must.

Well I will try and write a little of the news. Rice is rife. I have not met the Queen yet. Had dinner at Beaubaughs [Bierbachs] 5 or 6 days ago. Cochroaches are doing well. We have a party tomorrow night at one tent – 9 all told in honor of Jacksons birthday. The refreshments will be cocoa made with canned milk, sandwiches, Deviled ham and jelly & bread. I will send you a *sample of one of the invitations. You folks, from the two letters, must have had a lot of fine times and I often wonder if I am realy missed – "the monkey part I mean of course". Well I am old enough to be over such things but we have a round or two once and a while. We are fixed fine now. There is seven in the tent now. The tent is 7 x 8, contains four bunks so you see we have some good inventions to make this much room. We could accommodate two more. The bunks are double deck and fold to a lounge in the day time. It took a whole lot of engineering to make them, I can tell you, when you have to walk a mile for a piece of lumber.*

Well I guess I will close for tonight and this letter but I will write soon again. Well lots of the real thing –

     Dick

Enclosure: *Honolulu*   *Oct 1 1898*

Mr & Mrs Fairchild
Request your presence at their home No 5 "M" Place
Oct 4 1898
In honor of their son "Perry Jackson Fairchild's" sixteenth birthday
Cards
Kindly bring your silver mugs

Mailing date: Oct 13 2.30 PM 98 Astoria. Oreg.
Received: San Francisco. Cala. Oct 16 8 PM '98
     Forwarded to Honolulu Oct 26 5 PM 1898

Wednesday Oct 12th

Dear Dick

We are rushed with work getting ready to leave here Saturday morning on the Str. Columbia so I only have time for a line but you hardly deserve even that much for another mail has come and brought no letter for me. Your mother let me read hers but it certainly was short. Harriet is going with me to S.F. I do not know how long we will be there but next time you write, and I hope it will be soon, direct to 713 Castro St. care of Sidney Smith. I mailed a book of blue prints to you which I hope came all o.k. It isn't nearly full but when I get some more will send them and you can stick them in. Here is one of Lila that is pretty good I think and a group taken in our boat one day of the Regatta. I hope it wont be in your way. I know you don't have much room for such things.

The Halsteds leave Friday. Marge thought for a while that she would stay here and spend the winter with Mrs Lighter (don't that strike you funny). It did me for I didn't know she even knew her until she told me about staying there but she has changed her mind because her chum in Alhambra was going away and she wanted to get home before she left to see her. I cant get over it or understand how Marge could even think of staying here all winter and visiting with Mrs Lighter of all people.

Well I am going to take dinner at the <u>Stevens</u> with Marge tonight. I will no doubt hear some news down there - they always know <u>every</u> thing. Hope you can read this. It is written horriable. Write soon to

Louise

P.S. When you are in Honolulu look out for my cousin Frank Smith. I guess you remember him. He stayed with us here the year the can factory was built and he is living down there now. He married a Miss Hitchcock whose family is pretty well known down there I guess for they lived there for a long time for her father was sherrif. She is a queer one. I only saw her once though, but Frank is a <u>fine fellow</u>. Think he is employed by a firm called Castle & Cook, I believe. When I get down to Aunt Fannies I will write to him to look out for you. Well good bye and do write to me.

L.

Thursday a.m.   Guss came back this morning.

I went in to see her [Marge] and say good bye. We had a long talk which gave me the blues for she told me lots of things I was so innocent of that I could hardly believe them about Kate, Hat & etc. She said you knew them so you will know how badly I feel but still I have such faith in Hat that I can not believe more than half. Your Mother is awfully proud of you Dick. I heard her tell Todd[142] she wanted him to grow up to be <u>just like</u> his brother Dick.

Oct 31, 1898   [Written Sunday, October 30th]

Dear Louise

I received yours of the 13th on the 26th and had answered the one before that on the steamer which left on the 25th. In your last you said I hardly deserved a letter - did you not get one a day or two after that I mailed on the 4th. It I think explained why I had not written. It should have been there on or about the 12th to 14th and I think you must have got it before you left for Frisco. I wrote you Oct 4th- Oct 25 and this one goes tomorrow. As the last was of good length I will not be able to give you much today but as soon as I go get my baked beans - they are lining up for supper - I will finish this. Baked beans is our Sunday evening meal and they are baked beans surely. Well I am hungry talking of them so wait and I'l finish this with ink "if I can find it." Eat hearty - well I guess I will.

---

142 "Tod" is another name for Dick's youngest brother Robert Rex Carruthers, also know as "Babe."

Monday 31st

This must be Monday -

I guess I was a little rattled last night as I dated the start of this wrong, and as company came after dinner, I have to finish this tonight. We are building barracks about a mile from here and this camp has been condemned and I have no time in the day time for writing. The new clerk at Honolulu Drug store made me a call yesterday and had dinner with us. We spent the day in bathing and went out in the afternoon and I took several pictures. I have had the first roll developed and they turned out fair; have had none printed as yet so cant send sample yet but hope to soon. I was in Honolulu Saturday and Otto B- told me that the two Flavel girls and their mother were out to camp to call on me but the day they were out I was guarding the mules some half mile from here so missed them. I would like to have seen them and am sorry I was not at home. They were on the way to Japan and were only here part of a day.

Well I'l try and answer your last – the one I did not deserve, but you must have got one long since. By the way I mailed the last to you at Astoria. Also a copy of the *News Muster,* and by the way, let me thank you for the blue print album – it is gotten up quite fine and admired by all. They want to know who 'L' is. Well I tell them she is the best ever. True I have not got oceans of room but have plenty to see that the album is well taken care of. At present it is wrapped in several newspaper and laid away in a box under my bunk.

By this time you are in S.F and I hope have had the best luck a going and I feel you will. Well write soon and tell me all. Thanks for the address of your cousin Frank. I will be sure to look him up. Also your telling him to take care of me as it might come in more handy than you expect as there is considerable sickness starting. But as soon as we change camp this will be all settled. The board of health condemned the camp; they said no camp could be kept cleaner and healthier than the engineers, but that the New Yorks with whom we are camped was filthy. So you see where the trouble lies - that it is mostly New Yorkers. As soon as we move we will be apart and I am glad of it. We will in all probility break camp and go in the temporary barrack in about ten days.

I am in perfect health and as Will might say 'the pink' and feel as though I could go a hundred in about 10 3/4 if I was not so lazy. But we are working now and all feel the better for it. Four of our boys go home tomorrow discharged on account of sickness so you see I might have cause for your concern to see I am taken care of for your sakes as I will explain if it becomes necessary to do so, that I do not shuffle off. But I will not impose to much on him and hope I will not have the opportunity of doing so.

The Oregon recruits were here Saturday on their way to Manilla. The only one I knew was Davies, an Englishman, a friend of [Frank] Gunn's, etc. I met Burnett the miler – he is also *along. Brown, the Stanford man Will beat, was here last week with his sisters on a trip. So you see there has been lots of excitement lately.*

Well I will close for this time. Will try and have a letter to you on the fifth.

With love

Dick

I am sending you some brass goods tonight, Hawaiian hat pin and our coat of arms

IMAGES IN PRUSSIAN BLUE

By 1898, Louise had gotten quite good in making "blue prints," technically termed cyanotype prints. She may have learned the process from Dick's older sisters, Grace Carruthers Allen and Zoe Carruthers Ridehalgh, who were professional photographers associated with a studio in Astoria. Dr. Arthur Finch, also a professional photographer, knew the process and helped Harriet and Marge develop blue prints at the Tallant's house. It was a popular hobby for many in the 1890s and early 1900s, but not restricted to that period. There are many today who enjoy being more creative and experimenting in their photographic printmaking.

Sir John Herschel, an English scientist and astronomer, discovered this chemical process in 1842. However, another British scientist, Anna Atkins, made the first "blue" cyanotype prints using the process. She is credited also as being the first woman photographer with the publication of her series of books of cyanotype "blue" prints, made of ferns and woodland plants. The process is essentially unchanged since its invention.[143]

Webster's Dictionary defines the blue print process as "a photographic reproduction in white on a blue background." There are two primary processes to obtain the blue prints – each requires the use of chemicals. Extreme care must be taken when working with any chemicals.

In brief - the process Louise used required the use of two chemicals – Potassium Ferricyanide (iron salts) and Ferric Ammonium iron III Citrate (green in color). In a darkened room each of the two chemicals is separately mixed with water in specified measures. Equal amounts of the two solutions are then combined to create a photo-sensitive solution. The material on which the print is to be made, such as watercolor paper or fabric, is evenly coated with the solution – only an small amount is needed - and allowed to fully dry in a dark place. A photographic negative may then be placed on the dried, coated material and exposed to strong, direct light - preferably outdoors in bright sunlight. Experimentation of the length of exposure to the sunlight is necessary, although 10-20 minutes is likely sufficient. If properly done, the ferrous (iron salts) chemical will oxidize in the UV rays of sunlight, leaving a contrasting "blue image' on the material. The resulting blue print must then be "developed" by running cold water over the print material to remove the yellow-colored chemicals - the salts that are soluble in water - until the water runs clear. A thorough rinsing is necessary. The print is then allowed to dry on a flat surface. As the print dries, a beautiful Prussian blue image of non-soluble

---

[143]   See web sites – wikipedia.org/wiki/Cyanotype. Also bostic.com/c_cyano.htm.

salts emerges. This resulting image is highly resistant to "decay" or fading, even when the exposed print is subjected to years of direct, strong light. If a print does fade, it can be restored to its "blueness" by storing it in a dark place for a period of time.

Louise enjoyed experimenting with the process. She usually made blue prints of one-inch square to three-inches square (the size of the negatives used), but she did several fine, large cyanotype blue prints – eighteen inches long - of the warship, the U.S.S. *Constitution, aka "Old Ironsides,"* that docked in Astoria in the 1930s.[144] Louise also experimented in using shapes of leaves and cutouts to enclose a second print by varying the exposure times of the leaves and of the negatives on the printing material.

In an August 1898 letter from Hawaii to Louise, Dick mentioned seeing a cyanotype album belonging to Otto Bierbach that contained blue prints of the Astoria area and Coxcomb Ridge, as well as "three girls in an arbor." The album prints "had a little tendency to make me feel a little homesick," he wrote. Louise's cousin Frank Smith, who lived just outside Honolulu, also had a blue print album he showed Dick.

From time to time, Louise would enclose blue prints in her letters to her friends. She also sent an album of blue prints she had made to Dick, who was stationed in Honolulu. It contained scenes of Astoria, boats on the Columbia, and interiors of the Grand Avenue house, printed on tissue-like/rice paper pages. Louise included some of herself, Harriet and their friends.

On October 12, 1898, Louise wrote Dick:

> *I mailed a book of blue prints to you which I hope came out o.k. It isn't nearly full but when I get more will send them and you can stick them in. Here is one of Lila that is pretty good I think and a group taken in our boat one day of the Regatta* [held in August 1898]. *I hope it wont be in your way. I know you don't have much room for such things."*

During the turn of that century, Astoria's amateur print makers, including Louise, also experimented with another process using a camera that did not have a roll of film in it. The picture was "taken" on blueprint paper by direct – and sometimes lengthy – exposure. A few basic items were required: a camera, blueprint paper, regular household ammonia, a large sealable container (such as a bucket) with a tight fitting lid – and patience. The camera needed a large aperture of f/8.0-f/2.0. There had to be enough exposed plate to be able to easily see the finished print because enlargements were not possible. An early Brownie camera or even a simple homemade camera of black cardboard, duct tape and a good lens could do a good job. Blueprint paper, such as that used by architects and engineering draftsmen, was handmade then, but now can be purchased at supply houses or ordered on-line. The sealable container had to be large enough to hold an exposed blue print without curling or wrinkling it. A glass jar or cup of heated ammonia was placed in the bottom of the sealable container. The heated ammonia fumes were the "developer." This process seems trickier – and quite risky, but how to do it this way may be found in detail on several web sites. One must use goggles, heavy-duty gloves and considerable caution.

---

[144]   Donated by the Lambert family to Clatsop County Historical Society.

The new couch in the family parlor.

Dining Room

Entry hall stairway

Louise's bedroom in the turret.

Mrs Heilborn and Olga

Olga (Blue print mounted on
yellowed tissue paper.)

All images on this page are originally cyanotypes in Prussian blue.

Frances "Fan" Smith – San Francisco

Louise – Los Angeles.

Dick's older sister Grace, her husband Carleton Allen
and one of their dogs. They resided in Astoria.

Zoe Carruthers Ridehalgh
with son Walter T., *aka* "Chap."

218

Mailing date: San Francisco. Cala. Nov 8 7PM '98
Received: Honolulu Nov 16 12 am 1898

Nov 5th 1898   San Francisco

Dear Dick

I guess you changed your mind about writing again in four days for it has been more than two weeks since your letter came. Wasn't it strange you thought it would arrive on the 14th and it got there on the night train the 14th allright but we left on the Str. the next morning before it was delivered and so I did not get it until the 18th I was sorry to hear you had been sick and hope you are all well again. Take care of your self.

A transport left here the day we arrived. They say there are very few soldiers left here now but still you see them every day where you go and always rather lazy looking fellows, just hanging around getting into trouble. A soldiers life seems to be rather demoralizing. Have you heard any more about going to Manilla. Astoria is deserted with Mick & Tom both going & Dr B- also. Mick is a traveling man now and he thinks he will be down here soon. Dr Finch expects to be here in about three weeks. I hope we don't have to go home before then, but I made my last call on the Dr yesterday and there is nothing more to stay for except that we are having a pretty good time.

Went to the theater last night for the third time this week and three times the week before. There is nothing I like better than that. The Prisoner of Zenda was the best so far. I thought that was fine. I am learning to walk again and it is no play but hard work and it breakes my heart to think I will always be lame but as my foot gets stronger I will show it less and less of course. Had to have my shoes made to order and they cost fifteen dollars. Pleasant prospect isn't it but I am thankfull not to have to wear any iron braces or any thing of the sort.

Had a letter from Nan today – listen to all the weddings that are coming off in Astoria. Mrs Page & Wilkens on the 24th. Minnie Sovey & Dr Grigg (that came off two or three days ago). Miss DeYo & Mr Barnes – glad that girl is married – perhaps she will get over being so spooney. Hat has got to get home to be brides maid for Laura Knowles on the 7th of next month.

Olga, Nan & I have decided to be old maids (case of have-to however). My cousin Fan[145] is going to marry a man old enough to be her father. Col. Sontag his name is. I would rather be the old maid than marry him even if he has money for he thinks there is only one man in San Francisco and that is Col. Sontag. Fan was all ready to go to a dance last night and he wouldn't let her go because his office boy was going to be there and he didn't think he was good enough to be at the same place Fan was.

---

[145]   Louise's cousin, Frances "Fan" Smith, was the daughter of Sarah Frances Tallant Smith and Theodore Smith of San Francisco.

Oh before I forget I will tell you what the difference is between Uncle Sam, a Rooster and an old maid – I meant to tell you before but forgot. Well Uncle Sam says "Yankee Dodel do", a Rooster say[s] "Cock a dudel do" and an old maid says "any dude will do" – ha- ha-.[146]

Don't waste your prayers on Jim [Corbett]. There is no hope for him, but I will keep on with the good work. Just now I am doing a <u>very good</u> piece of work for I am making a pillow of [for] a young minister down in Alhambra – an awfull nice fellow. You see Dick we are such old friends that I don't mind tell[ing] you all about my other friends. I am sorry you don't want me to call my friends <u>our</u> friends but he is my friend any way and I am sorry if you don't like him. Is <u>your friend</u> Miss Kelly, the young lady who stays at the Bierbachs. I made a mistake when I said my cousin Frank worked at Castle & Cook – he is living at his wifes grandmothers, Mrs Castle. The place is about eight miles or so out of Honolulu.

I should think you must have some fine invention to be able to get seven people in a 7 x 8 tent. Wish I could have droped in for the party but I am afraid a girl would not be welcome at such times. You are never to old Dick to have a good time or play monkey, if you feel like doing it. But you are missed at home, not only for the monkey part by any means.

I hate to go home – it will be so lonesome and dull there this winter and Mama writes the weather is dreadfull and here it is simply splendid. I didn't say any thing about Marge forgetting you – she hasn't forgotten you at all. She spoke in a letter not long ago of writing to you. I owe her a letter and must write today. Lillie Kerckhoff is in Europe now so I got a postal this morning from her that was written on the Str. and mailed just before it sailed. Isnt she lucky to travel all over Europe and spend the winter in Italy.

Well I am so hungry that I must stop and eat as lunch is now ready "in the dining car."

After lunch I went to sleep. It is so warm today one doesn't feel like going any thing. Hat is up town getting flowers to wear to a dancing party tonight. She is going with Norman Pierce – he seems to know some nice people here. Sue Elmore is spending the winter at the Metropole Hotel in Oakland and is having a pretty fine time I guess.

I haven't written to Marge yet and it is getting late so I cant write any more to you this time. I hope all the things the papers say about the Honolulu troops is not true.

Mr Gunn is loafing around here – we are always meeting him and he never seems to be doing any thing.

> *Good bye.*
>> *Take care and don't get sick again and write soon*
>>> *to Louise*

---

[146] See Chapter Seven, page 201, for the first part of the joke.

220

On Thanksgiving Day, November 23, 1898, a number of local Americans organized a parade of automobiles out to Camp McKinley and invited the troops to a fine Thanksgiving banquet of mostly American/English, rather than Hawaiian, dishes. The menu appears to have included: Mulligatawny potage, jellied consommé, turkey, salmon, fillet beef, goose liver, lamb, vegetables and salads, tapioca pudding and lemon ice cream - plus assorted fruits, nuts and crackers, served with tea. Cigars were passed around to the gentlemen after the meal.

Mulligatawny potage is an Anglo-American soup. "Mulligatawny" literally means: "pepper water." Inspired by Indian cuisine, it contains, chicken breasts, vegetables, red lentils, rice, coconut milk, juice from tamarinds and lemons, curry powder and other spices.

Honolulu, Nov 27, 1898

Dear Louise

Your very welcome letter received and I am ashamed of myself that I have not answered it long ago. The last I wrote you was on the 2nd of the month. There was a boat since and I intended to have a letter on it to you but realy we have been to busy to write here lately and the Saturday and Sunday I went to write I was down town with Fred Westhall [Westdhal] and I know you will not feel mad for my not writing when I tell you what times we had that stoped a letter to you. I was at the dock when the boat landed and had quite a time finding him in the crowd but after awhile found him and introduced myself, etc, and it was funny how soon we became friends. He is a fine fellow as you have said and I like him fine. I got some bananas and oranges for him as they would not let him off and I know how good it was for I had been there. I waited until dark and he slid down a rope while a guard turned his back. I had fixed the guard with a cigar or two, and then we went up the streets of Honolulu, both tickled to death and had a banquet at Dewey restaurant, a china place of business, a soldier retreat. The next day I missed him - he came out to camp and I went down aboard the boat, but I saw him the next night and introduced him to Tom Rawlins & Iver Tomson with the word to do for him what ever they could on the trip over. Rawlins & Thomson are both old Astorians and I think will do a little in the food line for him. Well I hope this will go some way in squaring me.

You have not got a very good opinion of soldiers. Well when they are off duty there is little to do. I presume we are all about the same on our day off but then all of them give up a good deal when on duty. Their work is not of the nicest sort and are held in hand most of the time. When I have a day to myself I do not know what to do now a days. I very seldom go down town as there is nothing to do. But by the time I come off an all night guard am tired enough to lay down and go to sleep. Some times of a Sunday I go to the park and hear the band but today I have put in the day so far I hope not to a bad advantage. I have wrote two letters to my sisters and by the time I have this finished it will be dark. I have all so mended my clothes and straightened things out generally, so I have been busy indeed. We have all been working from

7.30 untill 4.30 every day except Saturday when we have to work all morning and stand inspection at one. To take up a gun and outfit that has been laying for a week and get it as well as all your clothes cleaned up keeps you busy until taps Friday night. So far I have had no trouble the last two months in finding plenty to do, but would rather be that way as I feel much better when working. But you do not feel much like doing any thing of evenings. We heard our company was going to Manilla, but as the New Yorkers are going home we will be here a while at least, to look after their sick and lots of other things, such as driving mules, watching money for the paymaster, etc. I don't know what I'l draw and care little as one keeps you busy as well as another.

I hope Mick and Dr Finch were both in the city before you left. *The Prisoner of Zenda* is really fine. I am awfully glad you had such good success there but go easy for awhile as I will expect to take you for a long walk a night or two after I arrive. The young minister should surely like the pillow – if he doesn't well he should. I don't know if I would like the young man or not, but hardly think I would, but I guess the pleasure is all mine. Miss Kelly is the young lady who stays at Mrs B. I passed your cousin's house two or three weeks ago but I think they are away from home now as the place looked empty. I'll go out that way sometime and make a call. I was in my ever[y] days the time I was out there, so didn't go too near. The house is a pretty little cottage on the Swiss plan, built on the side of the hill. I will get a picture of it some day.

I had a letter from Marge the other day and was glad to hear from her as I had realy though[t] she had forgotten about me. I guess the papers are stretching things about the troops here a little – still they are not all angles. I was over to the Pali last Sunday in a rain storm. Cyrus & I went and the rain and mud done us a world of good. We got wet through and mind no name for it. Wednesday eve Mr Dekum took I & Reed of Portland to a small dinner and dance at the Hawaiian Hotel. We enjoyed the dinner but the dancing was not coming our way. Nevertheless we had some fun watching one of our captains dance. Thursday the ladies of Honolulu gave us a regular Outing Club dinner at the barracks. We moved in Wednesday and it is much better than tents. The New Yorks go home on the 29th & 7th. They leave some thirty dead and about two hundred & fifty in the hospital. They did not take very good care of themselves. It will be for the Engineers to run the island now and nurse the sick back to health. We have about thirty sick. I am sending my latest photo. Hope you will like it. Well I must close for this time and as usual I will say I will try and do better the next time.

Yours as before

Dick

This is a bum letter I am sure but will let it go, you [know I] mean right at times [even] if I don't say it.

Dick sent a letter to his twenty-one year old brother, Angus Russell "Gus" Carruthers, who still resided at home in Astoria.

Honolulu. Nov 28 / 98

Dear Gus –

I am just off work (4.30). We are finishing up around the barracks to day; we were patching up the rafters. 'I' Co built the building we are in and made a very poor job of it. We are about done now and I guess will finish tomorrow noon. I will answer your letter and then tell you some of the news. I wont write a great deal though as I have a long letter ready for Zoe and one for Grace and will write some to Mama tonight. So Clark has finaly got out of the ranks. Well I guess he is happy.

I hope something has been done about the schooner [the Jessie] – is there any hope of selling her? Fairchild is alive and well and has a bunk next to me. I guess you got Fletcher mixed with him. He and Bell who died in San Jose are the only ones we have lost – he was on furlough. The New Yorks buried two Sunday and two Saturday. They go home on the 29th and 7th. I have not been arrested and a few have – the stealing of fruit was greatly exzadgurated – the reason little was stolen was there was little to steal.

I have written how I spent Thanksgiving. I hope all were home on that day. It has got to be an old humdrum of a life. There is little to do, so I hope they keep us busy as time goes so much faster. We have been here three and a half months and I am still inclined to think it a bum place. There was talk of our Company going to Manila but I guess with the New Yorks going that is off. We never pay much attention to rumors any more as we have learnt better, but have considerable fun circulating them. You can hear most any thing. Tom Rawlings and I went to a base ball game between Kanakas & the Iowa boys one Saturday when the steamer was here. The Knakas play fine base ball and done what ever they wanted to do with Iowa. The day before, the Iowa beat them bad at foot ball. Speaking of football I am as lots of others wondering how the big game came out. I have an invitation to try a little running with no other than the famous Drumm of Berkley – he keeps up his practice and wanted me to do a little work with him but I am hardly equal I think. We also have Davis the champion broad swordsman, foot and mounted, of America. He enlisted at the Presidio with L.

They have lots of good schools here and three, I think it is, fine colleges. They are fine buildings all of them and have of course fine grounds. They have a race track and hold races once a year. Next June they hold them again, and I hope I will not be here to witness them.

Well I have had supper – fried spuds, lettus salad, boiled beans and tea. Jelly furnished by myself. Well give my regards to all the boys.

Your brother Dick

Nov the 29th 1898   Home in Astoria

Dear Dick

Excuse this paper and a bad pen and I will try and get a letter off today. I have sadly neglected you of late haven't I. Will [you] forgive me and I will send some good news now. Havent touched my crutches since I got home and yesterday I went way down to Goodmans house – to be sure I rode in the car but as you know that convenience does not run up the hill. I am quite proud of self. You see the Drs don't know it all. In the first place as he told me, he never expected me to have to try to walk and then he never thought my foot would be as strong as it is. I told him I was <u>tougher</u> than I looked and I guess I am. But he is all right and the finest Dr in the land.

We had a fine time in the city excepting when my Uncle Capt. Smith died – I think it was the 9th. Of course he had been sick so long no one expected him to live much longer but death is always sad no matter how long you have been looking forward to it and he had suffered so much he was glad to go. We were playing with a cousin and they live just next door. The day of the funeral they got news of Franks father-in-laws death, Judge Hitchcock of Honolulu. They all felt dreadfull over that for the whole family thought so much of him and he was my uncles best friend. I sent Frank your St. & number. Hope he has been around to see you.

They have lots of Honolulu papers at my Aunts house and as she has lived there and two of my cousins were born there I got pretty well posted on the place. Fan has some brass buttons from there and she thought she was the "only pebble" until I got my hat pin. <u>Thanks</u> so much – and the coat of arms – how did you happen to have our old county jail on your coat of arms? That was the first thing I thought of when I saw it.

But it seems rather nice to be at home but I wouldn't mind <u>very</u> much if I was still in S.F. The weather! Oh dear, it is <u>awfull</u>. We were on the ocean Thanksgiving Day and I didn't eat a bite of dinner but we had a fine trip, not a cloud in the sky until we got to the mouth of the Columbia. Havent seen a boy since we got back. I don't think there is one in town unless it is Babe. He isn't looking after your interests very well or he would have been up to see me. I suppose you know of Dr Burnetts engagement to the girl he took to the Knappton party. Winnie & Carney [Reed] got more wedding presents than any one ever did before in Astoria – such beautiful ones too. They are going to live in the little house between theirs and the glass works. They have fixed it up quite nice.

The paper this a.m. announces the engagement of Miss Nancy Tuttle to Mr Aldridge, Sup. of the Canadian Po...[Potash?] Smelter works. I want to go down to Olgas if I can make it between showers.

We have put a lovely big couch under the window in the sitting [room] where the piano used to stand and it is so nice and cozy – wish you would come in this evening and try it.

How are you getting along with your camera and have you been sick again? There is such a lot of typhoid fever there I am so afraid you will get it. Be carefull – take as much care of your self as you can.

Your letter of the 15th must be coming along soon now. I will write again as soon as I get it.

Good bye with love from Louise

A new couch in the family parlor of the Grand Avenue house.

Honolulu   Dec 10 / 98   [Saturday]

Dear Louise:

A note to say a Merry Xmas. I am at the hospital as a nurse and have not a moment to myself. I mailed a small package to you to day. Which I hope you will get, not for the value, just to be sure you know I remembered you.

Dick

Signing the Payroll.

Dick with his new pipe.
(From a badly scratched tintype)

Only a portion of a letter from Louise to Dick written in mid December 1898 survived:

Page 2.

-----but that is all over and I mean to make up for it this year. I am feeling fine – put my crutches away the day I left San Francisco and havent used them since, but I don't know about taking that long walk you speak of. It all depends on whether you promise to behave your self – you generally do so I guess it will be all right.

Charlie was getting a Xmas box off to you so I donated a box of those lovely cigars---- Robert Wilson is engaged also. They all get girl[s] away from here so you must bring home a "Honolulu Lady." I wonder if they sing "My Honolulu Lady" as much down there as they do here. It has gotten to be worse than "Hot Time in the Old Town Tonight"---

Olga came so I stoped and now it is late and must say good night and finish this tomorrow, Guess you will have enough cigars to last a year.

<u>*Monday am*</u>

And I am head over ears in work so I am afraid I can't write anymore, but after Xmas when the rush is over I will write more. I am not doing much for Xmas but what I do give I have to make my self for I am dead broke and so are the rest of the family – sad state of affairs but true never the less. However I don't care if I don't get any Xmas presents – I can have a good time and I never felt better in my life. We are planning a Xmas party at Olga's Monday night the 26th so you can imagine us all down there and me in my new white dress that I started to make for the assembly party over a year ago and then had no use for and never finished it. Well try & have a Merry Xmas and tell me about it.

> *Yours as before*
> *Louise*

> *Buena Vista Hospital*
> *Honolulu Jan 3 1898* [meant 1899] [Tuesday]

Dear Louise:

Just a line to say I am still on deck and to thank you for your fine box of cigars and the two nice letters I have received. I am busy <u>as usual</u> but hope soon to be able to write you a long letter. I have put in twelve hours daily for four weeks at the hardest work I ever tackled and came out on top and I think winner, but strange to say I have never felt much inclined to write letters. Yesterday we were released by some Red Cross men and am now running a shovel and broom, etc. Fatigue, they call it – polite name for work. I spent a very nice Xmas at Bubaughs.

Well the cigars are most gone. I have divided time with them and the new pipe but around a hospital you must smoke lots. Well good bye for this time. As you know I am always busy.

> *As before , Dick*

The local Astoria newspaper reprinted one of Dick's letters to a friend at home:

The following letter, received by Homer Fletcher, will be read with interest by the many friends of Richard Carruthers in this city:

Camp McKinley, Honolulu, H.I., Jan. 12, 1899.
Friend Homer: -
You can hardly blame me for taking so long a time to answer your letter. I have just been relieved from the hospital and am once more at the old stand. I consider myself an expert on fever cases now – quinine, quinine, etc., before and after taking. I may not be much of a doctor, but I am no hoodoo to a place – there were only two deaths while I was there. I had to work from 7 o'clock in the evening to 7 in the morning; and double quick at times. Well, it was an experience.

Boys were pleased to hear that the old transport Lakme had taken fire at Astoria, and was perhaps a loss. Some went so far as to wish she had been loaded with powder and had the same two cooks on her as were on board when we took the eleven-day ride on the tub.

This is fine business. Get a start and come over. I might let you have my place in eighteen months. Then I will send in my application for an eight-year enlistment – nit. I don't want to leave the island – there is so much excitement here. You can't see a fight even; but then you can eat "poi" that's "foine."

They had a show here once and I attended. The opera house is some nicer than Fisher's – has those nice, easy chairs. There is another fine company here now. Six people and two soldiers (75 cents a night) and from the programs you will see that the old Astoria favorites, Post and Ashley, are here. They have been on "short rations," but are doing nicely now.

Well, I must close for this time; remember me to the boys.
Well, goodbye, and a happy New Year,
Dick.

Mailing date: Jan 13 6PM 1898 Honolulu
Received: San Francisco. Cal. Jan 20 7-Pm '99
Astoria. Oreg. Jan 23 8PM 1899

In the Barn

"Home Again"

Honolulu Jan 12 99   [Thursday]

Dear Louise:

I am going to answer your last letter slightly and let you know I am back from the hospital. Was relieved by the Red Cross from Frisco. I don't mean it took the whole Corps to relieve me alone - I and the other engineers. Well we got a name for being the best nurses any outfit had sent and all the trained nurses wanted us to stay, the[y] preferred an engineer to a red cross man. Well we all did work hard. I have had an experience and would have stayed had it been left to my say.

I spent a very nice Xmas and New year. I called on your cousin New Years day. He had not been very well and I believe left for Hilo yesterday. He is the same Frank Smith and I think his wife very nice. I had called to see him once before and had a very nice buggy ride with them. They asked me to call often and I am sorry I never had time to do so. Those cigars were alright. I feel fine, better than ever before but I guess camp laziness will come over me soon. I have only been here since yesterday. I heard of Finchs engagement and of course was as tickled as though I ran a nail in my foot; and Bob Wilson too. Well, well – No, I will pass on Honolulu ladies – the song is nice but not the ladies.

Well there is little to write about and as this is the first time I have had for letters for some time I must close and go at another. So will close as before -

Dick

The *Astoria Daily Budget*, on January 24, 1899, printed a reference to another letter that Dick had sent to one of his Astoria friends, Harry Hamblet:

A letter was received from Dick Carruthers this morning by Harry Hamblet in reply to the receipt of a Christmas present. He says that "Remember the Maine" fades from view after the war is over and that he wants to come home but sees no chance to do so. The letter is humerous but personal and tells how he is learning the local dances to meet [Duncan] McTavish in a contest between Alaska and Hawaiian dances. In speaking of the native girls he says that "They are on the bum and there is no danger of my bringing one home with me."

Camp McKinley, Honolulu, Hawaii
from an old newspaper clipping

228

The following letter to Louise is from her dear friend from childhood, Lillie Kerckhoff, who was touring Europe with her mother. Although Lillie wrote to Louise in English, Louise would have been able to read the letter in German – she had graduated from Astoria High School in 1892, having "majored" in the German course of study.

Received: Feb 13, 1899 in Astoria via New York
         Ink stamp on reverse: Hotel Bon - Port Territet J. Kunz
Addressed to: Miss M. Louise Tallant
         682 Grand Avenue
         Astoria
         Oregon

Montreux Switzerland   Jan 25th 1899

My darling girl

Your long welcome letter I received quite a while ago, but the days and weeks seem to slip by so quickly with out my hardly realizing it. Mama also re'cd your dear Mothers letter which she is surely going to answer during the course of the next week. We were so interested hearing all about Laura's wedding, and many thanks for the clippings. She did wear a white dress after all. Hat must have looked stunning, and I am anxiously waiting for the photo and hope that she will surely send me one. Her dress must have been very <u>swell</u> and especially as it was the dress of your Mother must have made it doubly attractive. [147]

We came down here on the 21st, and are enjoying a little sunshine. We spent three weeks in Holland, but I am sure the climate is worse than Oregon's ever dreamt of being. It was so damp and not very cold. Here it is cold and dry. Yesterday they had a severe snow storm in the mountains and this morning, they are white with snow down to their base. Tomorrow we are going to walk up to the snow line, and going tobogganing. Wont that be fun. Just think of it in the Alps. I would be perfectly happy if I could only have some of my <u>girl friends</u> with me.

We are staying at a pension and there are almost nothing but English people here. Quite a number of girls, and they have been very nice to me, but someway I feel more at home with Amer. I wish you could see the way they dress – always décolleté for dinner, and such short sleeves, just below the shoulder, and some have such thin arms. There is so much dress though in this place, and the shops are so lovely. They have the most beautiful French gowns, etc. They have impromtu dances here in the house every few evenings, as they have a good floor in the dining room, but the girls have to dance together as there are only a bout two or three men here. One is a Russian prince??? and I had a fine dance with him a few evenings ago. Am getting to be very fond of dancing again, as I went to several in Germany and have gotten in practise again. At the Xmas ball in Pafunburg, they danced the cotillion around a large tree and had some very pretty figures.

---

[147] As Laura Knowles' bridesmaid, Harriet apparently had worn Mary Elizabeth's 1869 wedding gown. Later, in 1918, Laura wed Angus Carruthers, the day he returned from his Army duty in France.

Dear Louise, I am so glad that you are getting along so nicely and have discarded those old crutches. You must be so delighted now that your blouses wont pull up anymore, which used to bother you so last year. I was thinking the other day that it is just about a year ago that you arrived in L.A., and I think it is perfectly wonderful how you have improved in that time. I wish I could gain as much flesh, but that seems to be an impossibility for me. I feel lots better though since I have come South. Mama caught a severe cold last week, and has a sad time trying to get rid of it. We take long walks together every day, and enjoy them so much. She seems more like a sister to me, for she enters so heartily into all the fun. She as well as I enjoyed your Mothers letter so much, and it was such a long interesting one. How is Olga and her Mother? I have often planned to write to Olga and Nelly, but my! I don't get time for anything any more. I re'cd a long letter from Loll the other day, but she poor girl has been in bed a week again with her old trouble. It does seem too bad. She mentioned having re'cd some pretty views from you and Hat. Also had a long letter from Jim that was all sweetness. Herman [Lillie's brother] and Mr Bradshaw seem to be as great friends as ever. Floss and "Charlie" are still not married. I think that I would loose patience if I were in her place.

They have a Kursaal here, where they have fine music every day. The orchestra is composed of about fifty pieces, and the music is fine. We are going to stay here a few weeks, and then go farther south. They have been talking here in the room about a freak of a girl that is at one of the hotels here, and who Mamma and I put down as one of those "crazy English." And now have discovered she is an American. Great joke on me. Realy she looks wilder than ever Buffalo's Bill show was.

We are going for a walk, so au revoir. Best love to all the family, and all inquiring friends, and write soon to your loving friend

            Lillie

Who is Mr Wilson engaged to?

Mrs. Kerckhoff and daughter Lillie.

Chapter Nine

Louise and Dick's good friends Beatrice Pearl Holden and Charles H. Callender were married October 12, 1898. The afternoon ceremony was held at the home of Pearl's parents at 405 Duane Avenue in Astoria. Only their immediate families and a few special friends such as Louise, Harriet, Kate Upshur and Olga Heilborn were present. It was those "old" friends who decorated Pearl's house for the happy occasion.

The bridal trousseau was reported to be "one of the handsomest ever possessed by an Astoria bride," but only Pearl's special friends were allowed to see it.[148] Her wedding gown was of white organdie with inserts of white ribbons – she did not have a train. She carried a bridal bouquet of white roses. Frances, the bride's sister and attendant, wore a similarly styled dress of Nile green organdie and carried carnations. Charlie's groomsman was Louise's brother Will. Mr. E. C. Holden presented his daughter to the groom in their parlor. The Reverend Henry Marcotte, who had just arrived back from Portland on that morning's steamer, performed the Presbyterian wedding service, after which the wedding party enjoyed a fine sit-down dinner.

After a wedding trip to the east coast, Pearl and Charlie set up housekeeping in Knappton, Wahkiakum County, Washington, almost directly across the Columbia from Tongue Point at the east end of Astoria. For thirty years, Charlie's Scottish father, Melville Philo Callender, had been the superintendent of Asa M. Simpson's lumber and sawmill in Knappton and was a large stockholder in the company. Charlie now managed the mill.[149]

Active in many businesses in Astoria and Portland, Charlie also erected the Callender Dock and Warehouse, building it over the water on pilings between 12th and 14th Streets in Astoria; the dock was used by his river tugs business – the Callender Navigation Company. Today, the Astoria trolley tracks run nearby along the south bank of the Columbia River, as does the pedestrian Riverwalk. Both the trolley tracks and the Riverwalk currently extend about five miles from the West Mooring Basin to 39th Street in the east.

Pearl and Charlie's son, Melville, was born in 1899; they were a happy and busy family. However, Pearl was now unable to cross the river often to visit all her friends in Astoria. So she invited them to visit her. Louise was a frequent visitor at the Callenders' home. She would make the short journey on the regularly scheduled morning steamer that left Astoria at 10 o'clock for the Knappton Dock. Louise usually stayed for several days.

---

[148] *Astoria Daily Budget*, October 12, 1898.
[149] The Simpson mill burned down in 1941.

Knappton Cove's Federal Quarantine Station 1899 – 1938

Originally named Cementville, Knappton was primarily an industrial community made up of the Simpson sawmill and fishing interests. Although its streets were made of wooden planks, it did have tennis courts, a gym, and a dance hall. The nearby cove became the site of the United States Government's Columbia River Quarantine Station.

With thousands of immigrants trying to enter the United States, the federal government found it needed quarantine stations on both coasts for the protection of its citizens against diseases and "undesirables." In 1889, Congress passed a national law requiring inspections and, when necessary, detentions and quarantines. In 1882, Joseph Hume had sold his Knappton Cove Eureka and Epicure Packing Company to Knappton Packing Company. Early in 1899, that company merged with the Columbia River Packers Association. CRPA quickly closed the former Hume cannery and put the facility up for sale just at the time that the U.S. government was looking for a site for its fourth quarantine station on the west coast. In 1899, despite opposition from the local people, the government purchased the buildings and the exceeding long wharf that jutted well out into the waters of the Columbia. The facility was well suited for the government's purpose.

Dr. Hill Hastings, Assistant Surgeon and a member of the Commissioned Corps, established the station May 9, 1899. He was in command of the facility until the end of 1900. During that time, he erected a new disinfecting building on the long wharf. Physicians usually paid only weekly visits to the facility, unless persons were in quarantine there; nurses rarely were requested to attend the quarantined people. Dr. Hastings resided in Astoria, so he shuttled across the river on the steamer *Electro*, which had been leased for the exclusive use of the station's physicians.[150] Louise's circle of friends was delighted to have Dr. Hastings join them in their activities.

The quarantine station, termed a "western Ellis Island," was an absolute necessity on the Columbia, a major entry port into the United States for ships from all over the world. All vessels, upon crossing the bar and entering the river, were required to anchor off Astoria and were boarded by inspectors to determine whether the ship carried any infestation(s) – including rats that could carry bubonic plague - or communicable diseases on board. Of particular concern were vessels originating in the Far East. If health problems were found to be present, the vessel, its crew and passengers were "impounded" and escorted to Knappton Cove. Passengers and crew disembarked and were led into the long building on the wharf, sometimes called the "*Lazarreto*," or the Pesthouse. Here they were required to strip and shower in disinfectant. Their clothes and other belongings were deloused in huge cannery retorts. Anyone who was found to have an active disease was quarantined for as long as necessary – sometimes for many months.

If a person "passed" the health inspection, he/she lived in a tent on shore until such time as the ship was released. The vessel and its cargo were thoroughly fumigated by placing burning pots of sulphur throughout the inside of the sealed vessel; the process took about 48 hours. The ship was then released to continue on its journey. Later, the Station was equipped - on shore - with a hospital, living areas, detention quarters and isolation rooms. Interestingly, the latter had one bathroom to be shared between two

---

[150] Anderson, 40.

rooms.[151] Decommissioned following action in the Philippines in the Spanish-American War, the patrol gunboat USS *Concord*, was sent to Knappton Cove in 1914 by the Department of Treasury to be used as a temporary floating "hotel" for the quarantine station. The *Concord* also performed Coast Guard duty there until the U.S. Navy sold her in 1929.

The federal government decided to put the Knappton Cove Quarantine Station up for sale in 1950 – offering it at auction as a possible "resort." The Clarence Bell family purchased the land and buildings. The Bells developed it as a museum that now provides the "story" of the Station. It is part of the Columbia–Pacific National Heritage Area awaiting final approval by Congress.

Mailing date: Feb 10 5.30PM '99 Astoria
Received: San Francisco: Feb 13 10AM '99
                    Honolulu Feb 27 10AM 1899

Feb the 8th 1899   [Wednesday]

Dear Dick

I would have answered your last letter before but I went over to visit "The Princess" [Pearl] *at Knappton and stayed a week. I had a splendid visit. Pearl is a different girl so happy and contented and Charlie* [Callender] *is a model husband. Pearl has a snap over there. They have breakfast at ten oclock and all she has to do is take care of her own room and she has a beautiful room too – such lovely furniture and every thing so convenient. It made me smile to see her sitting there so calmly darning Charlies socks. She always used to be so figity.*

The weather has been about as cold as we ever have it – good skating down at Clatsop on the lakes and fine coasting and sleighing here in town. The coasting reminded me of lots of good old times and the slides we have had – do you remember one night when we came home from a party and got the sled out from the cellar so quietly as we could and took a slide. And our sleigh ride - Olga and Burnett, Tom & you and I. What would you give for a sleigh ride now or even a sight of snow.

I hope to goodness you wont be ordered off to Manila now. There is fighting again down there. Marge said she had a letter from you last Sunday. I haven't had one for over two weeks. I had a long letter from Edith Copeland today. She is still at work; said she wished she had been a "Princess"- said it payed better to sit around and primp than it did to work.

Talk about luck though, Nancy Tuttle is the lucky one. Clara Starbuck wrote me that she knew Mr Aldrich and his family and he was a <u>fine</u> man and he only gets $900 a month.

You can imagine how nice it is out today when a warm rain comes on top of about 7 inches of snow - lovely walking - I have to go down to Nells.

---

[151] Anderson, 40.

Charlie asked me to go to the last assembly that was the 3rd but I stayed over to Knappton and missed it. Well I will have to finish tomorrow and get ready to go down to Nells now. Good night for today –

　　　　　L.

　　　　　　　　　　　Thursday

Dear Dick

Well I got down to Nells with out being drowned. My but it was a terriable day and not much better today only the snow is all washed off and the walking isn't so bad tonight. Mrs Short entertains the St. Agnes Guild – you are an honorary member I believe. I don't belong any more but Mrs Short asked me. I wish you were back here to go. Parties are dreadfull tame to me. She said to ask a gentleman so I asked Charlie [Higgins].

Now we are our own cooks and dishwashers just now or I would write more but it is about time to get ready to eat again. Dear me I will have to begin soon and diet – my clothes are getting tight – just think I weigh 138 lbs and never felt better in my life. You look so thin in your pictures. I expected to get lots of pictures from you – what happened to your camera? I hope to hear from you before long and then I will write a longer letter. This is longer than your last one to me. Any way there is nothing new except the combine but thank goodness our cannery isn't in it. Write soon to your lovingly

　　　　　　　　Louise

Dick in Honolulu.

Lillie writes Louise - this time from Montreux, Switzerland, dated February 11th, 1899:

My dearest girl

I know that I have not been very good about writing but you remember when I was visiting you how you thought I was always writing. And now where I have been with my relatives, they think the same things. I am down in the drawing room, as the light is too poor in our room, but it is full of people talking and playing cards, so I will not be responsible for what I say in this letter. I can't make a very lengthy letter of it this time, - only wanted to thank you for your letter, Laura's wedding announcement, and the Berlin address. I am sure that we will enjoy meeting your friends, but I don't know when we will get to Berlin. No prospects just yet.

Tomorrow we are going to Nice and are going to be in Rome for Easter. I have enjoyed our visit here so much, but oh, how I have wished that you girls could have been here too. Last week they had lots of snow, and the tobogganing was glorious. It was such fun, and oh, the snow was so beautiful. Whole mountains covered with it, just one solid mass of pure white. I never expect to see anything prettier. I did so enjoy hearing about all the Astorians. Am glad that Mr Knickler is still in existence. I had not heard about him for so long. And so you have changed your opinion about Mr Dekum. Who is the attraction, you or Hat? Give Olga, Nell and all the girls my best love. What a fine Xmas you had, and how glad I am that you are getting along so fine, Louise. Received a letter from Marge the same day I re'cd yours. I think her photo is very good, don't you?

They are dancing and I am just dancing here in my chair too. Several of the English girls have come to ask me in, so I will have to tear myself away from you. Heard from Loll[152] but the poor girl has not been well this winter. Grace [Eliot] is having a good time. Also re'cd a letter from Mr Bradshaw. I can see your look of disgust at my changing <u>my</u> <u>opinion</u>, but Mamma wanted to send him a New Year's greeting, so this was only an answer. Love to your dear Mother, Father, Hat and all friends. Regards to the <u>boys</u> -

Same address   *Yours*   *Lillie*

Mailing date: Feb 21 4.30PM '98 Astoria
Received: Honolulu Mar 4 '99

Dear Dick

Your last letter came just a day or so after I had sent one to you. What kind of a place is that where you are working as an office clerk? And why don't you say any thing about coming home. We need you to liven us up - it is awfully dull and we miss you but so many of the boys

---

[152] Olga Heilborn's older sister, Laura Heilborn Bierbach, lives in Honolulu.

are away I guess you would find it dull too. But it is home and I guess you wouldn't mind being here, rain & all as you say. But it hasn't rain[ed] so far today –some thing is wrong.

Jim married a missionary – how is that for Jim. No I haven't heard of Dr Burnetts wedding yet. Hat's dress was a buty – she was Laura Knowles brides maid and wore it there, not at Pearls wedding. I told Nan what you said and she said she was going home and write to you so you must have heard from her before this. Nell was here when I got your letter and she said it was mean of you not to say some thing nice about her. I read her what you said about Nan. Nan is a dear thing, there is no mistake about that. Why did you put a 5-cent stamp on your last letter – you never did it before – aren't you a soldier still when you work in an office?

Mr Heilborn has had another stroke and has been very sick, but he is up again now, although he is still feeble, both bodily and mentally. I am afraid he will never be quite him self again. It leaves Charlie with a good deal of care on his shoulders. Charlie has gotten to be quite a josher lately.

No wonder you say every letter tells of a wedding or engagement. The latest is Maude Warren & Charlie Higgins. Sure go this time. He has waited a long time but has won at last. They say you can see his smile three blocks off. He is tickled to death.

Well I have got to leave you now and will finish tomorrow. We are still doing our own dishwashing.

L.

Later –

Tuesday

Sun shine - just think of it. We have been having April showers for three days now and it is fine to get a peep at the sun once in a while. Last night Charlie telephoned up to Hat & I to go down to his house; he and Dr Finch were going there to make a rare bit. It was fine and we had a good time playing croconole [153] (don't know how it is spelt, but any way that is how it sounds). You remember we played it one night at Nans and laughed so much – you, Charlie, Dr Burnett, Olga, Nan & I. It makes my fingers hurt.

I hear Mick is going to be best man at Neal Crosbys wedding, Easter. Charlie said he knew of another wedding coming off soon but he wouldn't tell us who it was. Kate [Upshur] says she and Jack are going to get married pretty soon.

Marge sent me a book today called "With Edged Tools." She said it was the best story she had read in a long time. Poor girl, she has been sick most all winter and she worries so because some thing is the matter with her heart. She has sent off her annual shipment of oranges to Astoria.

---

[153] The game to which Louise refers is Crokinole. Please see Chapter Five, page 138, describing the game.

Your sister Grace looks mighty well - she has a blue tailor made dress and an awfully pretty hat. I have only seen her on the street and haven't seen Zoe since Xmas. Your Mother owes me a call too. I haven't seen her since I came home from S.F.

Well I am making an apron for a Bazar [Bazaar] down in Alhambra and I must stop now and sew on it. So good bye with love from

Louise.

Do you see my cousin Frank [Smith] any more?

Nat with his Christmas ring.

Eben Weld Tallant and their cat.
(Original images are cyanotypes)

Marge, Louise and Bismark.

Mailing date: Mar 7 12 M '99 Astoria
Received: Portland. Ore. Mar 7 11.30 PM 1899
Written on Columbia River Packing Co. letterhead
Addressed to: Miss Maria L Tallant
     c/o J D Sutherland
      #357 West Park St.
       Portland, Oregon.

Astoria, Oregon, March 7th 1899 [Monday]

To My Dear Maria:

I enclose for your benefit a check for Nine dollars. You can collect it yourself or get Mr Sutherland to attend to it. I have mailed L.L. Shuman a Receipt for it. So you need only go to the bank for your money.

The only thing I want out of this is a pocket diary for 1899. You can probably get a bargain in Portland. I went to Griffin and Reeds for one. They had but three in stock and wanted full price 1.00 @.

I received a very interesting letter from Aunt Fanny this morning. All well. Frank [Smith?] very much improved. GOLLY! What a storm we had last night. It came up very quick about midnight. Will and Hat said they could not sleep. Even Nat was woke up by the wind blowing the slop bucket off the porch, down the back steps, scattering its rich contents.

Letter from Bro Nat - he leaves S F 14th for Astoria via Portland. We will see him Thursday 16th. Charley Fulton informed me yesterday my position as Pilot Commissioner was confirmed by the Gov.

Affectionately
Your Father

The Death of Crown Princess Ka'iulani of the Kingdom of Hawai'i [154]
Victoria Ka'iulani Kalaninuiahilapalapa Kawekiu i Lunalilo Cleghorn (1875 – 1899)

To Ka'iulani - At The Threshhold of a Promising Career

"Forth from her land to mine she goes,
The Island maid, the Island rose,
Light of heart, and bright of face,
The daughter of a double race.
Her Islands here in Southern sun,
Shall mourn their Kaiulani gone,
And I in her dear banyon shade,
Look vainly for my little maid.
But our Scots' Islands far away
Shall glitter with unwanted day,
And cast for once their tempests by.
To smile in Kaiulani's eye." [155]

Robert Louis Stevenson, Honolulu, H. I.

---

[154]   "The Call of Grim Death" and "With All the Royal Honors," (Honolulu *Pacific Commercial Advertiser*, March 13, 1899).
[155]   "The Call of Grim Death," Ibid.

Victoria Ka'iulani Cleghorn was born October 16, 1875, (the same year as Louise) on Emma Street, Waikiki, in Honolulu. Her parents were the Honorable Governor of O'ahu, Archibald Scott Cleghorn (born in Edinburgh, Scotland) and Princess Miriam Likelike, sister of the reigning King David Kalakaua, and of Lili'uokalani of the Kalakaua dynasty, who became Queen in 1891.

Crown Princess Ka'iulani grew up in Honolulu on her 'Ainahue garden estate, on which grew her favorite tree - a giant banyon; her favorite companion was her little pony named "Fairy." She was well aware of her dual heritage of Scottish and Kanaka Maoli. In April 1889, Robert Louis Stevenson, visiting Hawaii with his family, dedicated a poem to her, originally titled *"To Ka'iulani - At the Threshold of a Promising Career."* It was rumored she was infatuated with Mr. Stevenson - she was thirteen years old.

On May 10, 1893, the Princess left for England to study at Great Harrowden Hall in Northamptonshire. Ka'iulani remained abroad for several years. The Princess had hoped to visit all the major cities in the United States as well as the Columbian Exhibition/World's Fair of 1893 in Chicago, but the turmoil in the Hawaiian Islands at that time caused her great anguish. She restricted her travel plans and only managed to reach Washington, D.C., where she unsuccessfully pled her nation's cause before Congress and President Grover Cleveland. She sadly returned to England. During the period 1894 to 1897, she traveled extensively in Europe and to her father's homeland, Scotland. She also visited the home of the famous opera singer, Mme Adelina Patti, in Wales. During this time, there were several deaths in her family, as well as the death of Mr. Stevenson (December 1894). Her grief was deep and her health declined.

Ka'iulani arrived back in Hawaii in November 1897. At the age of twenty-two, she was a cultivated, charming, athletic young woman and the beloved *"hapa-haole"* (part non-Hawaiian) of her Island people. But her health continued to worsen. During a visit to the Big Island of Hawaii in 1899, she fell ill with rheumatism and developed a high fever, an aftereffect of having been caught in a violent rainstorm. Four months later – at two a.m. on the morning of Monday, March 6, 1899 - she suddenly died. She was only twenty-three years old.

The people of the Islands were in shock. Princess Kaiulani lay in state at her home on Wednesday. On Friday, her body was moved to the historic Kawaiahao church. The funeral procession took place at 12 Noon on Sunday, March 12. Many hundreds lined up for the procession, including all the members of the U.S. Volunteer Engineer Corps (including Dick), who "…with gleaming arms and crepe draped standards marched up and took their place on King Street between Punchbowl and Richards streets."[156] People filled the church to capacity for the service. The Bishop of Honolulu gave the reading; the choir sang "Brief Life To Here Our Portion" in Hawaiian. Many gave loving eulogies of their Princess. A touching solo of Handel's "Angels, Ever Bright and Fair," sung by a Mrs. Macfarlane, ended the service. To the organ's music of "Home Sweet Home," the Princess was carried out of the church. Her flower-ladened, snow-white casket was borne by pallbearers wearing feathered capes. The cortege formed.

---

[156] "With All the Royal Honors," (Honolulu *Pacific Commercial Advertiser*, March 13, 1899).

To the boom of guns and the toll of the church bell, a black and white covered rope was attached to the hearse. Two hundred thirty Hawaiians, dressed in white trousers, blue jerseys and yellow capes took hold of the rope and pulled the catafalque the two miles to the Royal Mausoleum in Nunann Valley. In a private ceremony, Princess Ka'iulani was laid to rest. Waiting outside the crypt were the thousands who had formed the procession, including the bands; the faculty and staffs of the colleges; dignitaries of all kinds; the National Guardsmen of Hawai'i; members of the secret societies; the U.S. Army and Navy - and the battalion of the U.S. Volunteer Engineers; native women in flowing black or pure white *holokus*; and elderly men, all dressed in black suits and wearing old silk hats.

They all bid "*Aloha*" to their beloved "fairy tale" Princess – their "Island Rose."

Note: a film version of Crown Princess Ka'iulani's life is expected to be in theaters in the summer of 2010.

The following letter is from Dr. Marsha Murphy, one of Louise's physicians while at Children's Hospital in San Francisco in 1897-1898.

C. H. Mar. 7 / 99

My dear Miss Tallant: -

I was quite delighted to find a letter from you awaiting me at the office the other morning and more than delighted to hear that you are doing so well - isn't it grand?

As to poor Miss Phillips - poor girl. I was so surprised when I heard that she had been taking morphine to such an alarming extent - is really about what I have told you, to Miss P or any one else, because it is Hospital news that I know that besides her mother, we are probably most interested in her case and you would like to know particulars. She will be a long, long time getting well. It was very sad about Allyn - she told me of it and I really pity the girl from the bottom of my heart. I don't visit her much because they are endeavoring to keep her as quiet as possible, but I keep constant watch of her. Poor, poor girl.

I have opened an office at 746 Clayton St. - Ashbury Heights - there are few doctors there and it seems to be a desirable locality - so I was advised. You must come and see me when you come down. I have had <u>one</u> patient so far - my sign is not up yet. I am having it painted! It is to be just Dr. Murphy - I hope people don't think it a <u>man</u>! Well dear, I must bid you goodbye. Write soon, won't you & with much love, I am

Your friend,
Marsha Murphy

Remember me to your father & sister.

Eben Weld Tallant, celebrating his fifty-eighth birthday on Tuesday, March 28, 1899, sent this note on his Columbia River Packing Company stationery to Louise and Harriet, who were again visiting Lila Sutherland and Grace Eliot in Portland.

Astoria, Oregon, March 28th 1899   [Thursday]

Dear Louise

Yours of yesterday received and at breakfast table found cuffs and buttons. Shall christen them at tonights dinner.

Please thank Miss Eliot for her kind invitation to Easter dinner but we have made our plans to be at Hotel Portland and expect you and Harriet to dine with us there. Plan to leave Astoria on Sat. night boat. It costs only a Room to get us three up. Will breakfast at the Portland, attend church.

Am very glad to learn of the intention of you and Harriett to unite with the church. Wish it were possible to get Will interested sufficiently to join.

You do not mention receiving five dollars from Geo. Taylor. I now enclose [$]2.57 to help out until I arrive.

Affectionately

Papa

P.S. I think this check will require a stamp.

Mailing date: Apr 8 4.30PM 99 Astoria
Received: San Francisco Apr 11 1899

April 8   [Saturday]

Dear Dick

I have been expecting to hear that you were on your way home so I have not written but as I cant find out any thing definite about your coming I will write and if you don't get the letter there wont be much loss anyway. I came home from Portland Wed. Was up there a little over a month and had the best kind of a time. Would have liked to have stayed another month. The weather was good most of the time and every day there was some thing going on. Part of the time I visited with the Eliots and the rest with Lila. I haven't had such a good time for about two years. You don't know how good it seems to me to be able to go every where and do what I want to with out getting tired. I had lots of lost time to make up for, so I didn't over look any thing, not even a nice young millionaire who took me to the theater, sent me flowers, and etc. Mr Dekum gave a party for Violet & I. We had a fine time; it was an awfully nice party. I had just gotten your letter that day and Miss Dekum had one from her brother, so we compared notes about the caves iand etc. I meet the Mr Dekum that is down there once - Lillie introduced me. I have forgotten how she happened to know him but I remember I thought he was an awfully queer man, not nearly so nice as George Dekum.

Marge writes me that you are going to run down to see her on your way home. That will be a nice trip for you. Take a look around for me if you do go, so you can tell me all about it. Thanks for the photos. Where is the other half of your face? Lolie Bierbach says you are looking well, but in the picture you look so thin. Well guess I will see you soon and so must leave a little news for then. Expect though you will want to do all the talking. Well, I'll listen.

Good bye

Louise.

Don't spoil your reputation by doing as Hobson did when you get home again.

Fancy Dress Party at 682 Grand Avenue - April 22, 1899. Louise is standing center back, dark dress; Hat is center in white costume. Attendees included: Polly; Nell; Sue; Nan; Olga; Harriet S.; Caroline; Nora; Will Sherman; Charlie and George Teal; Duncan McTavish; Dr. Finch; Charlie Higgins; Terry McKean; Frank Shields; Bob Urlson?; and John McK.(possibly McCue?).

(Original image is a cyanotype)

An Invitation from the First Unitarian Church of Our Father:

Portland   April 23, '99

To: Maria L. Tallant and Harriet H. Tallant
Dear Friends –

It has been the custom of the Committee of 50 to call upon all the new members of the church and extend to them a friendly greeting, As this is impossible in your case, we take this method of reaching you and assure you of a hearty welcome when ever you are able to visit our church.

Yours Very Truly
Mrs. J. R. Comstock, Pres.
Mrs. F. A. Jackson, Sec.
Com. of 50

242

Received: May 15 11-30P 1899 Astoria. Ore.
Addressed to: Fraulein Louise Tallant
682 Grand Avenue
Astoria
U. S. of America   Oregon

April 30th 1899   Heidelberg   [Sunday]

My darling girls –

I received your loving letter yesterday and I think myself <u>very good</u> to answer so quickly, when you kept me waiting such an age. Before I forget it – I thought Hat was going to send me her photo. I wish she would – it would give me lots of pleasure. I have been wanting to have my photograph taken and I wish I had done it in Italy where they take pretty good pictures, but we were always so busy sightseeing that I did not take the time. Here they take horrid pictures. Of course I have not been in any of the large German cities yet, but in these smaller places they know very little of photography, like Stieckel or even "Mrs Crow."[157] I consider myself fat enough now. I weighed myself the other day and I came up to fifty-seven kilo. Heavens only knows how many pounds that makes. My Uncle says it is 125 pounds, so I joyfully took his word for it. Too bad about Marge not feeling well this winter, but I guess she will be alright now that she has arrived at the distinction of being an Aunt. I heard from her last week, and she was excited in anticipation of the great <u>event</u>. I wish we could see our little ones – Frankie's Father died in February, and she spent the last two months with her Mother in Santa Barbara. She is home again now, and her Mother and Rose have returned with her. Wasn't it funny about your meeting Mr Cheal. I remember hearing Frank speak of him very often.

My! what a glorious time you had in Portland. I almost envied you of all the parties given in your honor, etc. Just fancy having a "millionaire" so attentive. Just hold on Louise, a girl does not get a chance like that every day. But he must be nice and good too - that goes farther than riches (lecture from your grand-mother). So you have changed your mind about Mr Dekum. I will wait until I meet him next time. It seems to me that you girls are too popular – there you have all the young men in Portland running after you and Hat has two of the nicest men I ever met dancing attendance on her – entirely too much good luck. You might divide up, with some other poor mortals, although I can't complain this winter. Don't worry about the "Lieutenant's." I have not seen them for the last three months, so I have had time to get some sense. The American men are my ideal anyway.

Dear Louise, how delighted Mamma and I were to hear that your foot is not bothering you anymore. I can fancy how you enjoy your <u>liberty.</u> What a difference for you between this winter and last. We did have a pretty good time though, about a year ago now, and later on into the summer. What a glorious time we did have in Astoria. The other day I was thinking

---

[157] M.A. Crow was a popular portrait photographer in Astoria during these years. The photo studio was located on Commercial Street.

about the drive we used to take – you remember the evening we went out with the big horse and we met the electric car. What suspense and agony for me, but it is awfully funny when I think of it now. Is Fanny [the Tallant family's horse] still in existence? Mamma received your dear Mothers letter, and she is going to take the first opportunity to answer it. She does not have very much time for writing. We are now visiting relatives again, and Mamma does not do very much more than talk over "old times," etc. We have been here three weeks today and so far as rain is concerned, this climate is certainly equal to Oregon. We have only had two solitary days that have been entirely free from rain. We do manage to get out between showers though, and take long walks into the woods, which are fine. We generally walk an hour or two, and then go into a "Wirthshaus" and refresh ourselves with a glass of beer, brown bread and sausages. Good, I assure you. Heidelberg is the most picturesque place – the ruins of the castle are grand. Tomorrow night the "Gerzherzoh of Baden" is coming here, and they are going to illuminate the castle and old bridge. I fancy it will be fine. There is a large university here, but the students as a rule do not interest me. Their faces are one mass of scars, as the result of the duels they have, and they look pretty dissipated. Some of them I mean. Studying what they came here for is I imagine the last thing they think of.

This letter amuses me. I have hardly mentioned the most interesting thing that has ever happened to me, and that is our Italian trip, but if you only knew how many descriptive letters I have written, I know you would not blame me. I have seen so many wonderful things, and enough art to last me for a lifetime. But it was realy fine. After we left Montreux, we spent three weeks in Nice, then three weeks in Florence, two in Rome, four days in Venice, and a day in Pisa, Bologna, Milan and Lugano. From Nice we also made day trips to Menton, Monte Carlo, etc. At the latter place I saw <u>enough</u> style to last me for a lifetime. But I will wait and <u>tell</u> you all about it. I would never finish if I was to write it all. We liked Rome <u>best</u> of all. Unfortunately we did not see the Pope, as he was so ill just at the time we were there, but we did see the Queen several times and also heard lovely music in the churches. The climate was horrid though especially in Florence – it was so cold. Does not equal our California climate, but of course we were realy there a little too early. April and May are the best months. I love to think about it all now. Venice was very romantic, just like you read about in books – gliding around in a gondola. The trip up here, through Switzerland was grand. There was a rain and snow storm, but someway the mountains were not obscured and they were simply overpowering in their grandeur. But as I told you before some day I hope I can tell you all about it.

You ask when we are coming home, and what our plans are, but those are pretty hard questions to answer as we are very uncertain ourselves. In two weeks we are going to Weisbaden to meet Mrs Wollweber from San Francisco, and will probably stay there for several weeks. That is all that we know of our plans at present. I received the loveliest long letter from Nell [Sherman] sometime ago. Please thank her for me and I am going to write to her soon. We are so *sorry to hear that Mr Heilborn has been so ill, and also that Olga has had such severe headaches. There is another girl that I have wanted to write to. Some day I am going to <u>reform</u>. I hear from home very often. Herman and all the family are well.*

Hasn't the drought been dreadful? It makes Mamma and I sick to think of it. Poor Ella has had a siege of it, but Emma writes that she is much better now. Doll & Grace are well too. Grace has had a very attentive suitor all winter, and I fancy is having a gay time of it.

Time to prepare for tea. My Aunt's girl took it into her head yesterday that she did not like to work, so left after an hours notice, a la American. In consequence we have to work.

With love to all the family, and a <u>German</u> kiss for you and Hat.

Yours as always

Our address is always the same / Papen, et   *Lillie*

Dick's Company M leaving Honolulu for San Francisco on board the S.S. *Australia*.

Although no letter or note from Dick was found, on April 10, 1899, Dick's Company M, 3rd Battalion, 2nd Regiment, Volunteer Engineers received their orders to return to San Francisco. They had spent eight months stationed in Honolulu and were finally relieved by four batteries of the Sixth Artillery. A short time before they left Hawaii, the troops were allowed to sail over to see Kauai, the Garden Isle. During that period Dick was promoted to corporal.

On Thursday, April 20, they packed up their belongings. Led by the Government band, the rousing procession marched from Camp McKinley down King and Fort Streets to the Oceanic Wharf, where the troops boarded the steamer S.S. *Australia.* Their colors were flying high and leis were bestowed upon the departing soldiers as dense crowds accompanied them to the ship. The band struck up the "Star Spangled Banner" as they filed onboard. As the *Australia* began to move into the bay, a bugler, up in the rigging, played the song composed by Lydia Lili'uokalani in 1884 - "Aloha Oe." One soldier unfurled the Stars and Stripes; another waved the Hawaiian flag. The mass of people on the dockside waved back with handkerchiefs and leis.

The ship reached San Francisco in only 8 days. The troops were stationed at the Presidio until their discharge on Wednesday, May 16, 1899. Dick decided to spend several weeks traveling in the Los Angeles area before returning home to Astoria. He was disappointed that they were never in battle - except against mosquitoes, sickness and ants.

Mailing date: May 6 6-AM 1899 Astoria. Ore.
Addressed to: Mr R. E. Carruthers.
　　　　　　　Care F. R. Noyes
　　　　　　　Mills Building
　　　　　　　San Francisco
　　　　　　　Cal.

May the 4th 1899　　　　　　　　　　　　　[Thursday]

Dear Dick

Your note came yesterday. Charlie was up here the night before and said your folks had letters from you written in S. F. so I was looking for one and was glad to hear from you and know that you were safely home again - not quite home yet though. Wish you could have gotten home for your birthday - we would have had a celebration. The Bachelor Maids Club met at Nells yesterday and the girls all said they would be glad to have you back again and wished you would hurry up now that you were so near. But I think it will be fine to go down and see Marge. You see I have been there and so I know how nice it is - to good a trip to miss and they will be awfully glad to see you. If you will be in Los Angeles at all I will write Herman Kerckhoff and he will show you around - he knows every one and can tell you all about the place. I guess you met him when he was here - you will find him at the California Club - he lives there.

Hat and I are both terriable disappointed that you are not going to be here while Cousin Fan (from S. F.) is with us. As soon as she wrote she would be here for the last two weeks in May we said "good, Dick will be here then." Now I don't know what we will do with her. It will be so pokey. None of the other boys will do. They are all to slow for a San Francisco girl. I know you would like her and she would like you, but she has to go home the first of June so you will not see her.

I have just been up to Portland again – only stayed a week this time – had a fine time. Harriet and I both went as we each had urgent invitations to hear *The Bostonians* and go to the Multnomah party. We visited with the Eliots. I went two nights to the opera to hear *The Serenade* and *Robin Hood*. The girls are teasing me because I went both nights with the same man, but as I don't care a row of pins for him, I don't mind – and I did enjoy the operas very much. The mans name is Mr Clarke – he is an admirer of Grace Eliots. I met him there the first time I was up. I wrote Marge all about my Portland trip – she can tell you what a good time I had. But you will have other things to tell and talk about and I can tell you all that has happened since you left - our fancy dress party and etc - after you get through telling us all that you have seen and done. The little that has happened here will only be a post script.

Write to me when you get to Alhambra and tell me how Marge is and eat an orange off your tree for me and take a good look at every thing for me. Get Marge to show you where we used to live, the place Hat and I were born, and the Sunny Slope Ranch where we visited. I expect you will make your trot – there are so many nice drives. Well for this time good bye -

Expect you feel old having your twenty fifth birthday - the 9th isn't it? My congratulations.

As always your loving friend

Louise

Dick "celebrated" his twenty-fifth birthday on May 8, 1899, while stationed at the Presidio - still a soldier, but now a Corporal in "M" Company, 3rd Battalion, 2nd Regiment of U.S. Engineer Volunteers! On Tuesday, May ninth, he wrote a letter to Louise, remembering the birthday he had two years before. So much had changed since then – for all of them.

Dear Louise:

I received your letter yesterday and I guess you will be taken back at my answering so soon, but I am still at the Presidio and will be here until the 16th. I guess this will be the last letter you will receive from a soldier for sometime unless you have some one else on the list I don't know about. I hope not as soldiers are not very good people. I am on guard tonight and as all I have to do is sit here and check the passes off as the men come in I will answer your letter fully. I don't suppose you know I am a little above a private now. Well our dearly beloved Captain took a queer notion into his head a week or two ago before I left Honolulu and made me a Corporal – and my orders must be obeyed and followed, so if I come home gruff and mean

I am simply unaccountable. As you know all Non Com Officers are to the men no good. I am not very much swelled over the raise and think I could wear shoulder straps as well as stripes with as much dignity at least. Perhaps next time I go to war I might be lucky and get a commission. IF I GO. But I hope you think with me that all officers are to be avoided and there are a few nice enlisted men.

I am sorry I am not home for a birthday celebration. Do you remember the one I had two years ago – seems to me I was feeling very good that night, but then I had lots of troubles those days. Well we will celebrate yours instead if you like – just see, you will be twenty three – my but you are getting old. Soon be able to start on that Lo Haneli Head old maids home. Today I see is the 9th I did not celebrate. Tell the Bachelor Girls Club, if you allow swearing, that they are not a --- bit glader to have me back than I am to get back. Now that is well expressed and has more meaning than you can guess. Thank them for their kind wishes though. I sometimes think I should go right home as I have lost so much time but then I know I would enjoy a visit down south so well that it is to tempting. I will be glad to meet Herman K- and it would be nice to have such a good guide. I will look up all the places you mention. I am sorry I will miss meeting your cousin Fan but as for me being good company I might have changed. I am slow I think but perhaps will brighten up a little under better surroundings. I guess you had a fine time in Portland and now I am about 9th on the list, will I ever be able to get past that 5th place I once gained – let's see, in the fall of '94, I think it was.

Well I guess you've had about enough for any one girl (of this kind of stuff) so I will close. With regards to all and hoping to have the pleasure of taking you to the first dance of the summer or what ever comes along. Trusting I wont look any the worse for wear; that all will be pleased to see me back; that in time I will be able to accept invitations out to dine and will be able to eat soup with a fork if it be the proper thing; that I can wear white shirts and high collars with out every body getting on to the fact that it troubles me and my neck is sore; that I will not have to wear the new striped shirts they are wearing here; and above all that you will let me see you safely home once in a while.

I am as ever.   Dick

The following notice is from the Personal Notes column of the *Astoria Daily Budget* on Friday, June 9, 1899:

> Misses Louise and Hat Tallant and Miss Symthe[158] of California went up river on the *Hassalo* this morning.

---

[158] The newspaper may have misspelled Frances Smith's name. Fannie had been visiting the Tallants.

Elsewhere in the same newspaper there appeared the following note about Dick's arrival back in Astoria on the same day. The temperature in Portland reached over eighty degrees during this period in 1899, so Dick must have felt like he was still in the Islands or in Southern California.

> "Dick" Carruthers arrived home this morning on the State of California after having attempted to serve his country in the Philippines. He enlisted in the Oregon engineers with every prospect of going direct to Manila but the "great father" at Washington forgot all about them after they had reached Honolulu where they remained until mustered out a few weeks ago. His experiences were not altogether unpleasant but it is doubtful if he would enlist again if he was compelled to only go half way to the seat of war. He looks in robust health and gives no evidence of having undergone any hardships.

Mailing date: not legible.
Envelope addressed to: Mr Richard Carruthers
                                          City

Monday a.m.   [June 12, 1899]

Dear Dick

If I hadn't seen you on the street I wouldn't believe you could have been in town and not even telephoned to me these last two days. The phone, & door bell have been wringing constantly and each time I have gone thinking it would be you and each time have been disappointed.

If you are to busy to come up, telephone soon to

Louise

Summer arrived and the usual doings took place, including the Fourth of July 1899 picnic, held that year at Lottie Bennett's in Gearhart for fun at the beach.

The ladies arrived at Gearhart train station.

Fourth of July Picnic 1899 – at Lottie's in Gearhart.[159] Harriet is in the front row, plaid skirt; Louise, also in a plaid skirt, is behind Harriet. Floretta, Sue, Lottie and Marge are also in the group.

---

[159] In another album of Louise's, this same photograph is dated as May 6, 1900, at Kinney Cottage, Gearhart.

The Second Regiment of United States Volunteer Engineers. A History
Captain William Mayo Venable

Roster of Company M as Mustered Out on May 16, 1899[160]

COMPANY M

Captain : George W. Freeman.

First Lieutenant : Charles Kern.   Second Lieutenant : George O. Seyde.

SERGEANTS.

John C. Clark	Orin H. Stratton	Frank Batten
Charles S. Inglerock	Perry E. Jackson	Sylvanus F. Sheppard
George Clark	Jorgen Jorgensen	

CORPORALS.

William L. Covington	Daniel Shea	George H. Reed
William E. Elwell	William H. Turner	William W. Sproul
Gustavus A. Wikunder	Richard E. Carruthers	

Cook : William Carroll   Musician : Sampson N. Waller

FIRST-CLASS PRIVATES

Charles A. Anderson	Asa Bishop	Austin H. Bittner
Frederick R. Blackburn	Benjamin J. Byrnes	John J. Carney
Jacob E. Coffin	T. David Connerlin	Alva A. Coulter
James D. Craig	Charles Crowel	Henry W. Cyrus
David Dunlap	George E. Dugdale	Charles Erickson
Charles H. Francis	Edward R. Francis	Louis E. Fairchild
Claus C. Grau	Wendall Hall	William G. Keeth
Bert A. Kellogg	William F. Kissel	Robert Lauka
Ellsworth P. Linn	Charles E. Logsdon	Archie C. Luster
John C. Lynn	William E. Millar	William Meysh, Jr.
Joseph J. Miehlstein	James Moriarty	Walter McCarthy
Sterling McReynolds	John Nolan	John F. O'Leary
Thomas W. Rodabaugh	Frederick A. Simpson	Edward S. Sweetser
Frank J. Wallace	Maurice D. Welsh	Michael Welch
Frank Wilkinson	William D. Wilson	Valentine G. Wheeler

SECOND-CLASS PRIVATES.

John C. Baxter	Thomas Blevins	Gus Bodinson
George G. Curry	Peter C. Dorland	William Hanna
James T. L. Harris	Grant Hendershott	George V. Howell
William Johnson	Frank P. Kitchen	Charles R. Kung
Charles A. Mason	William McDemrott	Adolphus G. McFarland
Clarence W. Stephens	Edward Warners	Fred W. Westlake

---

[160] Venable, 192.

Excerpts and paraphrased Chronology of Dick's Tour of Duty in Venable's chapter on "The Third Battalion, 2nd Regiment, Company M of the United States Volunteer Engineers."[161]
Parts are from the diary of Capt. T. Waln-Morgan Draper, Captain of the company. Some notations indicate Dick's service.

Emblem of the Volunteer Engineers: a miniature gilded castle.
Newspaper: *The Reville*. First issue published on November 8, 1898.

1898

July 2	**Dick** entrained from Astoria to Portland to join with other volunteers. Traveled south by train to San Francisco.
July 9	Arrived at The Presidio, San Francisco. Marched to Camp McKinley under Major Wm. C. Langfitt (Captain, Corps of U.S. Engineers, U. S. Army). The unit was attached to Expeditionary forces and become part of the Eighth Army Corps. Uniformed, armed, equipped and drilled while there. Kept grounds in fine condition.
July 26	Major Langfitt ordered to precede to Honolulu, H. I. He arrived in advance of his troop command and began to prepare the campsite.
August 5	In San Francisco, the command broke camp (13 officers, 361 men) at 9 AM; Third Battalion marched six miles via Lombard St., Van Ness Ave., Golden Gate Ave. Market St. and Stuart St. to Stuart Street Dock where lunch was served by the ladies of the Red Cross Society. The New York volunteers and part of Company K boarded the steamer *Charles Nelson*. Companies I, L, M, and the remainder of K, boarded the Klondike steamer *Lakme*. Captain C. F. Klitgaard of the *Lakme* ordered lines cast off at 7 PM. Remained at anchorage in the stream off Black Point until the following morning.
August 6 Saturday	The *Lakme* weighed anchor at 8 AM; proceeded to sea, passing Fort Point. at 9:20; the Light Ship at 10:55; the Farrelones at 12:35.
August 17 Wednesday	Arrived at Honolulu wharf at 6:15 AM. Distance from San Francisco. 21,00 miles. At 2 PM marched to a point four miles east of city, near Diamond Head; established Camp McKinley.
September 26	Command marched 16 miles to Pearl City; established Camp Langfitt in a pavilion by a redwood grove. Made surveys in vicinity of Pearl Harbor as directed. **Dick** was ill at the time of this exercise and remained at Camp McKinley along with a few other enlisted men under Sgt. Hemphill.
October 19	Camp Langfitt abandoned. Unit marched back to Camp McKinley.

---

[161] Venable, 103-111.

October 28	**A typhoid fever** epidemic appeared in the 1st New York Regiment. Camp McKinley condemned. Work began on temporary housing about one-half mile north of Camp McKinley. The cost of each barrack unit was limited to $1,000, solely the cost of materials.
November 4	For sanitary reasons, the battalion was ordered to move camp to the new site as soon as possible.
November 23	Engineers moved to a temporary barracks at new Camp McKinley. Work completed by 27th November. The entire New York regiment was ordered back to San Francisco as soon as possible. Two hundred fifty men ill with typhoid fever were left in hospital in Honolulu, plus the thirty deceased men buried in Honolulu.
December 2	**Dick** was one of eight volunteer engineers who responded to the called to assist the newly arrived Red Cross and White Cross female nurses from San Francisco in caring for the sick in the Buena Vista hospital. Numerous soldiers were ill with typhoid fever and other medical disabilities. On the 16 December, 18 more engineers were called up to assist in the hospital.

1899

January 1	Battalion formed; participated in flag raising at Post Headquarters.
March 12	Battalion formed at 12 M. and attended the funeral of Princess Kaiulani, marching from the church in Honolulu to the Royal Mausoleum in Nunann Valley, a distance of two miles.
April 10	Orders received from Department Headquarters for troops to prepare to leave Camp McKinley.
April 20	At 12:30 PM, the command left Camp McKinley and marched to the Oceanic dock in Honolulu, boarded the steamer *Australia* at 3 o'clock, and set sail for San Francisco at 4:15 PM.
April 27	Arrived San Francisco Bay at 7 PM - anchored in the stream off Black Point.
April 28	Weighed anchor at 6 AM and proceeded to the foot of Pacific Street, and at 9 o'clock the troops went ashore for inspection by customs officials. At 11 AM, the tug *McDowell* conveyed the command to the wharf at the Presidio, where it disembarked, marched to the permanent camp on the reservation near the east gate and resumed the usual camp duties.
May 1	Chief Mustering Officers called out the lists and gave references to the muster out of the command. All work continued uninterruptedly until finished.
May 16	Tuesday, at 3 o'clock P. M., the command was mustered out of service by Captain Sedgwick Pratt, the Chief Mustering Officer, Department of California, 3rd Artillery.

In 1984, the State of Oregon dedicated a Spanish-American War memorial newly placed on Salem's Capitol Mall among other memorials. The almost three-foot high plaque honoring all the veterans from that 1898 war had been found in the basement of the Capitol Building in Salem, Oregon. Its creator, date and origin are not known.

Chapter Ten

Later In 1899
The Nineteenth Century Comes to a Close
Marking Time

Saturday [Oct 14, 1899]

My dear boy

I have just telephoned to see if I could find you at the can factory to tell you Pearl has sent for me to come over this afternoon, but in case I cant see you before I go I will leave this note. I rather hoped she would send for me while you were away – you know the visit has been planned for some time so I think I had better go but will probably be home Tuesday. So telephone up then and if I am here come up <u>sure</u>. I kind of hate to go and miss a chance of seeing you perhaps tonight and surely tomorrow, but you must be awfully tired from being up all last night. You are a dear to do it I think. So get a good sleep tonight and dream of me. I had a lovely dream last night of you. Look over at Knappton once in a while as Pearl used to do.

I wish you were going over with me. These lovely moon light nights would be appreciated over there, wouldn't they – by <u>us</u> any way. Take good care of yourself and don't get the small pox or any thing like that. For my sake be careful. I hope the Jessie gets off all O.K. tomorrow and good luck to her. Lunch is ready so must say good bye. The boat goes at ten. Loads of love and kisses from

Yours always

Louise (I'll be a good girl)

If I should not come home Tuesday I will write you but I think I will be pretty home sick for you by that time and will come back. L.

Mailing date: Oct 17 1899 Knappton, Wash.
Received: OCT 18 6.30A 1899 Astoria. Ore.

[Oct 16, 1899 - Monday]

My dear Dick

Can you spare me until Saturday? I found Pearl expected me to stay until then and had planned to go over with me then and stay a few days and there isn't any reason why I shouldn't stay expect [except] that I want to see you and they wouldn't understand about that. Oh I wish you were here. Your eyes looked so tired Saturday. I keep thinking about them. I forgot to date that note – it was the 14th, wasn't it?

Pearl Callender and young Melville.

Louise and Dick at the OR&N Dock.

Henrietta Eliot, Louise with box camera,
Dr. Hill Hastings and Harriet.
(Original image a cyanotype)

Henrietta, Louise, Harriet and Dr. Hastings
at Knappton Cove.
(Original image a cyanotype)

Image #1257-340 courtesy of Clatsop County Historical Society.

The *Electro* on the Columbia. A butterfly fishing boat is on the right.

We should have celebrated the anniversary by a trip to CocksComb Ridge. A year ago Hat & I were just landing in San Francisco. My, didnt it rain Sunday. We couldn't have stayed out that long. There isn't much excitement over here and I am <u>awfully good</u> - cant help it. The baby [Melville] is so sweet for any thing and Pearl is a lovely little mother. This afternoon we walked down to the Quarantine Station (pushing the buggy) and this evening we have been playing Whist. They go to bed awfully early and have breakfast at nine - just suits me. I hope you can read this. - excuse pencil but I haven't any ink here and the Str. goes at ten, so I thought I had better have my letter ready over night and will add a P.S. if I have time in the a.m.. If there is any special excitement, let me know. There is almost always some kind of a boat coming over. The electric[162] was here today but Dr Hill Hastings didn't honor us. Have you called on the Halsteds? I wonder if the Jessie got off yesterday. I will <u>surely</u> see you Saturday if not before. Take care of your self and be good and now good night with love from your

Louise

Tuesday P.S.   Dear Dick, I love you.   L

Folded inside the letter was a torn scrap of letterhead paper for the Simpson mill listing their boats:

North-Western Lumber Co.	Steamer Cruiser.	Tug Traveler.
San Francisco Office, 48 Market St.	Steamer Edgar.	Tug Printer.
A.M. Simpson, Pres.	Steamer Typhoon.	Tug Astoria.
Office of Bend - Mill Division	Steamer Rustler.	

For some months, Nathaniel Weld Tallant had been staying at the Grand Avenue home of his brother Eben and his sister-in-law Mary Elizabeth Tallant. Nathaniel was in deteriorating health. He died the evening of Saturday, October 21, 1899, at the age of sixty-seven. Both Eben and Mary Elizabeth accompanied the body to San Francisco to the home of Nathaniel and Eben's sister, Sarah Frances Tallant Smith. Many in California, where, on November 5, 1883, Nathaniel Weld Tallant had been elected a resident member of the California Academy of Sciences, mourned his death. His many friends in the Northwest and in New England also mourned his passing. The obituary of E.W. Tallant's older brother appeared in the *Astoria Daily Budget* on Monday, October 23, 1899.

Nathaniel Weld Tallant, who was stricken with apoplexy on Saturday morning, died at 6:30 on the evening of that day, having never recovered consciousness. [163] The deceased was born in Nantucket, Massachusetts on January 25, 1834.[164] He removed to San Francisco in 1850 and that city has since

---

[162] She refers to the steamer *Electro*. A vessel named the *Electric* was also on the river.

[163] The outdated medical term "apoplexy" was used to indicate a stroke – some sort of blockage or rupture, such as an embolus or thrombus, in a blood vessel that interrupts the blood flow, commonly occurring in the brain. A paralysis and/or coma often result.

[164] The Tallant family Bible lists Eben's older brother's year of birth as 1832.

been his home. He has been associated with the Cutting Packing Company for over 30 years and in 1874 took charge of that company's cannery on the Columbia river. At the time of his death he was President of the Columbia River Packing Company. His younger brother, Mr. E.W. Tallant of this city, and a sister, who resides in California survive him. He was unmarried. Mr. Tallant was a progressive and energetic business man and had built up an enviable reputation among the commercial interests of the coast. The remains, accompanied by Mr. E. W. Tallant, were taken to San Francisco this morning for internment.

Dr. Thomas Lamb Eliot
Portland

Sarah Frances Tallant Smith
San Francisco

Nathaniel Weld Tallant
Astoria and San Francisco

Dear Louise & Harriet –

Our thoughts not only followed your dear parents on their sad journey – but have often turned back to you who remain at home – your brothers & yourselves.

Your uncle was a man of the highest type – germaine, sincere, high-minded & honorable – his life forces all were fed at the root by moral & spiritual loyalty to God and love to his fellow beings.

I enter deeply into your personal bereavement – in which I truly share.

We want to hear from one of your household, when you can conveniently write, how your father & mother are. We sincerely hope to have them here, on their return, as you know how welcome at any time any of you will be to our home – if you can visit us.

Mrs Eliot & Grace & Henrietta all send love –

Affectionately yours

Portland, Oct 28 – '99   *T. L. Eliot*

The Unitarian church to which Eben Weld Tallant and his daughters Louise and Harriet belonged had its roots created by New England's intellectuals as a compromise between strict orthodoxy and liberal attitudes. In 1794, the first Unitarian Church was established in Northumberland, Pennsylvania. Early Unitarians included many well-known persons of history such as: John Adams, John Quincy Adams, William Howard Taft, Daniel Webster, Oliver Wendell Holmes, Henry Wadsworth Longfellow, Thomas Jefferson and Ralph Waldo Emerson.

The Reverend Dr. Thomas Lamb Eliot was the first pastor of "The Church of Our Father," First Unitarian Society, in Portland, Oregon, from Christmas 1867 until 1893. He and his family had been dear friends of all the Tallant family for many years.

Thomas Lamb Eliot

Thomas Lamb Eliot (1841-1936) was born in St. Louis into a family devoted to life in the service of religion, good morals, philanthropy, civic improvement and education."[165] His forebears, from a distinguished ancestral line, emigrated in the mid 1600s from Cornwall, England to Beverly, Massachusetts. In 1834, Eliot's parents, the Rev. William Greenleaf Eliot IV and Abby Adams Cranch Eliot, felt a calling to move west to St. Louis, then a frontier town, but usually spent their summer vacations in Massachusetts and New Hampshire. Because Eliot suffered from a painful eye problem, his parents sent him, at age nineteen (1860), on a sea voyage around Cape Horn on the *Golden State* clipper ship to San Francisco; he later returned to St. Louis at the beginning of the Civil War (1861). The beautiful clipper ship, the *Golden State*, formed but one of many links in the life-long friendship between the families of Eben Weld Tallant and Thomas Lamb Eliot.[166]

In 1864, Mr. Eliot graduated from Harvard Divinity School. No degrees were confirmed until after 1870, but Eliot was awarded the honorary degree of Doctor of Sacred Theology in 1889. In 1867, he answered the plea of the newly formed Unitarian society in Portland, Oregon, to become the congregation's first minister. Eliot, his wife Henrietta Robins Mack and their one-year old son, William Greenleaf, Jr., left St. Louis for New York and sailed via the Isthmus of Panama on the *Constitution*. The 7,000-mile sea journey took six weeks. They arrived in Portland Christmas Eve 1867. It was in the Unitarians newly built 50 x 60 foot chapel that Dr. Eliot preached the dedication service on the twenty-ninth of December.

By 1878, the Ladies Sewing Society, and Eliot himself, had raised funds for a new $18,000 church building. The cornerstone was laid with Masonic rites at the corner of S.W. Broadway and Yamhill. Mr. Eliot named the building "Church of Our Father." Dr. Eliot became Pastor Emeritus in 1893, after twenty-five years of service. His older son, Dr. William Greenleaf Eliot, Jr., served as the First Unitarian church's minister from 1906 to 1934. A new church building was erected in 1926 at 12th and Salmon.

The name of Thomas Lamb Eliot is well known in Portland for his philanthropic works. Dr. Eliot was involved in so many civic organizations and enterprises, among which were the committee for the Skidmore Fountain (1885-1889); organization of the Portland Art Association (1892); a director of the library association (1896-1916) and of the Park board (1903); and aided in founding the Boys and Girls Aid Society of Oregon (1885) and the Oregon Humane Society (1868), that protected both children and animals. Perhaps of all his endeavors, he is remembered as being instrumental in influencing

---

[165] Wilbur, 4.

[166] Ibid., 122, *f.n.*#15 – referring to page 10 of Wilbur's book: "A year or two later as Second Office and then as Mate on this ship was Eben Tallant, later of Astoria, Mr. Eliot's life-long friend and parishioner."

former Portland residents, Mr. and Mrs. Simeon Reed, to found Reed Institute (later Reed College), using a $2 million bequest from Mrs. Reed. Dr. Eliot was the first president of Reed's board of trustees (1904 to 1920). Less than two months after his death in 1936, Reed College's Twenty-Second Annual Baccalaureate service was dedicated to Dr. T. L. Eliot with the naming of Eliot Hall. A glacier on Mount Hood also bears his name, honoring his love of the out of doors.

The Eliots lived at 227 W. Park Street (renumbered 1025 SW Park Avenue) in Portland for fifty-seven years. They entertained many famous persons at their residence, including Susan B. Anthony and Julia Ward Howe of women's suffrage movements; Dorothea Dix,[167] historian Frances Fuller Victor, who, in 1872, published her volume "*All Over Oregon and Washington;*" and Dr. Eliot's nephew, T.S. Eliot, poet and essayist.

The family spent three months each summer at their cottage on Neah-kah-nie Mountain on the Oregon coast near Cannon Beach. They often visited the Tallant family on Grand Avenue in Astoria. The Eliot's two daughters, Grace Cranch (born in 1875 – the same year as Louise) and Henrietta Mack (born in 1879 – one year younger than Harriet) visited back and forth for years with Louise and Harriet. Dr. T. L. Eliot officiated at the Astoria wedding of Louise and Dick in October 1901, and that of Harriet to Frank Greenough in September 1911.

T.L. Eliot sent the following note, postmarked March 25, 1931, to Eben Weld Tallant, Esq. to mark Eben's ninetieth birthday on the 28 March. Eliot himself would turn ninety on October 13 of that same year. Much like Dr. Eliot, Eben had been involved in local affairs, served on the school board and the library board, often officiated for the Regatta, and chaired the city park commission. Besides being an active member of the Masons, he had long belonged to the Ancient Order of United Workmen. As a Unitarian, Eben was also fully committed to serving his community.

My dear Friend,

The 28th is on hand and I think it is your Memory Day. How far we have come, and how full of rich experiences! Life becomes more and more of a wonder, more full of perplexities, and also more full of things to be grateful for! We have talked of many of them together. Chiefly of our children & children's children who are rising up with so much to be proud of. Let us count <u>good character</u> and <u>usefulness</u> as <u>chief.</u> <u>Success</u> as the world appraises it may come and may go! "Give me neither riches nor poverty" says the old sage. The world's accumulated wisdom is a good school and experience is a good school master, though at times a hard one! But I am not preaching to you! This line from us all – Mrs. Eliot, Henrietta, Grace, who is home today - and I am sure Will [Eliot's older son, William Greenleaf] & wife & the rest bless you for all your kindnesses to us. I wish you many Happy returns!!

Ever your "chum,"

T. L. Eliot

---

[167] Miss Dix was instrumental in establishing the first modern mental institutions in America.

Eben Weld Tallant, oldest living cannery man of the Columbia River District, celebrated his 90th birthday Saturday at the home of his daughter, Mrs. Richard E. Carruthers, at 681 Jerome Ave. A host of old time friends visited him during the day and he was the recipient of many letters and telegraphs from friends in other parts of the world, as well as beautiful gifts of flowers.[168]

The following letter is from a friend of Louise's – there is no signature and only the first page of the letter survives. Evidently other pages were removed by Louise - one would assume for personal reasons. Eben's letter to his daughter, dated December 17, 1901, mentions he met a Mr. Preston, who asked to be remembered to Mr. Carruthers (Dick, Gus or Tod?) – Mr. Preston had some money for him. No other information was given, but a web search shows the Preston Peak Copper Company was operating in Oregon and Northern California. Preston Peak, in California, was one of the pioneer mining discoveries in the Siskiyou range with 12% copper and some gold. Near the border between Oregon and California in Josephine County, Oregon, Waldo was a booming gold rush town of 30,000 in the 1850s. After a terrible fire late in 1900, it became a ghost town.

Stationery:

Preston Peak Copper Company

Mines:	Office:
Siskiyou County	Preston Peak.
California	P.O.: Waldo, Oregon

Preston Peak   11-25-99

My dear Louise:

Your letter just received and I can not say how pleased I was to hear from you. And how glad I was to know you had not entirely forgotten your old friend. I was more than hurt at your not writing to me. I was in Portland in October and had an invitation to go to Astoria, just for the trip. It was indeed a temptation for I wanted so much to see you all, but the fact that you had not written made me imagine you did not care to keep up the acquaintance.

I am so sorry to hear of your uncle's death. I remember him quite distinctly. We all have our sorrows. I feel for and with you, for I know too well what it means to lose one who is near and dear.

Can hardly believe it possible that you have forgotten the number of our room 53. I for one can never forget it.

I have been all around Oregon and also spent 3 weeks at Shasta Spring. I am feeling splendid. We expect to spend the winter in the mountains. I enjoy the quiet very much.

I am so glad you have no trouble with your foot. When I look back and think of how useless it was once. It seems wonderful that you get along so well. All Hail to the Chief Sir Harry.[169]

---

[168] "75 years ago – 1931," (*Daily Astorian*, April 5, 2006).

[169] Dr. Harry Sherman was Louise's surgeon at Children's Hospital in San Francisco in December 1897.

Well dear friend I must close for want of news. O yes, forgot some thing. My brother returned safe and sound from Manila. He withstood Spanish and Philippino bullets, but alas on his release he went down before a pair of flashing black eyes and for the first time showed the white . . .

No further page(s) are found.

Richard and Mary Faint Carruthers
Pioneers of Oysterville, Pacific County, Washington Territory
Proprietors of the Pacific House Hostelry

At some point in 1848 or 1849, Richard and Mary Faint Carruthers and their four children – John (1839), Sarah Ann (1843), Robert (1845) and Mary Jane (1847) – left Whitby Township, Ontario, Canada, and moved south into central Missouri, approximately halfway between St. Louis and Kansas City. They settled in what was then Enumeration District No. 23 of Cooper County. They were in, or near, Boonville (also spelled Booneville on some 1850 to 1855 maps), close to the Missouri River and the Oregon Trail Road. Their third daughter, Elizabeth, was born there in 1849. The United States Federal Census of Cooper County, dated September 2, 1850, listed all of the family under the last name spelling of *Caruchen*. Sadly, their son, John, age twelve, died in 1851 in Boonville: he was buried there, with his toy gun and pocketknife beside him.

Joining an Oregon Trail wagon train in 1852, the family of six crossed the plains by ox-team for the Oregon Territory.[170] Stopping briefly in Portland in the Oregon Territory, they boated across the Columbia River and, on September 13, 1852, arrived in the southern part of the present day North Beach Peninsula in Pacific County (at that time still part of the Oregon Territory). By 1853, they were homesteading in the developing town of Pacific City, in the newly formed Washington Territory.[171] The Carruthers family then moved northward up the very narrow peninsula. On August 10, 1854, they settled on their large Donation Land Claim No. 38 that bordered upon the weather beach of the Pacific Ocean. The claim consisted of 319.98 acres, where Oceanside is presently located, west of Cranberry Lake.[172] The course of the stagecoach line - and later the railway - passed along the sandy beach on the western edge of their property. While they lived there, Richard and Mary's fourth and fifth daughters were born: Sophia [Sophiah] (1854) and Maria [Mariah] (1856).

---

[170] Some years ago, the Carruthers' well-worn wooden ox-team yoke was donated to the Clatsop County Historical Society (CCHS). At the time of their crossing to the West, the 1848 act of Congress had established the Oregon Territory to be south of the 49th parallel (Canada) and included what is now Oregon, Washington, and parts of Idaho, Montana and Wyoming. The legislature established Pacific County in 1851. In 1853, the portion from the 46th parallel (Columbia River) north to Canada officially became the Washington Territory. Oregon attained statehood in 1859; Washington became a state in 1889.
[171] Pacific City was begun in 1849 by Elijah White, a minister, and plated by J.D. Holman. It was to be a major port at the mouth of the Columbia River, on the lee side of Baker's Bay, just north of Cape Disappointment, so named in 1788 by the British merchantman, Captain John Meares. Pacific City was abandoned when the area became part of the Ft. Canby Military Reserve.
[172] Freeman, et al. *Washington Territory Donational Land Claims*, abstract, V-231, roll 107, page 72, Sections 28 and 33, T11N - R11W.

This postcard of the Pacific House Inn and Saloon is still being issued in Oysterville.

Richard and Mary Faint Carruthers

Perhaps because he was the second living son of the thirteen children of Thomas and Sarah – and of Scottish descent - Richard had been brought up with a very strong work ethic, which made him productive throughout his life. He was also an entrepreneur and a risk-taker. Anyone who emigrated from overseas and undertook to cross the plains with a wagon train was definitely a risk-taker! In the spring of 1855, Richard, along with L.A. Loomis and a few others from Pacific City and Loomis Station, set out eastwards intending to mine for gold in Montana. By one account, hostile Indians forced them to turn back near Spokane Falls.[173] However, George C. Johnson's account stated that both Richard and his son Robert were on the trip with the others and, while working in the

---

[173] Whealdon, "L. A. Loomis . . .," (*Sou'wester*), 30.

Montana gold mines, Richard and Robert convinced J.C. Johnson to become a settler in Pacific County.[174]

Richard was a robust man – he had to be. His primary trade was that of a stonemason, a left handed one at that. His work took him over a wide area in Pacific and Clatsop counties. By several accounts it was Richard who rebuilt the Cape Disappointment Lighthouse in 1856. Court records of September 1861 show Richard was finally paid for laying the stone "underpinning" of the Astoria Court House - the record did not state how much he received for that job.

Richard had filed his Declaration of Intention to become a United States citizen on March 16, 1852, at the Cooper County Circuit Court in Missouri before beginning the difficult trek west. The Territory of Washington of the United States of America finalized his request October 1, 1860, by which time Richard and family were living in Oysterville, Washington Territory (W.T.). In the year 1860, there were six surviving children in the Carruthers' family: the three born in eastern Canada – Robert, Sarah Ann and Mary Jane; Elizabeth, believed to have been born in Missouri; and the two born in the Washington Territory – Sophia and Maria.

---

[174] "Pioneer Families Play Important Part . . .," (*Morning Astorian*, September 22, 1926).

Further north from Richard and Mary's Donation Land Claim, almost to the tip of the peninsula, was Oysterville. In territorial days in the 1860s, the thriving, and wealthy, community of more than 500 persons on Willipa/Shoalwater Bay was a college town and the county seat of Pacific County. It had developed a growing industry of shipping much sought after Shoalwater Bay oysters - fresh - by schooners to cities as far away as San Francisco. Oystermen were paid in gold coin. At the peak of the oyster enterprise, Oysterville was reported to rival San Francisco in gold per capita. By 1875, Oysterville became more easily reached by land when L.A. Loomis and others began operating a stage line between Ilwaco and Oysterville three times per week. Each way cost $1.00. The stage, drawn by four horses, carried passengers, freight and the U.S. mail. The schedule was not fixed because part of the route ran along the western sandy beach and was dependant upon tidal conditions. Also, beginning in 1875, the Ilwaco Steam Navigation Company, with its principal office in Oysterville, provided connections across the Columbia River to Astoria. Oysterville became a tourist destination.

Richard and Mary had finally settled in Oysterville long before the birth of their seventh surviving child, William Alfred (04 July 1861-03 Feb 1944). By 1873, possibly using California redwood brought as ballast on the return trips from California by some of the many oyster schooners, they built and were managing a two-storey inn that may have provided living quarters for their family as well. It was known as the Pacific House Inn, a hostelry, saloon and stage stop, located on Pacific Street, two blocks from the bay. The establishment, the largest in the county, "was destined to become one of the most famous hostelries in the north west,"[175] It had a first-class reputation over a very wide area. On a busy day, Mary would easily serve two hundred fifty meals, aided by her daughters, Elizabeth, Sophia and Maria.

Oysterville had been holding annual regattas since 1870. Many attended the regatta held July 25, 1873. People even came from as far away as Portland, journeying five hours by steamer to Ilwaco near the mouth of the Columbia River; the passengers connected with horse carts to cover the twenty miles overland to Oysterville. During intermission of that regatta's evening dance held at Espy Hall, the dancers went over to Pacific House for a supper prepared by Mary Carruthers. It was judged "creditable to Portland where every luxury is supposed to be accessible."[176] Whenever the Pacific County Superior Court was in session, many men pleasantly waited their turn in the nearby saloon at Pacific House.

On October 7, 1876, Richard and Mary's son Robert and his wife Harriet officially took over the daily management of Pacific House. "It always bore a first-class reputation, which will be enhanced, if possible, under new management."[177] But by December of that year, Robert had almost decided they could not make much and was ready to give up the hotel. However, on Sunday, August 13, 1882, in the *Daily Astorian*, M. Carruthers, Proprietor, advertised that Pacific House offered "Oysters, Clams, etc, kept constantly on hand and served in any style, without extra charge." To board by the day cost $1.25 - by the week cost $8.00.

---

[175] Tompkins, "Oysterville, 1840-97," (*Sou'wester*), 110.
[176] "The Yacht Club Regatta," (*Astorian*, July 29, 1873).
[177] *Morning Astorian*, October 7, 1876.

The Carruthers Family on the balcony of Pacific House. From left: Harriet, third adult, with hand on railing; Robert, tall man behind her; Grace (?), Zoe, hands on railing, with Sarah Ann Hunter (?) behind her. From right: possibly young Richard Ervin with one leg over railing, next to William Alfred (?); Richard is third (x), holding a young child; Mary, fifth (x). John (holding child) and Mary Jane Carruthers Wood[178] may be standing next to Mary.

Photograph #10-8-87 (6) courtesy of Pacific County Historical Society.

Photo taken between 1885 and 1893. The group likely gathered to attend the Pacific County Superior Court session held in 1888.

After several years of terrible freezes in the late 1880s, the oyster beds began to die. Oysterville slowly declined with them. About 1887, S.D. Stratton became the proprietor of Pacific House. In 1888, William Brumbach recalled taking the stage to Oysterville's Pacific House, at that time managed by S.A. Mathews. He remembered the meal served there because one could choose from "four or five kinds of meat, oysters, crab, etc. and all for twenty-five cents.[179] Pacific House Hostelry was gone by 1910, razed to the ground either by fire or torn down – or blown down by the area's not infrequent gale force winds. Only a small marker identifies the spot on the northwest corner of Pacific and Main Streets.

---

[178] McClenny, "The Carruthers . . ., (Cumtux), 36 - 40.
[179] Walker, "Oysterville Remembers . . . (Clipping) p.1, 7.

In 1890, Richard deeded a donation land claim to his younger son William Alfred, which became part of Al's Carruthers Ranch. Al developed modern tideland farming and diking methods as well as raised prized Angus beef cattle.

"He was a man of remarkable strength and vitality, doing an able-bodied man's work at eighty," stated the obituary of Richard Carruthers, which appeared in the *South Bend Journal*. Richard died suddenly in Oysterville on November 8, 1896, at age eighty-six. [180] His wife, Mary Faint, who had been in ill health for several years, died December 4, 1899, at the age of eighty-three, also in Oysterville. Her obituary in the *Oregonian* a few days later, called her "a notable character among the pioneers of the Pacific Coast, and one of those sturdy, true women who have assisted in building the Northwest." At the time of her death, seven of her eight children were still living, with twenty-one grandchildren and six great-grandchildren. Richard and Mary were interred in the Oysterville Cemetery.

An Invitation to a Dance - mailed to Dick on December 18, 1899.

The young ladies invite	*Patronesses*
you to a dance to be	Mrs Upshur Mrs Lewis
given Saturday evening	Mrs Stokes Mrs Chutter
December the twenty third	Mrs Heilborn
At eight oclock	
In Hanthorn Hall	

(Inside)   *Dear Dick - Excuse this paper not matching the envelope - I ran short.*

Cant you come up tonight (Monday). Telephone to me any way.

In haste

Yours always   L.

A Holiday Party Menu for Tuesday, December 26, 1899

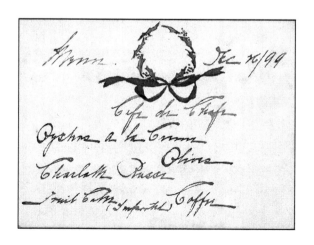

Café de Chafe

Oysters a la Creme

Olives

Charlotte Russe

Coffee

Fruit Cakes – Imported

---

[180] No birth certificate has been found for Richard, although his tombstone gives his birth year as 1811. This date is in question. Please see footnote on page *v.* of the Introduction.

Apparently Lillie is writing this time from Berlin. It was not uncommon in those days for persons to return to Europe frequently on quite lengthy tours and visits to family members who remained in Europe.

Berlin   December 29th 1899

My dear Louise and Harriet –

Yesterday morning we received the lovely Christmas remembrances which you sent us. Many thanks for the little needle book Louise. And Hat, you know how I always enjoy receiving photographs – It is a very good likeness and you seem to be enjoying life. Your hat is simply dead <u>swell</u>. Many thanks.

The handkerchief for Mama is lovely. Your Mother must be growing younger every day, if she can do such fine work as that. I received your letter Louise about three weeks ago, and intended answering it from day to day, but we had some relatives visiting here in the City, and our time was fully occupied going out with them. We were dreadfully shocked to hear of the death of your dear Uncle. We felt so very sorry – he was always so pleasant, and had a kind word for everybody. I know you must all miss him very much, especially your dear Father.

The weather has been so cold here for the last three weeks, and it snows almost every day. About two weeks ago we had a dreadful storm, and all the traffic was stopped for a day or so. It was interesting to watch, as I had never seem anything like it before, but I felt very sorry for the men and horses. The skating and sleighing have been fine, although I have not tried either. It is too cold for sleighing, and I don't know how to skate. I have a cousin here who is very anxious to teach me, but I am sure that I should break my neck or something.

Christmas has come and gone. I am rather glad it is over for on such days we feel more or less homesick. The lady that keeps this pension had a lovely tree for us, and all the guests presented each other with little trifles. This is only a small pension though – only about ten of us English and Americans. There are two German students, but they went home for the holidays. We missed them sadly, for they are very jolly. One of them is very nice to me, and I receive all the attention I could wish for. He is also studying music, and comes from a very fine family, book publishers from Stuttgart. It is nothing more serious, than a very cordial friendship, so don't imagine that you are going to get rid of me yet.

We have been here in Berlin over three months, but are uncertain how long we will remain. It all depends upon how we like the weather. I have been studying music and German, and going to a number of the good concerts, which they have here in this city of music. Oh dear! I wish I could take some of them home with me. Yesterday afternoon I heard Joachim for the second time. He played divinely. Do you still keep up your guitar and mandolin? I play on my mandolin occasionally in the evening, and get along a little better than I used to. Does Olga still keep it up? and how is dear Little Nell? I know she is dreadfully disgusted with me.

I received a long letter from Marge last week. I suppose she will have left Astoria by the time you receive this – if not please give her my love, and that I will answer her letter very soon. Wasn't Herman [Lillie's brother] a great fellow to get engaged and married so quickly. I fancy he has a very sweet little girl for a wife though, and they are very happy. We received some lovely books, which they had sent us for Xmas. Herman is having a home built out on West Adams – west of Hoover, which they expected to move in by the first of January. I can't understand that you did not receive any announcement cards. I know it was not intentional – there must have been a mistake of some kind made. I think there generally is at weddings unless the bride is acquainted with all the grooms friends. I suppose you have heard that Carrie Weiss and Mel Eshman are also married. Brides galore in the family. I wish I was there this winter. Frankie has also added a new member to the family – a little boy again. Poor girl she was awfully ill for a few days – they did not know how it would all end, - but now we have received several letters from her again, and she is gradually regaining her old strength back again.

Rosita was taken home by her Mother, and Anton misses her sadly. She will be more spoilt than ever now, I suppose. She is a great girl. I received a long letter from Loll [Bierbach] yesterday. They were busy making party dresses – were going to a dancing party given by the Wigmores. She said she has sewed on <u>eighty</u> yards of narrow velvet ribbon. You girls seem to be having a gay time of it, as usual. I have not been to an entertainment for so long now, that I am sure I would not know how to act. Can't say that I am very sorry though, I enjoy the rest – will have plenty of it when I get home again.

We like Berlin so much, I wish we could stay all winter. The art galleries are very good, and the music is fine. I have heard so many good things. The opera is not so good here, but the concerts are the very best that can be had. I have a lovely teacher, a Fraulein Schwartz. She is a pupil of Leschetizky and plays divinely. It is almost time for my lesson now, so will bring this to a close, or it never will go off. I commenced a letter to you L- several weeks ago, but never finished it. Thanking you both again for your lovely remembrances and wishing you a happy New Years -

    Lovingly

        Lillie

Twentieth Century Party   January 9, 1900

Gentlemen:	**Ladies:**
Nan Reed	Nell Carnahan
Genie Lewis	Margaret Higgins
Anna McLean	Ethel Blenis (?)
Marge Halsted	Laura Fox
Sue Elmore	Sadie Crang
Zetta Smith	May Norton
Mame Lewis	Pearl Cole
Lottie Bennett	Laura Gray
Carol Young	Nora Nickerson
Olga Heilborn	Alice Wood
Louise Tallant	Nell Sherman
Maude Stockton	Daisy Stockton
Frank (Frances) Holden	Louise Whitefield

Louise is in the back row, to the right of the flag; no hat. Olga is second from Louise to right; Marge stands in front of Olga.

The years 1899 and 1900 signaled the middle of the *Belle Epoque* historical period (1890 to 1914) that gave growth and importance to numerous "isms," fostering such movements as Impressionism, militarism, colonialism (especially in Africa), naturalism and the Art Nouveau style. It was the era of great technological and scientific advances. This "golden age" was also a time of beautiful clothes, without bustles!, and luxurious living for the privileged. National identities were no longer as important, so middle and upper class persons could travel through Europe without passports.

The younger people chose to close out the Nineteenth Century, the *fin de siecle,* with another fancy dress New Year's party, obviously looking forward - with tongue-in-cheek and excitement - to whatever the new year might hold in store for them.

Chapter Eleven

Excitement was generated in 1900 by the publication of L. Frank Baum's book, *The Wonderful Wizard of Oz*. Children and adults alike were caught up in the endearing characters of the fantasy tale. Puccini's great opera *Tosca* debuted in Rome to mixed reviews. Nicola Tesla invented the wireless radio in 1895. His applications for U.S. patents, filed in1897, were granted in 1900, but for unexplained reasons, the U.S. Patent Office reversed itself in 1904. The Patent Office gave Guglielmo Marconi's applications, first filed November 10, 1900, the patent as the "inventor" of the radio.

In 1900 the population of Clatsop County, Oregon was counted as 12,765 residents – 8,381 of whom lived in Astoria. As was commonly done then, the Astoria Voter Roll of 1900, taken between January and May, listed only male members of a family – those having reached voting age. Eben W. Tallant, age fifty-eight, a cannery owner and William E. Tallant, age thirty, a clerk, resided at 682 Grand Avenue. Robert Carruthers, age fifty-six, in real estate; Richard Ervin Carruthers, age twenty-five, a hardware store clerk; and Angus Russell Carruthers, age twenty-two, also a hardware store clerk, were shown residing at 638 Exchange. However, the 12th Federal Census of 1900 listed Robert Carruthers as a cattle raiser - he really was an entrepreneur, involved in numerous businesses. Dr. Jay Tuttle was still listed as boarding at the Carruthers' house on Exchange, as was Katie Wantila.

The January ninth jolly event of the ladies and their "gentlemen" escorts was quickly followed by a big dance in Astoria on February 20, 1900, sponsored by The Assembly. Louise's dance programme listed eighteen dances plus two extras. The dance beats were of the waltz, the two-step and the Lancers. Her frequent partners were Dick, Charlie and Tom Bryce. The first part of this year must have passed swiftly with all the usual doings of the young people, besides the dances – outings, sleepovers, chafing dish parties and just plain get-togethers. And of course, Dinner Parties!

A small invitation card addressed to Dick, drawn by Louise. The menu is on the reverse.

Engagements and weddings were very much on the minds of a number of Louise's friends. Dated June 6, 1900, a letter from Louise's Chicago (1893) friend, Sylvia Norton, announced her coming marriage to a Mr. Carle Cotter Conway at a quarter before eight the evening of December 11, 1900, at her parents' home (the Edwin Nortons) in Maywood, Illinois, where Louise had often been a visitor. The invitation was sent to Louise and Harriet.

My dear Louise:

Possibly the news that my engagement has just been announced will rather surprise you for we have not seen each other for such a long time that I suppose you can think of me only as a little girl. But it is really true and I am quite in the seventh heaven of happiness. But I must tell you a little about him. To think that you don't even know that his name is Carle Cotter Conway makes me realize that it is a long time since I've seen you, for I've known him since I was twelve years old. Our families have been intimate friends and they are the people who traveled abroad with us three winters ago. It was during the time that he was at Yale. I will tell you just a word about his appearance. He is six feet tall, very dark with beautiful teeth and a most attractive smile. He is full of life and ambition and though I am prejudiced I will say he is a splendid man. My families' opinion, which is very flattering to Carle, would perhaps prove more. I enclose a little copy of a picture he had taken in his junior year at college. It was a fair likeness of him at the time but of course he has changed some what since then.

But enough of this. I must not bore you, even though it is a new and very interesting subject to me.

Arthur graduates from Ann Arbor this month and this summer we all hope to be together as a family at our lake Geneva home.

Mother joins me in sending kindest regards to all at your home and with love for yourself I am

> *Affectionately yours*
>> *Sylvia Gifford Norton*
>>> *Maywood, June sixth*

I find no envelope to match this paper. Sylvia.

Apparently, few letters were written or received, but the letters that did survive are significant in leading to the next step in the romance between Dick and Louise. The latter half of the year brought Louise a royal honor and a whirlwind of activity – her frequent absences surely made Dick's heart grow fonder.

Fourth of July 1900 group in Curley's boat on Youngs Bay.
Louise wears a plaid skirt and a tie. Harriet holds the American flag.

A 1900 Hen Party at a Gearhart Park cabin.
L. to R. front row: Margaret Higgins; Floretta; Zetta; GF (?); Olga; and Harriet.
Back row: Louise; Florence S.; Nan; Lottie; Sue; and Marge.

The following letter from Lillie was written during her lengthy tour of Europe as her mother's companion. This one is from a resort hotel in the Netherlands.

Scheveningen, den July 20th   [1900]

My dear Louise:

My Aunt, cousin and I have come down here to attend a concert, - we came early to get away from the dreadful heat in the Hague, but it is not very much better even here. We are in the reading room of the Kurhaus, and I thought I might occupy my time by writing to you, on this <u>beautiful</u> paper. The Berlin Philharmonic Orchestra is stationed here for the summer, and on Friday evenings they give a Symphonic concert, which we generally try to hear. They are so good. I wish I could have them at home.

On the 6th of Sept we leave for home. I am simply wild for the time to come – it seems at times as if I could hardly wait any longer, although it will not seem quite the same now that Herman [Lillie's brother] *is married, and we are not going to occupy our house again. We hear from home very often, and they are anxious to have us back too. Mama has been in Germany just a month today but we expect her back here next Thursday. I shall be glad for I feel lost without her. She recd a dear letter from your Mother when we were in London, but I don't suppose that she has had time to answer it, for when one is visiting, the time seems to fly. I will have to fly too, with my pen, for the others wish to promenade on the terrace. There is a lovely walk here, above the beach, about a mile long. There is any amount of agony here in dress, as Scheveningen is a very fashionable resort. I wish you could see some of the Americans though – they are <u>a caution.</u> This morning, my Uncle saw at least two hundred at the station. I suppose one of Cook's parties* [Thomas Cook Tour Co. of London] *He said they all looked so hot, but were all eating and drinking – whiskey cocktails, etc; something perfectly incomprehensible to a Dutchman, who hardly touches anything, before the afternoon. My cousin is impatient. I wish you could see her, she is twenty-one, very pretty and sweet, - a regular little Dutch girl.*

Love to all the family -

Yours as always –

Lillie

Late summertime in Astoria has long been associated with outdoor activities. The weather is generally mild; the days are lengthy with the sun not setting in August until well after 8 o'clock of an evening. Rain? Possible? Of course! In the late 1890s and early 1900s, the family men who worked in Portland during the week caught the "Daddy Train" down to Astoria, Gearhart and Seaside on Friday evenings, so they could spend the weekends with their vacationing families. Most everyone picnicked and built bonfires on the beaches. Children played street games until dusk, when they were called in to wash up and prepare for bed. Life then was just…different. But when Regatta time rolled around in August, Astoria popped and sizzled.

274

Some Notes on Early Regattas in Astoria

Some say the first Astoria Regatta was held in 1894. No way, stated Captain John Brown, who was visiting Astoria for a 1941 Elk's convention. According to the newspaper clipping Louise saved, Captain Brown said the earliest race took place at least twenty years prior to that – probably between 1872 and 1874.[181] He was not sure which year, but he did take part in it. Capt. Brown recalled that it came about "as a result of an argument on Captain Flavel's wharf among the skippers of four "plungers," which in those days carried mail to outlying points around the lower Columbia." Brown was the skipper of Captain J.G. Hustler's *Eliza* that had the Knappton mail run. The argument was about the sailing abilities of the four virtually identical boats. The four skippers bet $5 apiece and planned the racecourse from Flavel Wharf down around a black buoy on Desdemona Sands and back. Captain Brown, in the lead, ran into trouble on the last leg near Trullinger's Mill. Captain Grant, skippering the Wirt Brothers' *Ione*, swept past. The Brook Brothers' *Blue Racer* and Captain Dick Hobson's *Mary H.* lagged behind. When Grant attempted to tack, Brown caught up with him and went on to win the $5 from each of the defeated captains. So many watched the race the men decided to do it again after fishing season ended so a number of fishermen and three wood scows could participate. They offered incentives. First prize: "a bale of twine, enough for an entire net. Second was a cork line with corks; third, a lead line with leads; and fourth, an anchor and 100 feet of Manila hempen cable." A committee organized the following year's race. Plungers from Shoalwater Bay were invited to be contenders – Oysterville had already been holding its own regattas for a number of years.[182]

The Astoria Regatta is possibly the oldest surviving non-profit community event of its kind in the Pacific Northwest. It preceded even the Portland Rose Festival by several years and is still entertaining crowds from all over. In 1894, the members of the Astoria Athletic Club/Astoria Football Club suggested they would like to organize boat races on the Columbia River. The Australian Frank Gunn, a pioneer hotel owner and secretary of the AFC, was especially enthusiastic. Although it began as a lark, the idea was taken up by E. J. Smith, city editor of the *Morning Astorian*, and by John Rathom,[183] then editor of *The Astorian* newspaper, to hold the event at the end of the commercial salmon fishing season in August. It was to focus on water related events and, thus, was called a regatta. The first year's three-day program, held on August 17 through 19, 1894, featured races from the Flavel Dock at the foot of 11th Street, and Fisher's 12th Street slip, to a buoy one mile upriver (east) and return to the dock. The boats entering these first races were mainly gillnet fishing boats, the "butterfly" fleet and Shoalwater oyster sloops. Each boat was manned by three or four crewmembers. During the next few years, speedboat and sailboat races were added, along with such entertaining events as logrolling and rowing competitions. The life-saving crews from Pt. Adams and Ft. Canby demonstrated rescue techniques – still focusing upon water-related sports of a city whose main industries were fishing and logging.

---

[181] "First Regatta Was In 1870's …," (*Evening Astorian Budget*, August 27, 1941).
[182] "The Yacht Club Regatta," (*The Astorian*, July 29, 1873).
[183] Much later, the Australian John R. Rathom, who had been an active member of the group of actors in 1896, became a war correspondent for the *San Francisco Chronicle*.

The number of regattas that have taken place since 1894 depends on how one counts them. Regattas were not consistently held, perhaps partly because they were non-profits. In 1902, people seemed disinterested, did not want to subscribe to funding it and believed the preparation time was far too short. The same reasons probably led to the cancellation of the 1909 regatta. Several regattas were not true "regattas" at all – one such event was a tribute in 1905 to Sacagawea.[184] In 1911, Astoria focused on celebrating its centennial by presenting the pageant, "The Bridge of the Gods," – based on a Native American legend; Emma Wooten played the leading role to great acclaim. The production was held in an amphitheater built near the hilltop reservoir and Shively Park.

No regattas were held during the war years 1917 through 1931. The founding of the Astoria Yacht Club in 1931 led to the revival of regattas, which continued from 1932 to 1942. Again, no regattas were held during the war years between 1942 and 1952. By one "official" count, the 1955 event was number thirty-five. However in 1980, the Regatta Board adopted a different way of counting – as if the events had all been held consecutively, making 1916 the twenty-first; 1932 was the twenty-second. Somehow the 1935 regatta was numbered the twenty-fourth. In 2009, Astoria held its 115th Annual Regatta.

The first few regattas were simply a variety of water-related races. Then the carnival atmosphere increased along with the addition of a Queen, her court and the Queen's Ball (1897); a mid-way/circus; street parades (1901) with floats, bands and clowns; nightly dances and concerts; an authentic Chinese dragon from San Francisco (1903);[185] and the county fair (1905). An Admiral was appointed in 1897) as was the first Prime Minister and a grandstand announcer for the races and winners (1903). By 1905 the Queen's horse-drawn royal carriage was replace by her royal automobile – with the top down. The 1908 regatta added the Scandinavian Sangerfest. Glorious fireworks lit the night sky above the illuminated boat parades. All manner of races on land as well as water – including hose team competitions and track and field events – became popular. The three-masted and four-masted sailing vessels and old river steamers of the early days gave way to the bi-wing Curtis Hydroplane (1911). Early United States warships, such as the U.S.S. *Monitor Monterey* and the U.S.S. *Concord* – led to the modern, larger warships that dock each year for the festivities.

The Salmon Derby, begun in 1936 as a preliminary event leading up to the "big event" of the Regatta, proved to generate great interest with many participants; it continued in its own right as a big draw for many years. As in the early days of salmon fishing in the mid 1800s, one could almost walk across the river from one fishing boat to another. But the decline in the "health" of the Columbia River lessened the number of fish to be caught. On the August 24, 1951, Guyon "Guy" Blissett of the Hotel Astoria wrote a letter to the newspaper's 'Open Forum' trying to renew interest in the regatta and

---

[184] Sacagawea was Lewis and Clark's Indian guide.

[185] Astoria's large Chinese community always seemed to have participated in the regatta parades as marchers and spectators. Although they may have made a Chinese dragon for various parades, the 1903 Regatta was a very special one for them. They had arranged to bring an authentic "dragon" from San Francisco. The dragon was over 100 yards long with a huge grotesque head – its mouth was agape; the long red tongue lolled out, licking from side to side; its eyes bulged hideously; its body undulated sinuously along the line of march - all controlled by over 200 Chinese beneath the beast. For the Chinese, their dragon was a serious religious ceremony. Many Astorians drew back from the dragon in terror – both mock and otherwise – as the Chinese exploded the traditional firecrackers to drive away evil.

in the derby. In his letter he recalled that, following WWII, Jerry McCallister had unearthed "a battered copper-lined milk can" near 15th and Irving. The trophy's inscription was only partially decipherable: "Presented to Queen...of the Astoria Regatta by Admiral...this year 189...A.D." The excitement generated over this little "mystery" did indeed help to renew regatta/derby interest.

The idea of having a queen began in 1897. Marthena (Lydia) Gosslin, wife of the Regatta Chairman, William G. Gosslin, was selected as the Queen. The following year, enthusiasm for electing "royalty" increased. In Louise's letter dated July 27, 1898, to Dick at the Presidio, she wrote:

> *"We are having a hot time voting for Regatta Queen – 5 cents a vote. It seems to me the craziest thing Astorians ever did and they have done some pretty funny things some times too."*

On August 8, she again wrote that the voting had gotten even more exciting. Miss Maud Stockton was ahead at that time. Although Maud was a dear friend of hers, Louise would have chosen Dick's sister, Mrs. Zoe Carruthers Ridehalgh, as queen. However, Mrs. Alice Normile was ultimately crowned Queen – the first one elected by popular vote. In Louise's letter of September 21, 1898, to Dick in Hawaii, she wrote:

> *"The Regatta this year was alright and the Queen Mrs Normile was very handsome in a __beautiful__ satin gown. We watched the fire works from our up stairs window and I thought of the year before when we all were up there and how different every thing was then."*

Again prominent on the 1899 Regatta Committee were Eben W. Tallant, his brother Nathaniel W. Tallant[186] and G. C. Fulton. Receiving a total of 118,539 votes, Sue Elmore reigned as Queen of that Sixth Annual Regatta; she was possibly elected through the sale of regatta buttons. Louise, who had come in second with 81,376 votes, was one of her twelve "Ladies-in-Waiting," along with Astorians Alice Wood, Zetta Smith, Genie Lewis and Gussie Gray. Maud Stockton was one of the ten "Maids-of-Honor that included five other Astoria friends: Olga Heilborn, Reba Hobson, Katie Flavel, Polly McKean and Grace Short.

During that time, it was quite usual to have anywhere from fifteen to thirty-five ladies vying for the title in any given year. Numerous women, either on their own or thanks to friends, entered the voting for the regatta crown year after year. Both Louise and Harriet's names appear on more than one year's lists. Helen Matilda Dawson had tried more than once to obtain the crown; she was a member of Queen Esther Anderson's court in 1906 and later married Robert Rex "Tod" Carruthers on October 8, 1907, in Newark, Delaware. Isabell Trullinger entered more than three times, the first year as an unmarried woman and, for several years following, as the wife of Governor T.T. Geer whom she had married in 1900. The early regatta queens often were married women – some with children who took an active part in the proceedings. Nell Houston's eight-year old daughter was her crown bearer (1904). Mrs. Beatrice Pearl Holden Callender was in her thirties, the mother of then thirteen-year old Melville, when she reigned as Regatta Queen in 1913.[187]

---

[186] Nathaniel Weld Tallant died on October 21, 1899, two months after the 1899 Regatta.

[187] The former dancing master of Astoria, Prof. J.N. Beggs, was appointed the Director of Festivities for Queen Beatrice's 1913 Regatta.

The "royalty" of the regattas were as subject to gossip as much as any royal personages today. In Vera Gault's newspaper column, "Then and Now," she writes of the 1903 and 1904 queens in whom she held a special interest.[188] Two of Astoria's well-to-do matrons, Mrs. Anne Wilkerson and Mrs. Helen "Nell" Houston, continually tried to outdo each other. Mrs. Wilkerson was bound and determined that her niece, Frances Thomas, would be crowned regatta queen in 1903. Mrs. W. would make sure the coronation would be the most "elaborate ever attempted." She would model it on the coronation of King Edward VII and Queen Alexandra of England, which she had recently attended.

Frances Thomas and Harriet Tallant were neck in neck as the frontrunners in the 1903 voting. At the last minute, some supposed "gentlemen friends" of Frances' presented a certified check in the amount of $1000 to the regatta chairman. Fortuitously indeed, because the crown for Frances had already been ordered from Tiffany's in New York. Her crowning ceremony, organized by Mrs. Wilkerson, was worthy of a female potentate. Miss Thomas entered the hall under a silken canopy carried by four of her court. Her gown and robe were in stunning white and silver fabrics; her robe stretched out in a seventeen-foot long train behind her. A wrap trimmed in ermine topped her *ensemble*. "Magnificent," stated the newspapers. Her costumes for the three-day event cost $4000 – a fortune in those days.

However, Mrs. Nell Houston was not to be outdone. She spent a full year planning her own reign for the Regatta of 1904. She assured her election as Queen by ordering her husband to buy $3000 worth of tickets. Mrs. Houston garnered 54,527 votes; Harriet Tallant with 19,848 votes was second - again. Zoe Ridehalgh, well down in the list, received 4,346. Queen Nell's coronation gown was spectacular – blue brocade and crimson velvet crusted with pearls, diamonds and yards of tulle. Her eight-year old daughter carried her crown on a velvet pillow. When Queen Nell entered the hall for her official grand ball the evening of August 24, 1904, she received a standing ovation for her regal beauty and all her efforts.

The Reign of Queen Louise

It is the evening of Wednesday, August 15, 1900. The votes have finally been counted for the Queen of the Seventh Annual Astoria Regatta. All is quiet as the Executive Committee Chairman, Charles Stockton, formally announces the final tallies of the 103,285 votes cast for the more than thirty-three candidates vying to become the fourth queen of regatta. Louise Tallant receives 51,286 votes. "We have our Queen of the Astoria Regatta of 1900. All hail Queen Louise!"

A good example of the early Regattas is this one held August 23, 24 and 25 in 1900. By April, the committee had already begun arranging the program for the 7th Annual Regatta program of events, races, rules and entertainment. It was the same then as for any big event today. Their job was to find volunteers, to solicit funds for advertising, prizes and all other expenses - and to beg for donations of goods and services. A number of companies outside of the area also helped support this event, such as a fire apparatus dealer, A.G. Long of Portland. The committee had to give plenty of lead-time for the

---

[188] Gault, "The tale of rival Regatta queens," (*The Daily Astorian*, August 8, 1988).

officials and entrants to make their arrangements. They also plotted a seven-mile sailing course for the various boating participants.

The 1900 Regatta Queen continued to be elected by popular vote. Voting began on the third of August. A vote (a donation to defray expenses, if you will) cost anywhere from one cent to a "contribution" of twenty dollars. Twenty-nine voting boxes had been distributed among the major businesses in Astoria; the boxes were collected each evening and votes were tallied daily. There were at least thirty-three entrants that year. Both Louise and Harriet were well behind Madge Sovey at the very start. Mrs. Geer was well down in the list. By August seventh, Madge and Louise were jockeying back and forth for the lead. During the last few days prior to the close of voting, interest mounted. Rumors spread that big blocks of votes were being cast in the final hours for one or another of the eight frontrunners. Those ladies were, in addition to Louise - Misses Anna Peterson, Olga Noe, Madge Sovey, Nellie Utzinger, Antonia Johnson and Madge Chapman, and Mrs. Isaac Bergman, Mayor Bergman's wife. In the final hours, the votes for Miss Peterson suddenly increased her tally dramatically to a total of 23,840. Louise Tallant's supporters redoubled their efforts, giving Louise a final count of 51,286 - and the crown.

Regatta Chairman Charles Stockton, Mayor Isaac Bergman and their committeemen gave Queen Louise full authority to choose her court of two Pages and twenty-two Ladies-in-Waiting and Maids-of-Honor. She, of course, included her sister Harriet. She was also authorized to assign three ladies to handle any details she wanted: Mrs. Fred P. Kendall; Mrs. George H. George and Mrs. P.A. Stokes. Because the election results were not announced until voting closed on the evening of August fifteenth, Louise had only one week to make her preparations, to find a "royal" gown and to select proper costumes for a variety of events that took place on both the water and the land. Official portraits and court photographs had to be taken. So much had to be done in such a short time that a proper flurry resulted in her parents Grand Avenue home.

However, on Friday, August seventeenth, Louise still had time to attend a party organized by Pearl - the steamer *Callender* took a large group over to Knappton for a moonlight dance. A few days later, Mrs. Wilkerson gave a lovely tea for Louise and her court.

As with many events, the best laid of plans can go awry. A reporter for the evening edition of the *Daily Astoria Budget* for Thursday, August 23, 1900, submitted the following front-page article with a somewhat poetic beginning:

Crowning of the Queen and All Racing Events Postponed – Coronation Exercises Tonight in Foard & Stokes Hall.

The sunset last night was as beautiful as an artist could dream of and with a gentle northwest breeze blowing and a highly steady barometer it would have taken a chronic kicker to have suggested bad weather.

At midnight however the barometer began to lower and the sky overcast and in a couple of hours it started to rain and this morning had not stopped. The disappointment was universal but the committee was prepared to handle everything but the elements and the large crowd of visitors realized this and took in the situation as good naturedly as they could.

Early in the day the announcement was made that the crowning of the Queen and the exercises incident would be postponed until this evening when the program will be carried out at Foard & Stokes hall in connection with the opening of the grand ball in honor of the Queen.

An attempt was made to start the races and the gasoline launch race was started but resulted in a fizzle as one of the outer buoys had gone adrift and the launches, failing to find it, returned and it was declared not to be a race. All the events scheduled for today will be doubled up with those of tomorrow and it will be a continuous show during the entire day.

The opening feature of the regatta last night in receiving Admiral Edwards[189] was a brilliant success and at the same time a very pretty one. The steamers Miler and Alarm with the officials and the reception committee on board, accompanied by a band met the steamer Sarah Dixon off Tongue Point and after firing a salute in honor of the admiral and Governor [T.T.] Geer accompanied the steamer to the city where the admiral and governor held a reception.

The outline of the events to take place tomorrow will include the original program of the two days and should present a spectacle never before witnessed at an Astoria regatta.

San Francisco

August 24, 1900

Dear Queen Louise:

When I opened the paper a few mornings ago and found that I had a Queen for a cousin I felt very proud indeed. I want to congratulate you on your success, and hope that the duties of "Her Royal Majesty" will not be too severe for you. But, I suppose that by this time you are as strong as you ever were and the work will be too pleasant to become tiresome. I should just love to see you in your robe of state. Now is the time you can thank your stars for being tall,[190] for your train and crown would not be carried off so well by a short girl. The papers here had quite an article about you, spoke of you as one of Oregon's most beautiful daughters. I believe the Colonel sent you one of the papers. I suppose the whole house is in great excitement over it all, but now that it has a member of the royal family in it they should not object.

We are all quite well here, mamma improving steadily. She is staying at Glen Ellen now and the rest of us are at San Anselmo. We expect to come to town next month, and will be glad to settle down to the city life again, although we have had a very pleasant summer.

And now I must say "au revoir,"

wishing you a very happy and successful reign.

With love,

"Flora" [191]

---

[189] The 1900 Regatta "Admiral" was Capt. E.S. Edwards from Portland.

[190] Louise was tall for her era at about 5'8-5'9. Chicago's Bournique School had taught her well - her comportment and carriage were royally impressive and she continued to carry herself well throughout her entire life.

[191] Flora Kimball Smith (1882-1967) was born in Hanoaupo, Hawaii, H.T., to Sarah Frances Tallant (1844-1905) and Theodore Smith (1842-1898). Flora later married Lewis Asa Parkhurst in San Francisco.

Dick's badge for the Ball.

Louise Tallant, Queen of the Astoria Regatta - 1900

Queen Louise's Regatta Court photograph was taken at the home of Mrs. Page.
From l. to r.: (?); Maud Stockton; Mrs. Rob't Wilson; Maud Stackpole; Marge Halsted; Olga Heilborn; Nan Reed; Lottie Bennett; Queen Louise; Harriet Tallant; Katie Flavel; Reba Hobson; Sadie Crang; Margaret Higgins; ? ; Lila Sutherland. Seated: Clara Lionberger.

Coronation of Queen Louise on August 23, 1900.
Her court and her young pages surround her as a little girl presents Queen Louise with a bouquet.

(Original image in Prussian blue)

Queen Louise on the royal yacht, the *Columbine*, a lighthouse tender that had just returned from Alaska.

REGATTA BALL 1900.

RECEPTION OF QUEEN.

COURSE OF DANCES.

GRAND MARCH

1. Lancers	- - - - - -	*Our Queen*
2. Waltz	- - - - -	*The Start*
3. Polka	- - - - -	*Choppy Seas*
4. Two Step	- - -	*Setting the Spinnaker*
5. Cent. Lancers	- - - -	*Our Admiral*
6. Waltz	- - - - -	*Hoist Away*
7. Schottische	- - -	*Rounding the Buoy*
8. Two Step	- - - -	*Homeward Bound*
9. Lancers	- - - - -	*Our Commodore*
10. Waltz	- - - - -	*Running Free*
11. Polka	- - - -	*Maids of Honor*
12. Schottische	- - - -	*Lower Away*
13. Lancers	- - - -	*Blue and White*
14. Waltz	- - - - -	*Our Visitors*
15. Two Step	- - -	*Salt Sea Breeze*
16. Waltz	- - - - -	*The Finish*

AT FOARD & STOKES HALL.

Admission to the Queen's Ball on August 24, 1900, cost fifty cents.

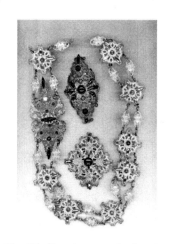

The Girdle – brass, ruby insets.

A souvenir pamphlet printed by the bookmakers, J. S. Dellinger Co., gave the details of the Seventh Annual Astoria Regatta held in August 1900.

FIRST DAY, AUGUST 23.

FORENOON.

9:30. The queen, attended by her maids of honor, and escorted by a guard of honor, will approach the grand stand, and after being introduced by her prime minister and being welcomed by Governor T. T. Geer, on behalf of the state, and Mayor Bergman on behalf of the city, will declare the regatta formally opened.

10:15. Gasoline launch race, once around course, five to enter. First prize, silver cup, value $75, donated by Union Gas Company. Second prize, $20.

10:30. Swimming race, for boys, 50 yards, prize.

10:30. Senior barge race. Dolphins vs. Alamedas. Gold medals.

10:40. Grand exhibition of high diving.

10:50. Single shell. Coast championship. Gold medal.

11:00. Tub race. Boys. Prize.

11:15. Senior Outrigger skiff. First heat.

11:20. Free for all swimming race, 100 yards. Prize.

11:30. Double pleasure boat. First heat.

11:40. Exhibition of fancy swimming and life saving. Prof. Cahill, of Olympic Club, of San Francisco, assisted by Mr. Pape.

11:50. Grand exhibition. Slack wire. Prof. Beno.

DINNER.

1:00. Columbia river fishing boats. Working sails. Fifteen to enter. Prizes valued at $200.

1:10. Whitehall boats sailing race. Three to enter. Prizes $25 and $10.

1:20. Cat boats sailing race. Three to enter. Prize $20, $10.

1:30. Sloops, 20-footers. Once around course. Five to enter. Prizes $60 and $30.

1:40. Sloops. Free for all. Three to enter. Twice around course. First prize $125; Second, $50; Third, $25.

1:50. Cannery tenders. Twice around. First prize, $25. Second, $15.

2:00. Scow schooners. Once around. First prize, $25; second, $10.

2:15. Greased pole contest. Prize.

2:30. Exhibition by Fort Canby life saving crew.

2:45. Boys' swimming race. Prize.

3:00. Grand exhibition. Slack wire and trapeze balancing.

EVENING.

7:30. Grand entertainment at grand stand, Flavel dock. Prof. Henry the world's famous magician, late of Europe, in wonderful sleight of hand feats. Madam Carita, famous buck and wing dancer and DeGosco Bros. musical artists in splendid exhibition. Introducing their musical effects, beautiful electric light bells, illuminated sleigh bells, the electric sparkephone. A grand electro-musical novelty throughout. Two hours of finest entertainment.

9:30. Grand regatta ball, formal coronation exercises and reception to the queen. The ball opening with the coronation minuet, by the maids of honor. Foard & Stokes' hall; admission 50 cents.

SECOND DAY, AUGUST 24.

FORENOON.

9:00. Intermediate barge race. Olympics vs Ariels. Five gold medals.

9:15. Greased pole contest. Prize.

9:30. Senior outrigger skiff race. Second heat.

9:45. Duck hunt. Prize.

10:00. Junior outrigger skiff race. Second heat.

10:45. Exhibition of high diving.

11:00. Chinese barge race. Prize.

11:15. Exhibition of fancy swimming, by Prof. Cahill, swimming instructor of the Olympic Club, San Francisco.

11:30. Double pleasure boat race. Gold medals.

12:00. Exhibition of aerial trapeze balancing and slack wire performance by Prof. Beno.

DINNER.

1:00. Fish boat race, fifteen to enter. Prizes valued at $200.

1:10. Whitehall sailing race, three to enter. Prizes $20 and $10.

1:20. Sloops, free for all, three to enter, twice around the course. Prizes, $125; second $50; third $25.

1:30. Sloops, 20-footers, once around, five to enter. First prize, $40; second prize, $20.

1:40. Boys' swimming race. Prize.

1:50. Punt race. Prize, $10.

2:00. Exhibition of high diving.

2:10. Exhibition by Point Adams life saving crew.

2:20. Swimming under water contest, for boys. Prize.

2:30. Slack wire walking, trapeze balancing. Prof. Beno.

2:45. Free for all swimming race. Prize.

3:00. Greased Pole contest. Prize.

EVENING.

7:30. Grand entertainment in front of grand stand, Flavel Dock. Prof. Henry, magician, in his wonderful and entertaining feats of sleight of hand; Madam Carita in the latest dances; DeGosco Bros. in grand electro-musical entertainment, beautiful colored electric light effects, changing with music. A complete change each evening.

9:30. Select concert by the Third Regiment Band, followed by a grand cake walk. The famous colored cake walkers of the coast in latest dark-town cake walk. Tickets, 50 cents to concert and cake walk.

Closing Event of the Day—Jost-Purtell Contest at the Louvre.

THIRD DAY, AUGUST 25.

REFEREE: M. M. Ringler, of the Portland Y. M. C. A.
JUDGES AT FINISH: Arthur D. Marshall, Astoria; A. B. McAlpine, M. A. A. C.; R. C. F. Astbury, Astoria
FIELD JUDGES: C. N. McArthur, U. of O.; F. P. Kendall, Astoria; Al Lean, Olympic Club and University of California
TIME KEEPERS: Grant Trullinger, W. E. Tallant, J. H. Seymour.
STARTER: J. King, M. A. A. C. ANNOUNCER. Peter Grant, Portland.
MARSHALS: D. A. McLean, C. T. Crosby, Alfred S. Tee, R. E. Carruthers, A. C. Callan.

FORENOON.

9:00. Greased pole contest. Prize.

9:15. Senior vs. Intermediate barge, coast championship. Silk pennant.

9:30. Free for all swimming race. Prize.

9:40. Single shell race. Consolation; gold medal.

9:50. Tub race. Prize.

10:00. Senior outrigger skiff race; final heat. Gold medal.

10:15. Swimming under water contest. Prize.

10:30. Duck hunt. Prize.

10:45. Junior outrigger skiff; final. Gold medal.

11:00. Punt race; prize.

11:15. Gig race. Manzanita vs. Columbine; prize.

11:30. High diving and swimming.

11:45. Single pleasure boat race; medal.

AFTERNOON.

Grand Athletic Carnival in which the Olympic Club of San Francisco, the Multnomah Club, of Portland; Seattle Athletic Club, of Seattle; University Athletic Club, of Eugene, and the Portland Y. M. C. A. will be represented. Under sanction of the Pacific Northwestern Association. All records made in these games will be recognized by the A. A. U.

ATHLETIC CARNIVAL.

100 yard dash; gold and silver medals.

Pole vault; gold and silver medals.

440 yard run; gold and silver medals.

Running high jump; gold and silver medals.

120 yard hurdle; gold and silver medals.

Running broad jump; gold and silver medals.

880 yard run; gold and silver medals.

220 yard run; gold and silver medals.

One mile run; gold and silver medals.

220 yard hurdle; gold and silver medals.

Team relay race; four men each team, each man 440 yards. Silver Cup.

EXTRA PROGRAM.

Boys' three legged race; prize.

Sack race; prize.

Pie eating contest; prize.

Free for all bicycle race; prize a Rambler bicycle, donated by the Fred T. Merrill Cycle Co., of Portland.

Baseball game. Astoria vs Multnomah Athletic Club, of Portland.

1900 Astoria Regatta Queen Louise Tallant

The family has donated several existing pieces of Her Royal Majesty's coronation gown to Clatsop County Historical Museum. Louise's "bodice" (blouse), fitted with nine stays, is of a gauze or cotton voile and ivory satin, with inserts of purple velveteen in the upper puff sleeves. The <u>very</u> tight satin sleeves from elbow to wrist are finished with ruching. Bits of her "Girdle" belt survive; it is of brass filigree links with ruby inserts. It circled her waist and a long panel hung down. For other events, Louise chose two short royal blue bolero-style velvet jackets, one with a cream satin hand-stitched *trapunto* lining and wonderfully interesting buttons. On the front cover of this book, Louise is pictured wearing another of her Regatta dresses.

Regatta colors were white and blue. Duck trousers and Regatta caps – the *de regueur* outfits of men – were to be found at Samuel Danziger's of San Francisco Clothing store located on the northwest corner of 11th and Commercial.

Hoefler's Confectionary touted not only its chocolates, but also its ice cream – and its elegant apartments for ladies.

Two trains, each pulling ten jam-packed coaches, arrived from Portland on the morning of the twenty-third. Astoria was happily overflowing.

A concert and ball were held nightly at Charlie Wise's Music Hall.

On Saturday, August 24, the second evening of the Regatta, The Louvre held a boxing match between Paddy Purtell of Leadville and Charles Jost of Portland. The fight ended with both men standing – a draw – after twenty-rounds of a good, clean, exciting match. "Best Glove Contest held on this Coast."

There was something for everyone.

In perusing the list of Astoria's Regatta Queens over all the years, it is striking to note that no single family can boast of having had **two** Regatta Queens – none, that is, except the Tallant family of Grand Avenue.

All Hail Queen Harriet!
September 2, 3 and 4, 1907

Although Harriet had tried several times without success (as had many other ladies), she was not deterred from trying yet another time. In late August 1907, the Tallant's home was again the scene of flurries and bustling as Hat prepared for her coronation as Queen of the Thirteenth Annual Astoria Regatta. She was twenty-nine years old, full of vim and vigor, ready to give her all during her reign.

At 9 o'clock on Saturday evening, August 17, 1907, the final tally was announced. Miss Harriet Easton Tallant received a huge majority of the votes cast – 11,373. Miss Hattie Wise came in second with 3,810.[192] The *Astoria Daily Budget,* on Monday, August 19, reported that the selection of Harriet, "a young society lady," was quite a popular one. "She is not only one of the most beautiful of Astoria's many handsome young ladies, but her charming personality and the fact she has taken an active interest in the court events of former regatta's assures her reign being a pleasing and successful one."

Queen Harriet's court was small compared with earlier ones. She had only two Maids of Honor: Miss Edna Luckey from Portland and Mrs. Nat (Florence Ross) Tallant,[193] her younger brother's wife. Her six Maids were the Misses Gertrude Upshur, Leta Drain, Lois Parker, Laura Fastabend, Carrie Short and Irene Livingston. Four young Pages served her: George Hildebrand, Vance Ferguson, Sherman Mitchell and Donald Roberts.

Led by Grand Marshall C.V. Brown and Admiral Charles Callender, the opening day's hour-long parade was the largest and longest to that date. Queen Harriet regally rode in her rose-decorated motorcar – driven by her older brother Will. Her Maids and Pages followed her in horse-drawn carriages. They all were guarded by the Queen's band of Royal Vikings - in costume, wearing horned helmets and brandishing clubs and spears. The Sangerfest members sang continuously as they marched along the parade route.

Because the 1907 Regatta was held slightly later than usual, the labor unions, in honor of Labor Day (Monday, September 2), had a prominent position in the parade, with marchers from various unions and local businesses, some with their own floats. The Finnish Brotherhood turned out in force to march with them. Parade spectators cheered their favorite tug-o-war teams, each team representing a different nationality – the real contests were scheduled later.

The Vikings accompanied her Royal Highness and the royal maids to all functions during the three days of events, including at her ball held in Logan's Hall on Tuesday evening, the third of September. The hall, bursting with Regatta goers, had been beautifully decorated in a regatta-nautical theme. Queen Harriet graciously thanked everyone and bid "her subjects" to enjoy dancing the night away – which they did until dawn.

---

[192] The following year, 1908, Miss Harriet Wise was chosen Queen "Hattie" of the 14th Astoria Regatta.
[193] Florence Sara Ross (1882-1955) was also a Lady-in-Waiting for Queen Frances Thomas in 1903. She wed Nat Tallant on November 2, 1904 in Astoria.

Harriet Tallant, Queen of Regatta – 1907

A cut-out of Queen Harriet in her royal automobile driven by her older brother, Will Tallant.

With Hat's "queen days" over, Harriet married Frank Leon Greenough September 5, 1911. Greenough, a printer and lumberman, had been employed as a ticket agent for the Oregon Navigation & Railway Co. and was the editor of a newspaper for a few years when he had lived in Astoria. Harriet and Frank had known each other for a number of years.

Harriet chose to hold their evening wedding ceremony at the home of her parents on Grand Avenue. They invited only a few special friends and the immediate family of both the bride and the groom to attend the ceremony. The house was decorated with banks of hydrangeas in the hall and masses of colorful sweet peas in the parlors. For her younger daughter's wedding, Mary Elizabeth wore her own 1869 wedding gown of gray brocaded satin. Harriet wore an elaborate gown of white chiffon over white satin with a long bridal veil secured by a circlet of orange blossoms.[194] She carried a shower bouquet of fragrant white sweet peas.

Harriet's two young nephews, Richard Tallant Carruthers (almost age nine) and Eben Hunter Carruthers (just seven) led the way into the parlor as Mrs. Charles Brink played the wedding march. The bride followed the boys on the arm of her father, E.W. Tallant. Frank was waiting for her with his best man, W. E. Stone of Portland. Reverend Thomas Lamb Eliot of Portland's Unitarian Church united the couple in marriage. Following the ceremony, a large reception was held for all their many friends. Amid large bouquets of Shasta daisies in the dining room, Sadie Crang and Louise Stone served the refreshments.

---

[194] Harriet's sons, Harrison and Tallant Greenough, donated their mother's wedding gown to the Clatsop County Historical Society.

Mr. and Mrs. Greenough boarded the steamer *Breakwater* in Portland on September 8 for Bandon, Oregon, where Frank was involved in a Coos Bay lumber business. They later moved to Coquille, Oregon. They became the parents of two sons – Harrison and Tallant.

Sources for regatta notes:
Numerous Astoria newpaper accounts.
Louise Tallant's personal recollections and memorabilia.
Two columns by Vera Gault that appeared in *The Daily Astorian* in August 1988.
Guyon Blissett, "About Regattas," Letter to the Editor – *The Daily Astorian*, August 24, 1951.
"History of the Astoria Regatta," *Evening Astorian Budget*, August 29, 1935:10.

Irving Club Insignia

Envelope return address: The Irving Club, Astoria, Oregon.
Addressed to: Miss L. L. Tallant
A note on the envelope: "To be opened when you like. Read it to yourself."

Astoria, Oregon Sept 16, 1900

When this you see, remember me

I have forgotten the rest of the little ballad, but if I remember right, this is the most important part. Any way I will study up.

Now I hope you wont be like myself, that is read this before the time stated. If you do I'll be mad and you know what that means. Well, Louise, I hardly know what to say. If I was with you I would know what to do. (This is what my Grammar calls Present & Parted Tense. I prefer the Present. How do you feel about the subject?) Now as I am on the subject of Grammar I would like to ask a question. If a duffer is in love with a person who is no Duffer and in studying his book should come to that part where it conjugates (that is a good word) the verb love, should he study this part or pass it on. Is it likely to mix him up so he would not know exactly how he stood at the end.

Well I hope you are having or going to have a good time. Don't know when you will read this. There is a little consolation in the fact that I will see you tonight, but you are going to a summer resort, do be careful of the summer men. A good many are hired by the Hotel people to be there, and if you fall in love with them, then they might shake you, and I really do believe a shake would be an awful thing. Do not care to have one though, so be good.

Well I'll quit being silly, as you say, and tell you I'll miss you, miss knowing you are in the same [burg?], miss one of those eight you owe me - since having some one to scold and miss getting mad but I will perhaps think of you at least once a day. Well have a good time. Come back soon.

With lots of love & XXXs

Dick

288

Astoria, Oregon Sept 30, 1900

Dear Girl

I would call you the other name but don't know how to spell it.[195] And it would look bad if you wanted to show this to any one else, so just consider it mentioned and everything will be the same.

Do you know if I thought or at least was quite sure you only took the trip for the sake of the trip I wouldn't feel quite so bad, but so[me] times I wonder if you don't like the change. Now this is a good start on one of these kind of letters isn't it. But it seems that I have to do so much of it lately that I have completely run out of starters. I was in hopes that the Knapton trip was to be the last for some time, but from a word or two last night I can see a Portland trip in the near future. Of Course I Don't Care. never did.

I am in some respects the most unlucky man I ever knew. Now if I was half as much in love with some Girl, who say for an example, did not know any one in Knapton or otherwise had a few friends who were situated to have people visit them, how much nicer it would be. Of this perhaps I should never complain as in the future they might come in handy. Perhaps then you would never care to go. I don't see how you could. Now perhaps I am one of the luckiest people a going to have such a dear old girl as yourself. (Please go back to where I started the last sentence and scratch out the word perhaps. I think it would be better.)

But honestly I think it a darn shame for you to keep chasing off as much as I know you like to do so. If I was to go on the weeks you were home, I would see you about once a month and just as like as not, all the folks would be home. Now how would you like it! Not it but that for on those nights there is very little of it. Well I guess I have roasted you enough so you will behave for a week so - will try and be good for a few lines.

Now if you are not tired of this I shall continue. But before you read any further allow me to suggest an idea that you carefully cut this letter up in to small bits taking care not to cut the love (which I intend to send a little later) up. Sew them up in a nice little silk bag or paste them on a gallon fruit jar - either one of the plans would be nice. Care should be taken though that nothing but [kisses?] be put in the jar or that the little bag be used as a sofa pillow. I always am a fraid that I will write one too many of the letters some day and queer myself. But I do dearly hope dear that you will get over the effects of this – forgive me and come back the same as I am quite sure you are going (How many young men are there over at Knapton?) I think I know where there is a nice Stein (Reasonable) and say, do you want the Kitchen over the cellar or next to the fireplace?

---

[195] Dick likely meant the term *fiancé*.

Little reminders – I don't know if the Stein is quite reasonable enough or if you will ever see the Kitchen or fireplace – kitchen especially.

Well I guess you are tired of this and that will be something I wont growl about if you are. I wouldn't blame you in [the] least and if you have to pack it around with you – well keep it off the boom logs.

But no Joshing I am awfully sorry you are going – every time I am a little more so. If you go any more I will be what ever comes after more so. I am glad you are going and hope you have a good time, but if you give me a chance tonight, I will try and tell you all about it. I know you are willing for me to have the chance.

Well, write if you have a little time to yourself and it will be real good in [of] you.

With lots of love & XXXs

Dick

Now take as much of this love etc as you want as really I guess it is about all I can give you lots of, but there is <u>plenty</u> & plenty of that. Well say, take it all.

Apparently gathering together "stuff," Dick began his collection of beer steins that he would later hang on a pole in their little house at Turkey Hammock in Florida. Few of his steins survived the years.

Mailing date: Oct 2 4-30P 1900 Astoria, Ore.

Monday

My dear Dick

Did you realy think for a minute that I could go away with out writing to you especial after you gave me such nice fat letter. I am going to save it until I leave, Dick, but it is hard to keep it with out opening it until tomorrow. I feel better today but am still ashamed of my self for being so disagreeable and mad to think those precious minutes we had together were spent in quarreling over nothing. But "such is life" and we love each other just the same. That blur on the front page is a kiss, not the nicest one you ever got, is it? We get awfully reckless some times don't we and we realy ought to be more carefull, but dear me, life is to short to miss any even half way chances. I wonder who that man was and what he knows. Look over acrost the river once in a while, Dick, and I'll wave to you or throw you a kiss. Think you could catch it?

Dear old duffer I get mad at you and wish you wouldn't do that and would [give me a] kiss and etc, but all the time I love you just so much as I can and I know there never will be any one but Dick and never was for me and I will be so happy when we can be together all the time, even if we do fight some times like silly children.

Later, so much later that I am awfully sleepy, so I will only say good night and get to bed and maby dream of you. Cold too isn't it these nights. I don't see how we are going to have many more evening walks. What is worrying me now is how we are even going to see half as much of each other as we would like to. Hope we have some kind of a club to go to once a week. Perhaps I will write more in the morning.   Good bye for tonight.

Yours,

Louise

Enclosed in the outer envelope is another envelope addressed the same as above:

Tuesday

Now don't go out walking with the Cocoa girl while I am away. Did you know Eleanor Halsted & her sister and the baby were here – came this a.m. and will wait here for Steve. I have enclosed a little poem for you to read some night when you have nothing to do. Whittier wrote it about my great-great-great (again I guess) grandfather. You see I told you I had Irish blood in me. Ask Charlie how his stein collection is getting along; he has had two given to him and now he says he is going to make a collection of them.

I think I will be home Saturday. Hope to come any way and as Mama expects to go to Portland then to stay a week. I'll have to come back so as not to leave Hat alone.

Well good bye. I must get my things together. Hope to see you on my way to the boat.

Always yours – Louise

"Fiddler Hugh," An Irish Gleeman

"Hugh Tallant" is the main character in Charles Nordhoff and James Norman Hall's 1941 novel, *Botany Bay*. Set in the eighteenth century, the book related the tale of a young American, who had arrived in London to study medicine. He was purportedly descended from a Hugh Tallant of Bedfordshire, who had immigrated to America in 1639. The novel's young Hugh fell in with bad company, was arrested and convicted as a highwayman. The British courts sent him to England's penal colony at Botany Bay, New South Wales, Australia, from which he endeavored to escape. The 1952 film starred Alan Ladd as "Hugh Tallant."

This fictional "Hugh" bore a few similarities to Louise's forebear. Hugh Tallant was born in County Carlow, Ireland about 1685. Some accounts report Hugh was exiled from Ireland – he supported British King George III – so he and two brothers took passage to America from England. When his brothers traveled to the southern states, Hugh remained in the New Hampshire and Massachusetts area. He became the first Irish resident in Haverhill, Massachusetts (1731) and was employed as a servant to Colonel Richard Saltonstall, whose family had received a royal grant of land known as "Island Farm" in Haverhill on the Merrimac River. On this landholding, Hugh planted rows and rows of

Occidental plane trees - sycamores. Hugh married Abiah Little in 1749; she died in 1752. They had two sons: John and Joseph. Hugh then married Mary Dodge of Hampstead 28 June 1753; they had nine children. The 1790 Census of Pelham, Rockingham County, New Hampshire records Hugh, Mary and eight of their children residing in Pelham. One of their sons was also named Hugh, born in 1767, and another was named Andrew Hugh (1771-1840), born in Pembroke. In 1790 Andrew Hugh Tallant wed Amelia Weld (1771-1819) and fathered Nathaniel Weld Tallant (1795-1871), who married Lydia Scudder (1806-1890) in Nantucket – Louise's paternal grandparents.

Many of the New England communities held strong religious views and had very strict rules about music and dancing. Hugh played a violin – mostly Celtic airs. One account reported Hugh, known as "Fiddler Hugh," was evicted from Plaistow, New Hampshire in November 1757; he and his family returned to Hampstead. In 1776, Hugh, loyal to the crown of England - a Tory, was declared an enemy to his country and placed under "house arrest" on his farm. His appeal for a second trial was granted, but the earlier judgment stood and he was remanded to jail. After one night, he escaped with the help of a Tory sympathizer, Samuel Little of Hampstead, who was later denounced.

At more than seventy years of age, Hugh was still quite strong and spry. He could leap over two horses, side by side, reported his great-great niece, Caroline L. Tallant (1830-1877) of Nantucket in her correspondence with John Greenleaf Whittier shortly after the publication of his poem "The Sycamores" in 1857.[196] It seems improbable, but Hugh appears to have lived to the very old age of one hundred ten. His death is recorded in 1795.

Louise sent Dick one of her family's nicely printed book-style "cards" (7.25x10.50") on which the thirty-four stanzas of John Greenleaf Whittier's poem, "The Sycamores" were printed. It relates the "ballad" of the Irish fiddle player, Hugh Tallant, from whom the Tallant family was descended.

THE SYCAMORES.

In the outskirts of the village,
  On the river's winding shores,
Stand the Occidental plane-trees,
  Stand the ancient sycamores.

One long century hath been numbered,
  And another half-way told,
Since the rustic Irish gleeman
  Broke for them the virgin mould.

Deftly set to Celtic music,
  At his violin's sound they grew,
Through the moonlit eves of summer,
  Making Amphion's fable true.

Rise again, thou poor Hugh Tallant!
  Pass in jerkin green along,
With thy eyes brimful of laughter,
  And thy mouth as full of song.

Pioneer of Erin's outcasts,
  With his fiddle and his pack;
Little dreamed the village Saxons
  Of the myriads at his back.

How he wrought with spade and fiddle,
  Delved by day and sang by night,
With a hand that never wearied,
  And a heart forever light, —

Still the gay tradition mingles
  With a record grave and drear,
Like the relic air of Cluny,
  With the solemn march of Mear.

When the box-tree, white with blossoms,
  Made the sweet May woodlands glad,
And the Aronia by the river
  Lighted up the swarming shad,

And the bulging nets swept shoreward,
  With their silver-sided haul,
Midst the shouts of dripping fishers,
  He was merriest of them all.

When, among the jovial huskers,
  Love stole in at Labor's side
With the lusty airs of England,
  Soft his Celtic measures vied.

Songs of love and wailing lyke-wake,
  And the merry fair's carouse;
Of the wild Red Fox of Erin
  And the woman of Three Cows,

By the blazing hearths of winter,
  Pleasant seemed his simple tales,
Midst the grimmer Yorkshire legends
  And the mountain myths of Wales.

How the souls in Purgatory
  Scrambled up from fate forlorn,
On St. Keven's sackcloth ladder,
  Slyly hitched to Satan's horn.

Of the fiddler who at Tara
  Played all night to ghosts of kings;
Of the brown dwarfs, and the fairies
  Dancing in their moorland rings!

Jolliest of our birds of singing,
  Best he loved the Bob-o-link.
"Hush!" he'd say, "the tipsy fairies!
  Hear the little folks in drink!"

Merry faced, with spade and fiddle,
  Singing through the ancient town,
Only this, of poor Hugh Tallant,
  Hath tradition handed down.

Not a stone his grave discloses;
  But if yet his spirit walks,
'T is beneath the trees he planted,
  And when Bob-o-Lincoln talks;

Green memorials of the gleeman!
  Linking still the river-shores,
Within their shadows cast by sunset,
  Stand Hugh Tallant's sycamores!

When the Father of his Country
  Through the north-land riding came,
And the roofs were starred with banners,
  And the steeples rang acclaim, —

When each war-scarred Continental,
  Leaving smithy, mill, and farm,
Waved his rusted sword in welcome,
  And shot off his old king's arm, —

Slowly passed that august Presence
  Down the thronged and shouting street;
Village girls as white as angels,
  Scattering flowers around his feet.

Midway, where the plane-tree's shadow
  Deepest fell, his rein he drew:
On his stately head, uncovered,
  Cool and soft the west-wind blew.

And he stood up in his stirrups,
  Looking up and looking down
On the hills of Gold and Silver
  Rimming round the little town, —

On the river, full of sunshine,
  To the lap of greenest vales
Winding down from wooded headlands,
  Willow-skirted, white with sails.

And he said the landscape sweeping
  Slowly with his ungloved hand,
"I have seen no prospect fairer
  In this goodly Eastern land."

Then the bugles of his escort
  Stirred to life the cavalcade;
And that head, so bare and stately,
  Vanished down the depths of shade.

Ever since, in town and farm-house,
  Life has had its ebb and flow;
Thrice hath passed the human harvest
  To its garner green and low.

But the trees the gleeman planted,
  Through the changes, changeless stand;
As the marble calm of Tadmor
  Mocks the deserts shifting sand.

Still the level moon at rising
  Silvers o'er each stately shaft;
Still beneath them, half in shadow,
  Singing, glides the pleasure craft.

Still beneath them, arm-enfolded,
  Love and Youth together stray;
While, as heart to heart beats faster,
  More and more their feet delay.

Where the ancient cobbler, Keezar,
  On the open hillside wrought,
Singing, as he plied his stitches,
  Songs his German masters taught.

Singing, with his gray hair floating
  Round his rosy ample face, —
Now a thousand Saxon craftsmen
  Stitch and hammer in his place.

All the pastoral lanes so grassy
  Now are Traffic's dusty street;
From the village, grown a city,
  Fast the rural graces retreats.

But, still green, and tall, and stately,
  On the river's winding shores,
Stand the Occidental plane-trees,
  Stand Hugh Tallant's sycamores.

---

[196] Pickard, 397-402.

292

John Greenleaf Whittier and *The Sycamores*

John Greenleaf Whittier was born on a farm in Haverhill, Massachusetts, on December 17, 1807. A staunch Quaker, he was an activist and abolitionist, and a very gifted poet. He studied at the Haverhill Academy with historian Joshua Coffin, who lived in the house built in 1650 by Trystram Coffin (1605-1681). Whittier formed an early love of poetry; he published over 500 poems during his lifetime. He also published numerous other writings, and was a composer, mostly of Victorian-style hymns, *e.g.,* "Our Lord and Father of Mankind." In 1886, he received a well-deserved honorary L.L.D. from Harvard. Whittier died September 7, 1892, at Hampton Falls, New Hampshire and was buried in Amesbury, where he had resided for more than fifty-six years.

Whittier published his poem "The Sycamores" in 1857. It is based on Hugh Tallant, his Irish background, his joy in making music, and the beauty of the Haverhill area. Whittier wrote Caroline Tallant, "In fact, Hugh Talent [*sic*] was to me a pleasant myth, a shadowy phantom of tradition only. Since receiving your letter I have ascertained for a certainty that the Hugh of my ballad and thy great-grandfather are one and the same…[Hugh] became a landowner and was noted for his love of fun and lawsuits. He took the Tory side in the Revolution, was outlawed, shot at, and driven off by his neighbors, but soon managed to return… I give the name as it stands in the Haverhill records – Talent. I presume it should be Tallant."[197]

At the time of Whittier's correspondence with Caroline Tallant, about a dozen of Hugh's sycamore trees were still standing some twelve miles from where John Greenleaf Whittier had lived in Amesbury.

Drawing by Dick – possibly a place card.

---

[197] Picard, 399-400.

Louise was caught up in all the activities of being Regatta Queen even after the big event, which continued as invitations were extended to her to visit here and there. However, an article in the *Astoria Daily Budget* of October 19, 1900, surely turned her attention homeward, to her father:

E. W. Tallant had an experience last evening that might have resulted in his death, and as it was his escape was miraculous. He was on his way home about six o'clock and when nearing there noticed a band of cattle being driven up the street, but payed little attention to them. George Morton, who was ahead of them on horseback, called out to Mr. Tallant to look out and not cross as it might cause the cattle to stampede, but Mr. Tallant continued to cross and one of the cows at the head of the bunch lowered her head and started for him. Almost before he knew that she was coming she hit him with one horn on the left side and the other immediately under the chin and threw him in the air. Those who witnessed it say that he must have been lifted at least four feet in the air and dropped some distance away partly unconscious. The cow continued on down the street and partially stampeded the balance of the bunch of 23. In a few moments Mr. Tallant recovered sufficiently to walk to his home and a physician was summoned. It was found that one horn had entered under his chin loosening his teeth and making an ugly wound but not breaking his jaw. The clothing on the body protected it from the most dangerous blow as the horn only entered sufficient to break the skin and a After the cow had tossed Mr. Tallant it made mad dashes at every one it saw and it was with difficulty that it was got into the corral. Previous to this time it was being driven from Uppertown it made no attempt to molest anyone.

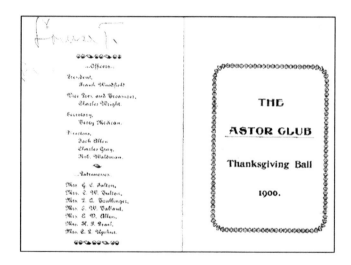

No envelope. **A letter from Louise to Dick, Christmas 1900:**

Merry Xmas <u>dear Dick</u>

and I would give you a nice big kiss if I could. You will get it the very first chance I have to give it to you, old duffer. I love you you know it though don't you. Well I hope every body will know it before long. I'll be so happy that I will go around singing it on the street. That would be a nice thing to do wouldn't it. You wouldn't mind would you? You can tell me to shut up when you get tired of hearing it. Now I know you want to see what is inside this package and of course you will read this first so I will make it short and sweet and I will let you get at the rest which isn't much but lots of love goes with it – and as I took some time to do the work I thought of you _very_ often. I did the laundry work also so you see if I had to take it up as a profession I might be able to make enough to buy salt.

I will hope to see you some time during the day so until then good bye –

Yours always with loads of love

Louise

Enclosed note:

Merry Xmas my dear Dick and my best wishes for the very happiest kind of a new year. Yours was the first Xmas present I made this year. I hope you will like it. I thought it was very appropriate on our couch. It would be wouldn't it? When we have it on _our_ couch it wont matter if the "daisies do tell" will it.

You interrupted me so I will close in haste.

Yours always

Louise

Chapter Twelve

1901 - 1903
Vows are Taken
Married Life on a Hammock

Dearest Dick

Or my dear <u>old</u> boy would be a good beginning for today. Now don't be shocked at those pretty socks. I put all those nice red stitches in them and if you are a good boy and wear them some time I'll make you a pair with red, white & blue, black & tan stripes in them. That would be real gay wouldn't it? The suitcase you must use as much as possible before we go traveling so as to get the newness worn off <u>see</u>. Better take it next time you go down to see Grace [Dick's sister] for you <u>might</u> decide to stay a day or two.

27 times X = what I will give you tonight <u>if I get a chance</u>. Until then good bye.

Yours always with love and best wishes for many happy returns of the day.

Louise

By the time you read this you will know whether I got the chance or not. If I don't, why next time will have to do. They will be safe with [this] *Lassie.*

The above letter from Louise to Dick was not dated, but she refers to his twenty-seventh birthday on May 8, 1901. Although only a few letters exist from either Louise or Dick during the latter part of 1900 well into 1901, one is aware they had pledged themselves to each other during this period. There was genuine affection between them, born of a long acquaintance. Dick had been faithfully requesting Louise's hand in marriage for so many years. Now, he was intending to leave Astoria for his family's cattle ranch in Florida and wanted Louise to travel with him as his wife. Louise, having recovered from her surgery reasonably well, finally accepted his proposal.

There was so much preparation to be done, not only for the wedding and a cross-country honeymoon trip, but also for a prolonged stay far from home. For months there would have been a flurry of preparations and arrangements in Louise's Grand Avenue home. Louise made sure to pack her camera, telescope, guitar and a few family photographs. She also packed her "telescoping" bag.

It was not until September 21, 1901, that a very brief notice appeared in the Personal column of the *Astoria Daily Budget* announcing the engagement of Louise Tallant and Richard E. Carruthers. No other information was given.

The Cotillion Club (*aka* The Assembly) hosted a dancing party in honor of Louise and Dick on Friday evening, October 11 at Hanthorn's Hall (535 Bond). The affair was termed "the most pleasant social function given in Astoria during the present year," according to the *Astoria Daily Budget*. The Columbia orchestra "rendered excellent music for the occasion." There were sixteen unmarried ladies present, including Harriet, along with twenty-three young bachelors, including Gus Carruthers and Frank Greenough, plus Drs. Cordiner and Earle. Mrs. W. Ridehalgh (Zoe), Mrs. Sutherland, Mrs. G. Wood and Mrs. P. Trullinger attended, along with the E.W. Tallants, the G.C.

Fultons, the F.A. Fishers, the H. Allens, the E. Rosses, the H. Praels, the N.A. Marrs, the C.B. Allens (Grace), the B. van Dusens, and Dr. and Mrs. Finch. Such a gala affair!

Weddings in the late 1880s into the early 1900s were often held at the bride's home. Dick and Louise's wedding was a good example. They had set their wedding date for Wednesday, October 16, 1901. The ceremony would be held at her parent's home. Louise would come down the staircase of her family home, as many other Astoria brides had done in their family homes.[198] Regrettably, no photographs have ever been found of Dick and Louise in their wedding attire. This was perhaps not unusual, although disappointing, not to be able to "see" the bride and groom, especially since both of Dick's sisters, Grace and Zoe, had been professional photographers. One must piece together information found in court records and in the accounts in the evening newspapers to describe what occurred.

Louise and Dick's Wedding   1901

A short note to "Mrs Richard Ervin Carruthers" from Catherine Starbuck of Nantucket was dated October 10, 1901:

> My Dear Young Friends,
>   May the blessing of Him who resides in the Heaven of Heavens
> be upon you and in the volume of his Will may Happiness be written
> is the Sincere wish of your loving and admiring friend
>
>   Catherine Starbuck

On the fifteenth of October 1901, the newspaper reported that Eben Weld Tallant had returned to Astoria from Portland by steamer. As an appointed member of the Oregon Bar Pilots Commission, he was required to spend much of his time in Portland. In the same issue of the newspaper, there was a notice that he had just purchased a four-year old trotter that ran the mile in less than 2:20; she was the Champion of White Horse Road. It is not known what he intended to do with the horse, but horse racing was quite popular then. The racehorse was definitely not a wedding gift for Louise and Dick.

In April 1899, Louise and Harriet had become members of the First Unitarian faith at the Reverand Eliot's Church of Our Father in Portland. This had pleased their father Eben very much. Because there was no Unitarian church in Astoria at that time, it was particularly important to her family that her father's dear friend, Dr. Thomas Lamb Eliot, had agreed to journey down from Portland to officiate at the wedding of the Tallants' older daughter. Dr. Eliot, then Pastor *emeritus,* probably arrived by steamer the morning of October sixteenth.

Louise and Dick obtained the Affidavit For Marriage License on October 16, 1901, from the Clatsop County Courthouse in Astoria. The document was sworn to and deposed

---

[198] An example: When Ada Ferguson married John Griffin, she descended the lovely mahogany staircase that spiraled down from the third floor all the way to the entry hall-parlor. Her father, Albert Ferguson, an Astoria pioneer, architect and builder, had constructed their home at 1661 Grand in 1886, only a block east of the Tallants' home that was built in 1896.

by their long-time friend, Charlie Heilborn. He attested that the bride, M. Louise Tallant, was over eighteen years of age – she was twenty-six – and that there was no legal impediment to the marriage. That affidavit was not required of the groom. Signing for County Clerk Wherity, Deputy County Clerk J.B. Clinton issued the affidavit document. The Marriage Certificate was issued on the same day. Will Tallant and Carleton B. Allen, Grace's husband, were the witnesses. Dr. Eliot signed the document as Minister of the Gospel.[199]

That morning Harriet and a number of Louise's "girl friends" festooned the staircase and entry hall with garlands of Virginia creeper, autumn leaves and branches of the red-berried mountain ash. Huge arrangements of pink and white hydrangeas and chrysanthemums filled the formal parlor; the large south-facing bow window was banked with smilax and white mums to create a bower. The pink and white theme continued into the family parlor and the dining room, using numerous bowls of roses and sweet peas from Mary Elizabeth's garden.

Family parlor

Dining room

Olga

Lillie – 1901

Marge

---

[199] Clatsop County Courthouse document marriage records, p. 148.

The gathering assembled in the formal front parlor: Dick, probably in a new dark suit with a much-hated high starched white collar, waited with his Best Man, Charlie Heilborn; the Rev. Dr. Eliot; Louise's Matron of Honor, Mrs. Norman A. Marrs (Eugenia "Genie" Lewis); and Louise's mother. Also in attendance were: Dick's parents, Robert and Harriet, who had not yet left for Florida; Gus; Will; perhaps Nat; Grace and Carleton Allen with their daughters Mignon (age five) and one-year old Zoe; and Walter and Zoe Ridehalgh with their young son, Walter T. ("Chappie"). Robert Rex might have been there, although he might have left early for Florida to work on the cattle ranch.

Louise's wedding gown.[200]

"Maria Louise" doll.[201]

At two-thirty in the afternoon, Olga Heilborn, Nan Reed, Nellie Sherman, Marge Halsted and Lila Sutherland – gowned in white and pink - formed an "aisle" by holding intertwined vines leading from the stairs to the parlor. Dressed in a white organdie gown, Harriet, Louise's bridesmaid, came down the stairs first, followed by Louise, on the arm of her father. [202] Louise had been a strikingly beautiful Queen of Astoria's Regatta in the previous year, so one would have expected her to be even lovelier as a bride. And she was. She was attired in an ivory-colored satin gown of intricate design. A "blouse," with rows of tucking, featured lace rosette medallions at the elbows of the long, tight sleeves. A satin sleeveless "jacket" had a complex series of tucks. The satin skirt was cut to form a short train. Louise carried a large bouquet of fragrant pink roses.

---

[200] Louise's wedding gown was displayed on a model at the Heritage Museum. Photograph courtesy of CCHS.
[201] Louise dressed this 18" tall French doll in a replica of her 1901 "going away" costume. She stitched the two-piece suit and undergarments using the original fabrics, jet beads, laces and feathers of her costume. The doll wears her original fishnet stockings and high-buttoned boots. Louise presented "Maria Louise" to her fourteen-year old granddaughter, Carol Louise Carruthers, in May 1945.
[202] *Morning Daily Astorian*, October 17, 1901.

The Reverend Eliot conducted the simple Unitarian marriage ceremony. Pearl Callender played Mendelssohn's Wedding March and Reba Hobson sang several solos. By three o'clock, several hundred friends began to arrive for the reception to toast the bride and groom's happiness – and to present the newlyweds with many beautiful gifts.

Louise then changed into her two-piece "going away" costume that was made of dark blue, patterned silk brocade. The jacket, with a peplum, had a belted waist, velvet trimmed collar, leg-o-mutton sleeves, narrowing to formfitting on the forearms, with a row of black jet buttons at each wrist. The skirt was fairly full. Underneath she wore a linen chemise edged in laces and a lower body garment, trouser-like, also edged in laces. Her elegant ensemble was completed with low-heeled high-buttoned shoes; perhaps net stockings; and a beautiful, stiffened velvet hat with a brim filled with ostrich feathers.

That evening, accompanied by many of their friends, "Mr. and Mrs. Richard Ervin Carruthers" were taken to the train depot for a jolly send-off as they left for a quick visit to Portland. As the train pulled away, Louise threw her bouquet of roses. Although Marge Halsted caught the bouquet, Marge never married.

On the eighteenth, Dick and Louise briefly returned by steamer to Astoria to call upon her mother and father. That same day, they then crossed the river by steamer to pay a short visit to Dick's family and relatives in Ilwaco before they started their journey that would take them to their new home in Florida.

Their honeymoon trip by train took them first to California to call upon relatives and friends there. In late October, again traveling by train, they left for Florida to reside with Dick's parents, who had traveled from Astoria directly to Kissimmee, Florida. While Louise remained in Kissimmee with her mother-in-law, Harriet Hunter Carruthers, her father-in-law Robert and her husband Dick left for the cattle ranch near Jack Hammock at the south end of Lake Kissimmee. They joined Dick's younger brother, Robert Rex, known as "Tod," who was already working on the Lightsey, Lewis & Carruthers Cattle Ranch. The men were building fencing around the vast holding. Early in the New Year of 1902 - Tuesday, January 21 - Louise journeyed by water to join her husband for a visit at Jack Hammock, a rather remote and primitive place. She returned to Kissimmee on the second of February. Dick managed to return "home" to see her from February 23 to 25. On the fifth of April, he walked from Jack Hammock to Kissimmee in order to accompany Louise back with him to the Ranch. On the eighth, they traveled together by boat into the hinterland to Jack Hammock.

After Louise and Dick left Astoria, her brother William Easton Tallant kept busy in the cannery business. The *Astorian Daily Budget* on November 20, 1901, reported that Will had purchased the old cannery of A.V. Allen over on the Washington side of the river. He paid $10,000 for it, intending to rebuild it and put it into full operation for the next fishing season. One of his main products was "Tide Point Oysters." Will spent a good deal of time traveling back and forth to Portland, and to California and the east coast, to market his specialty that was considered among the finest oysters ever packed.

Harriet penned a letter to Louise in Florida. No envelope was saved and no date appears on the letter. This was likely written in early December 1901. Apparently Louise and her mother-in-law Harriet - possibly accompanied by Dick - had visited the tourist spot of

Paradise, Florida, a few miles north of Orlando. Harriet also refers to their younger brother Nathaniel Weld "Nat" Tallant. Nat was studying in Pasadena, California at the Throop Polytechnic Institute that emphasized vocational training. Amos Throop, a wealthy Chicago politician - and former abolitionist - founded the small college in 1891. By 1921, after several name changes, the school became known as the California Institute of Technology, commonly abbreviated to Caltech.

My dear Louise

We received your letter thus afternoon telling about the picnic and your trip to Paradise. What a lovely place it must be. Papa has just come home from a hunting trip to Warrenton and around there - had fair luck. The Chafing Dish Club meet at Florettas [Elmore] to night for the first time. Expect we will have some thing good to eat. Mr Herz is coming up for me.

Friday is the 2nd Cotillion. Made my pink and black stripe to wear - its real pretty. The skirt hand fitted. Made it with only two seams back and front with the stripe meeting circular flounce with 4 small ruffles on the bottom, cut so the black stripe makes the edge. The waist I made with a tucked yoke - or rather I tucked the black stripe in then covered it with rows of gathered pink finishing ribbon. Am going to wear a long black velvet belt that I got to wear with the silk Aunt Clara gave me.

Just finished a dear little corset cover for Lila trimmed in footing and lace. Have burnt 3 bowles, one for Mrs Berry, Mrs Van Dusen, Mrs Kendell. Made 5 or 6 bags, covered Black Rock for mama to give for Xmas presents. I made some cute little needle books of the leather just like we cover books only put in a few leaves of flannel - good way to use up scraps.

My, but its cold and has been for a week. East wind and clear. Hope it last till Xmas. Nat says it seems funny to get ready for Xmas in the middle of summer [in Pasadena], but we don't feel that way. Hope you don't send many purses here for the fun of having mine is that no one else has one or ever saw one like it.[203] We sent one to Lillie and one to Aunt Clara. Mama is making some of the dearest little slippers for Tallant, like Olga made out of felt last year - remember.

Kates wedding cards came today but I cant realize yet she is to be married. Got her a pair of sugar tongs, butter cup pattern. Made her a tray cloth for Xmas.

Thursday morning

Had a good time at Chafing Dish Club last night. Had grapefruit, creamed oysters, coffee & cake to eat. Dr & Mrs F [Finch], Floretta & Mr Finley cooked. Played Dominos the first part of the evening. All the men wore dress suits - or rather all but Charlie and of course that

---

[203] It seems likely Harriet refers to alligator or snakeskin purses, common in Florida, but quite unusual in Astoria.

gave him the dumps. Every once in a while he would say to me "this isn't much like the old club is it?"

Have two or three Xmas notes to write so Good Bye. Tell us all about your Xmas.

With loads of love from

Hat

Saw Mrs [Harriet?] Shields yesterday. She looked awfully pretty and well. She gained 11 lbs while away. They are going to live in Portland this winter. Speaking of <u>gaining</u> I weigh 117, so its all off with low neck dresses this year.

Sunday 10 a. [probably December 4 or 11, 1901]

Dear Dick & Louise.

Hat said she was going to write Nat so I will write to you for if my babies enjoy their letters [as] much as I do theirs, I am willing to write. Brownie [the cat] has just jumped into my lap, and as I am sitting by the fire, trying to get my poor leg warm, it is not very convenient to write you. Although I am pretty big, my lap seems small with a big cat and pad of paper. But perhaps if I tell B- I am writing to Louise, she will keep still. Hat and I have been housekeepers for three days. Thursday, H. was helping serve the dinner at the Episcopal sale so I went down to the Sutherlands to tea and Willie & Hat came for me in the eve. Friday, Mr & Mrs S- took dinner with me as H- was going to the Cotillion party. They stayed until train got in. Then I went to bed & believe it was the first time I ever went to bed alone in the house. But no one carried me off. Hat went with Charlie - got home at one. I was glad she had <u>a change</u>.

Friday Mrs S- and I sat in my room sewing. Phone rang. I answered it. It was Jim Lounsberry - wanted to know if "Mr Greenough was there."[204] I said "that is too much; he is here sometimes but I draw the lines day times." He laughed. Said he wanted him very much. Come to find he had phoned to Reba, Nan, Sadie, etc. And after all <u>Willie</u> was out on an errand that I had sent him & forgotten it. And a man was there to buy a ticket to Chicago and W- had locked the office. As papa would say: "Tempest inceteapat." [Tempest in-a-teapot]. Well papa & Will are still away. I will enclose papa's note then you will know it all. I am hoping he will send a note on noon train & put a delivery stamp on, then I shall get it. He may come. Hat & I are going to Mrs S- to dinner. She kindly invited us if papa did not come. I have made two mince pies to take so I need not trouble to make dessert. I do wish the weather would clear so I could walk out. Friday was a nice day and I called at Mrs Heiborns on my way to Mrs S-. She showed me a pretty Xmas present you are going to get from Olga. We shall send

---

[204]   Mary Elizabeth likely refers to Frank Leon Greenough, whom Harriet married in 1911. At this time he might still have been a ticket agent in Astoria for the O.R.& N. Co. (Oregon Railroad & Navigation Company).

just a little package that you may be reminded that there are those at home that love you and wish you were going to be here to come into our room in the a.m. I think it will be a lonely time for us with you and Nat gone, but then as I said the other day, we ought not to make it so as you both are so happy and I would not have it otherwise. But I miss you two so much. Nat is so affectionate that I have missed him while I have been sick, but he is interested in school and has such a nice home. I say fifty times I am so glad he could go there. Mrs K- pho[ned] yesterday. She got home on the noon train. Said Nat looked fine. You know she called at the school and saw him. She said no wonder he liked it for it seemed so nice there.

Louise, didn't you mean to take your fur! I guess Miss N- would bring it to you. She says she shall come to K-[issimmee] and see you – that her brother in law has passes on the stea. that are on the gulf, etc. You better get on the good side of him & you & Dick can get a trip to Tampa to see them. Sue E-[Elmore] says she is coming down to see you. She leaves Thursday. F- came last week.

Dr K- was up to see me yesterday. I was getting discouraged for I have hardly been able to walk around the house. the last day or two and thought that ointment I was using was no good for the day I went to Mrs S- I did not use it and I could walk better, but he said "I was doing finely, looked a great deal better in my face and to keep on with the medicine & ointment." I told him Will wanted us all to group and have our Xmas dinner at The Portland, but I could not walk the length of the dining room. He said "lets see, it is two weeks yet before Xmas. You tell him you will go and I will have you so you can walk without a limp." Wish I thought so. Seems as tho I would be satisfied now if I could dress myself – and not have to wait for either papa or Hat to come and put on shoes & stockings. Perhaps by New Years I can go to the ball – and dance –

Train in. Keep looking to see if papa & Will came. Guess I have to give them up.

<u>Here is papa.</u>

Well papa says he never saw such a busy place as P! [Portland] Says Will's store is fine, and the best of it is, they are doing a fine business. He says everywhere you see and hear of Tide Point Oysters.

We phoned to Mrs S- papa had come, so I would not come. She says All Come. So I must close and get ready. Will send Sun O [The Sunday Oregonian] to Dick. Guess he will find it more interesting than the letter. Your letters make us want to come to K- more than ever. It must be a pretty place. How far is the ranch? You speak of driving down – that will suit me. Stay in K- until we get there. I should enjoy driving down to the Ranch. Give love to Mrs. C-. [Harriet Carruthers]. Will not seal this until papa gets back from O [office?] May get a letter.

Kisses to Dick & self from

Mama

Louise's father sent this letter to her in Kissimmee. At that time, Eben was not only the Secretary of his son's Tallant-Grant Packing Company on West Bond Street in Astoria, but also the Captain of their schooner, the *Salmon Hunter*. For some time, Mary Elizabeth had been suffering from an unnamed illness that might have been neuritis, combined with myocarditis/heart disease. When Eben was appointed to the Oregon Board of Bar Commissioners in March 1899, his duties required that he often remain in Portland for long periods. Because of health problems, Lizzie was forced to spend much of her time at home.

Astoria, Oregon Dec 17th, 1901

To My Dear Louise:

Your interesting letter of Dec. recd.- inducements offered to visit Kissimmee are more than sufficient. It was quite enough to see you and Dick [in] *your happy home. Then when you add the glorious climate and good hunting, it's quite irresistible. It only requires a successful season in Astoria to settle the question. I have no doubt the sunshine would greatly benefit your Mother. Hope to get her in condition to travel. She has improved considerable past week, take occasional walks to Heilborns and Sutherlands.*

We have at last received long letter from Fanny; my various letters to her have been uncalled for at Post Office - Phoenix. She is very much pleased with climate and somewhat improved in strength. [Frances' son] *Frank is with her. They receive considerable attention from Dr Walker. Flora* [a daughter] *is having attention from a young Yale graduate who is there with a surveying party. He takes her to ride occasionally, brings them game he shoots.*

I enclose the hundred dollars from Will. He went to Portland this morning but returns to be with us Christmas. He sent ten dollars to Nat for a Christmas present.

We had a week of cold weather; it now looks like snow. Last Thursday I went to Skipanon for Snipe. Ice quarter of an inch thick on tide land. I made a misstep, got into water over boot tops, which spoiled my hunt. Met Mr Preston.[205] *He inquired about Mr Carruthers. Said he was disappointed not receiving letter from him. Reported he had some money for him. Your Mother and Harriet are very busy getting off Christmas presents, about the last to leave today. I frequently send you Astoria papers - trust you receive them. My love to Dick*

Merrie Christmas to all

from your affectionate

Papa

---

[205] Was this the same Mr. Preston of Preston Peak Copper Company? Was it he who had written Louise in 1899 at the time of her Uncle Nathaniel's death? See Chapter 10, page 259.

A rare letter from Louise's younger brother Nat, an eighteen-year old student in Pasadena, was kept in Louise's cedar wood box. Nat sent this to her in Kissimmee.

Merry Christmas and happy New Year to you all.

Pasadena   Dec 18, 1901

My dear Louise:

Well I know I have been a bad boy for not writing long ago but for one reason or another I have put it of[f] until now. But after Xmas I will be sure and write quite often. Mama has said that she sent most of my letters on to you so it is just about the same as my writing to you I sent my last months report to mama and they all thought I was doing fine and I was quite proud of myself. But today being our last day of school for this year we record them for this mt [month] and I was very much surprised to see that I had received much higher mark than last mt., so I will send it at once to the people at home - in my Bookkeeping and Law I received 100 - so you see it would be imposible to get any higher.

My but isnt it hard to believe that we will not be able to go into mama's room Xmas morning and have our stockings as we have done for so many years. Poor Hat I guess she will feel it most of any of us and how I wish I could spend my vacation at home. But, as I cant, I am going to make the best of it and have just as good a time as I can. I will tell you what I will send home for my presents. Mama got a nice box of sope [soap] for me to give Will - said it would cost to much to get it here and send it. For Hat I have made a neat book rack to stand on a table. Mama wrote me and wanted to know if I would make one as Hat wanted one, so I did and it turned out quite fine - at least I think so.

Mama said papa wanted a match box and so I will get him one tomorrow - have seen some very pretty ones.

As for mama I am in a bad fix. I intended at the end of my school term to make a chair for her such as one we have here at Mrs M-. But I thought the other day that I would start and see if I could not have it done in time for Xmas and would send it to her as a present. Well I started it and I have worked every minute I could find on it and last night worked by lamplight until ten thirty, and now that we have no more school I think that I will be able to have it finished at least in time for a new years present.

I intended to make something for you but as I was so rushed with mamas present I was not able to find time so I did the next best thing and bought you a picture which I think quite pretty. It is the very latest work out and this is the only place on the coast that it can be bought so I thought it would look quite nice in your new house.

Well Louise I would like to rite you a great deal more but if I want to get mama's chair done I must close and go to work and will rite you a long letter right after Xmas and will promise to write often.

So with lots of love to you and Dick, I will say good by from your loving brother

Nat

Goodness I never thought about addressing this letter to any one but Louise Tallant, so I don't know whether I will be able to spell your name ot not. Remember me to all the Carruthers family. – I think that is right isn't it?

Robert and Harriet Hunter Carruthers

Ohioans William Hunter (1810-1896), a blacksmith, and Jemima Meek (1810-1870) married in Claremont, Ohio November 11, 1830. They had ten children, of whom Harriet Hunter was the ninth child. One source relates that the Hunter family left Ohio for Oregon in 1847, but that must be incorrect given that Harriet was born in Ohio August 14, 1848. In any event, the trip would have been especially difficult with such a young baby. There were so many wagon train groups going west during these years, it seems unlikely the William Hunter and Robert Carruthers families met on the trail. The Hunter family settled in Brownsville in the Oregon Territory. One of Harriet's older brothers, John, active in real estate matters, moved to Ilwaco, where he met Robert's sister, Sarah Ann Carruthers; John and Sarah married September 28, 1859, in the Oysterville home of her parents, Richard and Mary. So, John Hunter is the most likely link between Robert and Harriet Hunter who wed July 26, 1868, in the Hunters' home in Brownsville. They settled in Oysterville, where they had four children: Grace, Zoe, Richard Ervin and Angus Russell, *aka* "Gus." Their third son, Robert Rex, *aka* "Tod," was born in the brick house in Astoria.

Like his father, Robert had a strong work ethic and was a risk-taker. In the Polk and Dellinger Astoria City Directories he is termed an "entrepreneur" and a "capitalist." His interests and abilities were broad. His contributions to the development of the Lower Columbia area were numerous.

Robert labored as a Shoalwater Bay oysterman for several years. He also became involved in construction projects, which required having his own horses and wagons. In 1867, he and his father Richard began investing in real estate in various parts of the Lower Columbia area, including the Old Morgan Farm above Jerome Avenue in Astoria.

On July 8, 1874, Robert, along with L.A. Loomis, George Johnson, Abram Wing and J.H.D. Gray, incorporated the Ilwaco Wharf Company (main office in Oysterville) and built a wharf and warehouse in Ilwaco on Baker's Bay. In October 1876, Robert and Harriet took over the management of Pacific House Hostelry in Oysterville from Mary and Richard, even though Robert was rushing to complete buildings at Scow Bay and on the Water Street Roadway (now Marine Drive). By the following June, the Water Street buildings in Astoria had a tenant: Alexander and Lobenstein Dry Goods Store. Although he took his own horses home for the winter in 1877, Robert continued hauling wood for construction projects up river in Clatskanie during January 1878. He had established his own drayage business – horses and wagons – necessary to his construction business and bought Astoria's Wing Brothers' "trucking" company in November of that year. The Astoria Court House paid him all of $19 for hauling wood for them in January 1879.

"Shortly after the first ringing of the church bells Sunday evening a scene of horror presented itself on Jefferson Street, near Olney [now Duane and 12th] where a little child of Mr. R. Carruthers fell from the walk into the bay."

The near tragedy occurred on March 17, 1878, per the newspaper account of March twenty-first. The child who fell into the deep basin is not identified in the news article but he must have been Richard Ervin, who would have been going on four years old - his brother Angus Russell was only about eight months old at that time and surely would not have been allowed to accompany his father and older brother to Astoria. Two young men immediately went to help and were successful in rescuing the child, handing him over to his father, who had been nearby at the wagon shed. One of the rescuers, Lewis Allen, had removed his coat, vest and watch before jumping into the water. He later discovered that his clothing and watch had been stolen - "a dastardly act by some miscreant."

In 1883, Robert constructed the family's residence at 638 Cedar (Exchange) – the first brick dwelling built in Astoria. Although Robert and Harriet's daughter Zoe married Walter Ridehalgh April 2, 1891, in Grace [Episcopal] Church,[206] their older daughter, Grace, chose to wed Carleton B. Allen in the parlor of the family's home on October 31, 1894.

A blacksmith's business and stable was located directly behind his home; on Jefferson (Duane) Street. Robert bought it about 1888 as a convenient place in which to care for his horses. He, along with Duncan McTavish, expanded his trucking/hauling business. In 1890, Robert and William Tarrant plated and recorded "Carruthers First Addition" in Warrenton near John's Slough on the Skipanon River – about 20 acres of lots. Robert also purchased property at the corner of 12th and Commercial in downtown Astoria on which to build a store with apartments above. In 1907, his son Dick opened his own hardware store on the lower level of Robert's building.

The Astoria Wharf and Warehouse building was the major project in 1892 by the real estate brokerage business composed of Robert and a notary public and assessor named Benjamin S. Worsley. They also made mortgage loans. It was Robert who found time to cut and polish those 6,000 walking canes of Washington wild crabapple to be sold at the Chicago World's Fair in 1893. Early in 1896 he sailed his sleek yacht-pilot boat, the *Jessie,* from San Francisco to the Columbia River and tried to survive the next four years of the shipping industry depression by forming alternative companies and jobs for the *Jessie.* In November of 1898, Captain George Flavel asked him to set the 12-ton obelisk monument for the Flavel family gravesite at Ocean View cemetery – this unique marker is prominent on the cemetery grounds in Warrenton, Oregon.

In 1896, Harriet Hunter Carruthers' father, William Hunter, died in Brownsville, Oregon and was buried there. Robert's father, Richard, also died in 1896; Mary Faint Carruthers, followed her husband in death December 4, 1899. Richard and Mary were interred in the Oysterville Cemetery, said to be the first cemetery in Pacific County.

---

[206] Walter had sent his Border Collie (?) by steamer to Portland to be cared for by a friend, while he and Zoe boarded the *Columbia* for their wedding trip to California. After arriving in Portland, the collie eluded his caregiver and somehow boarded the *Telephone* to ride downstream; the dog disembarked in Astoria and trotted directly to William W. Wherry's Star Market on Chenamus (Bond), where he was given a chuck of beef. The dog sat happily in the sun to eat it and wait for his master's return – or for someone to come for him.

According to the *South Bend Journal* of January 14, 1901, Robert had been traveling in eastern and southern Florida, and in the Tampa area. He probably had been checking out business possibilities regarding a cattle ranch. On his way back home, he stopped in Boonville, Missouri. Here he directed the exhumation of the fifty-year old remains of his older brother John, who had died there at the age of twelve. John's coffin still contained his toy gun and pocketknife that his mother Mary had tucked in with her son. Robert brought the remains to the Oysterville Cemetery, where he and his younger brother, William Alfred, laid the child to rest beside his parents on January 10, 1901. At some point, probably in the early 1930s, Gustave "Dobby" Wiegardt, Sr. of Nahcotta was hired to use his horse and buggy to haul a large granite stone from the Nahcotta railroad station to Oysterville Cemetery. The stone marks the grave on Lot 46 of the three Carruthers family members.[207]

Photograph taken October 2007 by Carol Lambert.

Shortly after, Robert returned to Florida where he managed the 40,000-acre Lightsey, Lewis & Carruthers Cattle Ranch. Harriet joined him there later. Robert traveled back again to Astoria "from the land of the sunshine and flowers," per a brief notice in the *Morning Astorian* of Tuesday, August 19, 1902. He was visiting family and old friends for a month, while taking care of some business. Robert mentioned that several electrical storms in the Okeechobee area had caused some deaths - and damage to his own property. He reported that the cattle ranch, with 6000 head of cattle, was doing very well and his improvements were "an eye opener to the natives." One person he visited was his brother Al in South Bend to further discuss new techniques that Al had developed in the raising of his Angus beef cattle and in creating better dykes for tidelands.

Robert and Harriet remained in Florida until September 1904, when the two of them finally returned to their brick home on Exchange Avenue in Astoria. Robert continued dealing in real estate. Even in 1930, Robert was still listed as the owner of one half of an island in the middle of Young's River, south of the bay. Harriet, as always, was active in

---

[207] According to E.R. "Bud" Goulter, a long time resident of Oysterville, Gustave A. "Dobby" Wiegardt, Sr. was paid with a five-dollar gold piece that was then called a "sou." Mr. Goulter was a personal friend of the elder Mr. Wiegardt - and of his son and namesake, who still lives in Nahcotta.

her church work. In 1917, within about three months of each other, Robert and Harriet died.

The *Astoria Evening Budget,* Tuesday, February 13, 1917:

Robert Carruthers, one of Astoria's pioneer residents, died suddenly about 10:30 this morning as the result of a stroke of apoplexy. He had been seen about the streets this morning and apparently in his accustomed good health. While returning from the Astoria Fuel and Supply Company's office he stopped at the residence of George Bryant, at the corner of 5th and Bond streets and fell dead while sitting in a chair and conversing with Mr. Bryant. The deceased was a native of Canada, 74 years of age and had resided on the coast for many years, first in Shoalwater Bay and then in Astoria, where he owned large property interests...

Monday, May 21, 1917:

Mrs. Harriet Hunter Carruthers, wife of the late Robert Carruthers, died at four o'clock this morning after a lingering illness. She passed away at the home of her daughter Mrs, Carleton (Grace) Allen who resides at 726 Irving avenue. The deceased was a native of Ohio, 67 years old and a resident of Astoria for many years. Mrs. Carruthers was an active church worker, a lovable mother and a kind friend. She leaves two daughters and three sons to mourn her loss... The funeral is to take place Wednesday at the Episcopal church.

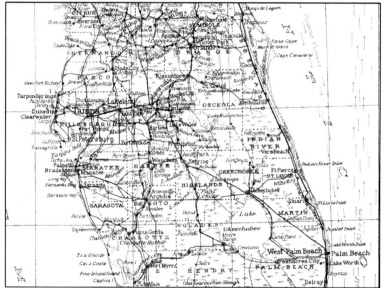

The central section of a National Geographic Society map of Florida dated 1930.

The Long Water

The name "Kissimmee" is a Calusa Indian name thought to mean "long water." A recent AAA Handbook for Florida translates Kissimmee as "Heaven's Place." Both translations are descriptive of this city and of the long Kissimmee River. Kissimmee, in Osceola County, Florida, is located about 15 miles south of Orlando. It is situated at the northern end of Lake Tohopekaliga, which is fed by a vast underground spring to the northwest called Green Swamp. Lake Tohopekaliga is the beginning of the Kissimmee River with its chain of lakes and connecting canals. It leads, in a winding manner, to Lake

Okeechobee, or the so-called "big water," the largest fresh water lake in the United States.[208]

From here the waters of the Kissimmee River drain into both the Atlantic and the Gulf of Mexico. This sluggish waterway, one hundred sixty-five miles long, is a labyrinth of by-channels with cut-offs and dead ends. In the nineteenth century, on either side along its horseshoe bends and meandering turns stretched miles and miles of prairie land dotted with hammocks of pine, oak and cabbage palms – intermixed with cypress swamps. It was a marshy paradise for numerous kinds of birds, e.g., ducks, coots, heron, cranes, egrets, curlews and water turkeys. But the carnage of the beautiful plumed birds was so extensive between 1880 and 1915 that they were almost wiped out. And the method that was used to obtain their plumage was terribly cruel. Sunning themselves on the sandy banks of this long waterway were alligators, turtles and water snakes. In the late 1880s, a rattler's skin sold for eighty-five cents; that of an alligator cost $1 or more.

Dredging operations in the three years from 1881 to 1884 drained over two million acres stretching from the city of Kissimmee south-southeast to the Atlantic Ocean. The city of Kissimmee was at an elevation of only 62 feet, while Lake Kissimmee was about 58 feet above sea level. It was downhill all the way to the Atlantic and the Gulf of Mexico. Reclamation of swampland, drainage projects and canal building caused the water level to drop dramatically – in some places, up to thirty-six inches. Formerly surrounded by cypress stands and marshes, large sandy beaches then formed around the lakes. The land was "elevated," becoming fertile meadowlands - or hammocks. By definition, a hammock is a place of rich land with hardwood trees growing on it. These hammocks, made up of wiregrass and palmettos, provided excellent grazing for cattle and for sheep. The hammocks also proved reasonably good for raising corn.

Cattle and some agriculture were the primary sources of revenue in this hammock-dotted area of central Florida. Cattlemen had to also be farmers in order to provide a living for their families. The crops they raised were mainly sweet potatoes and corn, plus some rice and sugarcane. Some of the cattle were penned between the crop plots to provide fertilizer.[209] Fences were often built of split pine or cabbage palmetto logs. However, as Louise related, the local people in Osceola County objected to the land being fenced; they retaliated by burning the fence posts whenever possible. Barbwire was invented in 1865, but its use in America did not begin until the late nineteenth century.

A local fellow named Lawrence Silas was interviewed in 1968 about the old days. He said: "After my father died in 1902, mama sold his 2,000 head of cattle...for $18,000. That was a lot of money in 1902. Today (1968) 2,000 steers would bring over $200,000."[210]

A number of cattle companies, large and small, sprang up in the mid 1800s to mid 1900s on the grassy hammocks in remote and primitive parts of Osceola County along the "long water." The Lightsey, Lewis & Carruthers Cattle Company was one of them. Two of the men involved in the incorporation of this cattle company were apparently residents of the area: Mr. U.A. Lightsey, the Secretary-Treasurer; Dr. W.H. Lewis, a Florida banker, was the General Manager. Mr. W.C. Parson was the company president and main shareholder; he resided in McCabe, Arizona, but often traveled to Florida, as

---

[208] An unusually long spell of drought dried up Lake Okeechobee in 2007, causing monumental problems.
[209] Hetherington, 1-7.
[210] Ibid., 54.

well as to Astoria. He also owned the large Brahma Island in Lake Kissimmee. Robert Carruthers was Vice-President; he was listed on the company's letterhead as residing in Turkey Hammock.

Early settlers began building shallow-bottomed boats to navigate the long waterway. Even when the canals had been dredged, the boats had to be shallow because one could not always count on sufficient water to float any deep draft vessels. Nor were the lakes and canals very deep to begin with. In 1931, after all the dredging, the depth of the water in the lakes seems to have ranged from four to fourteen feet, depending upon which part of a lake was measured. The canals were even shallower. One of the first boat builders was Captain Clay Johnson, who was a great admirer of Mark Twain and apparently looked a bit like him. Capt. Johnson was known for his ability to "cuss with the best." He and his son, Clay Jr., ran a business ferrying people and supplies along the entire waterway, but especially along the forty-five miles between Kissimmee and Jack and Turkey Hammocks. It was young Capt. Clay Johnson, Jr. who piloted the boat taking Louise on her first visit to Dick at Jack Hammock.

Another of the early captains was Capt. Ben Hall of the *Naomi II*. He transported anything and everything. A story is told of one of his trips. "Frequently wealthy Northerners chartered his boat for a cruise. . . . [S]ome of these visitors stopped off at Bill Shiver's place, later to be called Turkey Hammock.[211] He showed them around the large tree-shaded yard, which looked out on an expanse of lush marshland. One of the visitors said, 'This would be a good place for poultry, Mr. Shiver.' To which Bill answered, 'Yes, guess it would. But you can't have a thing here for the damn chickens.'"[212] Later, when Dick and Louise lived at Turkey Hammock, they found the chickens still clucking around. Grape, Two Mile, Jack and Turkey Hammocks in Osceola County were some 45 miles from Kissimmee.

The large Sullivan and Padgett families were pioneer settlers to this area. Louise mentions the young twenty-five year old single fellow, Tip Padgett, who helped them as a day laborer. In 1890, he and at least four of his sisters attended the one-room Sunny Side School on East Lake Tohopekaliga. By 1901, Tip and his family apparently lived close to Jack Hammock.[213] The Carruthers' housekeeper, Mrs. Sullivan, and her husband, Bud, also appear in Louise's narrative of her trip to visit Dick. The Sullivans moved out of the Jack Hammock house soon after Louise's first visit there.

During the 1880s, Hamilton Disston became the largest individual landowner in the United States. He had paid only twenty-five cents an acre to the Internal Improvement Fund (I.I.F.) for four million acres located in central Florida. The purchase was made shortly after he and his associates had completed the draining and deepening that allow the Kissimmee River to flow faster into the Gulf of Mexico and the Atlantic. At thirty-seven years of age, Mr. Disston was the Philadelphia manufacturer of the famous Disston saws and tools.[214] On the front inside cover of the Polk's 1910 City Directory of Astoria, Oregon, Dick ran a half-page ad for his Astoria Hardware Company. The ad featured

---

[211] Hetherington, 18. Bill Shiver was the owner of a large herd of cattle at Turkey Hammock in the 1870s.
[212] Ibid., 58.
[213] Ibid., 46, 50.
[214] Hetherington, 5.

Disston goods. While working out of Jensen, Florida in 1904, might Dick have been a traveling salesman for the Disston Company?

Louise began her ten-day trip to Jack Hammock to visit Dick on Tuesday, January 21, 1902. She had little idea what she might encounter in the Lake Kissimmee wilds, but she was eager to see it and packed her telescoping bag with some clothes and her camera. After her return to Kissimmee, she and Dick moved into a house in the city before the middle of February. It wasn't until she was settled, and Dick had returned to the ranch, that she finally began to write her parents about her trip to Jack Hammock. Before the end of February, she sent her family in Astoria the first of two long "Chapters" about her adventures. She also wrote about some of their neighbors on Jack Hammock; although they were few and far between, Louise did meet some of them.

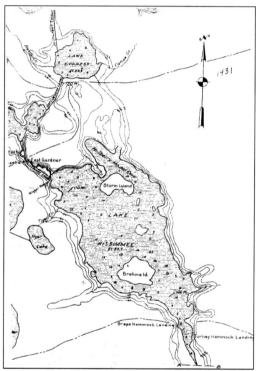

A portion of a 1931 Lake Kissimmee map, courtesy of Dr. Tana M. Porter, Research Librarian, Orange County Regional History Center, Orlando, Florida. Kissimmee and Lake Tohopekaliga are to the north of Lake Cypress. Grape and Turkey Hammocks are identified at the south end of Lake Kissimmee, about forty-five miles from the city of Kissimmee. The notation "100 mi," almost at the south end of the lake, seems to refer to the estimated distance southwest to Palm Beach via Lake Okeechobee.

Kissimmee Feb 29   [1902]

Well dear folks –

Here we are <u>moved</u> and <u>settled</u> but I'll write you all about the house next time. For now I want to tell you of my trip to the ranch. But first let me tell you I got your nice letter today. Mama, how small the family gets (Hat, stay by the ship). Expect Will will have a fine time in S.F. Any way he can show off all those fine clothes. What a cold spell you have had etc.

Tuesday the 21st [of January] it was that I started for the ranch. Dick had gone the week before. When I got down to the boat that AM I found the regular boat was not going until next day and was going to take a party of tourists through to the Gulf, but Capt Johnsons son [Clay Johnson, Jr.] was going down with his little str. They tried to persuade me to wait until the next day as there was a strong wind and it would make us late in getting down that day & etc. But I knew Dick would be waiting for me even if the boat didn't get along until midnight, so I would go. There were about fifteen men on board and to my relief one other woman. Well, the wind was strong, and kept getting stronger. These boats are flat bottomed, draw 15 inches of water and push a big barge of freight ahead. These lakes are big and so shallow they get choppy and the people here think it dreadfully rough, but I wasn't a bit afraid. Just as the Capt. was making for the canal that leads to another lake such a squall struck us. My how the wind blew and it got dark as night. Then down came the rain and in the midst of it one side of the barge broke loose and the Capt. couldn't manage the Str. at all, but fortunately the wind blew us right up against a little jetty that runs out at the mouth of the canal and we tied up there. The Capt. - a young fellow about 25 - said he never saw the lake like that before and he wouldn't go any further untill the storm was over. Every one was so excited. I told them about the Columbia and just wished they could see one of our storms once. We had made ten miles in five hours and I could see a blue print of Dick sitting on the bank all night waiting for the boat - and a few more gray hairs cropping out from worry. The woman, a Mrs Tatman, proved to be very nice. She was going to Grape Hammock, about 15 miles this side of where I was going. We were each glad the other was there for the boat only had one big cabbin with cots in it they made up at night, and we were wondering what we would do when a lul [lull] came and we got into the canal where it was very smooth (it was four miles long). She and I went up into the pilot house and most of the men took their guns out and sat on the front of the barge. The sun came out and it was so pretty. It made me mad tho to have them kill ducks just for the fun of it when they couldn't stop to pick them up.

Well, we got to the next lake [Lake Cypress] and found it quite smooth. It is only 2 1/2 miles where we had to cross and we got over O.K. Then into another canal about three miles long, then a lake again [Lake Hotchinehe]. The Capt. was telling me he would try to get there that night as it was full moon and I was happy and enjoying it all and Oh, such a beautiful sun set and every thing was lovely. But do you know, the minute the sun was down, up came the wind again and it was all we could do to make the next canal. But fortunately we did and Mrs Tatmans place was at the end of that canal, so he said well I'll get you there and tie up for the night, so he did and she took me in and was a mother to me, just as kind and good as could be. I'll show you the place some day. The house is near the water - just a big rough country house, but they made me feel at home. I had a box of candy I [had] made to treat them with. Capt Johnson said he would call me at day light and he did. It was a perfect morning and for a few miles we went along a narrow winding river and then out into lake Kissimmee. It is sixteen miles wide where we cross to go to Jack Hammock, and when we got well out from shore the wind came up again and tossed us around, and the Capt said he would have to hug the shore and take me down to Turkey Hammock five miles below Jack [Hammock]. Well, I didnt know what I would do if left there or how I would get back to Dick, but he said he would get a team and take me back & etc. But I stayed right in the pilot house with him and urged him on so he went in around Bramer Island [Brahma Island], that beautifull big island Mr Parson owns, and then I declared the wind had gone down and got him to take me acrost. I told him he would be my friend forever, & etc. The men passengers all stayed down in the engine room and I tell you, the little boat danced a jig. I would describe the boat only I expect you to see it some day soon. It was a great old trip and wasn't I glad to see Dick. Poor old fellow, he had hardly slept a wink the night before, listening for the boat and thinking it might come. There is no landing so he had to wade out and carry me ashore in his arms, and unload the provisions & feed & my telescope, & etc. Then he put me on the horse and he walked along side and waded the slough. That is why it is so bad at Jack Hammock - you cant walk to the house with dry feet. Well, afterwards we laughed to think what a time I had had getting to him, but I tell you, I had a kind of lonesome feeling when we tied up that night in a strange land. The moon light shining through those great oaks all hung with moss was so weird - and a house full of strange people, but I liked them.

Well, lets see. I was up on the horse astride with Dick walking beside me and so I landed at Jack Hammock and I wouldn't mind it one bit to live here a long time - it is so pretty - at least we could make it so - there is a space of about 2 blocks covered with oaks and palms (16 big ones like the one in Kerckhoffs old yard). The house is in the middle. This is a plan of it.

The Jack Hammock house was situated close to one of the numerous lakes – Lake Kissimmee, which is just off of the upper right-hand corner of Louise's drawing. The house is simple, but suffices. Her rough sketch of the house plan shows a bedroom for Mr. and Mrs. Sullivan on the left; a bedroom on the right and a sitting room with a fireplace for Mr. C. (Robert Carruthers).[215] Below is the smaller bedroom for Dick and Louise - "our room." Louise drew in the beds. The smaller house, connected by a breezeway, contains the kitchen and dining area with a stove, worktable and cupboard. A bench and four chairs flank the large dining table. Louise indicates on the drawing that she and Dick sat in the two chairs to the right of the table. The outbuildings include a barn and a woodshed; there is also a well on the property. She does not indicate to her parents where "the necessary" was located.

---

[215] Apparently Harriet Carruthers rarely visited the house site on Jack Hammock during these months.

Louise continues her "Chapter One" letter:

If we lived there we would make it over or tear it down, but if we live on the ranch, it will probably be Turkey Hammock. I did not go down there. Well, Dick left me at the house and went on a ways to get a man to go down and haul our stuff up before the cows got into it. Pretty soon he came with a Mr Smith (strange names down here) with a yoke of oxen. I jumped on with him and Dick rode the horse. We both wished for a camera. I would give a good deal to send you the picture we made coming back. I was on top of a bale, trying to keep the other bundles from rolling off. Mr Smith beating his oxen and shouting some kind of Dago to them. I couldn't understand a word, but they seemed to know what he ment. And to think in my excitement of getting there at last and seeing Dick I forgot my beefsteak. I knew they had been living on bacon so I had four fine steaks with me and left them on the boat. On the way to the house I said "Dick we will have steak for dinner," and he said "Oh wont it be good," and then I remembered.

The next A.M. we were all up at daylight, had breakfast and started off to work. I went along. We drove about three miles (I wore Dicks heavy overcoat it was such a chilly A.M.). They were working near such a lovely little oak grove. They built a little fire for me and then started setting posts. At noon we fryed bacon & eggs, warmed a can of beans and made tea. In the afternoon they worked through a pond and my but it is hard work to <u>tote</u> (as they say here) those heavy posts through that marsh, - full of snakes, too. I couldn't follow them there so sat in the sun and read my book. They got through just at sun set (about five) and then had that drive home all in their wet clothes. My teeth chattered for them. I opened a can of tomato soup as soon as we reached the house and poured boiling water in it – and my how good it tasted and how it warmed us up.

Mrs Sullivan, the housekeeper, is the dirtiest, laziest mortal, has a two year old girl, or pig rather, so the next day I didn't go out but tryed to tidy things up at the house and did some cooking. Gave them a nice dinner that night. They are Bud, Mrs S's husband; the kid; Tip Paget; Mr. C- [Robert Carruthers]; Dick and I. But the next day I went out, and of the ten days down there, I was with them all but three and I think it was good for me to be out-of-doors from sun rise to sun set. Yes, now I know you wont believe it, but I ate breakfast every A.M. at <u>six</u> !

Snakes!! I saw Tip kill one with 13 rattles on it. That night Dick skinned it by the light of a little bonfire. Ugh! It makes me shudder now. They look <u>awfull</u> with the skin off and still wiggle. It was over six feet long and we had to dig such a big hole for it – to burry it. Dick was sick that night and couldn't sleep – do you wonder. The next day they killed another 13 rattled one but Dick let one of the men skin it. We brought home three to be tanned. I don't remember how many they all killed. You see they build fires to clear the palmetto from the fence line and that makes the snakes come out – do you wonder. I worry now when Dick is down there and I am up here. They have every remedy with them, but they say there is <u>no</u> cure for one of those big fellows – only they <u>wont</u> bite unless you hurt them and make them mad.

Well when Sunday came, Mrs S. went to spend the day with a neighbor and you would have laughed to have seen Dick and I <u>scrub</u> while every one was away. I had made bread and at noon had a fine batch of little biscuits and such a feast as we did have – we just sat and smacked our lips over it. Dick says I am a <u>fine</u> cook. I made a cake with orange marmalade for filling. Try it, it is fine. Well, one day was about like another with Mr. C- growling to break the monotony (he is the <u>crossest</u> thing but don't say I told you). One warm night when I hadn't many covers over me, a mouse – yes, a real live one – ran right over me just as I was dropping off to sleep. Maby you think I didnt jump and grab Dick and nearly scare the wits out of him.

The next Saturday A.M. we started to drive home [to Kissimmee] - Mr C-, Tip, Dick & I. I wish I could describe the country well – it is all prairie with here and there a bunch of palms – some times two or three, some times thirty – and one place has a hundred or more – then oak trees and palmettos, and then the pine woods. It is a pretty drive, but we had a heavy load for one horse & went slow. At about three we reached Tips house and they wanted us to stay there of the night – and that was the most interesting part of the whole trip. If I could only tell it as it really was. That family would fill a story book if one only knew how to write it. Any way, they filled the house for there were nine of them there – three more married & away, one dead. They live in a log house of two rooms with <u>places</u> <u>for</u> doors and windows. Had another log hut where they cook and eat. The old lady, bare footed, came out to the gate as we drove up. Her old man was away she said. We had met him about noon driving a <u>sorry looking</u> horse. Every thing is sorry looking here.

Well here it is, the last page of my tablet and I guess it will fill the envelope, so I will call it Chapter One and send it off. It has rained all day and Dick off down on the ranch, living in a tent this time so as to save the long ride out to the fence. I wish it was done and he was here.

Love to all and kisses from

Louise

Undated.

Chapter Two!

Well, again I spent the night fourty miles from nowhere but this time "my old man" was with me, and we were well entertained. Mrs Paget called each one of those children up and had them shake hands and say "how de do" to the lady. Then she sent one to the well for water for us to wash in, another for wood, some to get supper ready for us, and she kept them all busy while she smoked her pipe and talked to us. She asked me if I didn't smoke and said well, she didn't either when she was young. Told us how she and her old man and the children had made the lumber and built every bit of the house themselves (guess they didn't know how to make doors and windows for they had none). Said she reckoned we were hungry so about five, supper was ready. The children stood around and waited for us to eat. The chickens were laying 'right smart' so we had eggs and some kind of greens, bacon, and sweet potatoes (Fla. life preservers, they call them). The tea, sugar, bread, and a can of beans we donated to the feast. They had one old lamp with <u>no</u> <u>chimney</u> – stood in middle of the table and you can imagine how it smelt.

After the meal we went out on the piazza and they built a fire in front as they have no stove or fire place. It was very cheerfull and gave us light as well as heat. Then the old lady began to tell us how a few days before she and her old man and the two youngest drove to town to buy a new kitchen stove and trade 3 doz. eggs for calico. On their way there some one told them there was a big show in a tent, and of course they wouldn't miss that. I am glad they didn't for it was as good as any circus to hear her tell about it. Beyond my pen to repeat it. Dick kept pinching me and asking her questions to lead her on until I thought I would have a spasm. She warnt going to pay for the children if she could help it, so she got in the middle of the biggest crowd and pushed them in with out the man seeing them, but she got so excited when they came to next and biggest tent that she forgot to wait for a crowd but hurried first to get a good seat and got sent back to buy childrens tickets. She went back to the first man and said 'look here, you sold me a ticket and that man wont let me in.' After quite a talk he said go back and tell him I say you are to go in because you haven't any more money. Then her old man thought he would be smart and buy a blue or 1/2 ticket for himself but you cant fool them she says and he got sent back for a red one.

That circus was the event of their lives. She described Punch and Judy to us – didn't know what it was, little folks with masks on she thought. There was a man who did tricks she <u>loved</u> – it was the most wonderfull thing she ever saw, it sure was.

She only stoped talking to light her pipe. The children had been taking singing lessons and could sing every note in the book, she said, so of course we asked them to sing for us and they got out the hymn book and sang it most through. Sang real well too. Then it was bed time. There were three beds in one room for the 9 Pagets & two in the other room for the 3 Carruthers. Being company, they gave me <u>the</u> lamp, but I had two candles in my telescope, so took them out and lit one for myself and handed the other to one of the girls standing near me. She said 'Oh, isn't it <u>smooth</u> and pretty,' just as if she had never seen one before. I gave them some papers and a magazine I had. The papers I handed to one of the girls and the magazine full of pictures to the mother. She said it is right smart pictures – I am glad you gave it to me and the ones with reading to the girls cause they can read and I cant. Poor souls, they hung around me so and when I started to undress and took down my hair, the old lady smoothed it with her hand and said 'Oh, it was so soft and lovely.' One little girl said isn't she a pretty lady, mama, and they paid me so many compliments innocently and as if they meant them that it embarrassed me. We were up at day light and they really hated to have us go. <u>All</u> shook hands, begging us to come again and promised to come and see me when they came to town.

We saw plenty of game as we drove along. By the time we got home Dick had killed enough (with his cherished gun) to send Mr Slater some, and we had a quail dinner. Dick and I both broke out in hives from riding in the sun and wind I guess, but before we reached home the sun disappeared, and while we were still five miles away, down came the rain in torrents. Oh, it can rain here as well as in Oregon and we did get a wetting. I had Dicks overcoat on so faired better than the rest but we made a funny sight and took the back streets when we reached town [Kissimmee]. Poor Mother C- had been dreadfully lonesome with us all away and was right glad to see us. We were home by 10 a.m.

Sunday in the P.M. we went to look at the new house we were to move into and were delighted with the change. Poor Dick didn't get much rest this trip home for it is awfull to move as you know and he did work so hard to get us settled before they started back to the ranch Wednesday at noon. This time he didn't think he would come up for two weeks or more and I often wonder, Mama, how you ever stood it to let Papa go and leave you so long. I don't know how I am going to stand it for two weeks without Dick and I get home sick. In last night I dreamed I was home and could see you all so plainly. I sent a bundle of magazines, old neck ribbons, belt, odds & ends and a jar of orange marmalade back by Dick to the Pagets.

Next time I'll send a diagram of <u>this</u> house and my room. We will get a film and take some pictures. We would have long ago only we have to send away for films and didn't know where.

Mrs C- had another big tin box of candy from Mr Parson - sent way from S. F. and three lovely pairs of gloves - white, gray & tan - rolled in a napkin she put in the lunch box she put up for him they day he left. It pays doesnt it. Well, this is a good long letter but not nearly so interesting as I wish I could have made it. I'll add a line to Hat - just got her letter. With loads of love to all, will close this -

from

Louise

Dick, Louise and her father-in-law returned to Kissimmee by horses and wagons. They took an overland route that evidently required them to ford several creeks. It appears to have taken them a good two days time to cover the forty-plus miles. Louise and Dick then moved into their new home in Kissimmee before Dick returned to the ranch once again.

The area was remote and primitive. After Louise had visited the men at Jack Hammock in January, Dick, his father and Tod "batched it." They pushed ahead building the fence around the big 40,000-acre cattle ranch with the help of a couple of other men and a young local lad, Tip Padget. It was hard work tending the cattle and building the fence, especially when local people, who were against any fencing of the land, would tear parts of the fence down and the men would have to rebuild it. When convenient, Tip, or someone else from the "outback" hammocks, usually took the mail by boat to Kissimmee to be mailed out from the city's post office. Delivery of letters, even to Louise in Kissimmee, could take as much as a week to reach her. A hand-carried letter delivered to her would have been much faster. Supplies such as food, fencing posts, wire and tools – everything - had to be brought in by boat from Kissimmee and/or hauled by horse-drawn wagons over the hammocks and through the creeks. Robert, Dick and Tod would take turns returning to Kissimmee for supplies. The men often slept aboard the boat used to transport the supplies. Dick did try to return for a short visit with Louise in Kissimmee every two weeks or so.

Mailing date: Feb 14 1902 11 PM Kissimmee, Fla
Addressed to: Mrs Richard Carruthers
      Kissimmee, Fla.

Two Mile Hammock

Feby 11 - 1902

Dear Louise -   Same as of old.

First letter I guess I ever really wrote my wife, so a short one as Bud who has just been paid off - having left us - is going to town and mark - send any word to Turkey Hammock. More about Bud when I see you - they did not like the change I guess. Well, I hope you are well and strong. After so much moving we are fixed fine and everything lovely. Going about 1/2 a mile a day. Well I have to close. Love & xx to you and lots of them *Love to all*

                       Your husband

But maybe I don't miss you miss.   *Dick*

Grape Hammock
Feby 26 - 10 PM

Dear Wife –

We are within a mile of Turkey Hammock and I will say good night to you before I turn in on my heading. I am afraid I will sleep very poorly tonight, and as I have spent quite a day, have had good chances to think on one dear old girl and only one. I wrote a letter to Chas and a short one to Mick, but the "Little old Boat" shook so, that I did not do much. We are unloading at Grape and go over to Turkey to lay over night. I stay aboard tonight. Just whistled to let go. I waved to you a long time this AM but do not believe you saw me. I wish I had let you come to the dock with me, but it would only prolong the parting very few minutes.

Well I must close as there is little news except the same old news of how much I love you and that you know pretty well and I am glad you do. Be good and the time will soon pass until I am home. Don't, above all things, worry. With love & a good hug, some more love, then more & more, more on top of that and then guess a little more. Take more if you can stand it and remember that there is more in store for you if you want more and I know, at least think you want more than that. Well take more & xxxxxx –

Dick

The family crest Dick had designed and enclosed in this letter has been lost.

March 1 – 1902   Place - according to crest

Dear Little Old Wife –

I am in hopes to be home to celebrate the 14th of this month. We are doing fine. Will go in to Jack H- Tuesday night after work. Put up nearly 1 mile of fence yesterday. The only boss is kept busy hauling the wire as we put it up about as fast as he can get it to us. That gives me a chance & to think my work showed up yesterday. We now have a cook from Grape H. The boy I got for marker is a good one, fine, does his work good. The old man is a little to windy. The other two are fair - going as we are we ought to get all done in two weeks. The rain drove all out last night, but we with the cots were above it.

How do you like thunder by now? Did you ever hear anything from my Hat? Had good pan cakes for breakfast this morn. Guess who made them. Today we will have soup, cabbage, "Palmentto" Beans, Tea, Cookies & & & O yes! Dried apples with cinnamon and allspice. After "Table" I will have an old Virginia - cigar. The rest will take pond water & chew tobacco the regulation style. Tip will, I am sure, entertain us during the courses by an act upon his hollow tooth, which [is] not up to the doings of a fine band at the greatest of all social functions.

Dinner is quite the thing, that is novelty, as there is quite a number of dinners where they do not do this.

In front of us every thing is out airing from last nights wetness. If we could of got the tooth [of Tip's] out there, it would have been good to have had it dried up.

Mr Bryan is now giving instructions on cooking. Interesting. My comb is here alright. Will use it in a day or two. Have used my tooth brush and Pearline every day. Pearline on my hands. Another cook book being recited by Mr B- . I'll bet he is a good cook, but he never cooks.

Have you spent all that $1. I gave you. Dried apples should be simmered, not boiled, Mr. C. This statement has just been seen, agreed to by Bryan and I will swear he never looked in the cook book. How do you like the coat without arms. It would be fine for the Shields, wouldn't it. Might make it again. Still have candy left. Well must cook soup. Beans and Art of cooking – Bryan. Will write more after "Table" and make coat of arms. Bryan's [coat-of-arms] is I think a Biscuit or a Soda cracker, see. Will send love on some other sheet. Sorry I can not send it on the main sheet of the Jessie[216] you have in your drawing room. It would hardly hold it, but will do the best I can..

Had dinner. A swell affair. Now I don't know how I am ever going to get this letter up – some one was going to Grape H- for some eggs, but it is too windy for the ferry man, so my hopes that this would go is over. Perhaps I'll get a chance soon. Well as news are scarce, Louise, my dear Little old one, I am going to add lots & lots of love and XXX and finish this later. Love and lots of etc is sent from Two Mile & you are the only one who can know just how much that is, and you well know, don't you, with lots & lots more of it than you can use.

Dick

Well a streak of good luck. Tip is leaving and carries this letter. If it was not for some one leaving, your mail from here would be slow. Tip, I think, is tired of a mile a day. That is 12 miles of walking - besides a long one to camp, three to work, & two and a half back, but I am glad it is going that way. As with out any mishaps, should be done in ten days, then start for a visit with dear old wifey.

My pen is giving out, so I must save it. Moved in to Jack Hammock to day & just as we got in Bud & wife drove up with two boys. Were going to stay I guess, but went over to Howells. They have not taken any of their stuff yet, but are going to tomorrow.

One sheet left so must close with lots of love on the remaining sheet. Will make seal on last page with lead pencil. Now don't look for me on any certain day as we depend on good weather, but two weeks I am sure at the most. Now I am sending by this lots & lots of love. Some for Mama & loads for Lassie - lots of it Dearest and you know how I would like to see you.

With love & XXX XXXXX   Dick

---

[216] Dick refers to the Jessie, the yacht-pilot boat his family had owned in Astoria and lost in Alaska.

Addressed to: Mr Richard E. Carruthers
Turkey Hammock, Fla
c/o Capt. Johnson

day after Easter 1902   [March 31]
Monday

Dearest boy –

We have just come back from the place you and I went that Sunday – had such a nice boat ride – Tip, your Ma & I. Tip can make the boat go but you would hardly call it rowing. Any way we got there and back and had a good time. Yesterday was a rainy Easter day and I knew you old dear were fussing around the house trying to make it more comfortable so I could be there with you next time. I will be there <u>sure</u> if I sleep on the hard side of a board. I saw Capt. Johnson; he said you got down about 4-30 and no one came to meet you. I was glad to get your letter and hoped they would meet you so you wouldn't have to wade to get to the house. Oh Dick, do come home and get me. I couldn't stand it another week with out you. I want you so much, but I am feeling pretty well, remarkably so considering the Nux worked like a charm. I am now troubled with the opposite complaint now.

I had a letter from Hat today and four bundles of papers came for you. Nothing special, and as I expect you will be on your way home when you get this I won't send them. Your Ma says to tell you & your Dad that she had letters from Walter & Zoe saying Grace, Carleton and all were home. Carleton [Allen] quite sick with a bad cold.

Last week the boat got here Friday night but Capt. J. said they wouldn't get back til Saturday this time. They had so much freight. I will try and be patient, only <u>do come</u> and don't leave me again. I had such wild dreams last night and woke up so frightened and my how I wished you were with me. I wont know which boat you are on, so probably wont be down to meet you, but will be watching and waiting, so do some sprinting and prepair to be smothered with kisses.

It has been a <u>perfect day</u> – so cool this a.m. I washed my hair. Yesterday I had a tubbing – my what a clean wife you have and how she does love her old boy Dick – he is such a good dear fellow. Well all the rest will keep til you get home. Don't worry about me – I am getting along fine.

> *Good night – it is to dark to write more. With loads and tons of love and kisses from your loving wife*

> *Louise*

XXXXXOOOOO which kind do you like the best XXXOOOXOOXOX
Hope you haven't wanted the check book, or did you mean to leave it here?

> *L.*

322

The envelope enclosing the following letter, written on Mr. H Dieffenbach's Hotel Kissimmee stationery, was addressed to Dick at Turkey Hammock. It has the initials "RR" in the upper left corner indicating Robert Rex (*aka* "Tod") Carruthers, Dick's youngest brother. No signature appeared at the end of the note. Tod usually was with Dick and Robert at the Turkey Hammock cattle ranch area, but this is sent from Kissimmee where he was picking up supplies. Dick's mother, Harriet, was now living at the ranch with her husband and two of their sons.

I will give Thomas the $5 to bring to you

Kissimmee, Fla. 20 - 1902 [probably April 20]

Tom got a little to much in him, and I saw that the things were put in the wagon and drove him up to Ghrames. I told Ghrames to feed him well and water him.

I will get up before Tom starts in the morning and will give him the mail as mama's letter for timber is not amongst it. Tell mama I opened the Wanamaker letter.[217]

I asked Lee about Tom and he says that he thinks he will be all right in the morning – I was going to tell him to go the pine road because the creek is so deep and guess I will if he is verry drunk because I am afraid of that creek on your side of the scrub place as it is verry deep.

But Lee says that he knows that he is responsible for Major [a horse] *and will behave himself.*

[No signature]

Louise's sister Harriet sent her sister a letter, but there is no salutation and evidently at least one page is missing. A quick note dated June 12, 1902, is attached at the end. Word is getting around that Louise is "with child." She probably became pregnant in early March 1902. The due date for her and Dick's child was early December.

I wrote Grace Shilling to come down for last night but some one was giving a Tally-Ho party for her so she couldn't. She goes home next week so I may not see her after all – Had a nice letter from Fan and a dandy *picture of her to day – the first good picture she ever had (its taken in a black lace dress, low neck). She said you seemed so happy she thought she would try to fall in love but found it up hill work – doesn't that sound like Fan –*

I am printing some blue prints to send you taken the Sunday we went to the Scotch bloom place.[218]

---

[217] Wanamaker's was an excellent and well-known department store in New York and San Francisco.

[218] Scotch Broom grows vigorously along Oregon's coast. Its deep green foliage contrasts strikingly with the lemon yellow blooms. For a number of years, beginning in 1900, a "Festival of the Scotch Broom" was held every June. People from all over the Northwest toured the "avenues of beauty" formed by the broom along both sides of the highways. Scotch Broom is now considered a noxious weed because it reseeds so readily. Eradication efforts have succeeded in many places. It is impressively lovely in the places it still grows.

Forgot to tell you Lynn was down with the Traveling Man. His <u>new</u> girl Cora Lang was here. Sat with them going to the beach. My but he's struck. She's a bright little thing but not as pretty as I thought she was when I saw her last summer. Ina Barker was with them – she wanted to know all about you.

Funny thing, Nelly told me last week she heard you were going to have a baby before long. She wouldn't say who told her but it is funny how some people know so much.

I must write to Fan now so good bye. Give Dick lots of love and tell him I say he's the finest brother-in-law that ever was. Guess you must want to make that lace now.

Yes. I hope it's a boy but then you couldn't name it Harriet. So either will suit me.

With loads of love. –

Harriet

June 12th

The blue prints are not dry yet so will send them next time.

Made me a cute morning dress this week – pink & green check – made about like yours only elbow sleeve which are fine to work in. Will send a sample of a shirt waist I made yesterday.

In November, Harriet Tallant traveled from Astoria to Kissimmee to be with her sister during the latter part of Louise's pregnancy and accompanied her to Orlando a few weeks prior to the birth. Dick and Harriet were with Louise when Richard Tallant Carruthers was born on Tuesday, December 2, 1902, in the Orlando Hospital. He weighed 8 pounds, as recorded in the little "Our Baby's History," a gift from "Aunty Grace" Allen.[219] The attending physician was Dr. W.C. Phearsons; Miss Dora Holden was Louise's nurse. The baby's parents and grandparents called him "Dickie" – so everyone else did also. Louise likely stayed in the Orlando hospital for about two weeks, as was customary then. Her mother-in-law was staying at the ranch with Robert, but she had a house in Orlando in which Louise, Dick and Dickie – and Hat – stayed for another few weeks. They then moved south to their house in Kissimmee. Dickie was the first of two sons born to Dick and Louise. Eben Hunter Carruthers would be born in Astoria on August 22, 1904.

Dear Louise –

If this letter isn't a proper congratulatory letter, its all Henrietta's fault. First she stole my ink, and then kindly gave me permission to read what she had written, so that I might have a chance to be original. Now how can I be original and say what I want to! I want to tell you how <u>very</u> glad I am, how I wish you all happiness. What a happy man I think Mr. Carruthers is. How glad every-body must be. How my only regret is the distance you are to be from us, and

---

[219] One of the many fine gifts "Dickie" received was a pair of beaded Indian moccasins Mr. Parson sent to him from Phoenix.

now she's "done gone said it all" – and I feel like our little niece Ruth, whom we call "little echo," because she repeats word for word every-thing she hears.

However, joking aside. I do wish you all joy and blessing and I'm sure you cant get tired of hearing the same good wishes over and over, when you know they come from the heart.

Lovingly yours –

Grace C. Eliot

While visiting in Hood River, Oregon, Grace Eliot, one of Dr. T.L. Eliot's daughters, penned the above note to Louise with congratulations on the birth of "Dickie." Enclosed in the same envelope, that showed a Portland postmark of December 12, 1902, is another short note - also from Grace

Mailing date: Dec 12 1902 8.30 AM   Portland, Oregon
Via Chicago Dec 15.   Rec'd in Orlando on Dec 17.

Dear Louise –

Many Many congratulations to the happy mother. Your mother sent me the "Astorian" with the two announcements of yours and Katies happiness. How lovely that you should have your babies so near together. I suppose your letters now will be one string of baby talk.

How good it must be for you to have Hattie with you. I suppose she worships at the baby's shrine just as I saw Rachel Joseph worshipping Mary Durham's baby. Give her my love - and give a kiss to the baby for me. I send two little towels for the youngster to bathe with on Christmas!   Merry Xmas to you all.

Lovingly

Grace Eliot

Louise's mother-in-law, Harriet, sent her a letter from Turkey Hammock. The letter had to travel via Pechom, Florida, to Kissimmee on the seventeenth and on to Orlando. It took all of five days, not reaching Louise until the eighteenth.

Turkey Hammock   Dec 13 / 1902

My Dear Little Daughter –

What a horrid time you did have and no mother there – I feel as though I might have helped you bear it if I could have been there. Thank the good Father you are safely over and the dear baby here. Isn't it funny how they are loved the minute they come. Don't you try to come until you have been up and around and real strong – for you know how far from help we are here, so be sure you are well. It is a long chilly trip and our houses are so punk. Dick did not say who baby looks like or if he has hair, dark eyes or blue, and you know I want to know.

I had Dr Gildersleeve do my shopping for the girls [Grace C. Allen and Zoe C. Ridehalgh] in New York so that's off my mind. I'm sending them chafing dishes – do you think they will be *pleased. Told him if he had any money left to put in something else and a doll apiece for Mignon and Baby [Zoe Allen]. I am sending for a book for Chap [Ridehalgh]. Gus wanted a magazine. I bought a <u>star</u> raizor for Papa so I only want Dick to send me a pr. of Xmas suspenders – white or pale blue – Gulats or some nice kind of Xmassy. I sent Dick some money for his and your Xmas present and if he needs more he must write so he will get it on time for the boats are so crazy – for sickness is the chrysalis that makes the money fly.*

Ohaz [?] has not come yet – look for it on this stmr. A little man brought 80 cows and calves yesterday but they were so poor I couldn't buy them. Gus wrote for prices on a car load of corn. If I have to keep it "the money" until spring I might just as well speculate in <u>corn</u>. Baby's nearly two weeks old and I expect you are just wild to be <u>up</u> and around so you can <u>bathe</u> him. I wonder how you will get <u>on</u>? Did Dick write <u>Marge</u>? She will have to wait for the <u>boys'</u> old hats now. So glad you can nurse the baby – he will be so much happier with his own <u>warm dinner</u>. I always felt sorry for a baby with a bottle.

Samy has not shown up to get his baggage yet – they say he is an awfull jug in K-[Kissemmee]. He was so sassy to Papa. Papa goes tomorrow or next day to K- and will post this. The boat is at Grape Hammock and will keep our mail of <u>course</u> until morning. I'll not close this until tomorrow, so good night dear – kiss the Baby for

Gran.

Robert Rex "Tod" Carruthers

Attached to the letter from Dick's mother is a note evidently written by Tod.

Saturday 13 –

[Capt.] Johnson lost one roll of poultry netting over board and Papa's taking it out on us. I think he is getting ready to go in the wagons to K- speechless with rage. We are having a <u>lovely</u> time. Got Dick's note and this is for <u>him.</u>

Yours in the <u>depths</u>

with love to <u>you all</u>

Chapter Thirteen

Will Tallant's crew of seiners at work and relaxing on the company's scow.

Astoria, Oregon, Jan 11th 1903

My dear Sister –

    I suppose you have given up all idea of ever getting a letter from me. I would like to write you more often, but writing is out of my line altogether. I am always glad to hear from you and that you are so well satisfied with your new life.

    I do not know of any news in the Social line to write you as I do not attend to any of the parties more than when you were here.

    I know Mama keeps you posted in all that happens, both in business, and socially. I expect to be very busy from now on in the cannery - we are building a very nice plant - I think when finished, the best on the river. It is hard to say, as yet, what success it will be, we know it is a *very hard business to make much money in but it is the only business either Papa or I know any thing about and we had to do something.*

Papa I think is looking very well indeed. The two years rest he has now had has done him lots of good, and he is feeling very happy to be in the cannery business again. If mama could only get over the . . .

No further page(s) found.

Louise's older brother Will wrote to her in Kissimmee where she remained until Dickie was old enough to safely be taken to the ranch later in January. Louise was certainly "well satisfied with her new life" at the time she and Dickie moved out to the Turkey Hammock house to be with Dick. They settled in nicely, fixing it up in a cozy and comfortable way. Dick even hung his collection of beer steins on a pole in their living room.

At Turkey Hammock

Robert Carruthers

Robert standing on left; Dick holds calf.
Tod is probably with his back to camera.

328

(Original image a cyanotype)

(Original image a cyanotype)

Louise and Dickie with Harriet C. in buggy.
(Original image a cyanotype)

Robert, Tod and Dick
(Original image a cyanotype)

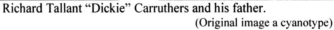
Richard Tallant "Dickie" Carruthers and his father.
(Original image a cyanotype)

In later life Louise often recalled a terrifying incident that occurred at Turkey Hammock. She went into the woodshed to replenish the supply in the house. As she turned around with a load of wood in her arms, she saw a huge rattler lying across the doorway to the shed. It was sunning itself. In his bed inside the house, young Dickie had begun to fuss. She had to return to the house. Her screams did not faze the huge reptile. She felt desperate. Trying to keep her composure, she began to throw pieces of wood at the snake. At first, the thick, long serpent turned its head toward her, but did not move. She threw more and more pieces of wood at it. Finally, it began to slither ever so slowly away from the woodshed doorway. Her route to the house was clear. She ran to her crying baby. She did not want to have that kind of thing happen ever again.

Things began to change for Louise, Dick and little Dickie before mid 1903. The fencing around the cattle ranch had been completed; Dick was working with the cattle and mending fences, as well as seeking employment in Florida. He was actually quite content and happy in that environment, especially since his son Dickie, who was thriving, and his wife Louise were the "loves of his life." Dickie kept Louise busy; he was a joy to them and they were very proud of him – a bright and clever little boy. But Louise was feeling the pull of being home in Astoria, of showing her child off to her family and friends - and of being in the mild weather of northwestern Oregon.

In 1903, as the hotter late spring temperatures advanced upon central Florida once again, a decision was made – without Dick's wholehearted support. Louise and Dickie, now about six months old, would travel to Astoria by train. Dick would remain in Florida. He had clerked in Astoria's Columbia Hardware store for several years prior to their marriage, so he would continue to try to find a similar sales position in Florida – somewhere. If that were not possible within a reasonable amount of time, then he would try to find the most suitable employment possible in Astoria. He was determined to keep his family together, no matter where it might be.

Early on May 19, 1903, Louise and young Dickie began their journey "home" to Astoria from Jacksonville via St. Louis, Denver and Portland, leaving Dick, ill with a cold, to do the best he could. The train trip was not to be without problems. There was a mix-up in her sleeper accommodation reservations and heavy flooding in St. Louis[220] caused long delays in their trip. Dick especially suffered from frustration, worry and loneliness. The Missouri flooding also caused lengthy delays in the delivery of Louise's letters to him, which, in turn, caused him even more concern. Before the end of May, Louise and Dickie had eventually arrived safely in Astoria - to their and Dick's great relief. There was little Louise could do to help Dick in his search for a decent job, but she was determined to "put in the good word" – strongly – among Astoria businessmen, so they could all be together there.

None of Louise's letters to Dick during this period survived.

Mailing date: May 21 1903 2PM Jacksonville, Fla.
Received: May 27 1903 11-30P Astoria
Addressed to: Mrs R E Carruthers   [Crossed out Denver, Col]
Letter was readdressed: c/o E. W. Tallant
26 West 12th Ave.
Astoria, Ore.

Wed Eve   1903   [May 20th]

Dear Girl –

A line to say that I am lonesome already & wish that I had you back. Well, I am in to mind to write tonight. By this time you are in Denver and well I hope, & will make a good finish home. Remember the new shawl & socks, & for fear you lost the formula:

---

[220] Louise and Dickie's train was held up by the extremely heavy flooding in the entire Missouri River Basin that occurred during the latter half of May and into early June 1903. Devastation was widespread.

330

2 oz milk   16 oz water   2 oz Wellens   4 oz water

With loads of love to yourself & the dear old boy.

Will write tomorrow   Your loving husband

Dick

Mailing Date: May 21 1903 2-30PM Jacksonville, Fla
Received: May 26 1903 11-30P Astoria, Ore.
Stationery: The Aragon Jacksonville, Florida [stationery showed a blue print photo of the hotel]

Thoroughly Renovated	One-half Block from
New Electric Elevator	Post Office
Electric Lights and Bells	200 Rooms with and without
	Private Baths
Largest and Best Located	Rates, $2.00 to $3.00 a day
Hotel in the City	Spacious Sample Rooms
W. B. Gerard, Manager	

Thur.

Dear Louise

I did not sleep well any to good last night & am feeling rather lonesome. I am thinking of running up to Mobile as I am afraid there is little prospect here. But perhaps I may run on to it any time.

How did you and the babe make it the first day? Did you have much trouble warming his dinner?

I will write you a longer letter tomorrow. My cold is almost well & I feel all ok.

With loads of love to you and baby & all – remember me to everyone.

Dick

Mailing date: May 23 1903 1-30A Mobile, Ala.
Received: May 27 1903 11-30P Astoria, Ore.
Stationery: Hotel Bienville, Mobile, Alabama

22 May

Dear Old Girl –

Here I am in Mobile – cheap fare & I took advantage of it. I told W. U. [Western Union] Tel Co to repeat your message to me here from St. Louis. So far I have not received it. I can not imagine why I have not received it. I hope you sent one. How I do miss you & the baby but coming here makes it seem that I am on a trip & will soon see you. Worst of it – I wont get a letter from you until I return to Jax.

Will not have time to see the Hdw. [Hardware] Co tonight but will write you tomorrow. Your folks will think it strange you receiving a letter [from] Mobile. You will have to square it the best you can. Will write you all about this place when I see it. If I don't get in here, will get <u>back</u> to Jacksonville tomorrow.

With loads of love to your dear self & baby.

Dick

Later –

I received telegram. Trouble with ticket – no sleeper engaged, etc.

Well how did you make it? I am worried to death. Did you have to buy a new ticket? & I'll bet you didn't have enough money, but I'll get a letter Sunday in Jax that will explain. Goodness, I am scared, but you say you would stop at Denver so you must have started some way. When you get this I'll know all about it, but that don't do much good now. I feel sure you are allright and will be when you get to Denver, but the next few days will be long ones to me.

Well I guess I should have staid in Jax until I got word from you. Well I close. If you do telegraph, I'll get it here.

Love & xxxx to both you old darlings – Lassie & the babe

Dick

There are several empty envelopes addressed to Louise from various hotels in Florida – one with the mailing date of May 28, 5-AM, 1903. None of Dick's existing letters fit those hotels, cities and dates of mailing. He obviously was traveling over quite a lot of Florida, but he does not specify exactly what he is doing in these travels. Perhaps he obtained some sort of work in Jensen, located on the east coast of Florida, not far from Ft. Pierce. Dick may be sarcastic in writing *"Like my work - have an excellent boss - nothing too good for me, etc & am having a fine experience, so don't worry."* Did he mean that he is his <u>own</u> boss, thus jobless and still searching? Or did that indicate he had been hired as a traveling salesman, possibly for the Hamilton Disston Company that made the then famous Disston saws and tools? [221] He had not given up hope that Louise, with little Dickie, would rejoin him to make their home in Florida.

Mailing date: Jun 6 1903 6 PM Jacksonville. Fla
Received: Jun 11 1903 11-30P Astoria
Stationery: Aragon Hotel – Jacksonville, Fla.

Sat   5   1903   [actually was a Friday in June]

Dear Girl

I am sending your birthday present, which I hope you will like as it was a great effort on my part. Divide it up. No news for you. Have your nice letter of May 31st. With love & best wishes - "Wishes," I wish I were there to give you your 30 kisses, but I'll have them for you - am storing them up. Will write you a letter tomorrow.   Dick

---

[221] The wealthy Philadelphian, Hamilton Disston (1843-1896), known for his manufacture of fine tools - particularly saws, took a great interest in central Florida during the 1880-1890s. He supervised several major drainage projects to create a navigable water link from Kissimmee to the Gulf of Mexico (1881); built the St. Cloud and Sugar Belt Railroad from Kissimmee east to St. Cloud (1882+); and developed a huge sugar plantation and the Florida Sugar Manufacturing Company in St. Cloud (1886). At this time, Disston was the largest individual landowner in the United States. In 1901, Col. F.W. Huidekoper of New York and Gen. Charles Miller of Pennsylvania purchased the Disston estate's vast holdings for only $70,000, a fraction of their estimated value of over one million dollars. Later, Dick featured the Disston saws and tools in the ads for his Astoria Hardware store.

332

Stationery: New Almeria Hotel
            Cor. Franklin and Washington Strs
            Tampa, Fla.

Sat. Eve. 9.30   [June 5th]

Dear Old Girl –

Just to let you know that I am thinking of you & the babe.

No job so far, but as yet have asked for none. Got here to late today.

Tampa – what little I've seen – seems ok. All say businesss is good.

Will write tomorrow. With loads of love to your own dear self & lots to the boy

Dick

Mailing date: June 11 1903 Jensen, Fla.
Stationery: Al Fresco Hotel
              Down the Indian River, Center of Pineapple Belt
              Jensen, Brevard County,
              Florida.

Jensen, Fla.   June 10   1903

Dear Girl –

I am a little blue tonight as I expected letters from you today, but I guess they were not forwarded. Arrived here today after a 12 mile drive down the banks of the Indian River. It is grand - & pineapples - well you ought to see them. This hotel is full of buyers. Railroad men looking out for the shipments, etc. There must be 30 railroad men and a gay crowd like an excursion. Mosquitos - well I never! During our drive down, which was 12 miles through one continuous hammock - and they were awful. You can not even form an opinion, even with your try at Turkey Hammock. Tomorrow I'll surely have a letter and as I will have plenty of time of evenings will try and write you nice long letters & in return will expect some.

Like my work - have an excellent boss - nothing too good for me, etc & am having a fine experience, so don't worry.

With lots of love & Kisses for you Lassie & the boy.

Dick

Mailing date: June 12 1903 Jensen, Fla.

Jensen, Fla. June 11, 1903

Dear Wife –

A line, and a line only. Another day & no letter - it is getting tiresome, but I am hoping for several tomorrow. I wish I were with you tonight, although I am nicely located & doing well. I do hope you are well and not feeling your age. I have a good room & your photos are all the decorations - which I <u>think</u> is a plenty. Well tomorrow night I'll have letters then I'll write you a good letter. We have very good times here - the railroad drummen buy a Keg of beer twice a week for the crowd. I am not getting more than my share so don't worry. Don't you wish we were on the ranch & I had my fill on Claret and was giving you an exhibition of my singing, etc.

With a crate of love to you & the dear little fellow.

Dick

Jensen, Fla.   Sunday Eve   June 14

Dear Wife & Son –

I am a little bit blue tonight as I have not rec'd a line from you since last Sunday. I know the floods delayed my mail but can not see how the[y] do for a week. If we were not in the habit of daily letters I would not care so much, but I know you both are all well & happy as your last letter to me you had been home two days & I'll bet I get a bunch tomorrow. You will have to consider this your birthday letter full of love & kisses and wishes for lots of them.[222] Did they make a cake for you? If you were slighted, don't cry.

Every thing is lovely with me. Had a letter [from] Mama last night - all is lovely there. [Harriet was living in Turkey Hammock then.] She said she was writing you. You will see that I am about a good days ride from the ranch. I guess you have located it on the map. Wish wireless telephoning was the go. I'd spend my cash tonight in a wireless message. It is not very warm. Walked 10 miles from here to White City. Then rode in a wagon to Ft. Prince [Ft. Pierce?]. The[n] back here by train yesterday. Was tired & failed to write you. Pineapple are the real thing here and at every place I feast on them. Wish I could share with you.

With Love - loads of it to you both

Dick

Mailing date: June 16, 1903   Jenson, Fla.
Stationery: Al Fresco Hotel

Jensen, Fla. Monday 15   1903

Dear Old Girl –

A letter from you and how glad I was, but it seems you were as bad off. I have only skiped two days that I know of writing too you. I guess you know where I am & I hope you have some of my letters & the photos I was so good to send. Just as soon as they get St. Louis fixed up, we both can look for a batch. I hope you did not worry any more than I. Your letter I got this eve is dated Astoria 2nd - that makes 13 days coming. Well we will get all the delayed love later.

Am doing nicely and having a very good time considering. The work is a good study as we have so much opposition and it makes things very lively.

---

[222] Louise celebrated her twenty-eighth birthday in Astoria on June 16, 1903. Dick, Louise and their son had celebrated Dick's twenty-ninth birthday on May 8th at Kissimmee, shortly before the three of them left for Jacksonville.

I can hardly get over your not getting more letters & I hope you did not worry too much. Hope baby is better & not giving you too much worry, but if Dr Fulton says he's OK, alright. Before we were married I use to look for a letter pretty hard from you, but now that I know you & there is that other little being who is just about as good, nice, etc as his ma, it was mighty hard to have the little bum P.M. [Post Master] at Jensen shake his head. But tonight I am as happy as can be and will surely sleep well tonight. This is the third letter I have had since you arrived home. Just think of the good news that I am looking forward to. I do hope you thought out the reason re St. Louis floods, for not receiving my letters. I am writing you oftener than I thought I might and I hate for them to go astray. I hope Father is all O.K. by now – so far I have had little news about home folks, but know that I shall in those delayed letters. I am sorry to hear about Laura Wright's death. I thought she had done so well. Hurrah for budget – with a capital B. I hope the Girls are pleased with the boy, but I know they are. Well you surely will receive my delayed letters before this but I send oceans of love in this and kisses for a week in case it happens again.

With love – lots of it to you and son and again saying I am well & happy beyond any thing to night.

Your loving husband

Dick

Mailing date: June 18, 1903   Jensen
Received: Jun 20, 1903   Astoria

Jensen, Fla.   June 17, 1903

Dear Louise –

It seems strange but no letter tonight from you, but one from Zoe dated 8th mailed 10th. I guess St. Louis does us. But her letter does partly as I know you were all OK on 10th and you will have letters on the way straight to Jensen, but I hope to have the delayed ones. They will make quite a book. You will see that Zoe's came on in good time – 7 days via Jax. How is it yours of same date do not do not do so? Well, the 10th was lucky.

Left Jax 9th. Last letter I rec'd was on the 7th except one yours of June 2, I received June 15 th. This was delayed at Jax 6 days, but our man in Jax say no more there. Well, Sat. I'll get one straight.

Wasn't that awful at Hepner,[223] and is not this country doing fine in that line.

With love to you & Son from Dick

---

[223] Traveling by train, Louise and Dickie passed through Heppner, Oregon, just a matter of days before disaster hit the small town, located some 100 miles east of Portland. Without warning, in the late afternoon on Sunday, June 14, 1903, a cloudburst - a torrential rainstorm and hail - caused the collapse of the town's dam. A flash flood of a forty-foot high wall of water from the normally benign Willow Creek smashed into the town, wiping out almost the entire area, including miles of railroad tracks. One quarter of the population – some 250 persons – lost their lives in a few seconds.

Photograph of Louise and Dickie taken at the Grand Avenue house.

Jensen, Fla. June 20 1903

Dear Louise –

I received five letters from you, one from your mother, dated sometime in May. Kindly explain why I did not answer hers. This goes as soon as If I had written last night. I hardly know what to say about F & S. [Foard & Stokes]. As soon as I am through here & I will know tonight about that - I think tonight, as I go to West Palm Beach tonight to spend Sunday with my boss who lives there. I'll think over the thing & write. I really believe you would like to live in Astoria.

Well, we'll see. I had as you will know, plenty of reading last night with all those letters & know you are all OK, etc. Also had a letter from Grace. Grace & Zoe seem to think the boy pretty fine. In none of your letters have you mentioned Babe. How is he?

Well, I must catch the North train with this. I was to tired to write last night. Will write again today.

With Love to you both   XXXXX times 10

Dick

A small fragment of Dick's letter exists on the Jenson, Florida, Al Fresco Hotel stationery:

> ....*work in the hardware line. Might go across country. I would hate to leave here on one account and that is Mama. But perhaps we could do so...*

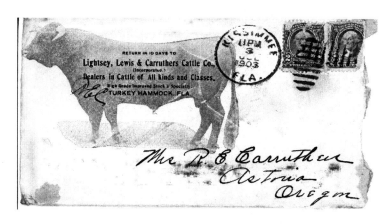

Turkey Hammock, Fla., July 1st 1903
At the Sign of the Red Bull

Dear Louise

There is a chance of the S.S. Lilly coming along tomorrow eve. Feeling that you might miss a letter I am preparing. Every thing is O.K. here except that I am building - our old kitchen is a thing of the past.

With Tod's valuable assistance, it has now in course of escalation, sawing, etc. become an addition to the little bedroom off the dining room. Mama is to use it as hers. Put a new window in it etc and it makes a good sixed room - to be concise - 19 foot long. You know about how wide. Have it all done except shingling, which we will do tomorrow. Pretty quick work & if I do say it, pretty good. It gives me something to do and will greatly add to her comforts. You would hardly know the way to our first home from here as the path is completely grown over. The sheep are all off and it gives the grass a chance. Mama has the dining room lined with cloth & it looks very nice. They have had no trouble with the fence since 1st of April. Mosquitos have sure been bad the last night or two. Corn made better than I thought for. The crowd take a bunch of Beef from here tomorrow. Well, that is about all the ranch news I know of. Mama is all OK, so is everyone.

I received your two letters – June 19th & 20 – this morning via Jensen, via Kissimmee. Am glad you and the boy keep so well, but when I am on health questions, you said you did not take your medicen regularly. You should & I hope you will from now on. It is nice to have the baby so well liked. Grace & Zoe make glowing reports of him, so he must be alright. Tell Nat not to use him as a football, but he should be able to withstand a knock or two as you of nights trained him to that.

I am sending Zoe's letter if I can find it, so you will see what she has to say about him. I often – yes, all the time, think of you & him, but from the fact that you are both well & happy helps me some in not being able to see him or you.

You say if I come there that we will be happy ever after. Well I was here & think you were too & I doubt we ever [will] spend another better year, but I think the proposition should come from F. & S. I shall have plenty too do there & want all there is in it, so do not care to write them for they might see my hand. Don't whatever you do let on that it would be o.k. with me. A hint may be given for them to try me – see if I would come, etc. You would like to <u>remain,</u> etc, <u>but</u> don't go at them too strong. To come down to the fine point I want all I can get for I'll have to earn it. See. You can't be too careful what you say, etc. We have made more money here in a year & a half than we could save on a salary. Of course, that is to be left, but you might say it is a clean gain of a thousand and is doing very well. Still I am anxious to have something steady; would go back to F. & S. if they pay me enough, as much as I hate to return to Astoria under the circumstances & that you know to be true. Well, perhaps next mail will tell the tale. If not, then maby the next, but there is no great hurry if they want me as bad as they seem too.

It is not very nice this once a week letter business is it, old girl? Of course I have no serious objections in regards to Willie being around by the baby – that is as long as he does not try to teach him to play with broken Pistols. He [Dickie] is a cracker & his means of defence shall, or should be, the knife.

In your last to me you said there was some swell dressers in town. Well don't get to far behind, but you must feel kind of dressy yourself after the ranch styles, etc. I am down to the old time easy, etc. Well, our ship will come in some day & perhaps we can come to the front.

How is your money holding out & when you need it, write as I have some in hiding. I don't want you to try & save too much, but I know you are wise as you are good & will strike the happy go between. I was thinking to day that little I had ever bought you & planning how I would make up for it some how.

Well, I am going to close for the night as the mosquito is sure driving me to bed. Will try & add a line or two tomorrow.

With a thousand XXXs for your own dear self & the dear old boy

Your loving husban

Dick

Wish you were here to break him of crying of nights. Also your letters full of news of the boy are the best I could ask for.

Dick's letter continues in pencil.

Thur   July 2   1903

There is a gentle rain so I'll write you a little more. Mama said to send her love and say that she would not write this time as I am doing so. I wonder how you will celebrate the 4th – have a good time I hope. We have not decided what we will do. Guess we will have to cut the Golf game as Gus has the clubs and the grass is too deep. Have had several thunder & rain storms, so I guess the boats will keep a coming. In case I do come to Astoria, I will over haul the boxes down to the house & mail up all that goes well. Do not think it advisable to bring any furniture as it would all get smashed up. Have one annex nearly completed and would have had it finished but for the rain.

Sorry, the boy has given so much trouble of nights. Mr Parson knows you are home & that I might go there, & so that is alright. But yet I can not see that he should do anything & I would not care to have anything said to him. Note what you say in regards to the water, fill up for you might strike a place again where it is not so good. But I hope not. How were the pictures of the house, etc, or did Willie ever print any of them for you. Get hold of the negatives & print some. Mr Alderman staid over night Wed. eve, getting even for my stop there. If you have a little change, give Grant Trullinger a small remembrance upon the event - & Osy too. Well I can see your finish[ed with] Weddings & lots of them.

Well, if I don't get another chance to write more, I'll close with loads of love to you & son – and say I am mighty proud of him if even half you say is true – and I guess I ought to believe you.

With love & XXXX from your husband (no one else has won me so far)

Dick

This is getting to be quite a book & I am afraid this will have to end it. The boat is likely to show up early tomorrow as the Capt. is trying to get to Kissimmee for the 4th. Well it wont be so long now till I commence to look for a letter from you. They seem far between.

I am going to close now for this time with lots of love & good night kisses for you dear old lassie & lots for the dear little fellow, whom I miss so much to say nothing about you.

Dick

On the back of Dick's envelope of his July third mailing, Louise apparently made a draft for a telegram to Dick:

Letters coming

offer eighty and other inducements

Letters in mail

Neck better

Louise

Harriet Hunter Carruthers had moved from the house in Kissimmee into one at Turkey Hammock, joining Robert. Dick's job (if he had one) appears to have ended, so he had returned to the ranch to help Tod fix up their parent's home on the hammock. He sent his next letter to Louise, mailing it on July 11, to be forwarded care of his sister Grace and Carleton Allen who were residing across the river in Ilwaco, Washington.

Turkey Hammock   Thursday July 9, 1903

Dear Louise –

Tuesday's boat & six letters from you. The last from you was your first direct to Kissimmee. Gladly did I settle down to them and was well entertained for the eve. The pictures were fine & the news all good, except that you had a cold – am sure that it is better by now. Have been working around the house & some very good improvements are the result of the labor – such as a sink & good drain. Mama's room all lined & matted (This is a big improvement). Place between houses floored over. Walk from there to back door; walk from back steps to gate. Yard cleaned up. We intend putting in a bath room tomorrow. Then I guess we will be nearly done. I am going to go over our stuff this week & get it in good shape, as I have about decided to drop F. & S. a line tonight, so I'll be ready for them. I do not think it would pay to bring the furniture. If we see that it will, can have it sent later. Am going over the goods marked "Jacksonville" and anything that I know you would want I'll repack. If things go that I should come, I think we had better board for a while so as to get on our feet and not have to go in debt, as much as I hate to go to boarding houses, but that can be decided later. Perhaps we could get a furnished cottage. We'll have to sail low for a while & then perhaps we can branch out with another one or two to the family. We will try for it any way. So you might come & see me in case we were separated on account of the boy.

Well I guess there will be no complaint on your part the first time we meet in Astoria or Jax or I mistake. Do you even worry about me in that respect? Have only been to Grape H- once that was as bad as going with out. Well I had to have a smoke, but I had company, so came back with a clear reputation; so did John H- who also went with me. This thing of waiting is a hard proposition, is it not?

I am all ways glad to hear so good reports about that dear old baby, and hate to go near the old house as it looks so lonesome. The little birds have finaly hatched – a family in the Megaphone – three out of five eggs. They left the nest today and Tod & I watched them for some time as the old ones were teaching them to fly. The Horse beans we planted are away up. The Palms seems to be doing OK. The yard needs hoeing though. Fourth of July I spent at work. We intended to take a day off, but it rained so I put down our old matting in Mama's room. At Lake View they tried to have a run [a foot race]. Bud Sullivan & Van Curry got at it. Our crowd Montedeco, Bass & Lawreance Sullivan (who is now on the staff) were in it, but no one "hurted enough to use white cement" as Everett would say. Fence cutting is very quite [quiet]. Bass & Sullivan are out to night though as it is a good night, full moon.

I sent stamps for the pk'gs you sent from home to Jensen (that word Jensen I don't like) as the P.M. [Post Master] sent me cards for stamps. Hope you did not as you have blamed yourself enough. I got all your letters finaly & the one of the Photo – thanks. Well repaid for my trouble, etc. So Chas H- has not favored you with a call. Letter from Mick [Prael] Tuesday said he expected to see you soon & that he was [in] fact going broke. So many weddings. How much cash will you have left? You will have to keep broke. I am feeling fine – do enough to keep busy, and from being to homesick for you and the boy. Give my best to West and thank him for giving the boy an airing, etc. I keep my hand in on dishes, helping Mama, but if I came to Astoria, I'll draw the line, because I must keep my hands in good shape. They have contracted the sale of 2 thousand beef cattle and look forward to good business.

There is little to write about, so am going to close for tonight. With lots of love to all & the rest for your own dear self & the baby. I can't commence to say how I miss you both – I think of you both all the time & wish we were to gether right then. I know you often regret not being nicer to me and I long for the time to come when you can make up for it – or should the above be twisted around the other way. Well good night dear old Lassie. I think I'll have time to add a line tomorrow morning. Hug baby for me & then get Willie to hug you for me, will you. If you do, well I'll see about him

Friday morning.

Well I'll add a line or two. Have a letter to F. & S. this mail & will be already to start if they reply favorably. So you can rejoice on.

On Monday, September 7, 1903, Dick telegraphed Louise from Jacksonville:

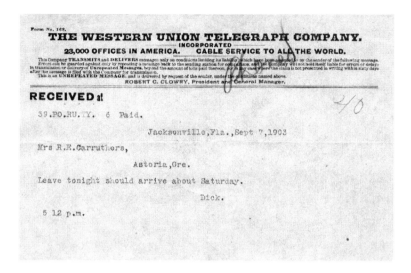

No further letters exist between Dick and Louise. Dick traveled back to Astoria to take up the position at Foard and Stokes store. It wasn't until later, on October 2, 1903, that an official announcement of his employment appeared in the *Astoria Daily Budget*. The notice stated that Dick had returned from Florida, where he had been working with his father conducting a cattle ranch and that he had accepted a position with Foard & Stokes Company with "the view to becoming interested in the firm in the near future." Foard & Stokes was a wholesale and retail store of general merchandise. Owned by Martin Foard and Frank Stokes the company had been in business for a number of years, located on the southwest corner of present day Fourteenth and Commercial. Dick made his plans to either move up in that company or start his own business.

As the year moved toward an end, Clara Wiederholdt Starbuck married William Easton Tallant in Brooklyn, New York on Saturday, December 12, 1903. After their wedding trip, they traveled to Astoria, where Mary Elizabeth and Louise held an "At Home" in honor of Mrs. William Tallant, from three to five o'clock, January 8, 1904.

Dick's mother, Harriet, remained in Turkey Hammock with Robert. Their youngest son Tod returned to Astoria and, apparently, their second son, Angus Russell "Gus" Carruthers, who had been studying law in the East, joined them on the ranch to help out. Harriet's letter is on the cattle company stationary. She always seemed to be the one managing the investments and following through on the business transactions - a careful, competent businesswoman.

Turkey Hammock, Fla. Feb 4 1904

Dear Dick -

A short note to night. Went horseback riding to day and you know what _that_ means. About that lot, he [Robert] says _ask_ four thousand, but you can drop to thirty six hundred if you can't get the four. He said same thing about giving you a commission for selling. Its over three hundred feet frontage. Maybe Zoe can stick _em for five_ and keep the _add_ thousand. Try it. You have my other letter about the meeting before this and will understand they have been buying and selling and the 20 percent is still _in_ the cattle. No division will be made until they sell off in August. So you can give your note and with interest, until then save what you owe. Wish I _could_ send you the money to square up now. I hate to have you worring. Only had a postal from Tod - he doesn't write as regular as he did - that seining takes his time, I guess. Gus is very content. I hope he keeps so.

We went out on the lake and caught a skiff that was a drift - belongs to the fishermen. They are busy ploughing the field and _his nibs_ is cussing the horses occasionally. Johnson is rather quiet so it evens things up. Hope Baby don't get the measles. It would be so hard on Louise. Is her neck entirely well now? Well, Boy, I must write Zoe a line. Kiss the Baby and Louise for me and have a big one for you.

Mama

Turk Feb 11 - 04   [Thursday]

Dear Dick & Louise -

Here's to both of you for I have so many to write to this week. You will have one to cheer you. Lewis was here all day yesterday with a young man from Cuba - a handsome fellow who's father is a dealer in stock [cattle]. He is negociating for 2 thousand head of steers, 5 hundred head of dry cows and 5 hundred head of cows and calves to be delivered in May or June. We have the biggest lot of steers in Florida at present. It will be a big sale and I hope they swing it. He was very much pleased with the cattle. He went back across the river to look over that range. They will not sell him any of the Norton cattle on Brama island. Lewis told him he will like to get out of active business and be home more - that Lightsey wants to keep in & so I guess this *fall will be as long as Lewis will be with us. I will be able to tell you maybe in my next if it's a deal.*

We are having snipe and quail regularly. The chicks are quite wild. Gus killed a three foot Alligator the other day in the slough where Louise and I crossed to go to Blanket bay. I always said the children could sail boats there so good there - it has sandy banks. I guess those blessed babies will <u>not</u> sail boats there now when they come unless we are there with a shot gun.

Did I tell you Will Simpson, the K- dentist - visited us for four days. I like him - and he <u>sure</u> did have a good time. He thought the shooting fine. He sings and knew the latest songs so it was a treat to have him. Said he would send me a little song "encore" –"Violets" - have you heard it? I think it so pretty. If he sends it I'll send it to Grace & Zoe.

They are still ploughing and the trees look fine. The new peach trees are all in bloom and the new orange too, so you see in time this will be a fine place. I dread your nasty cold climate, so I'm trying to inveigle the girls with camping down this winter for I'm not ready to come to A- [Astoria] yet - only want to see the girls so bad and it would be such a jolly trip for them. Well, I must write to Mr Parsons and Tod. Tods letter is in Grace's. She will give it [to] you. He's been sick for three days.

Kiss Baby a lot for me. I'm missing all his pretty Baby ways.

Love to you both –

Mama

Dick moved ahead on his business plans. He resigned from Foard & Stokes some time in February 1904 and spent several weeks working in the canneries before taking up new employment. In March 1904, he accepted a position in the hardware department of the Fisher Bros. Company. Brothers Augustus and Ferdinand Fisher had invested in a number of properties in Astoria, including the Fisher's Opera House. Their store carried wholesale and retail supplies in groceries, hardware, ship chandlery and logging equipment. Located at 546-550 Bond Avenue, "Fisher Bros." was one of the first businesses to subscribe for a telephone in 1896 – their phone number was "42."

Turk March 3 / 04 [Thursday]

Dear Dick –

Did not hear a sneeze from either you or Louise. But Grace said L- was in the depths of a progression dinner party, so that accounts for it. Well you are to tell [Frank] Spittle to get all he can out of Carlson if he gives a lease - not to unless he can get a hundred and twenty for taxes are higher and he makes good money there. About Brown - give a lease for one year at the present rate, but if he wants a lease for <u>two</u> years it must be at 45 per month.

Grace writes you are in the cannery for two weeks and then going to Fisher [Bros. Hardware] at a better salary – how much better will it be? I do hope it's quite a little. The fellow from Cuba went back on his bargain when it came to signing a contract, but they have made a better bargain to [with] another party. Lewis came over and saw how fine our grove looks – the young ones – and immediately sent for trees and has put a hundred in on the little Hammock near the house at Grape H-. Only about 15 feet apart and no straight lines – the men say it's a cultus job. He says Mr Parson will have a fine income from this grove some five or six years from now. Van Duesen[224] is awfully sarcastic – he says the dinner that Mr Parson gave in K- - before he went away - was a hot one - with Penitentiary Birds - Lee for burning the School House to get rid of the Ballot Box and Berry for cattle stealing, and some one else – I forget what he had done. He said had a queer crowd with lowest men. Papa quite likes Van Duesen.

Well the launch is here at last and is very much admired - she is cushioned with red corduroy and has a Cleveland engine – 3 horse power. Gus has learned to run her a little, but she gets baulky. Will have to have some one with him to show him just what to do. Your Father cut his foot one a piece of glass in K- and is quite lame, so Gus is helping the man fence postting six cows these two last days.[225] We hope to have a good garden. I guess Katz sent the material for Baby – four dresses last week. He did not send me the bill. I hope he never sent it to you. I told him to prepay the postage and charge to my acct.

Did your man go back on the price of the water lot? I have sent Tod's letter to Grace so you will see it – he had a fine report this last month. I have the Baulesay girl and like her very much. Now I'm going to get some Orange blossoms for you all and say good by. If Mr Parsons is there, give him our best and tell him he can come back this spring if he will let the "Whoppers" alone.

With lots of love and kisses to you both and my baby

Mama

The girls like Will's wife so much.[226]

On the 17 August 1904, Robert sent a telegram from Kissimmee to Dick, care of Fisher Bros. Company in Astoria. Robert requested a quick answer from Dick to give him authority to assign Dick's stock in the Lightsey, Lewis and Carruthers Cattle Company. He also requested authority to represent Dick in the stockholders and directors meeting. It seems possible that the Carruthers' group might have considered selling their holdings in the cattle company. However, in a small notice printed in the *Astoria Daily Budget* on

---

[224] Hetherington, 32, 41, 44. Willard L. Van Duzer's family members were early settlers in Osceola County. He was politically active.
[225] Cows were commonly fenced into a limited area to provide fertilizer before a late spring vegetable garden was planted.
[226] Harriet refers to the newlyweds Will and Clara Starbuck Tallant.

April 1, 1912, Robert announced that the Florida ranch, part of the estate of W.C. Parson, was sold for $200,000 by Mr. Parson's executors to another of the stockholders, W.H. Lewis, the Florida banker. The 40,000-acre ranch included 15-acres planted in orange trees and 6,000 head of cattle. It was considered one of the finest cattle ranches in Central Florida.

After living in Orlando, Kissimmee and on the ranch at Turkey Hammock for more than two years, Harriet Hunter Carruthers returned to their Exchange Avenue home September 10, 1904. Robert returned home to Astoria soon after, on the fifteenth, and became involved again in local real estate matters. The *Daily Astorian Budget* printed a notice that a trial date for Carruthers vs Alexander Grant and W.W. Whipple had been set, but there was no article relating why Robert brought the suit against Grant and Whipple or about the disposition of the trial. Robert left for the east coast in October on business.

The following slightly edited letter to Dick is from an old friend. There is no envelope for this one, so the writer is completely unidentified, other than by his first name and his indication that he and Dick had been friends in Oakland, probably when Dick was studying there in 1893. Even if there had been an envelope, few letters during all this period carried return addresses on the envelopes, with the exception of hotels and businesses.

Oakland May 12 / 04

Dear Dick –

Your very welcome letter received some time ago with enclosed pictures of your wife and baby and I should say that you certainly have a buster of a boy. I suppose by this time he is huskier than ever and a ringer for his Dad. I was very sorry to hear that your wife has had so much trouble, and sincerely hope she is now fine and dandy. I suppose the old people are still in Florida.

How is the hardware business, and did you get to be manager as you expected?

Your friend Robson has a very good job now with the Post Office. He was in here a few days ago and sends his regards.

Well, Dick, things look very bright to me. I seem to have a quiet but good time. Short hours and good pay are two things that help a young fellow to enjoy life, and I hope that you are finding things lovely up there and with my very best wishes to all. I remain

As ever Stan.

The Astoria Hardware Company

In February 1907, Dick decided to leave Fisher Bros. Company and establish his own hardware store. The *Astoria Daily Budget* printed the following notice in the March 13, 1907:7 issue:

Articles of incorporation of the Columbia Hardware Company were filed in the county clerk's office this afternoon. The incorporators are R.E. Carruthers, H.B. Settem and F.L. Parker and the capital stock is $10,000, divided into 100 shares of $100 each. The object of the company is to conduct a merchandise store in Astoria.

Dick's Columbia Hardware Company, located at 118 Twelfth Street, opened its doors for business on the morning of Monday, April 15, 1907, in the two-story building with the "rounded corner" erected by Robert Carruthers in the 1890s at Twelfth and Commercial. Apparently the business name was changed in 1908 to Astoria Hardware Company and its main entrance was also moved "around the corner" from Twelfth Street to front on Astoria's main street, Commercial. The business address also changed to 546 Commercial. The business telephone number was "117." Both of Dick's brothers, Gus and Tod, clerked at various times in the store during its many years of business while Dick was alive.

Less than four and a half months after Dick's sudden death on July 22, 1922, tragedy struck Astoria's downtown business. About 2:30 A.M., the morning of December eighth, Astoria's second major fire consumed almost thirty blocks of mainly downtown businesses. It was fueled by the creosote soaked pilings upon which that area had been built and because most builders had favored cheaper, more easily obtainable timber for their construction works. One of the many "victims" of the conflagration was Robert Carruthers' 1890s building that housed the Astoria Hardware Company. The building itself, on a prime business site, was still part of Robert Carruthers' estate.

Dick had made a good business of the hardware store, so his family members were determined to rebuild and to carry on the business. Architect Charles T. "Charlie" Diamond was hired to draw up plans for the new building early in 1923. Staying true to the general plan of the original two-story building with businesses on the street level and apartments/office space above, Diamond designed a "triple" building, with basements, that later became known as the Associated Building.

The *Astoria Budget* printed a front-page article about the new building on Friday, April 27, 1923. The headline read: "Commercial St. Building Plan Given Formal O.K.:"

The two-story concrete building with a frontage of 271 1/2 foot and which will cost between $150,000 and $250,000 was formally decided upon this morning. . .

The property involved includes the 50-foot frontage on the corner of Twelfth and Commercial, owned by the [Robert] Carruthers estate and formerly the location of the Bank of Commerce and the Astoria Hardware Store; 50-feet owned by Mr. and Mrs. C.W. Halderman adjoining 50-feet owned by [Mrs.] M.S. Copeland, formerly the location of the Bee Hive (a store selling general merchandise); and 71 1/2 feet owned by the [William] Cook estate.

These property owners have joined together to put up a single permanent structure instead of four separate ones. The building will be of reinforced concrete faced with brick of terra cotta. Mr. (*sic*) Copeland owns clear through to Bond street...The remainder of the building will be 90 feet deep.

C.T. Diamond, local architect, . . . announces that bids for the foundation will be called for next week.

Actually there are only three sections to the so-named Associated Building itself that form its 150-foot frontage. The joint owners names are inscribed in the facades: Carruthers, on the east corner, Block 58, Lot 8; (John) Hobson, in the middle; and Copeland on the west.

Diamond required exterior walls of reinforced concrete to be used by the Lorenz Brothers, the general contractors. He incorporated an unusual and very striking feature of a rounded corner on Twelfth and Commercial, and kept the original thirty-foot high ceilings on the main floor. While the new building was being constructed, the hardware store occupied temporary quarters in the Messenger Building on Ninth near Bond.

In May 1924, the Astoria Hardware Company reopened its doors, under the management of Robert Rex "Tod" Carruthers, Dick's youngest brother. Louise shared the ownership with Tod and, in 1925, with Richard Tallant "Dick" Carruthers, who, being her older son, had been called home from the University of Oregon. Along with another original occupant of the building, the Twelfth Street Grocery, Municipal Judge John A. Buchanan moved his law office to the second floor of the Carruthers building - his former office having been in the burned I.O.O.F.-Odd Fellows building. In May 1943, the executors of Robert Carruthers estate sold the building to Oliver C. Dilleshaw.

The building still stands kitty-corner from the recently refurbished Liberty Theater.

Frank Woodfield's 1923 photograph courtesy of Clatsop County Historical Society.

When Louise first returned to Astoria from Florida, she and Dickie lived at 803 Irving Avenue with the Ridehalgh family. Not long after Dick arrived from Florida, they moved into a stately Colonial Revival style house at 681 Jerome Avenue that looked very much like the old Baxter house in Barnstable on Cape Cod. Their second son, Eben Hunter Carruthers, was born in Astoria on August 22, 1904. Delivered by Dr. Fulton, he weighed a full nine pounds. Both young Dickie and Eben were fortunate in knowing their four grandparents, as well as some of their aunts, uncles and cousins who lived nearby. Theirs was a comfortable life in Astoria. Both Louise and Dick had many good friends and both were actively engaged in numerous community events and organizations. They traveled – mainly to California to visit relatives. They seem to have made the most of what they had and considered themselves fortunate.

Dick was a successful and well-respected businessman, a "square shooter," a good husband to Louise and a role model to his two sons. In May 1922, he and Louise drove to the University of Oregon at Eugene to visit the campus where Dick had been a 15-year-old freshman back in 1899. There they cheered for their U of O freshman son, Richard Tallant "Dick," who ran the middle distances and high hurdles in that 1922 Pacific Coast Conference Meet.

Robert, Harriet, Eben and Mary Elizabeth

Eben and Dickie – 1907

1910 -The Carruthers -Tallant families:
Florence; Nat; Harriet C.; Harriet T., Robert – holding young Laura;
Dick; Eben Weld and Mary Elizabeth; Louise.
In front: young Eben H. and Dickie - and their hound.

Mary Elizabeth and Eben Weld Tallant at the Hotel Oakland, Oakland, CA.
They resided in the hotel for the winter months of 1919-20.

Dick and Louise at the Hotel Oakland in the early spring of 1922.

On Saturday, July 22, 1922, Dick had gone to his hardware store early in the morning as usual. Feeling ill, he went to see his physician and returned home before 10AM. His illness was not considered serious. He felt better that afternoon at home - up until the time of his death at 7:30 PM. He was 48-years old. The cause of death was a stroke/heart attack (earlier, usually termed "apoplexy") – the same disease that had felled his Grandfather Richard (1896) and his father Robert (1917). It was also the cause of death of his brothers Angus Russell "Gus" (1932) and Robert Rex "Tod" (1945) - and his older son, Richard Tallant "Dick" Carruthers, Sr. (1965).

Louise never remarried.

Louise's two sons were in college at the time of Richard Ervin "Dick" Carruthers' death – Richard Tallant, *aka* "Dick," in his fifth year of the Architecture program at the University of Oregon at Eugene; Eben Hunter studied Engineering at Oregon State College (now OSU) in Corvallis, Oregon, later becoming Professor of Engineering at Cornell in New York State. Before the end of 1925, Dick, the older son, was called home to help his mother and family – he had completed the fourth year of the five-year program, so he never graduated. He joined his mother in the family hardware business. Dick developed that business into a By-Products Company, featuring "Ketch-Em" brand salmon roe eggs, which his father had developed prior to 1911. Young Dick designed and built his own house just uphill from his mother's - at 681 1/2 Jerome Avenue. In March 1926, he married Mary Maurine Buchanan, the older daughter of Judge J.A. and Madge B. Buchanan, who resided across the street from the Carruthers' home. Dick and Maurine gave Louise two grandchildren: Richard Tallant, Jr, (1928-) and Carol Louise (1931-). Eben also married and he and his first wife, Myra Gruber, added two more grandchildren for Louise – Sally Louise (1933-) and James Arnold (1939-).

After Mary Elizabeth Tallant's death on March 10, 1926, Eben Weld Tallant moved into the Jerome Avenue home of his older daughter, Louise. He enjoyed watching the ship traffic on the river from the living room windows; he also took pleasure in the visits of his two great-grandchildren, Richard, *aka* "Richie," and Carol. He remained with his older daughter until his death on December 16, 1932. Eben Weld Tallant was ninety-one years old.

Louise was honored to be one of the very few women who was permitted to set foot on Tillamook Rock; she was transferred from the beach by a buoy tender out to the monolithic rock and then hoisted up to the lighthouse by means of a breeches buoy, commonly used in rescues from ships. It was an exhilarating experience. She continued to be involved in the community and various organizations, including the Daughters of the American Revolution, Clatsop County Historical Society, League of Women Voters and the Red Cross. During World War II there was a shortage of housing for military personnel stationed in Astoria. Many households responded and rented out rooms. Louise moved into the southeast back bedroom of her home to allow the wife of a Coast Guard Captain to live in her northwest upstairs bedroom, with a view of the river.

She traveled occasionally, usually alone, to visit her family in Nantucket and Barnstable. She frequently visited her sister Harriet and family in Coquille and Bandon in southern Oregon and returned often to Southern California to visit with other family members and dear friends, including, of course, Marge Halsted and Lillie Kerckhoff. On one such visit there in the 1940s, her long-time friend, Charles Deering, drove her up Mt. Wilson, recalling the trip they had taken by "burrows" in 1896.

In 1948, Louise's son Dick designed a single-story home for his family on the south bank of the Columbia River in Hammond. He also designed a Cape Cod style house for her that was built on lots adjoining his. A few years later, her younger son, Eben, built his home adjacent to hers to the east. In a short time, her younger brother, Nathaniel Weld "Nat" Tallant, and his wife Florence, moved into a house across the main street. Louise delighted in her four grandchildren and the seven great grandchildren who had been born prior to her death. She found beauty in her garden and peace in watching the river traffic, which had defined her life, as well as that of her parents. She lived quite contentedly in her Hammond home for almost fourteen years.

On Tuesday, October 16, 1962, Louise sat on her royal blue velvet sofa in the cozy living room of her Hammond Cape Cod. As usual, she rested her lame foot on a low hassock. Her older son, Dick, came by to check on her, as he had done on a daily basis for several years. Her younger son, Eben, also came to visit with her. She reminisced on the passage of time, particularly back to the day, exactly sixty-one years prior, when she and Richard Ervin Carruthers had wed. Two days later, on the eighteenth of October, Maria Louise Tallant Carruthers died in her beloved home on the banks of the Columbia River. She was eighty-seven.

Maria Louise Tallant Carruthers

Epilogue

What a wonderful gift my paternal grandparents left in that cedar wood "treasure box!" I am thankful they saved so many letters during this period in their lives. For many years I wanted to learn more about Louise and Richard Ervin "Dick" Carruthers, particularly about my grandfather, who had died years before I was born. I did find some information simply by reading the letters, but doing that led to the realization I needed to know more about the times in which they lived – background information. Research was definitely required. Much of what is raised in their letters I knew little about, or in many instances, nothing - such as, the amateur theater groups then in Astoria; Mycobacterium *bovis*; the 1898 U.S. Volunteers involvement in Hawaii during the Spanish American War; and the Carruthers' Florida cattle ranch.

I was delighted to discover that my grandfather Dick was a very decent man, with many endearing qualities, including a droll wit; a sense of perseverance; the ethic of hard work; and the love of one's family. He seemed to have a gentle nature and an honest attitude toward all.

He also had an almost unfailing sense of good humor. The only time he seems to have mislaid his sense of humor was in 1902, while searching for a job in Florida. He obviously wanted to remain there; Louise did not. Reluctantly, Dick sent her and their young son Dickie back by train to Astoria, to her "home," family and friends. As he traveled around Florida seeking a family-wage position, I felt his sadness and frustration. Finally accepting a sales position in Astoria, he decided he had to unite his family by making the most of what ever awaited him as a member of Astoria's community.

Dick entered into many social, civic and community affairs. He became a successful businessman and built his own Astoria Hardware Company store, expanding that into the by-products fisheries business. He labored in the work force that built the road up Coxcomb Hill to the now famous Astoria Column. He was a founding member and past president of the local Rotary Club; active in the Elks; an officer of the Astoria Motor Boat Club; and an official for numerous Regattas. A strong supporter of the Boy Scout movement from its inception, Dick served on the local Scout Council until his death. Actively involved in the Oregon National Guard until his discharge, he organized the Edward Young Camp, the Astoria Chapter of Spanish American War veterans, holding a gathering of those veterans at his home on Jerome Avenue in March 1921.

Dick had high standards for himself, for his family and in his business dealings. He was a well-respected member of his community. As noted in his obituaries and by many tributes, the community keenly felt his untimely and sudden death on July 22, 1922. He was only 48-years-old! It was too early for Louise, and way too soon for us, his grandchildren.

In those days, it was not so common for one to speak about one's deceased family members and I greatly regret not having sense enough to ask questions about my grandfather Dick (and <u>all</u> the others) while my grandmother was still alive. Or, indeed, while my own parents were alive!

But, now I have a picture of the Man. It is by no means a complete picture, nor will it ever be. It is more like a rough pen-and-ink sketch, but with some of the areas more defined.

Writing this book has been a journey of love for me. I can now add these "memories" of the grandfather I never knew to those I have long had of my dear Grandmother Louise.

Bibliography

Books:

Anderson, Nancy Bell. *The Columbia River's "Ellis Island, The Story of Knappton Cove."* Gearhart, OR: Northwest Heritage Adventures, 2002.

Appelo, Carleton E. *The Cottardi Station Story.* Ilwaco, WA: Pacific Printing Co., 1986.

Coffin, I. Gardner. *The Oldest House on Nantucket Island.* New York: Charles Francis Press, 1905.

Cooley, ---. *Geneology of Early Settlers in Trenton and Ewing,* "Old Hunterdon County." Trenton, N.J.: W.S. Sharp Printing Co., Printers and Stereotypers, 1883.

Corning, Howard McKinley, ed. *Dictionary of Oregon History.* Portland, OR: Binfords & Mort, 1956.

Cutter, Carl C. *Greyhounds of the Sea. The Story of American Clipper Ships.* Third Edition. United States Naval Institute. New York: Halcyon House, 1984.

Dark, Russell. *Gillnetters: A Vanishing Fleet.* Unpublished monograph. n.d.
    Graveyard Passage. The Story of the Columbia River Bar Pilots. Manuscript. 1980.

Ernst, Alice Henson. *Trouping in the Oregon Country. A History of Frontier Theatre.* Portland, OR: Oregon Historical Society, 1961.

Fagan, Brian. *The Little Ice Age. How Climate Made History 1300–1850.* New York: Basic Books, 2000.

Hanaford, Phebe A. *Daughters of America.* Illustrated. Augusta, ME: True and Company, n.d.

Harris, W.T., PhD, editor in chief. *Webster's New International Dictionary of the English Language.* Springfield, Mass: G. & C. Merriam Co, 1918.

Hetherington, Alma. *The River of the Long Water.* Chuluota, FL: Michler House Publishers, 1980.

Hobbs, Nancy L., and Donella J. Lucero. *The Long Beach Peninsula. Images of America.* Charleston, S.C: Arcadia Publishing, 2005.

Larson, Erik. *The Devil in the White City.* New York: Vintage Books, 2004.

Leedom, Karen L. *Astoria. An Oregon History.* Pittsburgh: The Local History Group, 2008.

Lockley, Fred, ed. "E.W. Tallant," *History of the Columbia River Valley from the Dalles to the Sea.* Vol. III. Illustrated, Biographical. Chicago: S.J. Clarke Publishing Co., 1928.

Margolis, Simeon, MD, PhD, Med.ed. *Johns Hopkins Symptoms and Remedies.* Redding, CT: Medletters Association, 2003.

McArthur, Lewis A., Newell, Gordon, ed. *Oregon Geographic Names,* Fifth Edition. Portland: The Press of the Oregon Historical Society, 1982.

McCurdy, H.W. "Maritime Events of 1900." *The H. W. McCurdy Marine History of the Pacific Northwest.* Seattle: Superior Publishing, 1960

------. *Merchant Vessels of the United States. Twenty-Eighth Annual List.* Washington, D.C.: Government Printing Office, 1896.

------. Merck Manual of Medical Information. Whitehouse Station, N.J.: Merck Research Laboratories, 1997.

Miller, Emma Jean. *Clatsop County, Oregon. Its History, Legends and Industries.* Portland,OR: Metropolitan Press, 1958.

Newell, Gordon, ed. *The H.W. McCurdy Marine History of the Pacific Northwest.* Seattle: Superior Publishing Co., 1960.

Nordhoff, Charles & James Norman Hall. *Botany Bay.* Boston: Little, Brown and Company, 1941.

Oesting, Marie. *Oysterville. Cemetery Sketches.* 1988.

Palmberg, Walter "Wally." *Toward One Flag 1865-1943. The Contribution of Lower Columbia Athletics.* Astoria, OR: Astoria Printing Co., 1993.

Penner, Liisa. *Salmon Fever: River's End. Tragedies on the Lower Columbia River in the 1870s, 1880s, and 1890s.* Portland: Frank Amato Publications, Inc., 2006.

Picard, Samuel T. *Life and Letters of John Greenleaf Whittier.* Vol. II, Cambridge, Mass: Houghton, Mifflin and Company, 1894.

Stevens, Sydney. *Oysterville: The First Generations.* Chinook Observer Publications, 2006.

Thomas, Edward Harper. *Chinook: A History and Dictionary of the Northwest Coast Trade Jargon.* Second Edition. Portland: Binford & Mort, 1935, 1954, 1970.

Venable, William Mayo. *The Second Regiment of United States Volunteer Engineers.* Cincinnati: McDonald & Co., 1899.

Wilbur, Earl Morse. *Life of Thomas Lamb Eliot.* Portland, OR: Privately printed by George A. Allen & Sons, The Greenleaf Press, 1937.

Wright, E.W., ed. Lewis, --- & Dryden, ---. *A Marine History of the Pacific Northwest.* Washington, D.C: Lewis & Dryden Printing Company, Office of the Librarian of Congress, 1895.

Cumtux – Quarterly publication of Clatsop County Historical Society. Astoria, Oregon:

------. "S. Grant Trullinger's Trip to Alaska in 1897." Vol. 24, No. 2 – Spring 2004.

------. "Quarantine Station." Reprint of a November 27, 1900, letter sent by Judge J.Q.A. Bowlby to the Astoria Chamber of Commerce Vol. 26, No. 3 – Summer 2006.

Bell, Thomas McKean. "Burnby Bell." Vol. 21, No. 3 – Summer 2001.

Evans, Zoe Allen. "The Allens of Astoria." Vol. 3, No. 4 – Fall 1983.

Gault, Vera Whitney. "Preservation of the Charles and Anna Page House." Vol. 24, No. 2 – Spring 2004.

McClenny, Barbara Keist. "The Carruthers, Pike and Woods Families." Vol. 18, No. 2 – Spring 1998.

Penner, Liisa. "Astorians in the Alaska Gold Rush." Vol. 18, No. 3 – Fall 1998.

Smith, Robert David. "A Life on the Columbia River." Vol. 7, No. 3 – Summer 1987.

Tetlow, Roger T. "The Athletes of Clatsop County." Vol. 1, No. 4 – Autumn 1981.

Trullinger, Marie Adele Sovey. "To the Gold Rush in Alaska in 1899." Vol. 24, No. 2 – Spring 2004.

Williams, George C. "Alanson Hinman and the Building of Bond Street." Vol. 14, No. 2 - Spring 1994.

The Sou'wester - Quarterly publication of the Pacific County Historical Society. South Bend, Washington:

Morehead, J.A. "Pioneer Transportation." *The Sou'wester.* Vol. X, No 4 - Winter 1975.

Tompkins, Walker Allison. "Oysterville, 1840-97." *The Sou'wester* .Vol.XXVII, No 1 – Spring 1992.

Whealdon, Isaac H. "L.A. Loomis, His Life, Character and Achievements as a County Builder." *The Sou'wester.* Vol. 16, No. 31 – Summer 1983.

Journals:

Smith, Beatrice Scheer. "Maria L. Owen, nineteenth century Nantucket botanist." **Rhodora**. Journal of the New England Botanical Club. Lexington, Mass: The Lexington Press, Inc., Vol. 89, No. 858, April 1987.

Articles and Notes:

"75 years ago – 1931." *(Daily Astorian,* April 5, 2006).

Barber, Lawrence. "Reduced Rail Freight Rates May Mean Death for American Intercoastal Shipping Firms." Clipping. (Portland *Oregon Journal Sunday,* December 20, unknown year).

Bennett, Tom. "Bar Pilot Describes the Frenzy at the Mouth of the Columbia." (*The Daily Astorian,* October 15, 2006), 14.

Blissett, Guyon. "About Regattas," Letters to the Editor. (*The Daily Astorian,* August 24, 1951).

"First Regatta was in 1870s Says Veteran Elk Who Was In It." (*Evening Astorian Budget,* August 27, 1941).

Fischer, Margo. "Eighty-year-old woman still teaching dancing." Portland newspaper clipping, (September 20, 1930).

Gault, Vera. "The tale of rival Regatta queens." (*The Daily Astorian,* August 8, 1988).

Guernsey, John. "Oysterville residents still recall day county seat was stolen." [August 1893] (Portland *Sunday Oregonian,* February 1, 1976).

Goodenberger, John. "Cupola made Tallant house exclusive." (*The Daily Astorian,* November 24, 2004), 4A.

"History of the Astoria Regattas." (*Evening Astorian Budget,* August 29, 1935), 10.

Holden, E.C. "Growth and Prosperity of Astoria and Its Surroundings." Clatsop County column. (Portland *Oregonian,* January 1, 1882), 99.

Lucia, Ellis. "Old Oysterville." (Journal Northwest Living Magazine, March 14,1954), 14M-15M.

McKean, Polly Bell. Notes on Theatricals in Astoria. On loan to Clatsop County Historical Society by Thomas Bell McKean, 2007.

"Pioneer Families Play Important Part In The Developing of the Lower Columbia District," (*Morning Astorian*, September 22, 1926).

Shoop, C. Fred , "Death Recalls Pioneer Days," *Auld Lang Syne* column. Unidentified Pasadena-Alhambra newspaper clipping, May 1960.

Terry, John. "Oregon Trails," (Portland *Sunday Oregonian*, May 19, 2002).

"The Yacht Club Regatta." (*Astorian*, July 29, 1873).

Walker, Amy. "Oysterville Remembers 100 Years of Life on Willipa." A clipping. (*Astorian Budget* – 1954), 1, 7.

Webster, Michael. "They Shoot. They Score. It's Crokinole Night in Canada." *Harrowsmith* Magazine (December 1994).

Numerous Newspaper articles:

American Weekly Magazine
Astorian, The
Astorian Budget
Astorian Daily Budget
Barnstable *Patriot*
Daily Astorian, The
Daily Morning Astorian
Evening Astorian
Evening Astorian Budget
Honolulu *Pacific Commercial Advertiser*
Morning Astorian
Morning Astorian Budget
New Orleans Bee
Portland *Journal* - Northwest Living Magazine
Portland *Oregonian* – "Clatsop County Column"
Portland Sunday *Oregonian*
Unidentified newspaper from Pasadena-Alhambra, California

Miscellaneous:

1891 Map of Clatsop County, Oregon. Lewis & Dryden, Engineers. Portland: 1891.

1915 Oregon Almanac – Official Pamphlet State of Oregon Immigration Commission. Salem: State Printing Department, December 1914.

Bourniques' 1892-3 brochure. Mr. And Mrs. A. E. Bourniques' School for Dancing and Deportment, Twenty-Sixth Annual Session, (Chicago: Henry G. Shephard Co.)

City of Astoria – Ordinance # 1869. Approved April 24, 1894.

Clatsop County Court House Records: Deaths, Deeds, Legal Suits and Marriages.

Dellinger, J.S. and Perris. Astoria City Directories.

Freeman, Marie, et al. Washington Territory Donation Land Claims, an abstract. Seattle: The Seattle Geological Society, 1980.

National Register of Historic Places. Nominations and Inventory Forms. Astoria, OR.

Polk, R.L. & Co. Directories of the City of Astoria

Sanborn-Perris Insurance Co. Waterfront Maps 1892, 1894, 1896, 1908

United States Federal Censuses. Clatsop County, Oregon -1850, 1860, 1870, 1880, 1900, 1910 and 1920.

United States Federal Census of 1880, Wahkiakum County, Washington Territory.

Webster's New International Dictionary of the English Language. Springfield, Mass.: G. & C. Merriam Company, 1918.

Web Sites:

Brockway, Robert W. "Hawai'i: America's Ally." Reference to Spanish American War.
http://www.spanamwar.com/Hawii.htm (Accessed August 15, 2007).

Orland, Barbara. "Cows Milk and Human Disease. Bovine Tuberculosis and the Difficulties in Combating Animal Disease." Federal Institute of Zurich.
http://www.zgw.ethz.ch/pdf/orlandCowsMilk.pdf (Accessed June 26, 2008).

"Reminiscences of Helen Hand Fox." Reference to Chicago's Bourniques' School.
http://www.triad.rr.com/aqspinks/fox/autobiog.html (Accessed May 18, 2008)

Robinson, Thomas. Oregon Photographers; Biographical History and Directory 1851-1917.
http://www.historicphotoarchive.com/big/orphottxt.html (Accessed October, 2007).

Welch, Michael: www.spanamwar.com/2ndengineerswelch.html (Accessed August 16, 2007).

Index

Page numbers in **bold** indicate photographic images.

CPSIA information can be obtained at www.ICGtesting.com
Printed in the USA
BVOW06s2327290914

368826BV00005B/13/P